Good Sex,
Great Prayers

Good Sex, Great Prayers

Brandon Tietz

PERFECT
EDGE
BOOKS

Winchester, UK
Washington, USA

First published by Perfect Edge Books, 2014
Perfect Edge Books is an imprint of John Hunt Publishing Ltd., Laurel House, Station Approach,
Alresford, Hants, SO24 9JH, UK
office1@jhpbooks.net
www.johnhuntpublishing.com
www.perfectedgebooks.com

For distributor details and how to order please visit the 'Ordering' section on our website.

Text copyright: Brandon Tietz 2013

ISBN: 978 1 78099 530 4

A CIP catalogue record for this book is available from the British Library.

Design: Stuart Davies
www.stuartdaviesart.com

Cover design: Jamie Turpin
Author photograph: Chad Cogdill

Printed in the USA by Edwards Brothers Malloy

We operate a distinctive and ethical publishing philosophy in all
areas of our business, from our global network of authors to
production and worldwide distribution.

Brandon Tietz is the author of *Out of Touch* and *Good Sex, Great Prayers*. His work has been widely published, both online and in print. He lives and works in Kansas City, MO.

Visit him at his official website: www.brandontietz.com
Become a fan on Facebook: facebook.com/brandontietzauthor
Follow him on Twitter: twitter.com/brandontietz

For Wendy:
I only want to make dinosaur noises with you.

"Everything in the world is about sex except sex. Sex is about power."
-Oscar Wilde

"Religion. It's given people hope in a world torn apart by religion."
-Jon Stewart

Las Vegas, NV

"We should all know where we came from."

The prostitute puts on Christian lingerie: a pair of white nylons that extend to the upper thigh, too sheer to conceal all the various bruises on her shins and knees. Every badge of dishonor she's acquired in men's rooms and parking lots glares through the fabric. She slides one on, then the other. Material begins crumpled at the toes, and then she pulls them past her calloused heels, the tattooed ankles, over sore kneecaps garnished in hard scabs. Left, then right. Wrinkles smooth and I can see her chipped magenta nail polish and all those bruises—even the urine-colored ones that are nearly healed. Aesthetically speaking, white was a terrible choice.

I ask, "Do you know the origin of your profession, Serena?"

She sits on the hotel bed and shrugs on the corset, also white. Boning and underwire push her breasts and flabby stomach into place. Conceal a C-section scar. Serena shakes her head no and proceeds to tug on the silk ties crisscrossing her bumpy spine. Clammy little fingers loop, swoop, and pull. The corset narrows a little bit more, and I see excess skin spill over the top of the garment, much to my disgust. I try to concentrate on the color.

In this culture, white represents: purity, innocence, cleanliness. Virginity. When I forced the priest to bless these garments, I specifically asked him to endow them with those qualities. Only after I broke three of his fingers did he finally comply. The corset, the stockings, the garter belt and lace underwear—all are white and piously sanctioned. All of them were purchased at the Frederick's of Hollywood on South Las Vegas Blvd, formally ordained to make the wearer an object of virtue.

To Serena, I say, "From the ancient Mesopotamians, the first of your kind surfaced. Women of the land were required to sit in the temple of Aphrodite until a man chose them for fornication, paying them an undetermined amount which the whore could not refuse." She looks at me nonplused, waiting for me to tell her what to do since we're *officially on the clock.* "Masturbate," *I tell her.*

Serena lies on her back. She brings up her heels so they're resting on the edge of the bed, then pulls the crotch of the underwear aside, revealing clitoris, labium, and vaginal cavity. Unclean. Unwashed. From across the room, I watch Serena mash her fingers joylessly into herself, intentionally stammering her breathing. Purposely shaping her mouth in a wide 'O', as if to indicate spiking levels of arousal. She's 'phoning it in,' I believe the saying goes. There's no desire to climax, no inclination; I can feel this intrinsically.

"The man would cast money into the lap of the whore while verbally recognizing his tribute was being made in the name of the goddess," *I tell her.* "If the woman refused, that would be considered a sin due to the fact that the money was sacred. Now stick two fingers inside yourself. Plunge and repeat."

She does as instructed. Serena masturbates, staining white lace underwear in the fluids of weeping sores and enzymes. Cigarette vapors and the dried sweat of at least seven encounters contaminate the fabric of the corset, the garter belt and stockings. Fumes of disease cut into the air, a distinct molded flavor I can taste on the back of my tongue. If the Christian lingerie does what it's intended to do, if the ordainment holds, her illness won't pass over to me.

"The whore would accept payment," *I explain.* "And then she would engage in the act of fornication with the man—not for pleasure or affection—but faith. Faith is why you're here, Serena. It's where you came from," *I say.* "It's what I'm trying to discover."

The Inept

"I asked God and he had nothin' for me," Travis says, spitting a rope of tobacco into an empty soda can. He wipes the stray globs off his chin with the sleeve of an old cowboy shirt. Yellow plaid with pearl snaps. His bottom lip bullfrogs out, tongue packing the chew deep down under the gumline so it's buried and looking like a marble-sized tumor. Travis anxiously shakes the can, chaw-spit flopping against the aluminum sides as he looks to Father Johnstone with the same dirt-brown eyes his daddy had.

He says, "The wife and I already prayed about this, Father, so you can skip that piece of it." Travis spits into the can again and says, "I think we've done all we can do on our own."

In all the years he's known him, Father Johnstone can only recall two formal appointments with Travis Durphy. They've spoken many times, of course, the same way all folks do here in Pratt, usually at the weekly Sunday service. It's small talk and casual conversations anyone could have: how the single-A baseball team in the next town is shaping up or where the best fishing spots are located. Travis maintains it's the marsh bank on the east side of Larpe's Pond, just under the locust tree littered with carved crude hearts and the initials of high-school kids. All along the trunk, vows of eternal love (or perhaps *lust*) have been made in car keys and Swiss army knives. Serious inscribers use flathead screwdrivers, but Travis just likes to fish there.

"The dragonflies drive them so batshit they practically jump into the boat," he once said. It's nothing that Father Johnstone hasn't discussed with the other children and men of Pratt. Fishing and hunting gossip is frequent. For the women and wives, it's recipes: cobblers, pies, and during the winter months, stews and chili. Along with all things God, small talk is part of the church culture.

3

Personal office visits, however, are few and far between for someone like Travis, as he's never been the type to ask for help or seek personal counsel. Miles Conley, who owns the hunting supply store down the street, told it best when he said, 'That Durphy boy would cut firewood with a butter knife before asking a friend for an ax.'

Some folks say he's stubborn. Hard-headed. Travis would say he doesn't want to waste anybody's time if he doesn't have to. In the faith, Father Johnstone refers to it as *pride*, and he takes Travis's being here as a sign that, although he is not yet absolved, at least he's attempting to work through it.

Travis spits in the can again, sighing through his nose. "We're having the kind of trouble I never thought we'd need to worry about. Never in my life."

"I'm listening," he says, but it's only partially true. Despite himself, he's thinking back to that first meeting he had with Travis, which took place in the very office they sit now. The wood finish of the desk was a little bit brighter. The floors were a little less scuffed up, especially around the feet of the chairs, but it's mostly the same room Travis and Father Johnstone remember from all those years ago.

He was fourteen, and most people didn't call him Travis back then. Anytime he was spotted coming down the road, you'd usually hear someone say, "Here comes Danger's kid." Never "Travis." Always "Danger's kid" or "Danger's boy." His father picked up the name during his stint in the bull-riding circuit. "Daniel 'Danger' Durphy," they used to announce over the loudspeakers at the county fairs and rodeos. He always joked with the other riders that he could stay on any bull for eight seconds except for Mrs. Durphy, and then she'd slap him playfully on the shoulder with a slender hand while rolling her eyes. Everyone would laugh, drink, and then Mrs. Durphy would place her lips on Danger's cheek, leaving a lipstick signature. He never wiped them off, even when he entered the ring.

Most people in town regarded him as some kind of hero—not necessarily because he could ride, but because any time he went off to Dallas or Atlanta or Memphis for a competition, he always came back to Pratt. He never abandoned his roots.

"Good men grow up here," Danger said. "And my son will be a good man one day."

He was mostly right. Travis Durphy is known more for his hard work than for being bullheaded. Father Johnstone can hardly remember a Sunday when Travis wasn't one of the first through the doors for mass. If there was ever a dark cloud over the boy, that would have to be his father and the shadow he still casts. Even now, Travis is still thought of as Danger's boy by the older generations of Pratt, in both appearance and temperament. He's a constant reminder of what happened and a sort of campfire tale in the surrounding towns.

The story is that Danger finally met a bull that could buck him, and unlike the joke he often told, it wasn't by Mrs. Durphy's small frame. This was over 2,000 pounds of Red Angus steer. "A real mean bastard," the other riders said. Both Travis and his mother witnessed Danger get thrown to the dirt and shit of the arena after only a couple seconds, and before any of the rodeo clowns could swoop in and rescue him, a ton of steer slammed down on Danger's temple hoof-first.

Pratt's icon had passed.

As these stories do, it got more and more graphic with each retelling. Some people say you can still find fragments of Danger's teeth or little pieces of skull if you dig deep enough in the arena. They say there were real live cowboys throwing up corndogs and beer over the side of the railings that day, either sick to their stomachs or terrified. Hardened men broke down. Women wept, but none as much as Mrs. Durphy with her cheeks streaked with cheap, wet mascara and melted blush. She screamed and cried for so long she had to be sedated by the EMT personnel on the scene.

This is when young Travis was brought before Father Johnstone for his first appointment, so he could be coached through the grieving process. Places like Pratt don't have therapists or grief counselors; you have to make do with God (and that should be good enough for anybody). So Father Johnstone instructed Travis on the sentiment of the upcoming funeral and how Danger was in the Lord's Kingdom now. The pastor told him that Danger lived on through his son, concluding with a choice selection from the book of Exodus: *"Honor thy father and mother: that thy days may be long upon the land which the Lord thy God giveth thee."*

As Travis sits before his pastor about to pour his heart out again, Father Johnstone realizes this was the wrong thing to read to the boy considering the impressionable state he was in. The yellow cowboy shirt he's wearing was his daddy's, and so are the oversized belt buckle and boots, if Father Johnstone isn't mistaken.

Travis even began dipping chew after his father passed, despite all the times it made him sick the first few months. Sometimes he'd pack two school lunches just in case he lost the first one in the toilet. Plenty of underage boys in Pratt chewed, but Travis was the only one who didn't care if he looked tough or not. It was an homage. With the exception of riding bulls, Travis became his dad in every way he could, from the clothes to his bowlegged walk. He was paying tribute, just as he thought he was instructed to.

"The wife and I haven't consummated the marriage yet," Travis says. "We've tried and we've tried and it's like the Lord don't want us to—and I've prayed my ass off about this. Pardon the language, Father," he says. "Believe me, I've prayed the Lord give me the strength to be able to lie down with my wife as a man and…and…well, nothin'."

Father Johnstone leans in, lowering his voice to a little above a whisper, asking as delicately as he can, "What exactly is happening?"

Travis spits into the can again, wiping a brown string away from his lip. "It's more like what's *not* happening."

The second appointment was a little over a year ago. Father Johnstone remembers it because the daisy hill had just reached full bloom and he was holding Easter services at the church. He was watching the children hunt for eggs when Travis Durphy sidled him and said, "I need to talk to you, Father. Privately."

Travis looked possessed. He led the way through the grass towards the church, and Father Johnstone nearly had to jog just to keep up with him. The pastor's legs weren't what they used to be now that he was on the wrong side of fifty, yet, he kept right up with the Durphy boy, through the church doors and around the bend of pews. Travis entered the office, waiting for the pastor to cross the threshold before shutting the door behind him.

Father Johnstone hadn't even caught his breath yet before Travis blurted out, "I intend to marry Heather Graybel."

The boy was in love.

He's still in love.

"We've been trying ever since the wedding, but something's wrong with me, Father," Travis says. "It's like I'm afraid to do it—and no, before you even ask, I ain't no queer. Them queers make me sick to my gut," he says, spitting into the can a little more venomously than normal.

Travis Durphy and Heather Graybel were married on top of the daisy hill a year later, just as it had reached full bloom again. From far enough out, it looked like they were tying the knot on a pile of popcorn. They exchanged their vows with the assistance of Father Johnstone, and little Betty Graybel carried the rings on a small silk pillow. It was important to Travis that he knew his two fathers the Lord and Danger would bless this union, and he sought out Father Johnstone when he couldn't find the answer himself. Along with the cowboy shirts, chewing, and rugged good looks, Travis had also assumed his daddy's unyielding faith in the Lord.

The first two appointments with Travis Durphy were routine to Father Johnstone. Death and weddings happened often enough in Pratt, usually one or the other every year or so. A protocol had been established when it came to these types of events, anything from flower arrangements to biblical passages. Father Johnstone had a traditional line of questioning when it came to marriage and mourning, either to prepare or to cope. He preached love and devotion of the newly engaged, often stressing that a real marriage isn't always a day on the daisy hill. When it came to death, the bereaved took solace in knowing that the Lord is always present, always watching, and the departed watch with Him from the Kingdom. Death and marriage were standard. What Travis Durphy was asking of Father Johnstone was unheard of in the thirty-odd years he'd worked in the Lord's favor.

"This thing needs to be consummated, Father," Travis says. "So if you or the Man upstairs got any advice, I'm listening."

Father Johnstone is troubled. Granted, he could tell Travis to head over to the next town for one of those ungodly prescriptions, the ones for 'performance issues.' He's not going to do that though, and Dr. Keller would never endorse that sort of thing being the old-fashioned type that he is. If the Lord wanted man to have a four-hour hard-on, he would make it so without the aid of a pill or shot or however they administer that drug. It's unnatural. And yet, the consummation of the marriage is key, a bond between husband and wife and a heavenly tribute. Father Johnstone sees no reason why the Lord would keep Travis from that, however, can offer nothing by way of instruction to 'cure' the problem.

"Please, Father," Travis says. "I need help. Heather and I, we both need this. How are we supposed to have kids?"

And before Father Johnstone can utter a prayer, an excuse, a stalling question—before he can even think clearly, he says, "You need to fuck your wife."

A pause.

Silence. Travis Durphy's jaw hasn't dropped this low since he watched his daddy die right before his eyes. Father Johnstone is staring at him coldly, distantly, and Travis shifts his gaze to the pens on the desk, a small plate of lemon bars baked by Miss Paige. Anywhere but the man sitting five feet in front of him. He heard it—Travis knows that, but he's never witnessed Father Johnstone speak in that language. That tone. The can slips from Travis's hand, clanking hard and slinging chaw-spit on the front of the desk and over the hardwood floor.

The entire room seems to flinch and Father Johnstone asks, "What were you saying, Travis?" He smiles encouragingly. "I'm afraid I didn't quite hear that last part."

Processus XIII: Perceptio Virgo

The virgin female (feminam) *should first be removed of any impurities via the cleansing bath, either by fresh spring water or the milk of a cow or goat. Animal* (animalia) *milk should not be processed or pasteurized, and the providing species should be in good health as it may result in adverse effects otherwise. For water, the source must be derived from earth* (terra) *and not man-made or altered by man. Heated stones may be used for warming purposes, although not required. Petals of white orchid* (Orchis) *should be added to negate the scent of exiting impurities, which should diffuse over the course of a quarter-hour while the female remains in a stationary position. After purification, the female will exit the bath for crowning, the symbolic decoration of her virtue. Hair should be wound tight at the back of her head using wooden pins and interwoven with flowers of either: white, pink, or yellow. Never purple, blue, or red, as these denote the opposite of purity* (puritatem), *therefore, denoting the markings of a whore* (meretrix) *or one of whorish tendency. Using a sharpened bone (reference: forging tools), preferably elongated, the virgin will shave the vaginal region to denote youth, despite her chronological age. Hair should be contained in the appropriate receptacle (reference: storage) for later usage. She will then lie down on a bed of either: cotton, wool, or silk* (serico), *waiting for the male* (masculum) *to enter. The male genitalia should be purified by this point, and if desired, covered in animal fat or natural oils for lubrication and the necessary stimulation. He will approach the female, neither kissing nor touching her as these acts reintroduce impurities to the body. Neither individual will perform upon the other orally* (ore). *Neither individual will speak unless it is in that of the Divine Language, and only to formally pay tribute. It is imperative that the female do everything possible to accommodate the male's initial insertion, which must be delivered with great force in order to break the female's hymen. It is a well-known fact that virgins are infertile during their first intercourse* (clinopale), *so the male is encouraged to climax within her should he wish to. If the male climaxes internally, the female should immediately squat over a ceramic or wooden basin for the removal of the male's seed and retrieval of the hymen. In the event that the hymen has not completely broken away from the vaginal opening, use the sharpened bone of a chicken or other small bird (lagois) to cut it free. Store the hymen in either honey or amber. All other fluids should be bottled with non-altering preservation oils. The female's floral head décor may be dried and crushed for powder. Having served his singular function, the male is now insignificant. The female may either let him leave under his own accord or harvest him for supplemental materials.*

The Widow

Monday is the furthest away from God's day, which makes it more of a weekend for Father Johnstone. He sleeps in late, around 9:00 or 9:30—whenever his Yorkshire terrier, Mary, begins licking the pastor's hand to wake him up, a trick she learned many years ago. The two get out of bed. Father Johnstone fires up the coffee pot, having prepared the grounds and water the night before, and lets Mary out into the marigold-spotted pasture through the back door. She takes her usual three or four energetic laps around the yard before relieving herself, and the pastor grabs the newspaper off the front porch.

Reading *The Pratt Tribune* is part leisure and part homework for Father Johnstone. Over coffee—a teeth-staining black, no sugar or cream—he flips to the Local section, checking birth announcements, engagements, obituaries. If someone in Pratt passes on, there's an entire family tree that Father Johnstone will need to be extra sensitive to. He needs to know which townsfolk receive congratulations or condolences, which couples might request the services of the church for a baptism or wedding. The paper has always been his way of staying one step ahead.

As The Good Book says: *'Keep watch over your flock. Be thou diligent to know the state of thy flock, and look well to thy herds.'*

Although Father Johnstone stays well-informed through the daily news, the reality is that he usually knows the story before it's published, as was the case with Travis Durphy and his engagement to Heather Graybel. Today, there is no death or new life, no marital bond that he needs to concern himself with. The only thing of interest to him is the daily crossword puzzle (a favorite pastime of his) and an article reporting an overwhelming amount of pests eating the crops, which could severely hurt the town if not handled soon.

The pastor is about halfway through the first paragraph when he hears Mary scratching at the screen door, immediately darting for the fridge when Father Johnstone lets her back into the kitchen. She casts her eyes to the dish up top containing an assortment of brick red, beige, and pine-green milk bones, barking in anticipation and bouncing on her bony hind legs. Besides the afternoon walks Father Johnstone takes her on and the hard nap that follows, this is the highlight of Mary's day. Some of the men tease Father Johnstone for having what they consider an effeminate-looking dog, often saying something to the effect of, 'How the heck you supposed'ta tree a coon with that lil' rat, preacher?' It's all in good fun though. The people of Pratt have a certain amount of pity for the man who will never marry, never have kids of his own, and who will never know the love of a woman (physical or otherwise). He is devoted to God and the flock, but this can be a lonely existence at times, and so Father Johnstone snatched up Mary without second thought when he heard Shirley Adams was selling puppies for $50 a head at the market square.

It was nine years ago when Mrs. Adams plucked one of these little bears from a wicker basket by the scruff of the neck, handing her over to the pastor pale belly-first. She was barely bigger than a peach, black and tan. Soft. Softer than anything. Mary licked the print of Father Johnstone's thumb and acknowledged him with beady black eyes that squinted in the sunlight. Her nose was wet coal, framed in tiny strands of caramel. Then, right as the pastor was falling in love, Mrs. Adams said, "She's not for sale, Father. I'm sorry." And his heart cracked. A bruise spread over Father Johnstone's chest as he slowly extended his arms, palms up and full of fur, ready to hand Mary back over. She'd be with some other family by the end of the hour, he thought, seeing her only in passing on his walks through Pratt for years to come. She'd be 'the one that got away,' as they say. But then Mrs. Adams said, "No, I can't take money for that one," smiling mischievously at her own prank, and Father Johnstone let his arms reel back in where Mary settled in the crook of his elbow, nuzzling her face into his bicep. "I think you're just going to have to take the little lady home with ya," she said. "And I'll say a prayer that she doesn't chew up too much of your stuff."

There's not a piece of furniture in the house that doesn't have tears in the fabric or splinters of wood missing. Mary's teeth were particularly unyielding, especially in the first couple years, but he loves her, even during her destructive spells. He's grown to appreciate the markings of his little companion. Every scar in his coffee table or stain in the carpet brings a smile to his face. They give the home character, keeping that memory of the bear in the basket alive and well. Father Johnstone always makes a point to stop by the Adams place at least once a month to visit with Shirley. They'll chat over coffee while Mary plays with her siblings, Missy and Chips. The parents passed on some years ago from natural causes, and Father Johnstone could swear he'd never seen a bigger turnout for a dog funeral, let alone two.

After breakfast, Father Johnstone lets the dishes and pan soak in hot tap water and soap, continuing his morning routine of a shower and shave. He puts on his usual garb, a short-sleeve button down and dark slacks, black cowboy boots with gray embroidery. After giving Mary a little scratch behind the ear, he heads out the door.

The market is only a few blocks away from Father Johnstone's house, so he prefers walking over driving. Bringing out the car for such a short trip seems like a waste, and gas is fairly expensive in Pratt, being a small town and all. Besides Mary, the only other prize possession that Father Johnstone has is the 1970 Dodge Challenger sitting under a cloth tarp in his garage, which is probably in need of a good wash. He got it for cheap from a fellow a couple towns over in Barnes, mostly because the guy wanted it off his lot. "It's just killing grass and collectin' bugs sitting here," he said, giving the sagging tires a little kick.

The car needed work, a slew of repairs, and the kind of

attention only a non-married man with time on his hands could afford. A lot of pastors in small towns make this same move, either to cope with the loneliness or to give them some additional fulfillment beyond the flock. Instead of building a family, Father Johnstone built a car. He couldn't have a child, so he bought the closest thing to it. Substitutions like these keep the hands busy, keep the mind from wandering off the righteous path. The heart can love without drifting into the dark fields of *lust*. It is the delicate balance of being a man of God and being simply a man. Without Mary, without the Challenger and his routine, Father Johnstone fears the solitude would have taken over. Turned him somehow.

At Rawlings market, Father Johnstone picks up the usual: apples, yellow pears, a tin of strawberries to twist in sugar. He gets a loaf of sourdough and some lettuce for sandwiches. Mrs. Rawlings comes over while he's browsing through the wooden crates of produce, telling him he's got to try the new cider her husband made over the weekend. Father Johnstone obliges, putting a couple liters in his bag along with some ears of corn. He then backtracks two blocks to the butcher's, ordering a half-pound of lean turkey, some baby swiss, a few cutlets of pork, and one strip steak. Mary, of course, will be expecting her share of the leftovers.

A block east of the butcher's is the Presto Diner, a place that has had a recent swell in customers thanks to the addition of a new waitress, Miss Madeline Paige. She had been living in Portland up until a few months ago when her aunt Josephine got sick and passed on, leaving the house to her next of kin. The mortgage note had already been paid off. It just needed to be claimed, but a few property hounds were praying it wouldn't, considering its vicinity to the daisy hill and that beautiful view. Josephine used to always say nothing brought her more joy than watching that hill turn to popcorn every spring.

Auction murmurs ran rampant, but after a few weeks of

going through the paperwork, the town finally discovered the identity and whereabouts of Miss Madeline Paige of Portland, Oregon. She was asked to come to Pratt to settle the affairs of the property, and two Greyhound buses and a cab later, the twenty-four-year-old city girl walked down the main road turning the head of every boy she passed. "A smile that could start a campfire," they said. "And eyes just as warm."

Madeline fell in love with the town, the people. Life was simple in Pratt. The air was clean. And she marveled at the daisy hill, just like her aunt did. Father Johnstone personally took Miss Paige to the cemetery to pay her respects after she got her paperwork for the house in order. It was the least he could do since she missed the actual funeral. Madeline and her aunt were never that close, so she took it well. No tears. She placed white tulips on the burial plot and asked Father Johnstone to tell her stories about her aunt and the town.

"And they can't be sad," Madeline said. "I've had enough sadness in my life already, so you better put a smile on my face."

Father Johnstone spent that afternoon sharing coffee and pecan pie with Madeline, and for every memory he shared about the town and Josephine, he got a story in return about the city of Portland and all of Madeline's other travels. Despite her young age, she had seen much of the world so far: New York, California, Texas, and even Europe. Pratt was to be another chapter of that.

"I'll leave when it's time to leave," she said. "But for now, I'm home."

Father Johnstone would almost consider her a drifter if the term didn't sound so disparaging. However, Madeline settled into her new house quick enough. There was never a moving truck or series of packages delivered to the doorstep. She came to town with nothing but a leather satchel and the clothes on her back. Many of the women stopped by with casseroles and desserts to help fill the fridge. "Just to help you by until you get your feet on the ground," they said. A few days later she got the job at Presto Diner, and suddenly, all the young men were compelled to eat greasy eggs and burnt waffles in hopes of getting a peek at 'the new girl in town.' $10 tips were being left on orders of sour pink lemonade and not-so-sweet tea. It was quite the spectacle.

It remains so even now, all these months later as Father Johnstone walks in with his paper sack of groceries. Every booth, table, and stool is occupied, mostly by grain plant workers on their lunch break, but Father Johnstone recognizes a cluster of boys in the back corner as students. This doesn't hold his attention long though. The priest smells something in the air, a scent he's never encountered before in all his years of coming to Presto. It's the smell of cooking. Not burning or grease fire, but real down home cooking, and it almost makes the pastor wish he could sit down and have one of Mr. Farson's golden brown waffles or a side of perfectly crisp bacon that old man Clevenger is pushing down his gullet. Presto has never been known for its food. In fact, just the opposite. Often times you'll overhear people say, "Too short on time and money for a real meal. Gonna hit Presto."

Considering the boost in clientele and quality, the once-seedy diner is starting to look a little more appealing. Father Johnstone would be sorely tempted to sit down if it weren't for the lack of space, not to mention a few cuts of meat in his bag that are already losing their cool. A moment later he meets eyes with Madeline, who is in the middle of pouring coffee for a couple of plant workers. She gives the pastor a smile from behind the counter, holding up her index finger and mouthing, "One sec," before dashing back into the kitchen. She emerges seconds later holding a paper plate, wrapped in tinfoil and tied off in red yarn, announcing over her shoulder, "Be right back with more coffee, Mr. Curtis." He smiles and tips his hat.

"Father, I've got a confession to make," Madeline says. "My feet are killing me and I've taken the Lord's name in vain at least seventeen times today already." She smiles. Every man in the diner wants to be Father Johnstone right now as they attempt to stifle their *envy* with short stacks or home fries.

"Well then, I thank the Lord I know you're joking, Miss Paige," he says, returning a smile of his own. "And I'll pray for your feet."

She laughs. "Foot prayers? Really, Johnstone? If you do that I'm going to stop baking for you, although you've got so many fine ladies baking for you I'm not sure that's much of a threat."

"Do I sense some jealousy in our big city girl?" Father Johnstone teases. Even though the knives and forks continue to clink against the plates, he can still feel every eye in the diner on himself and Madeline.

"Well," she considers, "the way to a man's heart is his stomach, and from what I hear, nearly every girl in town has had their way with yours," Madeline teases back, placing the plate carefully in the grocery sack that's in the crook of Father Johnstone's arm. "Peanut butter, oatmeal raisin, and white chocolate chip—and let me know if the oatmeal is too heavy on nutmeg. Might've gone a little overboard."

"You really want to win this contest, don't you?"

"Johnstone, you're not a woman of Pratt until you've proven you can bake," Madeline says. "So I'm really counting on that overwhelming sense of honesty you have."

"I will surely do my best then," he nods, trying his damndest not to blush or grin like an idiot. The flock needs to know that at least one person can resist the charms and campfire smile of Miss Madeline Paige.

"I know you will," she says. "Now I've gotta get back. Feel free to stop by later with your pup if you're out for a walk."

"We might just do that," he says.

Father Johnstone exits the Presto Diner panging with hunger, and yet, oddly satisfied with his brief encounter with Madeline. She's injected new life into this town, increased its morale somehow. The women of Pratt love stopping by the Paige residence for a glass of cider, or even some wine if it's late enough in the evening. They'll sit on the porch swing admiring the daisy hill, and Madeline will tell them her tales of living around the country: the fast life of New York, the dirty glamour of L.A., and most recently, Portland's endearing weirdness.

"There's a place where they make a doughnut that has cough syrup in it," Madeline revealed once, and although the ladies laughed, there was much revolt at the idea of someone willingly putting that in their mouth, not to mention paying hard-earned money to do it. Portland might as well have been Jupiter as far as the ladies were concerned.

For these otherworldly anecdotes Madeline receives recipes, homemade wines, and directions on where to find the best ingredients in Pratt for a particular dish or stew. There's also the issue of town gossip, and due to the fact that Madeline is 'the new girl in town,' the women and wives delight in catching her up on who is shacking with who and any scandal, be it ever so trivial. It's smalltown drama.

Madeline Paige is viewed in a similar light as Danger was: bigger than the town of Pratt, and yet, a steadfast admirer of its people and charm. It's the ones like Madeline who can leave at any time that remind the lifers just how special this place is, and it makes Father Johnstone wonder if her coming here is simple coincidence or a gift from God. *Did the Lord see it fit to take Josephine so that he could send Madeline in her stead?* he wonders. *And how long will she stay?*

Consumed by these thoughts, Father Johnstone is very nearly home when he notices a red ribbon tied around Helena Wright's mailbox. It wasn't there before when he passed by on his way to Rawlings market—he's sure of it. The ribbon sticks out like blood on a sheet the way it's wrapped around the white post. It's been at least three months since he's seen it, calling out to Father Johnstone in just the way they had agreed upon: an emergency.

For a brief moment, Father Johnstone considers walking the remaining two blocks back to his house to drop off the groceries, but then he sees Helena in the window. Her finger has the curtain pulled aside, eyes staring him down. Beckoning. He can't leave, not when she's so obviously seen him on the fringe of her front yard. With the burst of the spring season in effect, her lawn is more wild than ever. The blades easily come halfway up his boots as he treads through, stomping towards the front door that's in dire need of a paint job. Helena already has the door cracked before the pastor can ready his knuckles to knock, and he enters stiffly, preparing himself for the same story he's heard before:

Mr. Wright was forty-one years old. He never smoked, drank only on rare occasions such as the tri-county carnival or a ballgame, but never more than a couple beers. The man knew his limits. He was a day laborer, and therefore, was considered 'an active man' by Dr. Keller. He was healthy, lived a low-risk life, and was one of the devout in Father Johnstone's flock. Then he died. All of a sudden, Mr. Wright keeled over and died for no apparent reason. It was one of the only times in Pratt that a body was shipped to the next town for an autopsy, considering there was no rhyme or reason to his death. It couldn't have been old age. He wasn't sick. Mr. Wright never showed a single sign of being out of sorts, so the speculation of what it could or couldn't be took over the town for the next few days. Then, almost two weeks later it was finally revealed: brain aneurysm.

It might as well have been an invisible bullet with the way that Mrs. Wright reacted. No matter how many times Dr. Keller explained to her what the condition was, she never grasped the concept. It was too random for her, and therefore, she could not find any peace in her husband's passing. Coaching people through the mourning process was something Father Johnstone did well, but it was easy when the cause of death was old age or sickness. And although people never like losing their family members to accidents, an accident is still technically an explanation worthy of closure. Travis Durphy knows that better than anyone.

Mrs. Wright, and more specifically, her husband were the recipients of what they would call 'plain old rotten luck.' This made Father Johnstone's efforts to console the widow Wright especially difficult, mostly because he didn't understand much of the science behind it either. God had always been the answer when talking through these things, but having something like a heart attack or cancer to explain how death added up was necessary. It's the mystery and unexplained nature of the brain aneurysm that keeps Mrs. Wright calling out to Father Johnstone, always with a red ribbon tied around the mail post, just as they agreed upon after the funeral.

"I'm hurt and will try to press on," she said, "but I'd be lying if I said I didn't think about ending it all." Mrs. Wright sniffled, crying. "I'm very alone right now...and I'm going to be alone for the rest of my days."

This is when Father Johnstone explained his own solitude, empathizing via his story of Mary and the restoration of the Dodge Challenger. To the common eye it would appear that these things are in his care; the reality is that it's just the opposite.

"Believe me," he said. "I am no stranger to loneliness. I'm probably an expert."

And so Mrs. Wright and Father Johnstone made a deal, that if she was ever lonely or depressed or felt like she couldn't take it any longer, she would display the red ribbon on the mail post. This method, believe it or not, would be more effective than calling as Father Johnstone is rarely around his telephone. Part of keeping watch over the flock is being a presence in their lives on a daily basis, not just on Sundays. He regularly tours the town, not only to play the role of the doting pastor, but to combat his own solitude via the revolving door of company and conversations.

"I pass by your home at least three or four times a day,"

Father Johnstone said. "Believe me, all strangeness aside, it's more practical than a phone call."

Most of the meetings consisted of Father Jones listening to the widow Wright talking through her husband's passing, the unfairness and erratic nature of it. She cried often, sometimes leaning into the pastor's body for many minutes at a time, sobbing until his shoulder was soaked in grief. In all his years in Pratt, Father Johnstone could not recall a more emotionally-charged yet aimless string of meetings. A pattern emerged: Mrs. Wright told the story, her confusion overwhelmed her to tears, and she'd eventually cry herself into submission. It usually concluded with her saying, "I'm sorry. I'm so sorry to put this on you," and then she'd thank Father Johnstone for his time, sending him away no closer to resolution than when he came.

The air in the home of Mrs. Wright is different now. Solitude lingers, but there's also a welcoming quality that the pastor thought all but removed. It's peaceful and clean. The usual smell of dirty dishes rotting in the sink and old laundry in need of attention has vanished, replaced by jasmine-scented candles and the oils of wood cleaners. The home is brighter and warmer than the pastor has ever seen it, more so than when Mr. Wright was still alive. Father Johnstone sits down on the couch in the living room, placing his groceries carefully next to the arm so they don't tip over.

"Can I get you anything, Father?" Mrs. Wright asks, less sad than usual. She's attempting to play host when she's normally exercising common niceties. "Cider? Pie?" she offers.

"No. No, thank you," he says. As much as he wants to assist Mrs. Wright, the pastor is hoping to do it fast lest his groceries spoil.

Helena Wright sits down on the couch next to the pastor, adjusting her sundress to tuck her feet under. She's wearing makeup today, and along with the clean house, Father Johnstone can't pinpoint the last time he's seen that either. Blush and eye shadow almost make it seem like he's talking to a stranger, right along with this new calm and controlled temperament she's exuding.

She says, "I feel better now."

"Good," Father Johnstone says. "I'm very glad to hear that."

"I'm still lonely, but I've stopped pining over Carl. I've stopped letting myself stew in misery," Mrs. Wright says. "I'm done trying to explain what can't be explained."

"You're letting go," the pastor says. "That's very good. I'm pleased to hear your life is turning around."

Then Mrs. Wright says, "But I'm very lonely, Father." She slides over on the couch one cushion length so that her knees are touching the pastor's leg. Mrs. Wright smiles, but not in any way that Father Johnstone is familiar with. There's aggression behind it, and then she leans in and plants her lips on the pastor. Her lips touch his, softly at first, and when Father Johnstone doesn't break away or resist, she clutches his face, pushing her tongue into his mouth. He tastes like stale coffee, but this matters little because she's finally able to touch, to kiss the man that talked her through so many hard nights. She's finally able to reciprocate all the attention and love he gave her, and then Father Johnstone mumbles something blissfully between breaths. He says a name, and Mrs. Wright is certain it wasn't *her* name. Definitely not. Lord as her witness, it damn sure was not her name that he just said.

Mrs. Wright tears her lips away from his and asks, "What was that?"

"That," he stammers. "That...it shouldn't have happened. I should go." But when Father Johnstone moves to stand, Mrs. Wright presses her hand against his chest, weighing him down.

"The name," Mrs. Wright says. "You said a name."

Father Johnstone blinks, dumbfounded. Distant.

"It sounded like you said Madeline," she says.

On the Road with Billy Burke, Truck Stop Preacher

"I don't care if she's fat. I don't care if she's got a stinky baloney cooter that cheeses right up like old potato salad left out at a BBQ. You fuck your wife. You fuck only your wife. That's the vow you made, and a man's only as good as his word. Lord doesn't welcome maligners into the Kingdom, and there ain't no good woman that deserve to be cheated on just cos her puss look like a pile of hair with chewed bubblegum dropped in it. There's plenty of men locked up that would chop their own ears off for a piece of ass right now. I've met them myself...out on the road. Met a man that was locked up for a twenty-year stretch, and he says to me, 'Billy, there were times I got so lonesome I stuck my pecker in the mattress hole while lookin' at my girl's picture. Lord as my witness, she's a pig, but she's my pig.' I want you to think about that while you're out there delivering our food and supplies and gasoline around our great country. You made a commitment to do a job. You made a commitment to your wife. Do your diligence, do right by the Lord, and be thankful you got more than a mattress to squirt into when you get home."

The Apathetic

"We've lost that spark, Father," Mr. Fairfax says, briefly glancing to his left for any objection from his spouse, but she's nodding in complete agreement. Mrs. Fairfax has been frowning for so long, years as a matter of fact, that even her mouth has crow's feet. 'The unhappiest woman in Pratt,' some people call her. And she's still nodding—perhaps a bit too emphatically, because her husband recants somewhat in his next statement, saying, "I don't think we're beyond help, though, and *that's* why we're here. That's why we're coming to you."

It's Thursday and Father Johnstone has yet to get a full night's sleep since the incident with the widow Wright. He's been getting to bed fine. Around ten o'clock the pastor brushes his teeth, says his nightly prayer (for good health and the strength to continue to guide the flock), and then proceeds to slide under the covers. Mary curls herself into a little ball adjacent to Father Johnstone's stomach, and the two of them fall asleep just as they always do. The problem is that Father Johnstone keeps waking up, typically every couple of hours with the aftertaste of nightmares soaking his pajamas. It's become such a nuisance that he even went as far as to buy a sleep aid from the local drug store, but all they've done is made him feel groggy and beyond the aid of caffeine in the morning.

"Do you think there's anything that we can do, Father?" Mr. Fairfax asks. "Any advice the church can offer us?"

Father Johnstone yawns. Shrugs absently. "Pray?"

He knows that he should be giving his undivided attention to Mr. and Mrs. Fairfax, but recent incidents distract him. Thoughts of Mrs. Wright and their encounter continue to haunt the pastor, and no matter how many times he replays it in his head or analyzes it, he can't make sense of the event. He knows what happened, knows very well that it was wrong, but the motives escape him. Not only was Mrs. Wright acting more ardent than she has since her husband passed, but Father Johnstone had never been that passive, so easily persuaded. Not since his early twenties, anyway. It's as if he forgot who he was and his role in the town of Pratt. He's supposed to be the guiding light, a pillar of the community, but that pillar has since cracked, apparently. *Lust*, no matter how brief, is still *lust*.

"It's confusing, Father, because—and I'm not trying to disrespect the Lord," Mr. Fairfax reassures the room, "but how exactly does one pray for a man and wife to be attracted to each other again? Wouldn't the Good Book classify that as *vanity*?"

"So," the pastor starts, "what you're saying is you've not even attempted to speak to the Lord in which you took your marital vows under? You're already thinking about loopholes? Am I hearing that right, Richard?"

Father Johnstone goes over it again: he saw the red ribbon and walked into the home of the widow Wright. She said that she was fine, that she was still lonely but had learned to accept her situation, and Father Johnstone was glad to hear this. He had been waiting for this kind of breakthrough for some time, but that was the point in which Mrs. Wright placed her mouth on his, and when he didn't resist, she proceeded to invade it. Consume it, devour him—but just as quickly, she stopped. The name. She accused him of saying 'Madeline,' however, he doesn't remember that. It continues to be a blind spot in his memory, and as insane as it sounds that he'd do such a thing, it's equally insane that the widow Wright would lie about it. Clearly, Father Johnstone did something to 'spoil the mood,' as they say, and logic dictates Mrs. Wright wouldn't attempt to seduce him in order to act hurt and offended moments later. It was the first time the pastor had seen her cry over a man not her husband, a new kind of guilt considering his nearly non-existent history with women. Father Johnstone has only kissed three in his lifetime, and the widow Wright marks the end of a thirty-four-year-old streak of benevolence.

"We've not yet prayed for something so specific," Mrs. Fairfax says. "I suppose we don't want to look, y'know…'petty,' I guess would be the word." She turns to her husband, "That sound right, Rich? 'Petty'?" He nods and she resumes consulting with the pastor, venturing, "Perhaps we pray the Lord renews our connection?"

"Yes, dear, a renewed connection," Mr. Fairfax chimes in. "That—yes, I couldn't have said it better myself."

The couple is tiptoeing now, being extremely deliberate with their word-choice. Father Johnstone is usually so welcoming, so open-minded and willing to listen. Couples counseling has never been something he's done in an official capacity, but over the years, more and more marriages were prolonged thanks to the pastor's insightful advice.

"Father?" Mr. Fairfax asks. "Does that sound right to you?"

The pastor is cold now. Distant and exhausted, and possibly coming off a bit mean with the way he's addressing the Fairfaxes. The impatience and callous tone are unlike him, so he has to remind himself not to make his problems the problems of others. They just want your help, he thinks. They need guidance.

"I believe that if you address the Lord with a pure heart and honest intentions, He will provide that which you seek," Father Johnstone says. "A vow is a promise of both body and spirit, but that's not to say that keeping a promise is always easy. The Lord favors those who seek His aid."

Mr. and Mrs. Fairfax sigh, smile. They ease into their chairs having heard their pastor say this, and Father Johnstone smiles back, even though it's a forced gesture. He had to dig deep for that last bit of advice. His counsel and ability to relate the Lord's Word have always had a certain amount of naturalistic elegance, never ringing false or untrue. It's how he became so revered as a bridge back to happier marriages. Father Johnstone has never claimed to be a miracle-worker; he simply reminds these couples why they got married in the first place. Regarding Mr. and Mrs. Fairfax though, his words feel empty. They lack their usual soundness, almost as if he's saying the right words but has forgotten the meaning behind them.

"And we *do* seek his guidance," Mr. Fairfax says. "We really do, Father."

"Our issue is that the marriage has become rather...lethargic, I suppose," Mrs. Fairfax says. "We respect our vows, of course, but it's like we're turned off by each other."

Mr. Fairfax turns to his wife, "Honey, I believe the word you used was 'repulsed'." Eyes turn back to the pastor, "I repulse her, Father."

"Well...yes," Mrs. Fairfax frowns. "I *might* have said that."

For some reason Father Johnstone can't help but be reminded of Travis Durphy and his own spousal issues, specifically, the lack of consummation. It's a matter of fear and self-doubt, he's surmised. Travis's problem is the same one Father Johnstone had the first time he popped the hood of the Dodge Challenger intended for restoration: he knew what would be under there, the function and the purpose of it, but the complexity of all those parts overwhelmed him into a state of impotency. He didn't know where to start, and therefore, dreaded touching a single spark plug for many weeks. For Travis, it's the same fear of the unknown.

Mr. and Mrs. Fairfax, on the other hand, have become so acclimated to each other, so conformed to the workings of their marital bond, they've slipped into apathy. Or, if Mrs. Fairfax's 'repulsive' comment is any indication, they've gone past that and into a state of animosity.

"I believe what you said was, 'I find you so repulsive that the thought of you touching me makes me want to vomit'," Mr. Fairfax quotes.

"That's because you smell like sweat and motor oil. You don't clean yourself, Richard. You don't warsh. It's disgusting," Mrs.

Fairfax reasons. "I know you're a mechanic and all, but honestly…warsh yourself. Just warsh the crud off your hands if you're gonna touch me. 'Cleanliness is next to godliness'," she recites. "That's what the Good Book says, right, Pastor?"

"Actually, it doesn't," Father Johnstone responds. It's a common misquote he's heard many times, but his patience isn't at its normal generous length. "And it's pronounced *wash*—not *warsh*. There's no 'r' in wash. Your husband can't *warsh* because it's not possible, Jean."

Crow's-feet stretch at the corners of Mrs. Fairfax's mouth, but out of shame this time. It's been a while since she's been reprimanded, not by Father Johnstone, but in any capacity. You'd be challenged to find anyone who'd want to cross 'the unhappiest woman in Pratt,' but Father Johnstone almost relishes the control he has. If there's one type of person she doesn't dare sass, it's a man of the cloth.

"This is petty bickering, plain and simple," the pastor says, scaling back the edge in his tone. "If all you see are the inconsequential problems, the marriage itself will become a problem. Wounds that go untreated will fester, which appears to be the case here, yes?"

Mr. and Mrs. Fairfax humbly nod.

"The issue isn't that you've lost the spark," Father Johnstone says. "Intimacy is a by-product of love and commitment. It recovers through prayer and devotion to your vows, understand?"

The pastor says this firmly, confidently, more like his former self. For the time being, his irritability has faded and he's back to an even temperament. Mr. and Mrs. Fairfax nod at the pastor, briefly looking at each other to acknowledge that they not only accept the words, but are ready to apply the advice they've just been given. They'll concentrate on the important aspects of their marriage, and Father Johnstone is hoping, praying in fact, that they will take their leave soon from his office.

"But Father," Mr. Fairfax leads in tentatively, "what about the sex?"

"Oh, peas and rice, Richard, give it up!" Mrs. Fairfax shouts. "I think we've pressed Father Johnstone enough for one day, don't you?"

"No, it's fine, Jean," the pastor says. "It's okay. Go ahead, Richard."

As much as he hates to admit it, Father Johnstone is intrigued by the various workings and malfunctions of sex, perhaps because he's never participated himself. Outside of the physical mechanics, the act (which is technically a tribute according to the Good Book) is mostly a mystery, so there's a strange dynamic at play when being asked about a subject he knows next to nothing about, nor personally experienced. Father Johnstone is learned in sentiment and emotive context, not the tangible application, which is where Mr. Fairfax's interests lie.

"How to I put this?" Mr. Fairfax considers, sighing. "We would…okay, how do we make it…*better*?"

"I don't follow," the pastor says.

"What my husband is trying to say, Father, is that we know this is a tribute to the Lord," Mrs. Fairfax says. "The tribute, however, is…well, it's become lackluster as of late."

"An empty tribute, Father," Mr. Fairfax says. "Like we're going through the motions but there's no meaning behind them."

"Hold on, you're saying you no longer find joy in this act?" Father Johnstone asks. "That it feels vacant?"

The Fairfaxes turn to each other, tilting their heads slightly considering if what they're about to say should be verbalized. Their admission might not be well-received, but they're also not the type to withhold information from their pastor. Guilt by omission, as they say. It's a grave sin to lie to a man of the cloth. By extension, that's a lie to God as well.

"Yes. More or less," Mrs. Fairfax says. "We won't bore you with the details but it's become a bit of a chore. A burden, almost."

"Tell us, is empty sex between spouses a sin?" Mr. Fairfax asks. "We've been wondering about that."

"No," Father Johnstone leans back in his chair, considering all the factors in the scenario. There's a parallel in there somewhere. He can feel it, almost as if God Himself sent the Fairfaxes to help deduce his own recent problems: the nightmares, the irritability, and a certain numbness regarding the wellbeing of his flock. Much like Father Johnstone, the couple before him have strayed from their usual selves.

"Empty sex isn't technically a sin, Richard," the pastor says. "But tell me something...how have you two been sleeping lately?"

Las Vegas, NV

The Christian lingerie fails.

Serena's disease transfers over to me after a one-week incubation period, manifesting in a steady discharge of cloudy fluid that is neither urine nor semen, accompanied by a mild inflammation at the tip of the urethra. Great pain now occurs during the process of voiding the bladder, a sensation akin to that of passing hardened splinters or pine needles. Pain also occurs during the act of climax, although much sharper on account of the speed the liquid exits the body.

If the Christian faith does in fact have the ability to prevent disease, then I have somehow miscalculated and must continue on with the experiment.

"We're going to try something a little different," I tell the girl on the bed—not Serena. This one goes by the name of Desiree, however, I've since devised the modern whore regularly exercises deceit in order to conceal their identity. She is ashamed of her endeavor, and therefore, distances herself from it on every conceivable level.

Desiree examines the items sitting on the hotel comforter: a Bible, a crucifix, a large bottle of water. "You want me to do what now?" she asks, flipping through the text with no intention of reading it, keeping idle hands busy. Wearing a fresh set of Christian lingerie, Desiree rests on her side and smoothes one leg over the other, flipping through Genesis...Exodus...Leviticus.

"Start with the Bible," I tell her. "And keep the Lord in your heart as you do it."

She glares at me for a moment, abhorred. "You're into some weird shit, mister," Desiree says, closing the book shut and rolling onto her back. The corner of the text mashes into her clitoral region, rubbing, applying stimulation to nerve endings. Responsive nerve endings that cause the vaginal cavity to salivate, becoming wet with enzymes.

I take a mental inventory: Christian text, Christian symbol of worship, Christian lingerie. A bottle of Holy water that I procured from a receptacle that was used for something called a 'baptism.' Under intense duress, the priest with the broken fingers finally admitted that my experiment was ill-intentioned and likely to fail. 'A nutjob,' he called me, which I can only assume is a derogatory term considering the context. I broke two more of his fingers, impressing upon him that another failed ordainment would come with consequences.

"This is too kinky," Desiree says, rubbing the spine of the Bible over the cleft in her underwear. Faster until the labia engorges with blood, flushing hot. Wet. "I'm not even gonna ask how this turns you on."

I smirk, adjust in my chair. "The crucifix now. Pull your underwear aside."

Desiree does as instructed, laying down the book and taking the cross in a manicured hand, palming the longest of the four ends. She exposes the vaginal canal: glistening meat. Clean unblemished skin. One wooden corner is applied to the clitoral region, rubbing methodically so as not to cut herself.

"This is totally unsanitary," she comments.

I stand up from the chair, approach the bed and take in the air filling the space between her knees. It is lacking contaminants. No disease. Modern chemical components are regularly being applied to purify the area, a process I'll later discover is called 'douching.' Vinegar, salt, and calendula herb. This particular whore cleans herself; aesthetic damage is minimal. No scabs or major abrasions, which might explain why she costs 300% more than Serena.

Desiree makes eye-contact, asking me in a smoky tone, "Do you like that, daddy? Does this make your cock hard?"

'Daddy' is an informal substitute for 'lover.' 'Cock,' in this instance, does not refer to the traditional farm bird, but the male sex organ. Much of my understanding of modern culture and dialect can be attributed to whores. Las Vegas whores especially tend to be especially worldly, hailing from all corners of the U.S. along with Europe, Asia, and South America. Their vocation is perhaps even more diverse than my own, which is saying something.

Desiree asks me in her smoldering voice, "This get you hot?"

peeling apart healthy pink labia, rubbing the tip of the crucifix over it.

I shake my head, lean down and adjust the idol symbol in her hand so that the Savior is facing downward. "Like that," I say.

"Is Jesus supposed to be eating me out?"

'Eating out' does not literally mean to bite, chew, and swallow. I made that mistake some years ago and have since learned it's the slang vernacular for oral stimulation.

I say, "Yes, he's eating you out." Reminding her, "And you keep Him in your heart while you do it."

Desiree complies. Legs butterfly-wing open, mashing the carved face of the Savior into that cluster of nerve endings, moaning convincingly. I grab the bottle of water from the bed, unscrew the cap, and proceed to dump the contents on her pubic bone. It cascades through her vaginal canal, past the perineum, onto the comforter where it begins to soak through to the mattress. Desiree suspends stimulation, glaring at me inquisitively.

"Holy water," I tell her. "To purify you."

She rolls her eyes, shakes her head. I unzip my pants and remove myself, bringing the tip of my penis closer to her. It's still drooling, leaking. Oozing disease. "You need to put on a condom," she says, bringing her knees together. Desiree props up on her elbows and waits for me to address the circumstances.

From my front pocket, I pull out a $5,000 casino chip. Based on the initial fee I paid her, this equates to roughly six encounters. It doesn't take long for Desiree to calculate that. Whores are reasonably proficient in math. She sighs, takes the chip in her empty hand and lets her shoulders touch back to the comforter. Legs spread and she gives the crotch of the underwear one final tug to the side, offering an adequate route of entry.

"You better not give me anything I don't want," she says, sliding the casino chip into the top of the corset. "I'm serious."

I nose the tip against her clit, smoothing it down to her labia, bathing in Holy water and organic lubricant. Hot disease and fever burns. Stings. I ask, "Do I really look like someone who would do that?"

pushing myself inside her.
    I implore God to stop me.
    To save the whore.

The Examination

"Let's check the ol' ticker," Dr. Keller says, pressing the end of a stethoscope to Father Johnstone's bare chest. He flinches slightly, chills spiking as Dr. Keller moves the metal pad down an inch, left another. It settles over Father Johnstone's heart, and the doctor squints while he listens. Dr. Keller raises his eyebrows and gives a satisfied little nod, plucking the eartips of the stethoscope and positioning them around his neck. "Sounds normal to me," he says.

Father Johnstone, however, has never felt more unlike himself. What started off as a general sense of fatigue and passivity has deformed into something much worse. He's getting headaches— intense migraines, to be exact, and this is accompanied by an unrelenting state of exhaustion that's since prompted him to start taking massive amounts of sugar with his coffee. This merely delays the problem for a short while, though. Moments of pain-free alertness are few and far between, and so the pastor finds himself cycling through caffeine, various pills, and the numerous prayers begging for a return to good health. He prays for strength and the will to go on, or even just a couple hours of uninter-rupted sleep when he's feeling especially desperate. So far, neither God nor the marvels of modern medicine have responded.

It's the first time in many years that Father Johnstone has seen a doctor for anything other than his annual flu vaccination. There was the one instance where a random nail in the basement snagged the pastor's arm. He got a tetanus shot and had some standard blood work performed. Besides that, Father Johnstone has always avoided Dr. Keller's table, either by living a life of low risk or the utilization of home remedy should illness arrive. It's always been easy to stay healthy in Pratt if you're careful, so the pastor's current condition is a bit of a culture shock compared to the common cold.

"And you said you've been experiencing insomnia-like symptoms?" Dr. Keller asks, wooden clipboard at the ready.

During the day, the pastor can barely stay awake. At night, he can hardly sleep for more than twenty or thirty minutes at a time. He's waking up so often that Mary has all but given up on her usual balled-up position under the covers, opting for the living room couch or a pile of dirty laundry if it's available. This is about the extent of what Father Johnstone feels comfortable revealing. Symptoms are required for Dr. Keller to make an informed diagnosis; it's none of his business as to what the nightmares are actually about. That's irrelevant, the pastor thinks.

"Okay, and you said that you're waking up about every half hour or so?" Dr. Keller confirms. "Can you give me a little more detail on that?"

"The symptoms have steadily intensified," the pastor says, buttoning his shirt back up. He sighs. "Honestly, if I could handle it or if I thought it would go away on its own, I wouldn't be here."

For the past three nights the condition has been at its worst. Father Johnstone is ripped from sleep, usually bolting upright so violently that it strains his lower back, always covered in sweat. There's so much of it he has to wring out his pajamas over the bathroom sink. This process is such a chore though, that he's since cast his modesty aside, either returning to bed in fresh briefs or completely nude. He prays the Lord forgives his indecency. Father Johnstone begs and pleads the Lord let him sleep for just a couple hours without a nightmare or migraine or fever sweating episode. He prays for the very simple ability to sleep and to sleep soundly, sometimes shouting into the dark about why the Lord would test him like this. He asks God about the nightmares, but as always, there's no response, verbal or otherwise. Not unless Mary's grumbling counts. Understandably, she's been especially cross with her owner with all the shouting and waking up in the middle of the night.

"It sounds like you're experiencing night terrors," Dr. Keller says, scribbling something on the clipboard. "That's what the symptoms indicate, anyway. The interesting part is that for a man your age, this is extremely unusual."

"How so?" the pastor asks.

"People get set in their ways after a while," Dr. Keller says. "Stuff like this doesn't hit men our age without a good reason. It usually means a trauma happened," he hints.

Even though Dr. Keller isn't technically one of the flock, he's a pillar in the town of Pratt, much like Father Johnstone. People respect him. Admitting that something happened, that there was indeed a trauma of sorts, would make the pastor look weak and incapable of leading. It could compromise him, both spiritually and professionally.

"*Did* something happen, Father?" Dr. Keller tries again.

He can't tell him about the blank spots in his memory, or the moment of *lust* he may or may not have shared with the widow Wright. His heated meeting with Mr. and Mrs. Fairfax has to be kept quiet, too. These are dark turns that need to remain secret, not only because these things would embarrass and discredit the pastor, but like Dr. Keller, there's a certain amount of confidentiality he must retain on behalf of the flock. Legally, doctors have to do it, but Father Johnstone answers to a higher power. He answers to God, and he'd prefer not to test the Lord right now with sleights of betrayal.

"I haven't really felt like myself, David, and I blame much of that on not sleeping…but as far as any trauma," Father Johnstone says, "I'm certain that hasn't happened."

"Well, the only other thing I can think of off the top of my head is that you might be Hypoglycemic," Dr. Keller ventures. "There's been links between individuals with low blood sugar and night terrors, although I doubt that's the case with you."

"What about the migraines?" Father Johnstone asks. "The

sweating…is that normal?"

"Technically, for you, Father, none of this is normal." Dr. Keller turns to a cabinet above a steel sink, removing supplies from the shelving: gloves, gauze, a syringe. He says, "I'd like to do some blood work, just to be thorough."

As Dr. Keller prepares to draw blood, Father Johnstone recalls Mr. and Mrs. Fairfax and their particular set of symptoms: irritability, detachment, and a growing sense of apathy. He had to be careful to not reveal too much about his own situation, taking the angle of the consummate caring pastor—not a man who's been having night terrors and snapping at anyone who rubs him the wrong way. As it turns out, the Fairfaxes have been having trouble sleeping too, just not in the same way that Father Johnstone is. As Mrs. Fairfax so eloquently put it: "Could you doze off next to 200 pounds of horse turd?"

Perhaps Father Johnstone was reaching with the theory that whatever affliction he's recently assumed that the Fairfaxes were experiencing the very same thing. The possibility that they simply have grown to despise each other is still plausible. In fact, it's highly likely, and no amount of counsel or prayer is going to save them. Some couples, no matter what they say, just don't want to be fixed.

Then Dr. Keller is snapping his fingers, saying, "Father, you're all set."

The pastor opens his eyes. He looks around the room, re-familiarizing himself with the paper-shrouded exam table and glass jars containing cotton balls, tongue depressors, and swabs. He asks, "What about the blood?"

"I took it already. Do you not remember that?" the doctor asks, possibly adding another symptom to the litany he's already notated on the clipboard.

"No," the pastor says. "I mean, *yes*, of course, I remember…just—like I said, haven't been as sharp lately." Father Johnstone stands up, noticing the cotton ball strapped to his arm with a Band-Aid along with a new weight in his shirt pocket: a foil pack of pills. He forces a reassuring smile so as to not arouse any further suspicion.

"Remember, only one of those per night, right before bed," Dr. Keller says. "I'll phone you with the results, okay?"

Father Johnstone nods, exiting the examination room feeling detached again. Another migraine thumps behind his eyes as he proceeds down the hallway, giving a half-hearted wave to the receptionist on his way out of the building. Not even a block away from the doctor's office, and already the pastor is regretting his choice to misrepresent his condition. The sweating and night-mares and headaches—those things are all true, but the pastor has also been experiencing periods of intense anger and sporadic forgetfulness. Mood swings are becoming more and more prevalent.

Sometimes he snaps at people without just cause. Other times he materializes not knowing how he got to his destination. Yesterday, for instance, Father Johnstone was at the butcher picking up hamburger meat, and not even a moment later, he was standing outside the Presto Diner watching Miss Paige serving breakfast through one of the storefront windows. He didn't remember paying for his groceries or the usual five-minute walk the restaurant. The pastor, for lack of a better term, had simply 'appeared.' At least, that's what it felt like to him.

Luckily, he was supposed to pick up a batch of peach cobbler from Madeline anyway. After his critique of her other desserts, she insisted the pastor try one more on the pretense of it being "a gigantic favor that I will be forever grateful for." Winning a category at the annual Pratt bake-off has become important to her, and so Father Johnstone has been doing his due diligence in the form of cookies, pies, and any other treat Miss Paige concocts in her kitchen. The apricot turnovers she made were exceptional, he recalls.

It would be easy to say that he is doing nothing more than

helping a girl out. To the casual onlooker, that's exactly what it appears to be, and it's not as if the pastor has never been on 'dessert duty' before with any of the other ladies of Pratt. Madeline, however, is a bit of a different case, and the relationship isn't exactly as formal as people are led to believe. In the wake of her Aunt Josephine's passing, Madeline and Father Johnstone bonded considerably. It's happened before; grief sometimes compels a person to want to connect with another, in a sense, replacing them. A death in the family feels like a phantom limb to some folks, and Father Johnstone tends to be viewed as an ideal candidate to compensate for these losses, as was the case with Travis Durphy.

Unlike most grieving families who are desperately reaching out for him, Madeline was the only person to which Father Johnstone reached back. And although he often asks the Lord questions of a 'why her?' and 'why now?' nature, the answers have yet to be revealed, and perhaps never will be. What he knows, what he's certain of, is that Madeline Paige is a fixture in his life. A positive force. In fact, the only time the pastor has smiled in a genuine sense in the past week was when he was conversing with Madeline or sampling one of her desserts. Otherwise, he is either exhausted, short-tempered, or in anguish.

And as Father Johnstone enters his home to the tune of Mary's welcoming barks, the pastor can't resist the allure of an early bedtime in light of tomorrow's Sunday service. His behavior over the past week may have shaken the confidence of some of the flock, so he wants to be well-rested for the upcoming sermon. The turnout should be substantial since the service will be followed by the annual bake-off, a contest which Father Johnstone also judges, hence, why all the women and wives of Pratt gravitate towards pleasing his palate. They're doing their homework for the big test, essentially.

Father Johnstone removes the foil pack from his shirt pocket, popping a slate blue pill into his hand. It reads 'HALCION .025' in an arc. He puts the pill in his mouth, chasing it down with some tap water from the sink, swallowing. It's not even six in the afternoon yet, but he wants to make sure that sufficient time is devoted to rest and catching up on sleep. A return to his former self is the most important thing right now, so for the sake of the flock, he prays the good Lord to allow him to do that.

"Allow me one night of peace so that I may do Your will tomorrow," he says, eyes shut and barely above a whisper.

Father Johnstone prays for sleep, prays that the Halcion will work better than the over-the-counter stuff he's tried so far. He begs the Lord to suspend the migraines and night sweats, to allow him to feel like himself again.

"Let me be not angry nor passive nor spiteful," he whispers. "Return my even temperament and allow me patience."

He then arrives at the final point of dialogue with God, the issue of his nightmares: those troubling thoughts that seem only too real in dreams. Even with the workings of doctor/patient confidentiality at play, Father Johnstone still couldn't admit the exactitudes of these so-called 'night terrors,' as Dr. Keller refers to them. They're too shameful, too intimate to be revealed to anyone. No matter what, no one can ever know that the topic of these nightly episodes is none other than Madeline Paige.

プロセス XVIII: 更改

For this, the female (女性) must have either a pre-existing emotional bond or a token vow of devotion (献身) by way of a ceremony. This doesn't have to be a wedding (結婚式), however, that is the most common example. A love letter, tea ritual, or mutual promise (either physical, verbal, or symbolic) would suffice. Whatever the individual circumstances may be, what's important is that the male (男) was, at some point, devout to the female in question regarding the three levels of fidelity (忠実): emotional, spiritual, and physical. No facet may have been deficient, as that would result in a negative impact or complete recoil. Both parties would experience much suffering, possibly death (死), but only in rare cases of extreme miscalculation. Materials to be used are temperamental. Ideally, if the two were married, the female would want a sample of the robe from the wedding ritual, although flowers, metals, or human samples would work too. Semen, if preserved correctly (reference: preservation methods), would be quite potent if taken from the first post-ceremonial intercourse (性行為). Regardless, the materials in question should be selected based on personal meaning and the significance of bond. Break these down (reference: reduction methods) and combine them with a wax candle. Do not simply crust the outside of the candle; the wax must be melted down, infused with the material(s), and then reformed. Burn this candle during the quarter-moon, taking care that it does not blow out. The process must be restarted from the beginning should the candle lose its flame prematurely. After a full moon cycle, the effects should manifest. The male will come to the female at her home (家), reverted to a state of complete devotion and love, although fabricated in its nature (資質). It will be the first instinct of the male to fornicate with the female. Should the female resist, the male will not be able to show restraint and take her against her will. He will not entertain reason or logic, as he has become a being of pure lust. *If the male successfully rapes the female, it's entirely possible that he will murder her after orgasm (性高潮) as penance for attempting to reject him. It would be in the female's best interests to comply with whatever he wants should she value her own life.*

The Feeding

As *The Pratt Tribune* reported on page C2 of the Local section, today marks the 11th annual bake-off for the church, which is more or less a fundraiser fueled by the allure of sweets and friendly competition. It's the only time of year the women and wives get to compete at something in which they have an established skill set. Bowling and darts are fun, of course, but cooking will always be an aptitude that's practiced on a daily basis. You'd be hard-pressed to find a woman in Pratt that's not serving up home-cooked meals at least six days a week. It's part of the reason why the Presto Diner never did much business up until recently.

"I'll be damned if my husband is going to bust his hump all day for greasy diner food," Mrs. Baines said once. "Least a good wife can do is make sure he gets one decent meal in his gut before he goes to bed."

Unless you were in a pinch, there was hardly a reason to go to the Presto—that is, not until Madeline Paige's employ began. The vast improvement in the quality of food didn't hurt either. Some people thought the diner hired a new cook, but all anyone had to do was peek their heads in to see that Buck Taylor was still working the line, just as he had been for the last twenty years. That got the rumor mill churning, and the peculiar shift from greasy spoon to renowned local favorite came down to two main theories:

The first is that ol' Buck was so smitten by the new waitress that he started putting a little effort into his cooking, believing this would be the best way to get Madeline to notice him. A sort of culinary compatibility, some people said. However, this theory only works under the pretense that Buck truly believes he has a shot with someone over twenty years his junior. And it's not like Madeline doesn't have her pick of the litter when it comes to men, so it's rather far-fetched.

The other theory—the more logical of the two—is that Madeline has been giving Buck private lessons in cooking, which would explain why the waffles now have a touch of vanilla to them and the sudden appearance of crepes on the menu. Even the syrup is less watery, but the case can also be made that management is simply ordering better syrup. Regardless of this, the fact remains that the food and service at the Presto Diner didn't get good until Madeline came aboard, and it's made some people in town view her as a legitimate culinary threat.

"I suspect our little world traveler might be giving Buck some tips," one of the wives said. "But you can tell her that pancakes don't win the ribbon."

The Pratt bake-off breaks down as such: there are three categories, one for cookies, one for pies, and one for cobblers. There can only be one entry per person for each category, and there's a $15 admissions fee for each submission. Desserts are then labeled with a number that corresponds to the person who submitted it, which is then presented to a panel of three judges for a blind taste test. Father Johnstone learned the hard way the first year that no mortal man can possibly judge three categories, which is why each dessert has its own trio of judges now. Even so, eating an average of fifty bites of dessert can be a task in itself, which is why the pastor leans towards farmers and laborers when he's soliciting for judges. Women have never fared well on the panel. A few years ago Mrs. Rawlings tried her hand at it, but took sick after only twenty or so samples. It was a notable disaster and spawned much controversy over who would have claimed the ribbon had she seen it through. The bake-off has always been a breeding ground for the dramatic.

"That Maddy Paige is this year's dark horse," Father Johnstone overhears one of the ladies say as he takes his place at the center judging table. Mrs. Tripp is talking to Gloria Vanders at the check-in line, each with their hands full of treats obscured by tin foil and cellophane wrap.

"I don't put it past her to try one of those fancy New York recipes out," Gloria replies. "Girl is crafty. Probably thinks she can waltz on in here and blow us all out of the water."

As much as Father Johnstone tries to be a non-partisan judge, he can't help but suspect there's a fair amount of truth to Gloria's claims. Madeline has made the pastor a variety of desserts: from cakes to cookies and even non-traditional things like fried ice cream. As she noted in the diner, nearly every woman in Pratt has had their way with Father Johnstone's stomach, so it's not really an issue of the pastor showing favoritism. If someone wants him to try out a dessert or new recipe he usually will, oftentimes giving a brief critique of what he thought. The divergence with Madeline's dishes specifically is that they're consistently good. Too good. Even the oatmeal cookies she feared had too much nutmeg in them were nothing short of perfect. The pastor has found himself skipping meals lately to save space for whatever treat Madeline may present him with next, a dietary transgression Dr. Keller would probably lecture him about if he were aware.

The joke around Pratt is that the annual bake-off is the only time you'll see the town overtaken by *gluttony*—all in the name of a good cause, of course. This year specifically, the church roof is in dire need of repair. Mother Nature hasn't been kind to the shingles, and after a particularly heavy thunderstorm in March, that's when Father Johnstone started to notice the puddles. One at the front of the main aisle and a few others scattered around the building. Three weeks ago the pastor had to deliver his sermon to the tune of droplets pounding into a metal bucket, and although the Lord is in the rain, Father Johnstone could have done without the additional noise.

The fundraiser should more than take care of the issue. According to Mrs. Tiller, one of the church's most active volunteers, the admissions fees have already exceeded the estimate the roofing guys gave Father Johnstone last week. The pastor isn't worried about the money aspect of it; his current problem is physically being able to consume the fifty or sixty samples of dessert he's supposed to eat today. His appetite has waned. He's tossing away more food than usual. Mary's share of the leftovers are so large she's been declining bites of steak and deli-cut turkey, opting to lie down on the couch to digest instead.

The myriad of desserts provided by Miss Madeline Paige are the only sustenance that the pastor seems to be able to completely finish nowadays, which is both a blessing and a curse. He relishes these dishes, but at the same time, knows the nutritional value of a carrot cake probably doesn't rank very high.

The pastor feels this may be the Lord testing him. Whereas there are many biblical instances in which men are challenged with starvation, Father Johnstone will have to face a gauntlet of endless sweets and sugars. Pie after pie after pie—and even though the last thing the pastor ingested was a Halcion tab close to nineteen hours ago, the idea of eating anything, let alone the finest desserts Pratt has to offer, churns his guts.

"Ready to do this, preacher?" Mr. Conrad says, slouching his 250-pound frame into a metal folding chair on Father Johnstone's left. Thankfully, he's taken the liberty of washing his overalls. The odor of manure and sweat the hog farmer is known for has been replaced by soap and fabric softener, courtesy of his wife who's checking in her own submission at the moment.

Father Johnstone gives Mr. Conrad an encouraging smile, one that reminds the hog farmer he's done this many times before. It's old hat, just as his sermon today on 'The Feeding of the Multitude,' or 'The Feeding of 5,000,' as it's sometimes referred to. Due to the *gluttonous* implications of the annual bake-off, Father Johnstone always makes a point to cover that particular miracle of Christ: the instance in which thy Lord and savior fed an entire town with nothing more than five loaves of bread and two fish. It not only demonstrates the power and compassion of

Christ, but serves as a reminder to Father Johnstone's congregation that food is a blessing not to be viewed trivially. The people of Pratt have a tendency to forget this in the presence of such abundance.

"Soooooooooo," Mr. Conrad says, drumming his fingers on the plaid tablecloth, "that was, um...quite the sermon today, Pastor." He clears his throat, shifting in his chair a little. "*Quite* the sermon," he repeats.

Father Johnstone doesn't have enough of a rapport with Mr. Conrad to know if he's just making idle chit-chat to pass the time, or if there was something truly interesting about his delivery today that diverged from the norm. 'The Feeding of the Multitude' reading is one he's given many times—perhaps too many, as it often draws a few groans or irritated sighs from the longtime members when he states the title, and today was no exception. Rather than probe Mr. Conrad for more information, the pastor gives a grateful nod, assuming he meant his comment in a praising sense. Before Mr. Conrad can elaborate or correct him on what he actually meant though, Jeremiah Wills approaches the table. He offers his hand to both Mr. Conrad and Father Johnstone, shaking them in turn.

"Good day to pig out, eh gentleman?" Jeremiah says with a smile, taking a seat to the pastor's right. He's wearing a lime green polo shirt and loose-fitting jeans, which is far cry from the meat-stained butcher's coat that Father Johnstone is accustomed to seeing him in. It's also one of the few times he's been without an edged object, making the handshake an uncommon occurrence. Jeremiah is what the pastor considers a non-practicing member of the herd. That is to say, he is a believer in the Lord, but admittedly, Jeremiah barely prays, he seldom asks forgiveness for his sins, and he never attends the Sunday service.

"Business is just too damn hectic that day," he explained to Father Johnstone once. "Everyone's doing cook-outs and tailgating around their radios for the game. Couldn't make it if I wanted to. No offense, preacher."

Being that he's a judge this year for the annual bake-off, Jeremiah attended today's sermon under the pretense that it was the least he could do for being bestowed "one of Pratt's highest honors," as he put it. A sense of obligation may have been at play, but regardless of the motives, the butcher showed up in his Sunday best having left his oldest son in charge of the shop. Father Johnstone could tell he was a bit nervous about the whole arrangement, joking with the pastor before the sermon, "I guess I should pray he doesn't burn the place down while I'm gone, right?"

Father Johnstone notices that the check-in line has wound down to a final handful of ladies: Heather Durphy (formerly Heather Graybel), Mrs. Tenley, Miss Ashcroft, Mrs. Conley of Conley's Hunting Supplies, and Miss Madeline Paige, who appears to be submitting desserts for all three categories. She spots Father Johnstone from her place in line and gives him a smile, but there's nerves behind it. It's not the usual campfire warmth he's seen before. There's fear in her eyes. Maybe even guilt.

"So tell me something, preacher," Jeremiah says. "Today's sermon…was that how it usually goes? Or are you trying a new angle on this whole thing?"

"Yes, Father," Mr. Conrad chimes in. "I was actually a little surprised that you took the reading in the direction you did. I mean, no offense," he backtracks. "It was just, well…*not* what I'm used to seeing from you."

Father Johnstone isn't sure what they mean. He performed the reading as he traditionally does, reciting:

13 When Jesus heard what had happened, He withdrew by boat privately to a solitary place. Hearing of this, the crowds followed him on foot from the towns. 14When Jesus landed and saw a large crowd, he had compassion on them and healed their sick.

¹⁵ *As evening approached, the disciples came to him and said, "This is a remote place, and it's already getting late. Send the crowds away, so they can go to the villages and buy themselves some food."* ¹⁶ *Jesus replied, "They do not need to go away. You give them something to eat."* ¹⁷ *"We have here only five loaves of bread and two fish," they answered.*

¹⁸ *"Bring them here to me," he said.* ¹⁹ *And he directed the people to sit down on the grass. Taking the five loaves and the two fish and looking up to heaven, he gave thanks and broke the loaves. Then he gave them to the people.* ²⁰ *They all ate and were satisfied, and the disciples picked up twelve basketfuls of broken pieces that were left over.*

²¹ *The number of those who ate was about five thousand men, besides women and children.*

(Matthew 14:13-21)

After this excerpt, Father Johnstone then praised Jesus and described to his congregation why this was a miracle. He conveyed the importance of food through the eyes of the hungry, making sure to remind the flock not to lose sight of this in the face of key lime pies and Mrs. Jasper's famous sugar cookies, which drew a few congenial laughs. He then capped everything off with a short prayer.

So this 'new angle' that Mr. Conrad and Jeremiah are alluding to is news to the pastor. He can't recall this supposed divergence they speak of, and attempting to remember it is making his skull pulse with the familiar throbs of a migraine. Harder, until he can barely keep his eyes open. He squints, pinching the bridge of his nose, breathing. Breathing too fast. The pastor feels his clothes distend and stick to his body as he sweats, droplets carving down his forehead and neck. Heavy and wet. It's never happened during the day before. Never, he thinks.

"Uh, Father, you got a little something..." Jeremiah says, touching the spot just under his nose.

The pastor slides a finger across his upper lip, sniffing and turning away from the audience so they won't see blood on his hand. He pulls out a handkerchief from his back pocket—originally intended for pie crumbs and various fillings, but scrubbing the blood away is a more pressing. Father Johnstone sniffs, forcing himself to give Jeremiah a reassuring smile. He snorts hard again, testing his nostril for the familiar glug of fluid attempting to spill out, but the flow has broken for the moment. The fever, however, does not relent.

Jeremiah puts a hand on Father Johnstone's shoulder, asking covertly, "Do you need me to get someone for you? I can fetch Dr. Keller," he says, but the pastor is already nodding him off. He doesn't need anyone because God is in control, and his faith in that must remain steadfast.

The pastor prayed for strength last night. He begged the good Lord give him rest, give him the ability to carry out His will and lead the flock. He asked for nothing more than the simple blessing of a good night's sleep, if only *just* one. And he found rest, but it came at a price.

"Goddamn, Father, you're bleeding again," Jeremiah says, but not in the mildly concerned tone he used before. He's panicked. The man that's surrounded all day by meat and fat and animal carcass is afraid, enough to make him blaspheme without shame. Heat spikes in Father Johnstone's body again, sweat pouring and convening with the torrent bursting from his nose. He mashes the handkerchief to his nostrils as Jeremiah tells Mr. Conrad, "Find Dr. Keller. Get him here now."

The handkerchief soaks blood until it's draining down his wrist and forearm, down to his elbow, and now he's sprouting pea-sized yellow blisters. Pustules surface on his face and neck, on his chest, all of them bulging with hot fluid. He can feel each one sing as the sweat washes over them, and the blood hasn't stopped or showed any signs of slowing down. The migraine tapers off, replaced by a feeling of lightheadedness that threatens to take him under, back into those dreams where Madeline Paige does the unthinkable.

Father Johnstone feels his weight roll out of the chair, falling towards the soft grass of the church grounds, falling back into nightmares, but Jeremiah catches him just before his head claps against the earth. Blood spatters against the lime-green polo, but the butcher ignores this and begins smacking Father Johnstone's cheek, slapping him repeatedly, saying, "C'mon, stay with me. The doc is coming."

Going to Dr. Keller, accepting his 'help' and those ungodly pills—it was all a mistake, the pastor thinks. He should have never turned his back on the Lord, despite any momentary discomfort he was experiencing. The bleeding and the migraines and the night terrors, it's all punishment for losing faith. He's paying the price for his complacency.

"I need the fucking doctor here! He's losing blood!" Jeremiah screams, but it's faint. It's all turned down. The pressure of the handkerchief and the screams are dim; the mass of people crowding are blurry silhouettes. Father Johnstone can barely keep his eyes open, the weight of his head fully supported in the crook of Jeremiah's bloody arm. Blood everywhere. It tickles faintly as it traces the pastor's jaw line and around the curvature of this neck. He's fading, falling back into that dark place, and then he sees Madeline emerge from the crowd.

The pastor's eyes open slightly, watching her lean frame move closer until she's standing over Jeremiah Will. She squats down, allowing her legs to fold under her so that her knees are buried in blood-stained grass, but the smile is back. Madeline Paige is smiling again, bringing her lips to Father Johnstone's ear until she's practically breathing inside of it.

She whispers, "See you on the other side, Johnstone."

On the Road with Billy Burke, Truck Stop Preacher

"For you single men, the road is lonely. Believe me, I know. Ain't got no one to talk to. Got nothin' and no one waiting for you at home. Just you and your thoughts, right? And that's when the goddamn Devil decides to get in your head. He gets on in there...burrowin' deep. He makes you hit the bottle and snort that meth you love...stirs your thoughts around. You forget yourself...forget the Lord. You start thinking with your pecker. So there you are: sitting in the cab of your rig...drunk, spun, and lonely...then the knock comes. It's some dirty lot lizard just checking to see if you want some company. She ain't got no shoes...got about half her teeth left, and they're yellow and worn the hell down to little nubs. She got sores around her mouth. This little piece of trash says she'll let you bust a hard load in her mouth if you give her a taste of that meth. Just a bump to keep her spirits up. And even though you can smell the cock on her breath from the last guy—it's tempting. For a little meth, you could fuck this girl's mouth and not be lonely anymore. You don't have to suffer by yourself. That's the Devil thinkin', my friends. I promise you, soon as that little girl spits your wad out in the ashtray, she's gone...off to the next man. You're worse off than before. That's how clever the Devil is: makes you want the thing you don't really want. He takes advantage of you when you're alone, weak. That's why you're here today. Take it from ol' Billy Burke...you are not alone."

The Hospital

Father Johnstone wakes up.

There's very little sunlight breaking through the shades, making it difficult to tell if the day is shifting to dawn or dusk, but it matters little. The pastor is in the white, sterile confines of the hospital, and therefore, not going anywhere in the near future. Dr. Keller is a bit of a stickler when it comes to regulations. That's the word around town, anyway. Whether you're a housewife, a plant worker, or even a man of God, there's no excuse in the good doctor's mind that justifies an early release.

"Sometimes living longer means putting your life on hold for a bit," Dr. Keller tells his patients, but that doesn't always go over.

The sense of responsibility runs deep in Pratt. Men work hard and the woman and wives do just as much keeping their homes in line. Little things like illness and injury aren't any kind of reason to take a day off or not cook. Even Father Johnstone has been known to give a few sermons while under the weather, and they were certainly not his best. However, this inclination to carry on through the afflictions of life is best illustrated by Mrs. Deebs. After being hospitalized with a nasty case of walking pneumonia a few years ago, she would sneak out the first time Dr. Keller's back was turned. That woman ran the streets of Pratt barefoot and wearing nothing but a hospital gown, mooning everything in her wake, all for the sake of fulfilling her duties as a wife.

"I was sick as a dog, I'll tell ya," she said. "But if my hubby don't get his supper, well, you'd be lookin' at a dead woman, I'd s'pect."

Of course, Mrs. Deebs was being a tad facetious. Half the reason why the Presto Diner exists is for those rare occasions the women and wives need a night off from the stove. No shame in that. It's more a matter of personal *pride*, which is the same reason Dr. Keller refuses to bend the rules for any of his patients. "Regulations are regulations," he'd say. It's his firm approach to conveying that when it comes to your health, there are no gray areas or shortcuts.

So when Dr. Keller enters the room with his trademark clipboard and white lab coat, Father Johnstone knows the inquiry as to when he can check out is anything if not premature. That's not going to stop him from trying though. At the very least, he needs to make arrangements for Mary—perhaps not for her usual nightly walk, but someone is going to need to replenish her food rations and fill her water bowl.

Dr. Keller must be able to read his concern because the first thing out of his mouth is, "If you're worried about your dog, don't be." He takes a seat on a rolling stool near the foot of the bed, giving it a little scoot towards the pastor so he's lined up with his waist. "Mrs. Adams is taking care of her...says Mary has been getting along just fine with Missy and Chips to keep her company." Then, for the sake of full disclosure, Dr. Keller admits, "Had to borrow your house keys though, I'm afraid. Hope you don't mind that I took the liberty."

The pastor sighs deeply, shoulders easing into the soft mattress of the hospital bed. He says, "No, it's fine. Thank you, David."

"Least I could do," Dr. Keller says.

Carted machines beep softly on either side of the bed, the only one that Father Johnstone recognizes being the heart monitor. White wires stem from the base of the mechanism, leading under the wool comforter and sheet to his torso. The pastor takes a particularly deep breath, feeling the stickiness of the patches pulling at his skin and chest hair. There's also a bag of clear fluid being intravenously fed into his body via the needle planted in his hand. Thankfully, the entry point is obscured by medical tape. Father Johnstone can't even get a flu shot without turning away and clamping his eyes shut.

"I guess we'll start with the easy stuff first," Dr. Keller leads in, positioning the pen against the legal pad, ready to take notes. "How are you feeling?"

Father Johnstone considers the question, keeping in mind the turmoil he's experienced over the past week or so. "Better than I have been, I guess."

"Care to elaborate?" Dr. Keller asks.

There's no headache. There's also no fever or that feeling of emotional instability he'd been experiencing. Not right now, at least. He feels calm considering the fact that he's waking up in a hospital. Father Johnstone also notices the distinct pang of hunger in his gut, and it's calling out for something other than the decadent baked goods of Miss Madeline Paige. He needs something salty and heavy, a cheeseburger or a bowl of Mrs. Gentry's famous pot roast. Maybe even some of that diner food everyone's been raving about. His appetite is back with a vengeance, that's for sure. Best of all though, the pastor feels rested. Whatever happened between the Pratt bake-off and now, it seems the good Lord saw it fit to grant Father Johnstone's prayers. If he had any complaint, it would be the slight tenderness in his ears and nostrils. His throat is a little sore too, but he ultimately keeps these symptoms to himself, thinking this will work towards an early release (Lord forgive the lie). He wants to see Mary.

"I feel good," Father Johnstone says. "Hungry though."

"I'll have one of the nurses get you some food just as soon as we finish up here," the doctor says, still making notations. "I'm afraid I can't give you anything substantial just yet…fruit and Jell-O for the time being. Maybe some toast."

"You think maybe we could go a little heavier?" Father Johnstone asks. "I haven't had anything in a while. Honestly, I haven't had much of an appetite up until now."

"Take it easy," Dr. Keller says. "Even if you feel fine right now,

I don't want to push your body any harder than we have to. Now, do you feel dizzy or lightheaded at all?" he asks, putting pen to paper again.

"No." The pastor shakes his head.

"Any bone or muscle pain?"

"No," he says, giving his legs and arms a little flex, testing them. "No pain…more like I'm a bit weak. Joints are kinda stiff, too."

"Normal," Dr. Keller says. "You've been off your feet a few days."

"A few days?" Father Johnstone confirms.

"It's Wednesday," Dr. Keller says. "Going on Wednesday evening. Mr. Conrad came in here Sunday afternoon on the verge of keeling over, saying you were having some kind of a fit at the bake-off. Do you remember any of that?"

Madeline's sweet whisper: *"See you on the other side, Johnstone."*

"Vaguely," the pastor says. "It all happened a bit fast."

"That's an understatement." Dr. Keller peers back down at the clipboard and makes a few additional notes. He sets it down on the bedside table next to the lamp, crossing one leg over the other so the ankle is resting on a knee. "This town has been chattier than normal…rumor mill's a churnin'," Dr. Keller says, smiling gravely.

"How do you mean?" The pastor suspects this is in reference to him and what happened at the Pratt bake-off. Obviously, there's going to be quite a few people concerned about the wellbeing of their town preacher, and it's not like he has a replacement that can step in at a moment's notice. Far from it.

"Look, you know I've never been one of the flock," Dr. Keller says. "And I don't make a habit in getting involved with people's personal lives…keeps things simple for me, but from one pillar to another, I can't just send you back out there to those people unprepared."

"Okay," Father Johnstone consents to the subject. "So there's gossip then?"

"Gossip is whatever *is* or *isn't* happening in the bedroom of the Durphy household," Dr. Keller says. "You got all sorts of people telling different versions of the story. This thing here about you—everybody is saying the same thing, more or less. They say you did something a man in your position shouldn't be doing."

Dr. Keller could be referring to a few things: the moment of *lust* he shared (be it ever so brief) with the widow Wright, or the less than stable nature he's been exhibiting around select members of the flock. It might even be his relationship with Madeline Paige, which could be viewed as fraternization amongst certain rumormongers in Pratt. The lonely and bored have an affinity for making mountains out of molehills, regardless of the truth or validity of these claims, and word gets around quick. Both men can attest to that.

"Do you remember what you did on Sunday at the sermon?" Dr. Keller asks.

"I do. 'The Feeding of 5,000' reading," the pastor answers. "The same reading I always give the day of the bake-off...to remind the people what a blessing food is."

"I'm familiar with that reading. Jesus arrives, cures the sick...he then proceeds to multiply the bread and fish until the entire town is fed. That about right?" Dr. Keller asks.

He's paraphrasing, but for a non-devotee such as Dr. Keller, it's surprising he'd know even that much. Pratt's chief medical expert has never made it a secret that he doesn't subscribe to the Good Book or its lessons, ambiguously citing how he's neither for nor against it. "I'm a man of science. Always have been, always will," he tells people, but the reality is that he prefers the simplicity of keeping faith and the workings of modern medicine separate. A doctor should rely on his training and skill, not omniscient beings or empty hope. Things like 'miracles' and 'acts of God,' although rare, can still be scientifically explained. Dr.

59

Keller had always believed that, up until recently.

"That's roughly the gist of it, yes," Father Johnstone says.

"And do you remember what you did *after* that reading?" the doctor probes.

"Well, I imagine we prayed and I did another recitation," the pastor says, although it lacks confidence, almost sounding like an assumption to Dr. Keller. "The tithe plate was passed around, hymns were sung—I forget which ones exactly...the usual Sunday, David. I don't know what you're looking for."

"When we brought you in here, you had lost four pints of blood already," Dr. Keller explains, frowning. "We call that a Class IV Hemorrhage, Father. Do you know what that is?" he asks, but the term is thrown out in a rhetorical fashion. No one in Pratt has ever suffered one, and therefore, the terminology has never appeared in the *Tribune*. "It means you'd lost roughly 40% of the blood in your body...all through your nose, ears, and mouth. And your skin was as white as that sheet you're under, all except for the pustules, that is. You may have noticed they've left some minor discoloration."

Father Johnstone can somewhat recall the episode: the sudden burst in his nose and the lightheadedness that followed, that feeling of weakness and intense migraine, and then the fading. He faded to that other side where Madeline was waiting for him, just as she said she would.

"Make no mistake, you were very nearly dead," Dr. Keller says. "I know you hear these TV doctors say that all the time for effect—but sure as shit, you were dying right in front of me. You had only minutes to spare," he explains. "Luckily, you got in when you did and we were able to replace the blood you lost."

"I appreciate that, David. I surely do," Father Johnstone says. "But what does any of that have to do with the sermon?"

"I'll say it again: you were gushing blood and breaking out in pus boils right in front of your congregation," Dr. Keller says. "You almost died. The people out there...they're saying you're not sick. They're saying God punished you for what you said in the church."

"What is it that I *supposedly* said in the church, David?" Father Johnstone snaps. "Because I think I'd remember if I did something differently."

Just as soon as he says this though, the pastor doubts himself. After all, he's been forgetting quite a bit over the past week and a half, blacking out and appearing places not knowing how he got there. Forgetting conversations. Forgetting extended periods of time.

"They're saying you questioned God," Dr. Keller reveals. "They're saying that you did the reading—just as you've always done, I imagine, but afterwards, you proceeded to openly question the miracle."

"Wait...I *questioned* it?" Father Johnstone asks, sitting up proper in the hospital bed. "How would I even do that? I've never done that."

Dr. Keller tells the pastor, "You refuted it. People are saying that for the better part of an hour, you walked around the church asking members or your congregation to scientifically explain how Christ could multiply bread and fish. 'Sorcery,' I believe, is the term you used to describe it. That's what they tell me, anyway."

"Well, I don't remember saying anything of the sort."

"I don't doubt you believe that," Dr. Keller says. "Everyone in that church has the same story though, and now that story has spread all over. When you walk outta here—the town won't be looking at you the same way." He offers the only consolation he can, telling the pastor, "You may not like it but at least you know now. You can prepare."

"Prepare for what exactly?" Father Johnstone asks, clearly new to being a topic of controversy. A quicker succession of the beeps emanate from the heart monitor. He says, "I haven't done anything wrong, David."

Dr. Keller gives a desperate chuckle. "We've got a whole town that believes the local preacher just defied Christ in a church," he says. "What are you going to do? Call them liars? You gonna say you don't remember any of it and hope things get back to normal?" he asks. "Hell, even the people that *weren't* there won't believe you."

Father Johnstone remembers the reading from that Sunday. He can see himself reciting the words and how they sounded in the acoustics of the church. There was a prayer afterward, and the congregation prayed with him, just as they always do. They are his flock. They do what Father Johnstone says, but what followed after the first ten minutes of the sermon is hazy. It's bits and pieces at best, lacking continuity, and trying to remember is making the pastor's head hurt again, so he stops. He lets go, and the pain goes with it.

"I don't wish to patronize, but maybe you could play the 'I was just testing you' card," Dr. Keller offers. "Either that, or you can say your illness put you in a state of delirium. I'm willing to back that up if you think it'll help."

"And what, pray tell, is my illness?" the pastor asks, giving the bridge of his nose a slight pinch to relieve the pressure.

Dr. Keller picks up his clipboard from the bedside table, flipping a couple pages. He explains to the pastor, "Over the past three days you've been in a coma. No surprise there with all the blood you lost. It happens when circulation is cut off from the brain, and in your case, you had it coming out of every damn hole in your head there."

"Right," Father Johnstone cuts in. "But what was the cause of it? What's wrong with me?"

"Nothing," Dr. Keller says. "On paper, you're healthy."

"How is that possible? You just said that had a Level IV Hemorrhage or whatever, and that I almost died, right?"

"That's *Class* IV, Father," the doctor corrects him. "And I said on paper you're healthy. That doesn't mean you're okay. I just can't find anything *medically* wrong with you." He displays the clipboard, saying, "I ran tests. The tests are supposed to tell me what the problem is and how it came about, but after three days, I haven't found any explanation. In fact, I've got more questions than when I started."

At first, Father Johnstone feared an official diagnosis from Dr. Keller. Men around his age start to fall apart. 'The machine breaks down,' as they say, but not knowing the root of the problem, being hospitalized for no specific reason—this is much more alarming for the pastor. It's fear of the unknown.

"We could be dealing with something entirely new here," Dr. Keller says, setting his clipboard back down on the nightstand. "Whatever it is, I just hope that the worst of it has passed."

It's the Devil, Father Johnstone thinks. The Devil courses through his blood now, causing fever and migraines, causing pus-blisters and bleeding episodes. During the day, he torments him with lethargy, and at night: acute restlessness. When he does manage to sleep (with the aid of those ungodly pills), his dreams are infected with *lust* and violence. He makes the pastor forget, takes control, perverts the Lord's Word in front of the flock. The Devil is steadily ruining him, on a physical level and by tarnishing his character. Pratt has it all wrong, the pastor thinks. God isn't punishing him at all. It's not a test. This unknown affliction that Dr. Keller speaks of is pure evil, and a non-believer would never be able to detect it.

"There's one other issue I need to discuss with you," Dr. Keller says. "It's about your blood type. Do you happen know what blood type you are, Father?"

"Shouldn't you know this?" the pastor asks.

"Yes," Dr. Keller nods. "I should. Can you answer the question please?"

It was one of the few times that Father Johnstone willingly let himself be penetrated by a needle: years ago, the pastor recalls, for the Pratt blood drive. Dr. Keller solicited the church under the pretense that the flock would likely be more receptive to the idea, what with their moral obligations to their fellow man. All donors were given a vanilla crème cookie and juice, provided by Mrs. Keller, and the doctor and pastor hosted a post-drive BBQ on the church grounds. The doctor paid a small fortune at the butcher's, and the two men spent the afternoon talking all things medicine and God, grilling burgers and hot dogs. They even shared a six-pack of domestic, which hit a little harder than normal because of their respective blood donations. This was how Father Johnstone became acquainted with Dr. David Keller, and it taught the pastor two distinct things: that believing in the Lord and His Word isn't necessary in order to do good, and that the pastor's blood type is AB positive. He distinctly remembers the technician telling him that it's the rarest type there is.

"Maybe about 1% of people have it," she said.

Father Johnstone conveys this information to the doctor, mentioning the blood drive and technician to put the knowledge into context. Dr. Keller says, "Right, and there was also the time you snagged your arm on the nail in your basement. Remember that?" he asks. "I took some blood to make sure you hadn't become infected."

"Yes, I remember that," the pastor says.

"AB positive again," Dr. Keller reveals, and then he slips his hand inside his lab coat, pulling out a piece of paper that's folded into quarters. He looks at it for a moment, frowning. "These are the results from when you came in last week...and there's an irregularity."

"I thought you said I was healthy," the pastor says.

"Right," Dr. Keller says, unfolding the results and giving them a quick scan. "No viruses or anything that would indicate you're sick. The blood itself is fine."

"Well, what's the problem then?"

"The blood isn't AB positive."

"So you're saying my blood type isn't the same anymore?"

Father Johnstone asks.

Dr. Keller nods. "Correct."

"Is that a rare occurrence?"

"It's an *impossible* occurrence," the doctor says. "Blood types don't change. It doesn't happen."

The Devil, Father Johnstone thinks. The Devil is in the blood, changing things, mutating his system. "Could there be an error?" Father Johnstone ventures, but he already knows he's grasping at straws with this. Dr. Keller is a thorough man.

"No. I quadruple-checked. You're an O negative now," he says. "You've gone from universal recipient to a universal donor. Not exactly the worst thing in the world, but still...it's disconcerting."

But what Dr. Keller really wants to say is that it's a medical miracle, and although he's never believed in the so-called 'act of God,' he can't deny that a man's blood type changing may fall into that category. At the very least, Father Johnstone is living proof that scientific law has been broken, and it's a contradiction that won't be taken lightly should it become public knowledge.

"You can't tell anyone about this," Dr. Keller says, but his concern is uncalled for. Father Johnstone has no inclination to share the news with anyone, member of the flock or no. As bad as the rumors are going around Pratt, a medical impossibility would only add fuel to the fire.

"I think I've got enough on my plate right now," the pastor says.

"Glad we can agree on that." The doctor folds the test results back into quarters, stowing them in his lab coat. "It's possible you could be discharged tomorrow, but I hope you don't mind if I reach out to you for any additional tests I might want to run. As far as I can tell, you're healthy, but there's still plenty to figure out."

"That's fine, David. Of course," the pastor says. "Whatever I can do to help."

"Good." Dr. Keller nods, resuming a standing position and pushing the stool towards the wall. He retrieves his clipboard from the bedside table, looking upon the pastor and seeing little hope in his eyes. Evening is almost upon them, and Dr. Keller realizes that whether he likes it or not, his profession as Pratt's chief medical expert has transcended into new territory. Father Johnstone is more than just a patient; both men know this. Both men fear the situation they've found themselves in. They don't even need to verbalize it. Like Mrs. Deebs, the pastor must persevere and return to business as usual, no matter how much of an interruption the Devil may pose. He'll pray for good health, that the Lord remove this evil from his blood. He'll pray for a renewed relationship with the flock and dreamless sleep, and then Father Johnstone remembers how he's been in a hospital for the past three days. He remembers waking up in the middle of the night, screaming, drenched in sweat with the occasional nosebleed to plug, but he was always in the confines of his own home. Now he's been in a hospital for three full days, seemingly under close observation by Dr. Keller and his staff.

"Did anything happen, David?" he asks. "While I was under...did I do or say anything out of the ordinary?"

"Nothing much. Occasional flinch here and there," he says. "That's normal. It's rare that a coma patient will speak, but you did."

Madeline, the pastor thinks, waiting on the other side just as she said she'd be. It's always Madeline.

"Tell me Father," Dr. Keller says, "who or what is Pollux?"

Las Vegas, NV

The disease passes to Desiree.

I'm notified of this when she arrives at my door two weeks after our initial encounter, accompanied by two dark-skinned males. Large men. In Las Vegas, they are technically referred to as 'muscle,' not to be mistaken with a bundle of fibrous tissue or mollusk meat. Their intention is to inflict physical harm, and potentially extort a sum of money out of me. I know this before I even open the door. Sensing intentions—the intangibles—is something I've managed to hone over the years.

Upon entering the suite, the two men take me by the shoulders as Desiree scolds me, asking, "What did I tell you, huh? I told you you better not give me anything I don't want. I fucking said that, didn't I?"

I smell her anger, her disease. I smell treated cow hide and fumes of the marijuana plant fuming off of the two men's jackets. They grip the fabric on my shoulders to hold me in place, keep me from running. They're disgusted for reasons I haven't deciphered just yet—not because of the disease. Something else.

Desiree draws a finger to just under her left eye, indicating the swollen area. It's plum-colored. "See this?" she asks. "This is what you get when your boss finds out you're not fit to work. He's sick, too. We're on four different kinds of antibiotics because of you."

I'm familiar with what she's referring to: Ciprofloxacin, Ofloxacin, and Nalidixic acid. Silly components cooked up by silly little men in white lab coats who think they understand the human body. Their methods are inferior. I could cure Desiree but lack the inclination and the required materials to do so.

"And don't even get me started on your little fetish. You're fucked, man," she says.

"Dirty motherfucker," one of the muscle whispers. He shakes his head, judges me.

This is the source of the muscle's repulsion: the Christian lingerie

and biblical stimulation. Perhaps the Holy water, too. Desiree mastur-
bated with the cross, then I fornicated with her, climaxing deep inside
her vaginal cavity. I instructed her to squat down on the bed and push
out the seminal fluid, excrete it upon the front cover of the Christian
text. An abundant puddle of foggy white was produced. Desiree was
then asked to lap at the wet leather as an homage to God and Christ and
the Holy spirit, licking it clean until only the glisten of her saliva
remained. The longest end of the crucifix was then inserted into her, so
far the hips of the Savior were buried in her cavity. Three minutes of
silent prayer was observed, allowing the wood to soak the remaining
fluids and enzymes. I have since carved the idol symbol down to a stake-
like point.

"You hear me?" Desiree asks. "You're fucking sick, man. No wonder
you have to pay for it."

The muscle holds me in place, but they do so in a way where they try
to make as little physical contact as possible, as if to touch me would
infect them somehow. It's obvious the whore disclosed the details of our
encounter, if only to make her lapse in judgment excusable by
comparison. This is when Desiree reaches into the back pocket of her
jeans, which are crusted in a decorative plastic known as 'rhinestones.'
She pulls out a straight razor, unfolding it and displaying the blade.
Reflected on the steel are myself and the muscle, stretched out and
distorted due to the curve of the object. I start to get excited. The sting
at the tip of the urethra dims and I feel myself growing thick, hard.

"I can either cut your cock off or slit your throat," Desiree says. "It's
up to you."

The whore's usage of the word 'cock' reminds me of back home, the
coop where the hens would lay eggs while others were harvested for
materials. Feathers were used to stuff pillows. Poultry was either cooked
on a spit over a wood fire or baked; gizzards would be floured, seasoned,
and deep-fried in animal fat (a delicacy). Other organs and spare parts
had their usages, too: the feet, the beak, and the wattles.

Desiree steps close, placing the edge of the blade against my neck and
dragging it down. It's her very poor attempt at trying to instill fear in

me. She says, "No begging? You're not gonna try to buy your way out of this?"

"I could." I tilt my head as if to consider it. "I choose not to."

She smiles. Desiree curls her lips—not with joy—but out of anger. This is not the response she was hoping for, and therefore, she will not do me the great favor of ending my life swiftly. Cutting the carotid artery (which stems from the brachiocephalic trunk) would prove mortally compromising, and therefore, lacks the sufficient amount of suffering I'm expected to endure.

"We'll see how much you like this town when you're a dickless freak." Desiree unbuttons my pants and draws the metallic pull-tab downward, separating the teeth of the zipper. Her hands graze my genitalia, prompting her to look me in the eye, look down again. "You're hard?" She looks at the muscle on either side of me, shocked. "This guy is fucking hard right now!"

In response, their disgust swells a little bit more. Tips of the muscle's fingers pull away from my shoulders, compromising their grip. I patiently wait for Desiree to remove me, pull me out and examine. Her fingers—now chewed, chipped, and unkempt—excavate a slab of meat, covered in sores. Skin glistens where pustule patches bloomed, popped, and became infected, resembling that of a vermilion pickle. Oils in Desiree's fingers soak into the wounds, sting. A sharp constant pain. When the penis flops over the waistband, opaque fluid squirts onto Desiree's wrist. She recoils, dropping the blade on marble floors and wiping the skin dry against her shirt. Scrubbing vigorously.

"Oh God, that's so fucking gross." Her nostrils flex once, twice, picking up the smell in the air. Infection cuts through residual marijuana fumes and the lilac body spray the whore wears on her neck, wrists, and chest. The muscle peers down and notices the weeping wounds and areas crusted in yellow scab, relinquishing their grip just a little bit more. Gag reflex chugs over my left shoulder, an opportune moment to unleash my own attack.

Unlike Desiree, I am quite handy with a blade.

I spend the next many hours showing them.

The Release

Father Johnstone is nude upon a bed. It's a bed he's been in many times recently: silk sheets in a garish shade of crimson. Pillows bulge at the headboard like they've never been used before, lacking that canyon years of sleep would impress upon them. The island is smooth, fenced off by pale candles at various stages of melt. They provide just enough light to see every fold and ripple of the fabric, but beyond the fringe of fire is black. Infinite nothing. The pastor subconsciously draws in his legs to cover himself, looking to random points of the void for a way out. Then he notices Madeline Paige lounging behind him, draped in the silk bedding. She gives the pastor a reassuring smile and tells him to not be afraid. Madeline says, "You'll be fine here."

This is how the dream starts.

It's what Father Johnstone feels he can't divulge, even to someone like Dr. Keller who maintains that he'll never judge, never repeat any of the information he's given. He simply wants to know if one variant corresponds with the other for medical reasons.

"I leave things like rumors and speculation to folks with too much time on their hands," he said this morning at the hospital. "So if there's something you want to tell me, you can be sure it won't be repeated."

The content of these dreams, these 'night terrors,' as Dr. Keller refers to them—Father Johnstone is certain they aren't the root cause of his recent health problems, least of all a changing blood type. Dreams are in the mind, and so they must be dealt with through prayer and a consummate devotion to the Lord. As certain members of the flock turn to God to extinguish their impure thoughts and fantasies of violence, so too must the pastor, despite any pain or anguish that may follow. He's accepted the fact that another migraine or bleeding episode is a possibility, or perhaps another coma. The path to purity may land him in the Pratt Medical Ward again, but a man with the Devil in his blood cannot shepherd the flock, cannot be expected to lead as the Lord intends. He must begin the cleansing process, even though the mere mention of her name heats the pastor's blood.

Madeline. Always Madeline.

She lies on the bed, bidding Father Johnstone to come closer, to press his body against her own. He refuses at first, opting to remain at the far corner of the bed with his knees pulled bashfully to his chest. His heart beats faster; the sweating begins. It's not heat. This isn't a particularly warm place. Father Johnstone is *lusting*, and Madeline smoothes the spot next to her on the bed with a hand, as if to say, 'You can lie here safely…right next to me,' and so the pastor moves closer to her, skin and blood hot, almost boiling. He accepts her invitation, dragging palms and knees across the silk surface. Little dark blotches of sweat trail from the corner of the bed, diagonally to where Madeline is waiting. He feels himself grow firm as he gets closer. Closer still, she reaches out to him, a hand curling around the back of his neck and pulling the pastor's face to her own. Father Johnstone can smell her sweet breath, the heat in his skin and blood spiking when she says, "Kiss me. Hard."

This part of the dream is also consistent.

At the beginning of these episodes, Father Johnstone would usually wake up in his bed, alarmed and covered in sweat. Sometimes out of breath or shaking. These were the first whispers of sex he'd experienced in years, making his lungs and heart flex uncomfortably, almost painfully as they had long been out of practice. The excitement of sin, even imagined sin, accelerated his body to the point of exertion. So Father Johnstone would need to take a moment to calm down, breathing slowly in the dark as Mary tried to get comfortable again. He'd splash cool water on his face in the bathroom, changing into fresh pajamas if necessary, and wait for his organs to stop rattling inside himself.

Father Johnstone would return to bed, breathing and praying. Breathing slowly in the dark, and praying to the good Lord for dreamless rest. He prayed these excursions with Madeline didn't get any worse.

The Lord wasn't listening.

Back to sleep, back into the dreams where she's waiting, lounging nude upon the bed, it happens again. Father Johnstone is naked and disoriented, drawn to the only familiar aspect within the void of candles and silk. Madeline clutches the back of his neck and they kiss, sometimes sweetly, other times lewd to the point of it being unnatural if he resists. It's those instances in which he tries to keep to the Divine path that it turns nefarious, he's realized. Madeline pushes her tongue into the pastor's mouth, then further, deep down into his throat so that it's pressing against his trachea. It makes a crunching sound and Father Johnstone's breathing stops, his neck visibly bulging. Most of the time he'll suffocate on tongue and wake up in his bed again. Other times he'll bite down, flooding his mouth with wet meat and blood. The pastor's gag reflex kicks in, pushing the elongated lump out of his throat onto the bed. Meat flops around on the mattress while Madeline pulls back, laughing girlishly with blood seeping through her teeth, saying, 'You'll learn to like this one day, Johnstone.'

Again, the pastor would wake up, wet and shaking and scared. Again, he'd try to tell himself that these are just dreams. They are grotesque in nature and disturbing, yes, but dreams all the same. No real harm can come from them. He'll always wake up in the safety of his own home, heart beating in his ears and unnerved, but safe all the same. And so the cycle would begin again: calming the body, clearing the mind, and praying to the good Lord once again that when he returns to sleep, there are no terrors waiting for him. He prayed sweet Madeline be not on the other side ready to do the unspeakable, to tempt him into sin, and yet the pastor is unsure if he truly meant it. *Lust* may have eclipsed the sentiment, that carnal need to experience in dreams what he vowed never to do on earth. He wasn't 'learning to like it,' as Madeline said, but he couldn't deny that he was becoming acclimated.

As Father Johnstone has said before, "A man who does not fear sin is destined to commit them."

The Devil plays off the will of the weak and complacent. He allows you to accept sin in your life, eventually pushing you to a point of indulgence, and before you know it, your life is consumed by *lust* or violence. It becomes drugs and alcohol and pornography. You covet, fornicate, and murder without regard, but these dark paths always start with that sliver of welcome, which is why we must reject all sin in all forms. Every version. Even in dreams.

Father Johnstone has reiterated these warnings numerous times in his sermons and private counseling sessions, usually in regards to marital fidelity. In fact, he doesn't doubt Mr. and Mrs. Fairfax are destined to go down this road themselves, what with their mutual disgust and ever-increasing animosity. It seems only natural they'd venture outside of their marriage in search of those earthly delights they no longer find in each other, but this is a slippery slope as most sinners are repeat offenders. Only those true to the Lord and His Word repent with the intention of adhering to virtue, and Father Johnstone doesn't see this in the Fairfaxes. Their immediate happiness is all that seems to matter to them, which is making them lose sight of the final destination of their souls.

The pastor will not make the same mistake.

He has emerged from the hospital with a mission, one that takes precedence over retrieving Mary from the Adams' household or his still-panging gut. These things can wait for the time being. As Dr. Keller says, "Sometimes living longer means putting your life on hold for a bit," however, Father Johnstone's task at hand has nothing to do with blood types or anything regarding his physical self. He needs to heal his spirit, to cleanse his blood of the evil that's so obviously inhabited it, and so he now finds himself en route to the First Church of Pratt.

Today, he must save himself.

The pastor is wearing the same short-sleeved dress shirt and black slacks he had on at the bake-off, though they've since been washed and pressed. Not a trace of blood remains, and he hopes Jeremiah Will's wife had a similar amount of luck with the lime-green polo. Although he can't be sure, the pastor suspects Jeremiah bought the shirt specifically for his judging duties at the bake-off for the sake of impressions, and he makes a mental note to pay him a visit later to atone for the inconvenience he caused. Only after he's taken care of himself though. Mary and the hunger and all the apologies he owes can wait. He needs Lord's house and His counsel. He needs his spirit mended and the Devil seized from his blood.

No more Madeline Paige, he thinks.

No more dreams of seduction and *lust*, the pornographic reel of her pressing breasts to his mouth, forcing his head between her legs and commanding him to lick, chew, and suck, and if he resists, he knows blood is coming. She bleeds from her breasts, soaking the pastor's mouth with boiling hot copper that blisters his tongue, but sometimes it goes beyond the scope of his imagi-nation, and this is how Father Johnstone knows it's the Devil at play. The Devil inhabits his mind, feeding him anti-fantasy of his mouth on the vaginal cavity of Madeline Paige, reluctantly licking, saliva leaking down and pooling into the crimson silk. Her hands will be clamped on the back of his head, pulling him to her, inside of her, and if he resists, a bouquet of maggots blooms out of Madeline's canal. The maggots chew the inside of his cheeks and burrow into his teeth, devouring him, eating his throat, and they taste like sugar. They taste like all those dreamy desserts Madeline feeds him, and she's laughing, writhing on the bed as the pastor chokes on the sweet moving obstruction. She says, "Don't worry. You'll get used to it. They all do."

Walking the dirt dusted roads of Pratt, Father Johnstone catches himself mumbling prayers, saying, "Lord, remove these demons from my mind. Lord, grant me clarity and peace."

He walks with Divine purpose, and at the halfway point between the hospital and the church, the pastor notices people stopping in their tracks on the sidewalk. They're gawking, looking at him like a man back from the dead. Last they saw, he was bleeding and falling apart in the arms of Jeremiah Will, bursting blood, so a rumor of his passing isn't exactly far-fetched. Or maybe they think he's sick. Their faces shift through a range of expressions upon seeing Father Johnstone, always starting with recognition, but then turning to either pure fear or the indecision as to whether or not to say 'hi' or wave or give a cordial smile. He's storming by too fast anyway, granting onlookers the reprieve of being able to pretend they didn't notice each other. The smalltown niceties he's grown accustomed to over the years have been tossed to the back burner, replaced by a sense of disdain or avoidance. No one wants to be the first to reach out, to offer the hand of acceptance that the pastor so often preaches of extending.

Dr. Keller wasn't exaggerating; Pratt has been talking.

Mr. Farson notices the pastor coming his way, prematurely flicking a cigarette to the street that's not even halfway finished. He enters the hardware store, smoke carrying over his shoulder while another couple of onlookers halt their conversation mid-sentence, staring conspicuously at Father Johnstone. The pastor is still walking and mumbling, praying to the good Lord as Mr. Radford throws a disapproving glare his way from a porch rocking chair. He elevates today's edition of *The Pratt Tribune* just below eye-level, spying the man stalking past and chattering to himself in the street. There's hatred in their eyes. Hatred and fear, and then something firm pelts the pastor's shoulder blade, bursting wet and staining the crisp white shirt. Father Johnstone catches a few tendrils of fruit and seeds flying through the air, but cares not enough to identify the assailant who's launching tomatoes at him.

He says, "Lord, allow the flock to forgive me, and allow me passage to forgive myself for resenting them. Give me time and peace to restore my spirit."

Another tomato pegs Father Johnstone in the lower back, and then an egg whizzes by from his left, just missing his head and shattering against the tire of a tan Chevy parked outside the painting supplies store. Someone, a teenage youth from the sound of it, yells out from behind him, "Get the hell on, preacher!"

The wind kicks up the dust, and dirt clings to the wetness of the pastor's shirt as he trudges on, praying. Another egg sails past him, but he neither speeds up nor slows down his pace. He never looks any other direction other than forward, the path towards sanctuary. Father Johnstone is on the road to redemption and clarity. His pale eyes spot the church lawn up ahead, just as a third egg is chucked his direction. It clips the back of his right arm, and veers off to the street where it shatters to snot and white shrapnel.

"Are you testing me, Lord?" Father Johnstone asks. He looks to the sky and the sun wavers, like a mirage. "Am I to turn my back on the flock now that they've turned on me? Shall I seek exile?"

A rock strikes the back of the pastor's thigh—not big enough to cause any real damage, but it stings and will surely leave a welt of some sort. Wincing slightly, Father Johnstone prays for relief, staggering towards the church as another rock clips his elbow, and then more eggs and fruit sail past. His boots are sticky with the guts of tomatoes and wet dirt. He can hear the shouts of children and men behind him, cursing his name and demanding he get out of their town. He can feel their hate, even without the death threats and promises of brutality should he not heed their warnings. Acrimony fills the air, and it's all directed at Father Johnstone for his actions: his sacrilege, his disease, his public scrutiny of the Good Book.

He enters the church knowing full well that he is indeed the most despised man in Pratt, attempting to turn his heart to embrace of God, but his thoughts remain on Madeline Paige and what those dreams could mean. Perhaps she has dreams of her own where the pastor, like herself, does the unspeakable. Maybe in her mind Father Johnstone is the aberrant aggressor, but the very idea of posing such a question to her directly goes beyond the lines of simple intrusion. Madeline has always been the open-minded type, a free spirit really. To inquire as to whether or not she molests a man of the cloth in dreams might offend her, potentially damaging the relationship beyond repair or apology.

Kneeling down before the oversized crucifix at the head of the main aisle, the pastor begs for enlightenment specific to Miss Madeline Paige. He prays for the origins of these dreams to be revealed, whether they be the product of Satan or otherwise. His soft words echo through the rafters and arched boughs of the church, asking for guidance to truth, for salvation of spirit. Father Johnstone opens his mind to the Lord, saying, "Forgive me, but I must share my nightmare with you."

Madeline is on the bed.

The bed is wrapped in silk and surrounded by candles. Father Johnstone is comfortable this time, feeling no shame or self-loathing for his indecency. He makes his way over to Madeline without being asked. Normally, she has to lure the pastor over, but not this time. Instead, he lunges at her mouth-first, kissing her. He kisses her hard, just as she would instruct him to, and he feels himself grow firm. Father Johnstone is completely hard, but he wants to taste her first. He wants to put his mouth on that vaginal cavity that usually emits such sugary horrors, almost daring her to do it again now that the Lord is present. His tongue plunges into her, past the labia, pushing deep inside of Madeline, and she's moaning and gripping the bedding in tightly wound fists. The pastor pushes his face and tongue between the legs of Madeline Paige, sometimes pulling back and inserting two wet fingers inside of her, plunging them in and out. In and out, and she tells him to fuck her. Fuck her now, and because the Lord needs to see how bad this can get, he does it. For the first time, real or imagined, the pastor inserts himself inside a woman and begins thrusting into her. Fornicating. Fucking her. She coaxes him to fuck her harder, and the pastor does it, a part of him waiting for the terror to happen: for the vaginal cavity to grow teeth and castrate him or perhaps a boiling hot fluid to gush out of her and burn him awake. He's expecting this, but all that happens is pleasure and Madeline's eyes locking into his. They're just as warm as the campfire smile. And Father Johnstone pumps her, pumps her harder, building, coming closer to release, closer until he bursts inside of her, soaking her insides, and she's climaxing too. Madeline's looking at Father Johnstone, peering into his eyes, smiling and telling him, "See? I knew you'd learn."

And then he wakes up.

Father Johnstone wakes up in the church before the oversized crucifix of thy Lord and Savior, pants down and erection wilting in his hand. Warm milky fluid is running down the backs of his fingers, pooling on the dark flooring. The pastor panics, quickly tucking himself back in and hoping that nobody noticed. He prays that there was no one around to witness his *lust* manifesting itself, that this mortal sin transpired covertly, and that's when he sees Mrs. Tiller standing off to the right by the spare office, tears streaming down her face.

She's clutching the doorjamb, white as a sheet.

Prosess XI: Mann på Mann

For this process the primary male (mann) must first inebriate the servile (or submissive) male, either by way of natural poisons (reference: deadly plants and spores) or man-made chemical compounds (reference: fabricated toxins), keeping in the mind the physical side-effects beyond the servile simply becoming unconscious/unresponsive. Some of the effects (effekter) could even backfire upon the primary, as with certain spores that transfer illness via bodily fluids: blood, semen, or excrement. The primary should research and choose their inebriation method carefully before introducing it to the servile. Some recommend a high dosage of spirits or whiskey, however, this can be a timely endeavor, especially if the servile has an established tolerance (toleranse). Once the servile male has become incapacitated, the preparation process of the physical body is ready to commence. The primary male should completely disrobe the servile of all artifacts of clothing for purification (rensing). Using floral oils or warm animal fat, coat the servile and remove all body hair with an edged rock (onyx or hardened magma is said to work best; shale may also be used). Hair (hår) may be stored for later usage (reference: storage methods). After all hair is removed, turn the body of the servile so that it's belly-down. Bring in a male goat (geit) with either a brown or white coat (never black), and align the neck of the animal over the buttocks of the servile. Slit the neck of the goat with a blessed blade (reference: ordaining tools) while chanting the Prayer of Sacrifice in the Divine Language. The goat blood (blod) will be used for lubrication, however, oils and liquefied animal fat may also be used. The primary male may now penetrate the anus of the servile. Please note that it is perfectly acceptable to imagine the servile's anus is that of a female (kvinne). Climaxing is all that is important, so the primary may do whatever he wishes in order to achieve that. Homoeroticism is not humane or natural, and therefore, should not be practiced unless absolutely necessary or to establish dominance (dominans). Once climax has been achieved by the primary male, he should harvest both the servile and the slain goat for materials. Horns of a sacrificed goat, for example, are especially valuable. No matter what the primary decides regarding the organs and materials of the servile, it's in his best interests to slay (drepe) him (no specific method recommended). A servile that realizes they have been anally penetrated is likely to be angry, and will attempt to seek revenge on the primary through violence (vold), burning his farmlands, or taking members of his family hostage. The servile must be destroyed (ødelagt) or permanently disabled.

The First Sign

Mrs. Magda Tiller, widow of Al Tiller, is at least ten years older than the pastor. Based on her physical appearance, though, as well as her taste in certain older films ('the classics,' as she refers to them), the pastor believes she's in her early to mid-sixties. He's accepted that he'll probably never know for sure until her birthday is etched into a headstone, and that's fine. The pastor has always written this off to a form of *vanity* specific to women. They hide their chronological age and even go as far as to conceal the tangible signs of it, usually spending their afternoons at Lana's Salon on 3rd Street, either getting a quick manicure, hairdo, or full-on makeover. Lana's has long been regarded as Pratt's leading beauty resource, not to mention a proverbial hive of gossip and loose talk. Even after her husband passed on (God rest his soul), Magda continued her weekly salon trips just to stay in the loop on the current events not reported in the *Tribune*.

Her official affiliation with the First Church of Pratt began after her husband died three years ago, and it was more a product of busying idle hands than doing the Lord's work. Mrs. Tiller has always been a regular at the Sunday service and a fixture in the community, both in the church and the town at large, but her husband's passing seemed to inspire a sense of insatiable diligence that her normal routine couldn't fulfill. If she wasn't involved in a project, if there was no task at hand or activity to partake in, Mrs. Tiller feared the grief would overcome her.

"Staying occupied helps me keep my head right," she said to the pastor. "And crying never did no good for anyone, so why bother with it?"

Mrs. Tiller used her sewing circles and church projects the same way Father Johnstone used the restoration of the Dodge Challenger: to combat her despondency and solitude. And it was odd the way folks couldn't see what she was doing. On the surface she was carrying on like normal, taking part in baking contests and volunteering for the church. Like clockwork, she'd be at Lana's every Tuesday getting her hair done and dishing gossip with a wicked smile. She'd shop at the market and mingle, waving off condolences in a 'these things happen' type of fashion.

Women all around Pratt were saying, "I sure as hell hope I'm that strong when my man passes," and Lord as their witness, they were a little *envious* of her austerity. Father Johnstone was the only one that knew the truth: Mrs. Tiller, despite all her normal behavior, was falling apart. She could barely sleep at night as those were moments in which there were no tasks or light conversations to keep her husband's memory at bay. Just her and a half-cold bed. That's right around when she offered her services as the church bookkeeper and event planner.

"You don't even have to pay me," she said. "You'd actually be doing me the favor here."

Knowing what the pastor knows of combating solitude, he accepted Mrs. Tiller's offer, and over the course of three years there's never once been an error with the books. Granted, the numbers aren't exactly as complex as other businesses here in Pratt, but Father Johnstone is grateful that he no longer has to toil over these himself. He's never been particularly fond of mathematics anyway, and Mrs. Tiller seems to find a certain joy in the process checking and re-checking figures against longhand calculations. This was her coping mechanism, and if doing the church's taxes and planning events keeps her sane, the pastor wasn't going to stand in the way of that.

Of course, there were those moments when Father Johnstone felt like he was taking advantage of the situation, openly displaying his malfeasance in the presence of Mrs. Tiller pining over the books. She'd always point her finger at him and say, "Preacher, you get those sad puppy eyes off of me and go work on your sermon. Flock ain't gonna lead itself now," and then she'd wave her hand at him palm-down, shooing him away like a stray mutt.

It took about a year before the pastor stopped having spells of remorse, after he finally came to understand that the work made Mrs. Tiller happy. She was doing a job that needed to be done, and Lord as his witness, she did it well. The numbers were shipshape and event planning had never gone smoother now that there were two people at the helm. Her behind-the-scenes efforts allowed the pastor to lead the flock better than he ever had, and considering what a bright woman Mrs. Tiller has always demonstrated herself to be, the report Dr. Keller gives regarding her mental health comes off slighty fictional.

"Physically she's fine...little bump on the head and a bruised arm," the doctor says. "But mentally she ain't what she once was. Things aren't clicking like they should be."

It's Friday evening, the day after Mrs. Tiller's episode at the First Church of Pratt, and the two men are discussing her current condition over warm whiskey in Father Johnstone's kitchen. The pastor has never been much of a drinker, limiting himself to no more than one or two per sitting, and only in social situations: cook-outs or the occasional tailgate party. You'd never find the pastor sitting alone at a bar or drinking in an attempt to 'get hammered,' as some say. Booze becomes the Devil's drink when taken in excess, and so the pastor has always made an effort to indulge in moderation. This is how he used to operate, anyway. Father Johnstone has been drinking since yesterday afternoon.

"Never knew you hit the sauce so hard," Dr. Keller says, looking—diagnosing the pastor's level of sobriety. "You okay?"

Since witnessing Mrs. Tiller faint in the church, the pastor has taken to the more rudimentary methods of numbing unwanted emotions. Not only did he befoul the Lord's house, but he hurt a person he cares very deeply for. His inability to control his *lust* endangered someone, and no amount of praying or repenting can change that. The guilt will remain, but that's not going to stop him from muting it.

"Still having trouble sleeping," the pastor says, slurring a bit.

"Just don't mix that with any of the medication I gave you," Dr. Keller says. "And not that I need to say it but I'm going to say it anyway—don't drive," he adds, taking a sip of the whiskey.

"Didn't plan on it," Father Johnstone says.

"Hmm, well, there's quite a bit that isn't going to plan these days," the doctor says. "I think you'd know that better than anyone."

Father Johnstone polishes off the last of his whiskey and immediately pours himself another, remarking, "My blood?" He drinks, taste buds barely registering the harshness of the liquor. "Or how this town has turned on me?" Aggression edges into his tone—not from the mood swings, though. From liquor. 'A mean drunk,' the barflies of Pratt call it, but better anger than guilt, the pastor thinks. He'd rather feel mad at the world than ashamed over one person.

"I told you what was waiting out there for you, didn't I?" Dr. Keller says. "Didn't I tell you it wasn't going to be the same? You know just as well as I do how Pratt gets when it's faced with something it doesn't understand."

Dr. Keller explains this in a calm tone, reminding the pastor as opposed to arguing with him. It's his way of saying, 'It's not your fault,' and to a degree, he's right. People in this town have a tendency to blow things out of proportion at the behest of their own boredom or self-loathing. It's always been that way.

"I just never thought it'd be me, David," the pastor says. "And now everyone's saying I put Magda in the hospital...like I did something to her."

"*Did* you do something to her?" Dr. Keller asks.

"Yeah, David," Father Johnstone snickers drunkly. "She caught me defiling myself in the church and passed out from the shock."

The doctor gives a depraved smirk, believing it to be a joke.

"Let's not get blue, Father."

Refuting the truth isn't something the pastor is concerned with. Nobody knows what really happened in the church besides himself and Mrs. Tiller, and it appears she can't recollect what she saw, convenient as that may be. This brings him back, once again, to that fork in the road in which he tries to justify his recent transgressions. The Devil could very well still be in his blood: feeding him nightmares, compelling him to *lust*. The Devil makes him drink and shirk his obligations to the Lord and the flock and Mrs. Tiller. Or maybe he's sick in a way he doesn't understand and Dr. Keller has yet to diagnose, which isn't exactly a comfort. To be medically unwell sounds only slightly better than being spiritually contaminated, but just as threatening. It's the first time Father Johnstone has ever truly feared for both his body and mortal soul. His ultimate end could stem from the evil within or an external source, more than likely a misplaced tribute of violence in the name of Mrs. Tiller. Pratt can be equally cruel as it is kind, and being a man of the cloth doesn't make one exempt from public retribution. Father Johnstone knows this. Not first-hand, but he's seen it. And his exile wouldn't be the first time someone was ran out of town due to low public opinion.

"You remember Mason?" Father Johnstone asks. He takes another pull of whiskey and his blood goes cold. "You remember...what he did to that girl?"

"I remember stories," Dr. Keller says.

"And you remember what they did to him, right?" the pastor asks.

It's a fair question. The answer, however, is dependent on who you believe. People in Pratt talk, and sometimes they alter details or add new sections entirely to enhance the story. Maybe this is the town's way of giving forewarning, that you don't touch little girls or make them do things the Lord didn't intend, and Mason certainly seemed guilty of that. They found an old cigar box full of pictures stashed away in his closet, and that was all the proof anyone needed. So over the many days that followed, people heard things: that he was taken out to the fields and stuck with pitchforks or hung from one of the big oak trees out by Larpe's Pond. Another version involved Travis Durphy and the sheriff holding Mason down while Tuck Graybel beat the ever-lovin' shit out of him, and when it looked like Mason couldn't bleed or breathe or move anymore, that moment just before slipping to full black, one of the men poured a BBQ grill of glowing red coals over Mason's body. 'Couldn't even scream he was so broken,' they said. But there were so many versions of this particular revenge that it almost seemed like a game of who could make it sound the worst: a horror story where men torture the monster. Sometimes Mason merely got the shit kicked out of him; other times he was castrated and forced to eat his own genitalia (*Lord, let that be a lie!*). Pratt took a sick sort of joy in its own *wrath*, and the pastor all but avoided the subject in his sermons. Although some of the flock would disagree, Father Johnstone has never viewed the Lord as a vengeful presence, despite how some people 'get what's coming to them,' as they say. He'd witnessed exactly what this town was capable of, though, and that put a deep-seeded fear in his blood. Pratt could hurt you if it wanted to. It could make you disappear.

Mason Hollis was never seen again, corpse or otherwise. There was no body, and therefore, no funeral for him (as if anyone would show other than to spit on his grave). No Last Will & Testament. His home defaulted over to the bank and most of his property was auctioned off at a garage sale. Leftover personal items such as his high-school football trophies and family photographs were tossed in an old leaf-burning barrel, soaked in gasoline and torched to the tune of drunken cackles. Men spent days combing his house, making sure there wasn't one iota of Mason Hollis or his misdeeds to haunt the town. Even the cigar box pictures, which most agreed were considered official police evidence, got tossed to the flames. Little Betty Graybel's nude body was visible for only a few seconds before it curled and bubbled to ash. No one knows if she remembers what Mason did to her, but no one plans on asking, either.

During those times, Father Johnstone remembers people praying for two specific things: that little Betty Graybel block out anything that was done to her, and that Mason Hollis spend an eternity burning in hell. The latter of those two went on for a stretch, fueled mostly by malice.

"And so now you're wondering when your time will come, Father?" Dr. Keller asks. "Are you really having trouble sleeping, or are you keeping an eye out for the men with torches and pitchforks on the horizon?"

"Perhaps I should be," the pastor says. "When it comes right down to it, what's to stop them from treating me like another Mason Hollis?"

"Your faith, I thought," Dr. Keller says, but not in a way that's patronizing. He can sense the pastor has lost his way, and even though he's never been a member of the flock himself, he realizes that people depend on Father Johnstone for guidance. He must put down the bottle and get back to being the shepherd.

"I'm trying," the pastor says, picking up the glass of whiskey once again. He holds it a moment, about six inches over the kitchen table before setting it back down. The pastor nudges the glass away, repeating, "I'm trying."

"I got a woman in my hospital that's out of her mind, and then I got you here...can't even begin to explain what's wrong with you," Dr. Keller shakes his head. He nervously rubs his chin and says, "I got people giving me the stink-eye, too, preacher. They don't take 'inconclusive' as an answer. To them, that means you're incompetent. Got half the damn bingo club talking about how we need to hire on a new doctor, so don't think you're the only one that's catching hell over this."

The pillars of Pratt have always been under a certain amount of scrutiny that other folks aren't. Grain plant workers and farmers screw up all the time, but those are always regarded as blips in the gossip chain. The law and the Lord and medical authority—these pillars of Pratt as certain figures refer to them—one error is all it takes before someone is calling for a new sheriff or district attorney. Rumors of an affair with a young waitress nearly got the mayor yanked from office, and rumors was all it ever turned out to be. Father Johnstone is dealing with a bit more than minced words and edited information. The Devil inhabits his blood, hurting him and those around him. Souring the town. Inspiring hate and public backlash. Dr. Keller may think he's overreacting, but Pratt isn't afraid to take the law into its own hands if it's compelled to. And desecrating a church is something they'd find quite compelling. Different than what Mason Hollis did, of course, but perhaps just as loathsome in their eyes.

"Can you tell me anything more about what happened to Mrs. Tiller yesterday?" the doctor asks. "Was she acting strange? Did she say anything out of character?"

"You're reaching now," Father Johnstone determines.

"Indeed, I am," Dr. Keller says. "Pratt demands an explanation, and given the circumstances, you should want to figure this out just as much as I do."

"What's wrong with her?" the pastor asks, immediately realizing the phrasing is redundant. "I mean, her symptoms. You said she wasn't clicking right?"

"Her memory is impaired. She thinks her husband is still alive," he says. The doctor pauses for a moment, allowing that bit of information to sink in. Technically, this isn't something he should be revealing to the pastor, however, his need for information trumps his usual practice of confidentiality.

Father Johnstone tilts his head down, staring at the flecked patterns of the table and feeling his guilt swell again. His neck tingles as sobriety overwhelms him, flushing the numbness from his system and bringing him back to reality. He sighs, admitting,

"That is…unfortunate." He says, "I'll pray for her."

"I'd like you to come to the hospital tomorrow," Dr. Keller says.

"For more tests?" the pastor asks.

"No," the doctor shakes his head. "To see Magda. I'm hoping it'll jog her memory. It's slim but it's worth a shot. It also might quell some of the rumors going around about you if you made an appearance."

"Me going to the hospital won't stop that," Father Johnstone says, unconvinced.

"Maybe not, but you're holed up in your house, drinking and looking like shit. You haven't even bothered to shave or shower or pick up your dog," Dr. Keller says. "These are the behaviors of a guilty man."

He assumes a standing position, gesturing that he'll be on his way, and Father Johnstone follows in suit to walk him to the door. The pastor is also curious as to whether or not people are lingering outside of his home. News has already spread all over town about Mrs. Tiller's incident in the church, and so the local youth may already be in the pre-execution stages of their vandalism: purchasing eggs and toilet paper, or procuring spray paint from their fathers' garages. The tomatoes and rocks chucked at him in the street were only the beginning. Formal warning shots carried out in haste.

"I do hope you'll consider stopping by the hospital tomorrow," Dr. Keller says, standing on the porch's worn 'welcome' mat. The white lettering of 'God Bless This Home' has deformed over to a dirt brown, edges fraying. The doctor braves a smile at the pastor, shaking his hand and telling him, "Remember: no meds."

Father Johnstone concurs, assuring he'll do no such thing with a promising nod, and the doctor begins his trek into the night. At the curb he trails left, either going home to pay his wife a visit or back to the hospital. Another long night of poring over blood samples and lab reports, pertaining to both to the pastor and a regressed version of Mrs. Tiller. Father Johnstone didn't have the heart to ask Dr. Keller if he broke the news to her yet about her husband. Maybe he's hoping she'll regain her memory and he won't have to, although that puts the pastor right back in the frying pan. He doesn't doubt in the least that his actions were the source of her trauma. Mrs. Tiller will either remain mentally unwell for the definite future or she'll snap out of it, enabling her to expose the truth. Either way, his actions will catch up with him, and this inspires the first thoughts he's ever had about leaving town.

He's seen Pratt destroy men who wore out their welcome before, and the last thing this town needs is another Mason Hollis. If his own exile would circumvent another spell of *wrath*, then for the sake of the people and the Lord, Father Johnstone will pack up and sanction a quiet exit. No long farewells. Swift action must be taken before he harms anyone else, before the disease can spread further than it already has. If he can't remove the Devil from his blood, the least he can do is remove himself from Pratt before more suffering occurs. No one is safe.

Even now, the ashen and slate-toned flurry of moths that would normally be fluttering about his porch lamp are absent. They lie underneath the yellow cone of light on the cement stoop, barely flexing their wings. Dying slowly, like they've been sprayed by pesticides. It's yet another odd occurrence in a series of them, but instead of dwelling on dead bugs, Father Johnstone backs into his home and shuts the door behind him.

He turns to the living room and Madeline Paige is standing before him. Perched on one of her arms is Mary, sitting saddle-style. Madeline gives her an affectionate scratch on her ear, clicking her tongue and cooing, "Such a good girl you got here, Johnstone."

It's the first time the pastor has seen Madeline since the Pratt bake-off. He was bleeding and breaking out in a fever, falling apart in the arms of Jeremiah Will, and then Madeline emerged from the crowd, squatted down and spoke into his ear: *"See you on the other side, Johnstone."* He never determined whether that was real or imagined, but it felt real enough. Unlike all those excursions on the silk bed where she does wonderful and terrible things to him, that version of Madeline seemed authentic.

"How'd you get in here?" Father Johnstone asks.

"Back door," she says.

"Back door's locked." The past 24 hours have been a drunken blur, but he specifically remembers securing all the entrances of the house, even the windows. "How'd you get in?" he asks again, firmer this time.

"Relax, Johnstone," Madeline says. She gives Mary another scratch behind the ear before placing her on the nearby arm of the couch. Normally, after going so long without seeing her master, Mary would be yipping and jumping all over the pastor in excitement, but not this time. She sits on the arm of the couch, remaining loyally by the side of Madeline.

"Why are you in my house?" the pastor asks, anger edging back into his tone.

"Because you're right," Madeline says, pacing slowly across the room. She flashes the campfire smile and warm eyes, and says, "This town plans on hurting you."

"And you're here to what—warn me?" he asks.

"No," she says. "I'm here to make sure you don't leave."

On the Road with Billy Burke, Truck Stop Preacher

"Times have changed. As our prayer and faith evolve, so too does the Devil. We cannot rewrite the Good Book; we cannot recite it and remain ignorant to the fact that we live in a different era. We've got Internet pornography and female NASCAR drivers. We've got pharmaceutical companies hawking us pecker pills. We've got gays getting married for the first time; we've got straights getting married for the sixth or seventh time. Holy union don't mean shit anymore. We celebrate sin. In San Francisco, I saw two bull dykes rubbing their hair pies together on a parade float...and the city applauded. Last night in my motel room, I watched some fat son of a bitch try to eat three pounds of sandwich while a crowd cheered him on. The Good Book never prepared us for that—any of that. We can judge, we can cast stones, but they ain't never going away. Evil evolves. Disease evolves. In this day and age, the Devil swoops in with his cock covered in herpes and warts, dripping with gonorrhea and AIDS juice, and fucks our women over a nightclub urinal while MTV films it. The Devil is everywhere...taking many forms. We need to adapt, gentlemen, and ol' Billy Burke here is gonna help you do it."

The Box & the Bee

Flowers surround Mrs. Tiller: yellow roses, white orchids, a few clumsy bouquets of daffodils tied off in yarn, more than likely assembled by the Sunday school children at the request of doting mothers. Balloons flirt with the ceiling, a few of the cheap rubber variety that say 'Get Well Soon' surrounded by high-end foil bumblebees exclaiming 'Bee Well!' and inflated chimps dressed as doctors, hovering and moving with the timed shifts in air-conditioning. Looking around this space, there's no question that Mrs. Tiller is a woman beloved by this town, and it's here that Father Johnstone recalls his own recent stay in the hospital. Yet, not a single card or flower came. Not one visitor. When Pratt turned, it did so in a sense that was not only swift but absolute.

"I'm still waiting on Al to come visit," Mrs. Tiller says, gingerly eating vanilla pudding with a plastic spoon. Her fingers are bone-thin, allowing her wedding ring to rotate with the weight of the stone. She's lost over thirty pounds since her husband's funeral, usually citing how she 'forgets to eat' or that she's 'still learning how to cook for one.' Flimsy excuses, but no one is going to challenge them. It's like that with widows: they either starve themselves skinny or pack on a bunch of weight in their attempts to smother their depression with comfort food. Mrs. Tiller had always been one of the former, up until recently.

Father Johnstone braves a smile at Mrs. Tiller, telling her, "I'm sure Al would be here right now if he could." He believes this to be true, but the mere indication that her husband is still alive inspires another wave of guilt to crest through the pastor's neck.

"He'll be by soon enough," Mrs. Tiller says, nodding confidently. She carves the bottom edges of the pudding cup with the spoon, placing it in her mouth and letting her lips drag over the curvature of the surface. "But *you're* here, Father," she says, pointing the flatware at the pastor and smiling at her consolation prize. "And I'm glad for that."

"Of course, Magda," he says. "In fact, I should have been here sooner."

"Oh, phooey," Mrs. Tiller waves him off. "You may be the busiest man in Pratt leading the flock all by your lonesome. I'm thankful you came by at all."

She remembers none of it, the pastor thinks. It's like it never happened.

Dr. Keller's official diagnosis, although a bit whiskey-soaked, was that Mrs. Tiller 'wasn't clicking right.' Even in laymen's terms, the pastor isn't sure what he meant by that, but he assumes it's a form of trauma that was brought on by the incident in the church. Clearly, her memory has been compromised, and Father Johnstone can't help but feel responsible for that. He also can't help feeling a bit relieved, as well. As Madeline said, the town plans on hurting him, and Mrs. Tiller could be the difference between the light taunting he's encountered so far and unmitigated violence.

"I'm sorry this happened to you, Magda," the pastor says. It's not the broad sympathy one usually shows during unfortunate times, nor a sentiment born out of common courtesy. Father Johnstone's apology is direct—he knows he's to blame, but it's not even a dent in the amount of penance he feels Mrs. Tiller is entitled to.

"It's fine," she says, giving the pastor's hand a little pat. "It's not your fault."

And for a moment, Father Johnstone is tempted to correct her. His inability to control the *lust* and the Devil in his blood is what led her to this place, and the Lord wants Father Johnstone to confess these sins. It would serve as an act of contrition for his misdeeds, but cowardice prevails. The last thing he wants is to cause Mrs. Tiller any more suffering, even if that means damning his own soul. She's endured enough, and Father Johnstone won't be around much longer anyway. He's already made the decision to retire his position as leader of the flock and depart the town of Pratt—not only for his own safety, but the safety of others. He can't have another Magda Tiller hanging over his head; he won't allow it. And so most of last evening was spent packing and drinking strong black coffee, sobering up and preparing to make amends. Despite being instructed otherwise, he had to see Mrs. Tiller one last time.

"Pretty flowers," a familiar voice says from behind Father Johnstone. It's Madeline Paige, standing in the doorway with an arm clipped to the doorjamb, almost as if she means to block the pastor from running out of the room. She gives him a little smirk, saying, "No card, Johnstone? How inconsiderate."

"Oh Maddy, don't tease," Mrs. Tiller says mirthfully. "I was just telling him how I'm glad he even came by at all."

"I wouldn't be so quick to let this one off the hook, Mags. He ain't all snips, snails, and puppy dog tails like everyone thinks," Madeline says, hint of sarcasm in her voice. "Perhaps an apology is in order?"

Father Johnstone shoots Madeline a look, curious as to how the two of them came to be acquainted, especially in light of Mrs. Tiller's faulty memory. She doesn't recall the passing of her husband, and yet, she and Madeline seem to have a rapport reserved for old friends. It doesn't add up.

"No, she's right," the pastor says. He turns to Mrs. Tiller, telling her, "I should have brought something."

"Oh, you're too kind," Mrs. Tiller says, "the both of you."

Madeline takes a few paces into the room, the heels of her boots clicking against the linoleum, she sidles the pastor. Pastry fills the air. Father Johnstone can smell caramel and robust chocolate cutting through the orchids, roses, and pansies of the room. Warm sugars permeate the space, getting stronger as Madeline digs around in her leather satchel. She produces a small take-out box composed of lavender heavyweight paper, and places it on the makeshift counter in front of Mrs. Tiller. It sits between the empty pudding cup and spoon, fuming sweetly and radiating heat.

Madeline throws a mischievous grin at the pastor, saying, "At least one of us came prepared today." And as Mrs. Tiller sits up in the hospital bed, beaming at the elegant box before her in wonder, that's when Father Johnstone feels something small and dry press into the palm of his hand. Madeline steps in front of him, concealing the exchange and says, "I made it extra special for you, Mags," and Mrs. Tiller begins to pry the tabs of the box open with an expectant smile.

"Awww, Maddy, how thoughtful," Mrs. Tiller says. "It smells wonderful," but something about that box and its contents don't seem right to the pastor. Taking into account all his recent encounters (both real and imagined) with Madeline Paige, Father Johnstone has become wary of her. The trust they shared has been compromised. Even the seemingly innocent cupcake Mrs. Tiller is holding seems to harbor some threat, but before the pastor can voice his concerns, Madeline looks over her shoulder, very clearly mouthing the word: *read*.

He looks at his hand, to the small strip of white paper that Madeline snuck him moments ago as Mrs. Tiller marvels at the cupcake: a decadent mocha, caramel, and (possibly?) tree bark. Father Johnstone smells something earthy, like dirt or old firewood mingling with the sugars and flour. Then he brings the strip of paper up to his face, using Madeline's body as cover, and in cursive scrawl, it reads: *She won't remember if you let her eat it.*

Mrs. Tiller takes the first bite of the cupcake, exclaiming though pastry and frosting, "Mmm! Mmm, swo gwood!" She smiles, brown icing streaking the edges of her lips, and Mrs. Tiller takes another bite before her current mouthful is even swallowed. Pink filling oozes from the middle of the dessert, leaking out into the metal baking liner. It's flecked with green and brown granules. Father Johnstone knows he should say something, knows he should stop her from eating all of it, but he's stifled. Not by cowardice, though. By curiosity.

After the second bite is swallowed, Mrs. Tiller's smalltown generosity kicks in, offering the pastor the remaining chunk. "It's really good, Father. You should try this."

Madeline immediately swings her hand back, fingers locking over the pastor's crotch and threatening to squeeze. "This one is allergic to vanilla extract, unfortunately," she lies, pouting out her bottom lip in a teasing fashion. She purses her lips at the pastor, very slowly letting her fingers come away as Mrs. Tiller wolfs down the last bite of the dessert. Madeline mouths the words: *watch this.*

Father Johnstone stands behind Madeline, waiting for some horrible effect to manifest and preparing to feel guilty again. If Mrs. Tiller drops dead or becomes violently sick, the pastor's inaction will be to blame. And yet he can't help wanting to watch, wanting to see what happens next.

"Ooh, I think I ate that too fast," Mrs. Tiller says. Her cheeks flush and she squirms a bit in the hospital bed, a hand rising up to her temple. Fingers massage in a circular motion, slow and clockwise, and now Father Johnstone is deeply regretting not intervening.

She's going to die, he thinks. Right here, right now.

Madeline holds up a finger, motioning for him to wait. Have patience. Don't move or panic or try to help her, it seems to indicate. "Just breathe, Mags," she says, taking a small step away from the bed. "Breathe," she repeats, soothingly, and Mrs. Tiller follows the order, closing her eyes as if in a trance. She hunches over so far her nose practically touches the makeshift counter in front of her, silent. Still and peaceful, almost sleeping, and that's when Madeline tells the pastor to pick out some flowers.

"Grab those orchids," she says, motioning to a bouquet just behind him. "Quick, before she comes out of it."

Father Johnstone doesn't question her this time, thinking a handle of flowers to be harmless enough. He steals them from the decorative vase, asking Madeline, "What did you do to her?"

"You'll see," she says.

The two of them stand silently, waiting for Mrs. Tiller to regain herself. Madeline checks her watch, taking a step towards the bed in expectation. A few seconds pass before Mrs. Tiller's head twitches and then slowly starts to tilt upwards. She bends at the waist until she's upright again, blinking with a sluggish look in her eye, as if awakened from a very deep sleep. Mrs. Tiller turns to Madeline and Father Johnstone, taking in the two of them standing next to her hospital bed.

"What is your name?" Madeline asks.

"Magda Elizabeth Tiller," she says in a fixed, even tone. "Maiden name: Bertrand."

"How old are you?"

"Sixty-three years, four months, nineteen days," she answers.

"And where are you from, Magda?"

"From the town of Pratt," she says. Again, fixed and cold. "I've lived here all my life."

"Do you like it here in Pratt?"

"No," Magda says.

"Why's that?" Madeline asks.

"Because the town is small and dirty," she says. "Because the people are judgmental gossipmongers. Everyone is in everyone else's business. There are too many degenerates, hicks, and trailer trash. Pratt is a town in which you're considered a success only when you manage to leave it."

Father Johnstone hears this, and although it's a bit disconcerting to witness someone verbalize it so bluntly, he can't help but agree with her answer. This is the opinion that most have of the town, even if it's only shared in drunken whispers amongst close friends. People long to escape, yearning for the bright lights of big cities, the locales Danger Durphy often visited but never seized for himself. Pratt was his home, but it's also a dirt-speck on the map that no one would miss.

Madeline presses on, asking, "Why haven't you left Pratt?"

"Because I'm like everyone else in this town," Magda says. "I'm afraid of change."

"And what if I told you change was coming here?" Madeline asks, leaning in slightly. "What if that change was something terrible?"

"The town would reject it," she says. "Pratt does not welcome change or abnormality or outsiders."

Father Johnstone finds himself nodding his head in agreement, recalling what an 'abnormality' Mason Hollis was and how the town responded to that. There was also a colored man some years back who came looking for work at the grain plant; he was ran out in a matter of days.

"Who was the last outsider to come to Pratt?" Madeline asks.

Madga raises an arm to point, formally identifying the answer. She says, "You, Madeline Paige."

"And why was I not rejected?" she challenges.

"Because you tricked everyone," Madga says, vague and cold. "People are saying all the time how crafty that Maddy Paige is."

At this point, Madeline turns away from Mrs. Tiller, leaning her mouth towards the pastor's ear. He's stock still, idly clutching the bouquet of orchids that Madeline instructed him to grab. She whispers, "Now I'm really going to show you something."

Madeline turns back to Mrs. Tiller, ushering the pastor forward a bit by the small of his back. She asks, "Madga, who is this?"

"That's Father Johnstone," she says flatly.

"And what is Father Johnstone holding?" Madeline asks.

"Six white orchids that were delivered yesterday by Mrs. Parks," she says.

Madeline snaps her fingers at Mrs. Tiller's face. She blinks once, slowly, eyes glazing over. Madeline tells her, "No, *Father Johnstone* brought you the orchids. Try again. What is Father

Johnstone holding?"

"Six white orchids," Magda says, a tad slower than she's been speaking. "Father Johnstone...he brought them."

Out the side of her mouth, Madeline says, "Hand her the flowers," and Father Johnstone extends his arm out, placing them in the hands of Mrs. Tiller. She doesn't smile or react or smell them.

"What do you say, Magda?"

"Thank you, Father Johnstone," Mrs. Tiller says, dropping her chin ever so slightly in acknowledgment.

"When's the last time you saw Father Johnstone?" Madeline asks.

"Two days ago in the First Church of Pratt," she says.

"And what was he doing?"

Father Johnstone's stomach drops. He knows what's coming next.

"He was touching himself in a way that would be considered 'impure'," Mrs. Tiller says.

"Masturbating?" Madeline insists.

"Yes." The answer comes out strained. Even in this state, Mrs. Tiller is resistant to lewdness.

"And what happened when you saw that?" Madeline asks.

"I fainted from shock," Mrs. Tiller says.

Madeline snaps her fingers in front of her face again, saying, "Maybe you didn't faint from shock."

Mrs. Tiller's eyes blink slowly again. She pauses; her thoughts reorganize. "Yes," she says. "Maybe I didn't faint from shock."

"In fact, I think you imagined Father Johnstone doing that," Madeline says. "I think you passed out from the heat."

"It's very hot in that church," Mrs. Tiller says, even and cold. Not one shred of emotion or voice inflection. She bends to Madeline's will. "The heat makes you see funny things," she says. "If I saw anything out of the ordinary, I probably imagined it and should keep it to myself."

"Because we don't like gossip and rumors, do we?"

"We do not, Madeline Paige."

"So if anyone asks, you passed out from the heat, right, Mags?"

"Yes," Mrs. Tiller says, nodding slightly.

"And what are you going to say about Father Johnstone if anyone asks?"

"That he's a good man and that he brought me these wonderful flowers," she says. "Father Johnstone was the only person around when I passed out and bumped my head. He *saved* me."

Oddly enough, Mrs. Tiller stresses that one word, the word 'save.'

"That sounds good," Madeline says. "I think your husband is on his way to see you. Would that make you happy?"

"Yes," Mrs. Tiller says. "That would make me happy. I miss Al."

"Then why don't you wait here for Al," Madeline suggests. "And we'll come back tomorrow to check up on you."

"I'll wait for Al," Mrs. Tiller says, the flatness leaving her voice. She almost sounds excited.

"Goodbye, then," Madeline says, retrieving the lavender take-out box from the makeshift counter in front of Mrs. Tiller. She refolds the tabs and stows it in her leather satchel, telling the pastor, "Say bye, Johnstone," as if he shouldn't have to be reminded to do this.

"Uh...bye, Magda," he says, staring at Mrs. Tiller, attempting to figure out what Madeline did to her, if it'll ever wear off. She blinks and gives a little tilt of her chin again, letting her back meet the mattress of the hospital bed. Mrs. Tiller holds the orchids to her chest, eyes fixated on the ceiling, and that's when Father Johnstone feels himself being tugged out of the room. They're leaving her. They're leaving her alone in that room waiting for a husband that will never come, and the guilt tries to flush back, but it's overtaken by the pastor's concern for Mrs. Tiller.

"Don't worry," Madeline says, speed-walking down the hospital corridor with Father Johnstone in tow. "It only looks bad because you've never seen it before. She'll be fine."

"What did you do to—"

"No questions," Madeline cuts the pastor off. "Not right now. I know you've got a million of them but they'll have to wait."

She's right, of course. What the pastor just witnessed has opened up a floodgate of queries. In all his years, Father Johnstone has never seen anything like that, in Pratt or otherwise. The effects were almost drug-like, although not in any way he's heard of or read about. This wasn't your average backyard skunkweed or old man Clevenger's bathtub moonshine. Whatever was in that dessert, it anesthetized Mrs. Tiller in such a way that it left her reality open to suggestion, allowing fact to become fiction and vice versa. She would have believed anything, and that's when Father Johnstone remembers that he's been eating cookies and cobblers at the behest of Madeline Paige for weeks.

At the hospital exit doors, she says, "Keep holding my hand. Stay close."

Father Johnstone does so, adjusting his grip so that their fingers are interlocked even tighter, palm to palm, and Madeline proceeds out of the building with the pastor by her side. They head north on Statham Street, nearing Pratt's market square with all the fruit and veggies and other various projectiles. He can see people in the distance, pausing their shopping to get a look at the two of them, and the pastor begins to tense up. His footsteps slow, but Madeline gives him an encouraging little tug on the arm, telling him again, "Stay close."

She says, "I'm not mad you snuck off to the hospital, by the way. You pastors are anything if not predictable."

Last night, when Madeline paid an unexpected visit to the

pastor's home, she already knew what he was planning. She could tell that he was going to run away, escape Pratt. It would have been so easy to pack up a couple of suitcases, put Mary in the passenger seat, and then drive off in the Challenger. A few hundred miles later, Father Johnstone would have arrived in another small town, maybe somewhere in the south where it stays warm all year. Places like that all over in Texas and New Mexico. Although you never hear much about them, there's thousands of little dirtball towns just like Pratt, and you can be anyone there. You can reinvent yourself.

That's when Madeline intervened.

She confirmed what Father Johnstone had been fearing all along: that the town has plans for him. For his blasphemy and corruption, he would suffer—maybe even die. It was just as Mrs. Tiller put it: "Pratt does not welcome change or abnormality or outsiders." The pastor only believed that to a degree, but he wasn't about to test it. Even a man of the cloth isn't exempt from the whims of smalltown violence, and all cowardice aside, he didn't want to become another Mason Hollis. Another campfire tale. Madeline, however, had no intention of assisting the pastor's exit.

"I'm here to make sure you don't leave," she said, explaining to the pastor that exiling himself would only make things worse. His plan would backfire. "And the flock must have a leader," she told him. Father Johnstone was instructed to stay in his house and not leave (no matter what), but he had to see Mrs. Tiller. He had to make amends.

Arriving in the market square with Madeline clutching the pastor's hand, she says, "I just showed you something not very many people get to see, so naturally, I know you're wanting an explanation."

Navigating the market, the faces are familiar: Mr. and Mrs. Bratten, the McCloy children, Mrs. Rawlings and her husband, who is currently unloading cider from his pickup truck. The pastor sees the Fairfaxes, shopping like they don't even know each other. By the apple display, Mrs. Yates is inspecting fruit for blemishes while keeping an eye on the pastor and Madeline. The faces are routine, but they've never looked at him like this before. Like an enemy, a betrayer of their trust, and it's all the more reason to keep up pace with Madeline as they pass by the peach and plum crates, currently selling at two for dollar according to the chalkboard sign.

"Drugs," Father Johnstone says to Madeline. "You drugged Mrs. Tiller."

She shakes her head, still pulling the pastor along. Madeline says, "Not even close, Johnstone. Although that would save *me* a lot of time," she snickers. "Don't worry, you'll get your answers soon enough."

Past the honeydew and watermelon crates, and right on by the spice display where Shelby Dunbar is loitering, the pastor and Madeline cut through the final lengths of the market, exiting on the other side unscathed. Father Johnstone feels like he just dodged a potential bullet. He's tempted to look back at them, to examine their faces for hatred or disapproval, but then Madeline says, "Don't," and gives him another yank. "Keep walking."

The pair hang a right on the corner of 6th and Main, just a few blocks away from Madeline's house. Father Johnstone can make out the trademark water-blue shingles of her home in the distance, and at the end of the road: a pile of popcorn. The daisy hill. A few bystanders stop reading their newspapers or halt conversations to watch them, marching hand-in-hand, and the pastor is waiting for it. He's expecting another rock or tomato to come flying his way, but nothing happens after a block, then two blocks. Father Johnstone's paranoia decreases as they distance themselves from the main population, nearing that serene slice of Pratt known as the daisy hill. Just looking at it brings him peace that no outsider could understand. Besides the church, standing on top of the daisy hill in full bloom is as close to the Lord the pastor can get. It is beyond landmark; it is sacred, a place where one can experience harmony with the world.

Madeline says, "I know it's tempting for you to want to leave. Believe me, I know. I've been on the run for most of my life."

Hand in hand, they reach the end of the road, stepping onto a warning track of heavy gravel. Plumes of grass become more frequent as they walk, sprouting up between clusters of rocks and hard dirt. The sporadic green shifts into pasture land, safe for barefoot walks and picnics, just at the bottom of the hill.

"Sometimes, Johnstone, when you leave a place, it's possible it won't be there when you return," Madeline says. "Like a sandcastle on a beach. Turn your back for a minute and the ocean washes it away."

Father Johnstone has never seen the ocean nor has he built a sandcastle. Unlike Madeline, he's never been anywhere of note, and he was very much looking forward to changing that with his impromptu road trip. This isn't to say her metaphor is lost on him, though.

"You speak of Pratt?" the pastor asks.

Madeline pauses, peeking over her shoulder, and says, "Yes."

"You're saying if I leave, it won't be here if I come back?"

"Yes," she says, turning her attention back to the hill. "I'll show you."

She tugs Father Johnstone's arm again, but less assertively this time. Madeline's fingers push into his palm suggestively, less brazen, asking him to walk with her on the daisy hill. It's safe now, and the two of them leisurely move on along the incline, higher until they're level with the summits of the houses. Then they're above them, able to see the expanse of this little dirtball town. Weathered residences and buildings no higher than three stories compose the mosaic, mostly shades of brown with off-white trim. Only the church displays any character with its stained glass windows and architectural divergences, and for a brief moment, Father Johnstone almost feels calm again. Then

Madeline brings him back.

"According to what you believe, God created the earth in six days," she says. "Then we came along and invented destruction. We created the hydrogen bomb and nuclear warheads." Madeline sweeps her arm from left to right, motioning to the town, "It took years to build all this. We could wipe it out in seconds."

"You're saying we're about to be bombed?" Father Johnstone ventures.

"No," she says. "I'm merely illustrating that it always takes longer to create something than to destroy it." Madeline squats down, telling the pastor, "And what do we become when we're destroyed?" Her fingers near the petal of a nearby daisy, one in which a bumblebee is clinging to, unmoving. Even when Madeline's digits threaten to clip down on its body, it remains still, allowing her to pluck it off the flower and place it in the palm of her hand, never moving. A corpse.

"Our bodies return to the earth," the pastor says. "As told in Genesis." He's not sure if she's looking for a biblical answer, but that's the one he's always given. Through prayer and the Word, almost anything can be solved.

Madeline stands up, bumblebee cupped in her hand. She asks, "And how's that passage go again?"

The pastor recites: *"In the sweat of thy face shalt thou eat bread, till thou return unto the ground; for out of it wast thou taken: for dust thou art, and unto dust shalt thou return."*

"Now open your hand," Madeline says, dumping the bee into the pastor's palm. It lies on its side, inert.

"It's dead."

"Then you won't mind crushing it for me," Madeline says.

"Why?"

"Just do it, Johnstone."

The pastor relents, curling his fingers in and the tips press into the body of the insect. It doesn't slowly give way to pressure—

exoskeleton pushing against organs, but shatters rather. His palm feels dry and powdery, like it's filled with talcum, and when Father Johnstone straightens his fingers he discovers why.

"If you leave, that's what your town will become," Madeline says.

Father Johnstone examines the contents of his hand, gray cinders littered with shards of black and yellow. Ashes scatter when the wind picks up, like a memorial, dusting the earth from whence it came. Ashes and dust. He takes another look at the expanse of Pratt and realizes that Madeline is right, that this could all be destroyed so easily. It could become oblivion, swept under the rug of the earth over time.

No one would even notice.

Las Vegas, NV

Everyone that gets too close to me either dies or takes ill.

Sometimes this is a spiritual degradation. Other times the illness manifests physically, like that of Desiree and her vaginal affliction. In Las Vegas, this would be known as having a 'dirty cunt,' which is to say the female is a harbinger of disease and should be avoided, sexually-speaking. This also earned her violent reprisals from her employer—or 'pimp,' as they are referred to. Although my endeavor to discover the intricacies of faith surpass the life of a common whore, I can't deny that Desiree's passing wasn't without consequences. Adjustments had to be made. In the face of physical threat, certain adaptations became necessary to prolong the experiment.

"What would you like me to do first, Mr. Thomas?"

Tonight's girl is named Sasha. She is young. Healthy. Physically healthy, that is. No disease. Not yet. Emotionally, however, she is unbalanced and erratic. I can feel this just being around her, the intangibles. And like every other whore in Las Vegas, she too employs a false identity for the sake of personal safety. I decide to adopt this same deception in the form of Mr. Thomas, a common-looking man with an overtly ordinary name. He is not a 'hooker-killer' or 'diseased fuck.' He is without reputation, and therefore, 'below the radar,' as they say. I've since left Caesar's Palace, checking into the Bellagio under this new identity. Much like these whores move from hotel to hotel for their various sexual encounters, I will exercise this same method.

"Be an obedient little slut and put on the mask," I tell her.

Sasha lounges on the bed in vinyl underwear, most likely purchased from Frederick's of Hollywood or a similar erotica outlet. She wears metallic nipple clamps, trapping blood so that brown skin flushes purple. This gives her pleasure, apparently. Gravity arcs the connecting chain between the two clamps just above her belly button. She's almost entirely nude, all except for the patch of vinyl concealing her genitals and the mask.

"Like this, Mr. Thomas?" she asks in a high whispery tone, as if her vocal chords haven't fully matured past teenage years. Sasha pulls the mask down over her eyes, modeling it. She wants me to be pleased. She wants to be hurt.

"Yes," I say. "Exactly like that."

I've momentarily suspended the usage of Christian lingerie for now, opting for an alternate approach that does not require the aid of a clergyman. The mask, for instance, was crafted from the leather and cardboard of a hotel Bible. Candles were stolen from a vigil being held at a nearby church. Bottles of Holy water fill the fridge, although I'm beginning to suspect it may lose its power when removed from the basin, like that of a flower plucked from the earth.

"Would you like to start with the wax?" Sasha asks, looking at no specific point in the room. The Christian eye mask was intentionally crafted without holes, thus, impairing the wearer's sight while increasing sensation. The body compensates for the lost sense by amplifying another. Basic knowledge where I come from. Understanding the body and bringing it to its full potential was part of our academia. Women like Serena, Desiree, and Sasha are designed to help me further that education.

"My tits first, please." On the bed, Sasha is propped on her knees and puffing out her chest, not totally unlike the Frigatebird. Hands push breasts together, narrowing the gap in the chain dangling from her nipples. She yearns for stimulus. "Pour it on me, Mr. Thomas."

From the nightstand, I select one of the Christian vigil candles that have been lit for the past hour. Their bodies are thick, white—indicating purity, peace, and affection. Wax is hot and of a milk-like consistency, sloshing around the raised edges as I position it over Sasha, her breasts. They ache for feeling, for pain. I tilt the candle and pour the contents on her chest, her tits. She flinches, inhaling sharply, and then letting the next breath ease slow, stammering as the wax hardens. It coats the meat of her breasts and nipples, becoming firm before cracking and flaking to the bed.

"More," she says. "Please. More."

Sasha's pain sensors are a rarity in that they're linked to her pleasure center. It is why her services cost more than $10,000 for the evening. Her skill set and physical makeup are unique, and therefore, more expensive than the common whore: the streetwalkers and escorts and models attempting to make ends meet. Another dollop of hot Christian wax and I can feel blood moving in Sasha's body, flushing to her labia. She tugs on the chain at her nipples, letting one hand wander to the space between her legs, stimulating the clitoral region through the vinyl.

"Hurt me, Mr. Thomas," she begs.

By the property of generalization, flame originating from a Christian-based object yields its attributes. Any pain will be ordained with the power of the Lord Christ, and so I let the fire lick one of Sasha's breasts to which she flinches backwards, coning the scorch mark with her palm and rubbing, relishing the feeling.

"More, Mr. Thomas," *Sasha says. Unlike Serena, this is not an act for her. Sasha's desires are genuine. Odd, but genuine.*

I burn her again, longer this time, which results in her experiencing a small yet thrilling orgasm. I feel this happen and am fascinated by it: a machine I don't fully comprehend. Sasha laughs, caressing a bubbling nipple. It fills with fluid to counteract the injury. She giggles, and then I start to wonder just how far she can be pushed. I wonder where the threshold lies.

Sasha says, "You may puncture me now, if you wish."

I find myself all too eager to explore her, setting down the Christian vigil candle and grabbing a fresh copy of the Bible along with a Swingline stapler, a modern device traditionally used to bind paper together. It will not be used for that.

"Remember," *Sasha tells me,* "our safe-word is: chili dog."

In the current sexual culture, a 'safe word' is an emergency exit clause utilized when either party feels threatened or convinced the experience has entered perilous territory. For the sake of keeping the endeavor laced with Christian undertones, my initial suggestion was the word 'God.' Sasha, however, thought this to be a poor choice.

"It should be a something you'd never normally say during sex," she told me. "Like...chili dog. Let's go with chili dog."

On the bed, Sasha gets on all-fours, arching her back to make her hind quarters more prominent. I unfold the stapler at the hinge and rip out a page from the book of Matthew, sandwiching the paper between steel and soft flesh. My fist pounds the top, piercing skin. Paper hangs from her ass, beading with fresh blood.

"Again," she says. "Do it again."

I repeat. I rip out a page, sometimes two, press it against Sasha's body and staple. On Sasha's ass, thighs, and lower back hang various excerpts from Mark, Luke, and John. Romans, Corinthians, Colossians. They overlap and hang off her body like a wooden electrical post covered in adverts—and she's bleeding, rubbing her clitoral region and oozing from those puncture wounds. Another page, another staple through the skin. Blood, then more blood. Orgasms.

Sasha flips onto her back, "Puncture and fuck me at the same time."

Her legs tilt open, the outside of her knees very nearly touching the comforter of the bed. Into her thighs: James and Peter. Her stomach: Titus. On the pubic bone: Revelation. I staple her, and Sasha pulls the vinyl underwear off to the side, edging forward. She desires traditional penetration now, and so I unbutton my pants and remove myself.

"Just a little more wax," she says.

Again I reach for the nightstand, grabbing a candle and turning it upside-down over her vaginal cavity. Sasha screams. She climaxes. The liquid is already thickening, becoming more opaque as I prepare to enter her.

Sasha sighs, stammers her breath. "You're fun."

Symptoms of the disease have intensified: small pastures of sores are in various states of bloom, covering roughly 80% of the penis. They're deep red, infected. Discharge from the urethra has gone from milky white to yellow, indicating an infection. Sharp pain throbs at the tip; this pain increases notably during urination and climax. There's also a sour smell, which is why I've employed the usage of candles.

"Fuck me, Mr. Thomas," Sasha says.

Naturally-occurring oils in my hands seep into the sores, stinging, making it so I can barely stand to touch myself. I wonder if Sasha would enjoy it. I wonder if it would add another level to her bliss.

She tilts her head up, tipping the mask off her eyes, shocked. Sasha screams, "Chili dog! Chili dog!"

I snap. My arms wrap around both her thighs and pull hard, entering her. Enzymes hit the sores, searing with pain, as if I'm cooking in the flames. Fluid oozes, coats the vaginal walls and spreads infection.

"Mother fucker!" Sasha screams at me. "Chili dog!"

The Catalyst

Father Johnstone's house is covered in raw egg, white shell shrapnel baked to the aluminum siding via the unseasonable heat. Whoever did this used at least three cartons of Grade As, most likely procured from the market he and Madeline passed through only moments ago on their walk back from the daisy hill. Roughly half an hour was spent up there, the pastor searching for something living while Madeline chastised him for wasting valuable time, as she put it, but he had to be sure. After the sixth or seventh crushed bumblebee, Father Johnstone finally surmised that he wasn't being tricked and no sleight of hand was at play. Death was officially in the air, in Pratt, and the proof was staining his palms and fingers cement gray. It was an unsettling realization, so much so that his response to finding his home vandalized is considerably mild. The cracked double-pane windows and bashed-in mailbox don't register like they should, nor does the crudely spray-painted word 'fagot' across his front door.

"Look at that." Madeline points at the middle where a 'g' is absent. "So, your graffiti artist is a shitty speller."

Father Johnstone digs his keys out of his pocket, saying, "That hardly narrows it down." He looks at the spot underneath the porch light, noticing the pile of dead moths from the prior evening. Their wings and bodies are disintegrating now, slowly deforming to ash like a cigarette without the smoke or smolder.

"The bastards even teepeed your little dogwood tree," Madeline says, motioning to the thin sapling in the yard, which tops out around four feet. It's draped in toilet paper. Half a roll lies discarded a few paces away from the trunk. She mentions, "I should whip up some poison muffins just in case they come back."

"You don't have to do that." Father Johnstone pushes the key into the deadbolt. He can hear Mary inside the house, barking and scratching at the door just as she always does when company arrives. As the pair enter though, it's Madeline she greets first, jumping at her leg and whining to be picked up, which she gladly does. Father Johnstone inspects the living room, moving into the kitchen to see if there's been any kind of a break-in, but all appears to be normal. Everything except for the luggage next to the couch, that is. Yet again, Father Johnstone battles the allure of a hasty departure. It wouldn't take but a few minutes to pack everything up in the trunk, stick Mary in the passenger seat, and liberate himself from Pratt. He could disappear completely—to another town a few hundred miles away, and no one would be the wiser. They'd never find him.

"Temptation is the pull of man's own evil thoughts and wishes," Madeline says with Mary cradled in her arm. She scratches the spot behind Mary's ear, which elicits a blissful grumble.

For a second, Father Johnstone thinks she's just said something oddly poignant, but then he remembers the source. There's even been a few occasions where he's uttered the words himself, although not in regards to his own cowardice. "Book of James," he cites.

"Don't mistake your own self-indulgence for self-preservation, Johnstone," Madeline says. "You're in this now. You can't leave knowing what you know."

"What do I know? Honestly?" he asks. "You've hardly told me anything."

Madeline approaches the pastor, forfeiting Mary over and taking Father Johnstone's ring of keys from his hand. Only three are on it: one for the house, one for the church, and a large black-handled one for the Challenger. They're accented with a white rabbit's foot, a somewhat morbid token Father Johnstone received from a member of his congregation that Mary has used as a chew toy once or twice.

"We'll take the car then," Madeline says. "I'll drive."

"Wait a minute, who said you could drive my car?" the pastor objects.

"It's a 1970 Dodge Challenger, right?"

"Yeah," he nods.

"110-inch wheelbase? V-8 engine?" she confirms. "And you probably sprung for the 426 block, right?"

"With a Hemi," the pastor says, unable to withhold a *prideful* smirk.

"I know my cars, Johnstone. It's gonna be fine," she says, heading towards the garage, keys jingling against each other. "Bring Mary. She's coming with."

"And where would you be taking us?" he asks.

"Well, you complained about not knowing anything," Madeline shrugs. "I suggest you get in the car if you want to learn."

She enters the garage, peeling the cloth tarp off the Challenger and revealing a glossy blue finish with black trim. Chrome wheels and handles. Tires are practically virgin, showing hardly any signs of wear. Madeline runs her finger down the body of the car, grinning in anticipation, and carefully inserts the key into the lock, taking care not to scratch the paintjob. She opens the door, a faint wave of Armor All and pine air freshener wafting out, and slides into the leather confines of the driver's seat. Madeline leans over to unlock the passenger side, and Father Johnstone eases in with Mary, clutching her tighter than normal against his chest.

"I have to ask you something," the pastor says. He sighs, turning to his left and asking, "Am I *letting* you drive this car? Or are you somehow forcing me to let you?"

"That's good, Johnstone." Madeline sticks the key in the ignition and turns. The engine fires up, revving when she gives the gas pedal a couple taps to test the car's integrity. She says, "Most people don't figure it out that fast."

Madeline presses the button on the garage door opener clipped to the visor, flooding the space with afternoon light. It gleams off the various wrenches and power tools stationed on the walls. She backs the car out of the driveway to an audience of a few random passersby on the sidewalk, giving old Mr. and Mrs. Bellows a wink. Madeline shuts the garage before peeling out, heading westward, towards God only knows.

"What exactly did I figure out?" Father Johnstone asks.

"That you might not be completely in control," Madeline says, taking Main St. towards the end of town, where homes and buildings become sparse. "Some people can't deal with that. Like, you live by this plan all your life, but what happens when you find out it's the wrong plan?"

The Challenger bolts smoothly down the road at a steady 55mph, the sign for Route 9 appearing over a small crest after a few minutes. Madeline eases off the gas, letting the vehicle cruise along the last of the worn blacktop of Main Street. She hangs left at the intersection, heading south to where the farmlands are located, acres and acres of wheat that are spotted with a few small cornfields. Father Johnstone considers what Madeline said, the part about living your life by the wrong plan. He can only assume she means God and the Good Book. Up until recently, Madeline has always been what Father Johnstone considered a close friend, albeit one he felt a certain paternal obligation to, probably due to her age and solitary nature. Never though, has she been one of the flock, nor has she been to a single sermon, despite the pastor's consistent pressure otherwise. In fact, the closest Madeline's ever been to participating in a church function was the Pratt bake-off. Even then, it was purely for the sake of carrying out a social agenda, or perhaps something more corrupt. Mrs. Tiller could attest to that, if she could remember what transpired this morning.

"You're being quiet over there," Madeline observes.

"I'm thinking," Father Johnstone says, still holding Mary to his chest. She gives him an affectionate lick to his cheek, pressing her little coal nose against his skin. He can see the wheat fields in the distance, golden on the horizon.

"Thinking, as in: you're hoping I'm full of shit," Madeline says. "But you're also afraid of what it could mean if I'm not. That about right?"

The fields begin streaming by, a golden blur.

Father Johnstone nods, looking out the window.

"And what do you do when you're afraid?" she asks.

"Normally, I'd pray." Father Johnstone turns back to his left, looking at Madeline in the driver's seat: young, beautiful, calm. She's in control. "My prayers haven't been working so much lately, but you probably knew that, didn't you?" he says, a hint of accusation in his tone.

"Maybe you're doing it wrong," Madeline says.

Father Johnstone doesn't respond. There's no right way to address the fact that a suspected atheist is telling a man of the cloth that he's praying incorrectly—not without it sounding completely rude, at least. She has no frame of reference to say such a thing.

"This car, for instance," Madeline says. "It's composed of specific parts: an engine, tires, gas tank, spark plugs. It works because all the pieces are in the right place."

"Okay," the pastor nods.

"Take one of the pieces away and the car doesn't function," she says.

"Right, but what does that have to do with anything?"

"I'm saying that maybe your prayer is missing something. Maybe it's not so simple as just saying the words."

Madeline eases off the gas, allowing the car to slow down, it goes from 65, to 55, then 40. They hear the transmission downshift, and the wheat around them become less blurred as they decrease in speed. Father Johnstone can make out the individual strands of grain, and the Challenger starts to edge off the road, easing onto the grass shoulder between the crop and the chalky gravel of Route 9. Madeline gently presses the brake, bringing the car to a full stop and killing the engine. The pastor has never been to this part of Pratt before, but he can assume that many of the town's teens looking for late night privacy have. Local law wouldn't take the time to patrol these roads unless they were specifically called out, and even then it would have to be something a little more serious than a run-of-the-mill MIP charge. The fields are desolate, almost making it seem like Father Johnstone and Madeline are alone in the world, even though they're only about ten or so miles from the main population.

"Let's take a walk," Madeline says. She puts the car in park and gets out, gently shutting the driver's side door behind her.

Father Johnstone does the same, letting Mary down onto the grass. The fields are so rarely travelled that the pastor feels safe letting her go without a leash. Of course, the first thing she does is meet Madeline on the other side of the car, sidling one of her boots.

"She's precious," Madeline says. "Do you remember when you first got her?"

The pastor recites this story to Madeline: the bear in the basket. He doesn't care if he comes off soft or weak. Mary is the closest thing to a daughter he'll ever have, and when he looks down at her, trotting along through the grass, he can't help but smile fondly.

"Can you remember a time you were upset with her?" Madeline asks.

"I used to kennel her when I left the house to run errands," the pastor says. "It got to a point where I thought I could trust her to be out by herself. A couple hours later, I came home to find the coffee table all chewed up and a few books that were on the lower shelf torn to shreds. Poop and pee everywhere. I was livid…screamed my head off at her."

Mary looks back at the pastor as she runs along, almost as if she can recall what he's talking about. It wasn't one of their best days.

"So she disappointed you," Madeline concludes. "How'd you deal with that?"

"She was a puppy. Puppies chew things and tear up stuff. It's in their nature."

Madeline traipses along, giving the pastor a smile. "Well put, Johnstone," she says. "Real love means understanding the other person—or pet, I guess, even when they disappoint you."

"I think I'd agree with that," the pastor nods.

"Good, because I'm going to need you to be more under-standing than normal," she says. "A lot more."

"Do you plan on disappointing me?" Father Johnstone asks.

"Maybe," she says. "I hope not." Madeline stops walking, squatting down so one knee is buried in the grass. She says, "Mary, run out there a bit. I need to talk to your daddy in private." Mary goes into a heavy jog, fur pushing back against the wind. She's swift when there's room to run. Madeline stands back up, pointing upwards, asking the pastor, "What do you see?"

It's blue. Not a single cloud.

"Nothing," he says, but he starts to feel his stomach churn, knowing that Madeline is building up to something. "The sky," the pastor adds with a shrug.

Mary is around one hundred feet out, still trotting along through the tall grass. Madeline yells, "Mary, stop!" and she does, walking a few paces back before she sits on her haunches. "When it rains, when the sun rises or the earth floods—what is that? What causes it?"

"The Lord," he says. "The Lord is in everything."

Madeline takes the pastor's hand in her own, interlocking their fingers. She says, "At all times, yes? Even when it hurts someone?"

Father Johnstone nods, pangs of doom in his stomach. "At all times," he says. "Even when it hurts His creations. He giveth and He taketh away."

"So if one of your flock were to ask you about a natural disaster, and all the people it hurt, and all the homes it ruined," she says, "then you would say that's God?"

"We don't always understand His plan, but we have to have faith in that there is one and there's a reason for His actions," Father Johnstone explains. "Yes though, even in the instance of disaster. We're fortunate in that we can at least somewhat predict these things now."

"Warning signs," Madeline says.

Father Johnstone nods in the affirmative.

"Now look out there," Madeline says. "Look at Mary sitting on the grass under this clear blue sky. Doesn't she look peaceful?"

The pastor nods, sighing deeply as he watches Mary out on the grass. She sits alone amongst the gold and green. It's like a painting. Places like the daisy hill and the golden fields remind the pastor just how beautiful the world is. They're out this far for a reason though, to see something, and the anticipation is making his guts churn.

"Keep watching," Madeline says, her hand gripping the pastor's a little bit tighter. His hand starts to tingle, almost buzzing. She says, "And remember what you said about the Lord being in everything."

It happens.

A column of white erupts from the earth, just underneath where Mary is sitting. Brightness stings the pastor's eyes as lightning shoot upwards, breaking unevenly as it reaches into the heavens. Into the cloudless blue. Madeline continues to squeeze the pastor's hand, squeezing so tight it hurts the bones in his fingers. Compresses his knuckles to mush. His palm aches like it's bruised, and then the light dissipates with a thunderclap. It punches his eardrums. And he can see Mary in the distance. Collapsed. No longer a caramel brown. No longer herself. Father

Johnstone rips his hand away from Madeline's, feeling significantly weak, but his adrenaline is pumping with fear, the kind that overcomes age or health or fatigue. The fear invigorates him. He runs, terror charging through his heart as he pleads, "No, no, no, please, no." He sprints towards the pile of burnt fur and flesh, covering half the distance in what seems like hours. A strip of white cuts vertically through his vision from the lightning, partially blinding him, but he continues to run. To pray and beg and hope. The pastor says, "No please no God no please no," and he's already crying, breaking, because he knows what's waiting for him. Tears stream sideways across his cheeks. Mary is unmoving, scarred by light and lying upon burnt, black grass. The pastor falls to the ground in front of her, hands reaching out but not touching. He doesn't dare touch. He can feel the heat on his palms, smell the char in the smoke rising off the carcass. Mary's eyes are sealed shut, oozing a dark brown fluid. Hot blood stains her teeth, and the pastor is sobbing, saying, "No...please no...please," blinking hard. Tears hit the earth, and he looks at Mary's body, the wet pink skin where fur has been burnt away. Bone pokes through fried skin. The edges of her mouth are cooked and bubbled, and he says it again, begging, "Please God, no...no...please." But there is no prayer, nothing he can say or do. She's dead. Mary is dead. Father Johnstone balls up in the grass, burying his face in the earth and cries. Sobbing in agony.

He knew the day would come where Mary would pass, but it wasn't supposed to be like this. It wasn't supposed to be a product of abrupt violence and gore. She was to slip away peacefully, in the comfort of their home where the pastor could wrap her in blankets and hold her close. Her body was to remain immaculate—not with scars and burns and charred fur. Not disfigured. The pastor can't even look at her now. So he shuts his eyes—shuts them tight, and he cries. He sobs into the earth until she comes for him.

Madeline's footsteps approach from behind, slowly, as if she's being cautious to the fact that Father Johnstone could snap at any moment. She puts her fingertips on his back, then her palm, smoothing it down his shoulder to the middle of his spine. His torso quakes, still sobbing into the grass and dirt, too heart-broken to be angry. Too destroyed to speak. Grief eats him as Madeline kneels. The pastor can smell sweet perfume mixing with the earth and char in the air, and she says, "We can fix this, Johnstone. We can bring her back."

The pastor doesn't move, doesn't respond.

She's lying, he thinks. She has to be lying.

"I know you think that's impossible," she says, "but consider this: how many times have you read about seas being parted or the sick being cured by a touch?" Madeline rubs her hand in a circular motion on the pastor's back, attempting to comfort him. "Have you ever personally seen anyone walk on water?"

No, the pastor thinks. He hasn't.

These are stories. It is the fodder that compels the flock to follow. This is what they need to hear in order to believe in the power of the Lord, to have faith in something greater than themselves. Because when you get down to it, no one has ever been worshipped for being ordinary. The mediocre are never deified.

"Miracles aren't random. There's a method to this, Johnstone," Madeline says. "A formula. It's like the car: all the parts have to be there in order for it to work. We can bring her back, but I need you to believe it. Believing it is an extremely big part of this."

For some reason Father Johnstone thinks about Dr. Keller and what he said about his blood type changing, that it was an impossible occurrence. He said that it's not medically feasible. By extension, that makes the pastor a walking impossibility. A phenomenon. A living contradiction.

"Don't ask for her to be brought back," Madeline says. "Demand it. Know what you're entitled to."

Good health and the strength to lead the flock, peace of mind, body, and spirit—these are the requests Father Johnstone has made over his many years as pastor. Commonplace prayers. He's served the Lord's will for over three decades, not once asking for something of a selfish nature, even in desperate times. To guide the flock is to lead by example, but perhaps Madeline has a point, he thinks. Maybe his servitude has earned him this favor.

"Give me your hand," she says. "You don't have to look at her, but I need you to concentrate and remember, okay?"

Father Johnstone offers his arm and Madeline grabs it. Again, the tingling sensation begins to generate in his palm and fingers. Again, she squeezes so tight it hurts. It burns and stings. Prickles like needles in his palm, spreading throughout his wrist and forearm, his elbow, but then he thinks about Mary and it begins to fade. Her life flashes before his eyes: the bear in a basket with the pale belly; she's brought into the pastor's house and he holds her, scratching behind her ears right where she likes it; she's out in the yard under the sun, she urinates and the pastor praises her, offering her a treat; if she does it inside on the carpet or kitchen tiles, the pastor scolds her, but in a way where he's only pretending to be mad; in truth, he's not the least bit upset with her; she has a water bowl, a bowl of kibble, a leash for walks; her little legs tire easily, and then she lies on the couch for a long nap, sometimes twitching her feet in her sleep, dreaming of running through pastures; she misses her mom sometimes, but as the days go on, as she and the pastor become more acquainted, the memory slips; he's the one that makes her happy; he's the one that takes care of her and scratches her ear and gives her breakfast meats; she hears the people call him 'Father' and he refers to her as 'Mary'; she learns that when he says Mary, he's talking to her; sometimes he chirps it in a high-pitched voice while slapping his leg, and then Mary will zip across the yard and jump at his knees; he throws a tennis ball, she learns to fetch it and bring it back to him; Mary likes to roll around in the grass and flowers, and sometimes the pastor will watch her do this, drinking his coffee and smiling.

You're doing well, Johnstone.

They celebrate the holidays; Halloween is the night in which she finds herself barking at strangers all night, familiar scents but oddly disguised; the small ones shout "trick or treat" when Father Johnstone opens the door, and he hands them a food token of homage; it reminds Mary of how Father Johnstone would give her a milkbone or bacon rind for relieving herself in the yard as opposed to inside their dwelling; the small ones visit all night, but sometimes they collect Mary's turds and burn them on her owner's doorstep within a womb of tan paper; this makes him angry, but thankfully, it is but a rare occurrence; Thanksgiving is a far more enjoyable affair; it is much like Halloween, except the roles are reversed in the exchange; the pastor and Mary are showered with random company, each bearing some kind of dish or other food offering; Mary receives many bites of turkey from all the different visitors, eating to the point of excess, but the occasion that she's given such delicacies is rare; she takes to hoarding these nibbles of the white meat under the bed for later consumption, much to the disappointment of her owner; Father Johnstone tells her, "Don't worry, I can't eat all these leftovers myself," and Mary seems to understand that this feast will last many days, opting to curl up on the couch to digest her meal; she's loved and adored by many of the different visitors, mostly female; they coo and rub her belly, always affectionate; Mary reaches her first snow, the cold white powder stings her paws if she stands still for too long; she puts her face in it and comes out with a little Santa beard, it makes the pastor laugh; afterwards, they'll lie on a blanket by the fireplace, the pastor reading the paper or working on the crossword while Mary lets the heat dry her fur, she's balled up next to the pastor's stomach, drifting in and out of sleep; he puts Mary in a festive sweater, buys her an extra large bone wrapped in a bow for an occasion known as

Christmas; Mary hears that word a lot as the cold takes over; the smell of pine consumes the home as Father Johnstone stations a tree in their main room; it sits in a metal water bowl, not unlike the one that Mary has; she learns quickly she's not allowed to drink from that water bowl, nor is she allowed to get too close to the various boxes under the tree; they hold no real interest to her, but her owner still shoos her away if she lingers by them for too long; guests pay homage as they do on Thanksgiving, only this time ham is the main dish that they feast upon, a salted meat with a hint of sugar that Mary enjoys; it reminds her of bacon somewhat; these feasts and the people and lying by the fireplace are pure joy for Mary; she loves the holidays, and the pastor can't imagine spending them without her now. She's family.

Keep going...almost there...

Mary gets bigger, her baby teeth fall out and the color of her coat changes, shifting the ratio between caramel and black; they develop a routine and a relationship unlike either have ever had before; sometimes there are missteps: Father Johnstone won't immediately pick up the signal that the water bowl is empty just as Mary will sometimes gnaw on items not meant for her; she noses her bowl if it's empty now, he buys her toys and elevates his valuables out of her range; they reach an understanding that one is caring for the other, although it often feels mutual; there's an emotional void in her owner—Mary can sense it; he's lonely, or at least he was lonely, but there's only so much she can do; Father Johnstone will speak to her sometimes just as he does those of his species; unfortunately, she can only understand reoccurring words: her name, 'sit,' 'lay,' 'treat,' 'outside,' and things of that nature; commands, and then other terms like Christmas or Thanksgiving; long passages of speech can only be interpreted through tone, so when the pastor breaks, when he says, "You're all I have and you're all I'll ever have," Mary can only decipher what he means through the tenderness of his voice, the way he gently scratches the back of her ear and under her jaw; she has absolutely no idea that what the pastor is really saying is, 'If you died, I would die, too.' That is what a prayer is: a sentiment, an emotion that doesn't need to be put into words. It's communicating with your heart, your soul, your very existence. It transcends print, goes beyond the Good Book. The prayers that really matter are the ones we write ourselves.

Madeline says, "Now look, Johnstone."

But he doesn't have to. The sensation is familiar. In fact, he's felt it every morning for the past ten or so years: a scratchy wetness with fur grazing against his fingers. Mary always licks the pastor's hand when she wants him to wake up.

Prozess IV: Selbst Liebe

*The female (Frau) will disrobe, placing herself on her back facing east, the direction of emergence and origin (Entstehung). She may use an elongated mirror (Spiegel) for assistance in the seeding portion, however, it's imperative that the mirror be removed for the actual process, as the effects may backfire. The speculum (derived from Greek; reference: tools) will be used to expose the vaginal cavity, and must be blessed and cleansed before application. Once the cavity is exposed, the female will insert the tribute (Geschenk) which consists of: one male lock of hair bound in a white bow, one small personal item of the male, three male fingernails, one photograph (Foto). The tribute items may not be sourced through multiple males. All items must be wrapped and bound in an earth-sourced binding type (reference: materials), however, animal hide has been said to yield the best results. Once the tribute has been seeded, the speculum must be removed along with any reflective surfaces. The female will then proceed to rub the clitoris with her dominant hand counter-clockwise for twelve revolutions, clockwise for five revolutions, repeating as necessary. She must fill her mind with the image (Bild) of the intended male of tribute and only him. Should the female lose count or concentration, the process and intended effects will either be flawed, weak, or non-existent. The female's climax infuses the tribute with her essence (Essenz), and she may now proceed to the main residence of the male for planting. It's important that the female not remove the tribute from her body. Planting must occur between midnight and sunrise, and it is recommended that it be done during the quarter or full moon (**Mond**). Do not plant in the rain as it will negate the infusion. Snow also has detrimental effects. Using her bare hands, the female will dig a hole in the earth (**Erde**) no more than twenty feet away from where the male sleeps. The depth of the hole must be at least a foot deep but no more than three. The female must now plant the seed by positioning her vaginal cavity over the hole, pushing the tribute out of her body and into the earth's soil. Once this is accomplished, the soil* *must be swept over the tribute and packed tightly to contain the essence and feminine infusion. Effects will manifest in three days time.*

The Formula

"How did you do that?" Father Johnstone asks.

Madeline steers the Challenger down Route 9, her right hand gripped steady on the wheel while the other hangs out the window, arm at full extension. She shakes her hand like a ballplayer that's just caught a line drive with a little too much zip on it. Her fingers wrap into a fist, clenching tight, and then wilt loose. Dusty wind cuts through her fingers and licks her palm dry.

She says, "What *we* did, Johnstone. The two of us."

It's as if it never happened: the lightning and the thunder. The aftermath. Mary lying dead, cooked to a fine char on the once lush grass. Mary smoldering, smelling of burnt hair and hot meat. He could see her bones and organs through the tears in her flesh. Mary's eyes flash-fried and burst to brown ooze, streaming like tears across what was left of her face. It was the very thing nightmares are made of and over just as quickly.

A miracle, for lack of a better term, but the pastor isn't so ready to accept that as an explanation, despite the proof he's holding. Mary's licking his face, propped up on her hind legs and lapping at him like she's just returned from a very long trip. Her little docked tail wags in a blur of joy, and as much as Father Johnstone wants to return this affection, he can't stop examining her body for scars or burns. He pets her, hand smoothing down her ribcage, but it's with the ulterior motive of investigating for damages. He searches for any lasting impressions of what he just saw—what broke him to pieces. Yet, there's not a single brittle hair or patch of discoloration on her skin. At a casual glance, she looks healthier than before. Her coat is shinier. Eyes brighter. Father Johnstone pushes a thumb into Mary's mouth to get a look at her gum line, an area once plagued with brown strains and muddy patches, but they're clean now. Mary's teeth glisten like new, playfully nipping at the pastor's fingertips.

Madeline gives her left hand another shake and brings her arm in from the window, using the steering wheel to pop her knuckles. She looks at Father Johnstone and Mary in the passenger seat, giving the two of them a smile something like relief, as if what just happened could have gone another way. Mary could still be dead, the pastor thinks, but then a more important issue surfaces. Everything happened so fast that Father Johnstone had forgotten about the lightning.

"You knew," he says. "You knew it would hit that exact spot."

Madeline scoffs. "Let's just sit here and think about what you just said."

She flexes the fingers of her left hand again, keeping her eyes on the gravel terrain of Route 9. Father Johnstone had put it together that Madeline must somehow know when certain things are about to happen. The scope of that, he's unsure of—but she knew that lightning would strike at that exact place, at that exact time, and she put Mary in the path of it to teach him a lesson. She wanted to show him that God would let an innocent creature get hurt, even if such a creature was all the pastor had in his life to call his own.

"*God is in everything,*" he said. "*Even when it hurts His creations.*"

Madeline had brought Father Johnstone out to the fields for one simple reason: to get him to forsake his idol. Because it's difficult to keep worshipping the same thing that hurts you, especially when you've been led to believe you're exempt. Maybe that's the pastor's *vanity* at play, but he never thought the Lord would intentionally hurt him, or Mary for that matter. It's a cruelty he never anticipated.

"You're thinking about this the wrong way," Madeline says. "Consider this: how many times have you seen lightning strike on a clear, blue day?"

Never, he thinks. A singular bolt of lighnting without the

presence of clouds isn't just unnatural, it borders on impossibility. However, 'impossibility' has taken on a very different definition as of late.

"How scared would the people back in town be if they had seen what we just did?" Madeline asks. "They'd freak."

She clenches her left hand again, balls it up tight and shakes it loose. The palm is singed, reminiscent of a sunburn. It reminds Father Johnstone of the sensation that went through his own appendage, like hot needles threatening to burst out of his skin. White hot pin-pricks.

Madeline says, "There couldn't be any witnesses, Johnstone. They're not ready yet."

"Ready for..." the pastor trails off, thinking about what just happened with new perspective. She's right, he realizes. He has been thinking about this wrong. Madeline didn't predict the bolt; she caused it. *They* caused it. Together.

Madeline glances over to the passenger seat where the pastor is clutching Mary, holding her tight to his chest. She says, "Figure it out, did ya?" noticing the look of panic on his face. The wheat continues to blur in gold as the Challenger speeds along, and Father Johnstone remembers what she said about praying: that he was doing it wrong. Just like the car, if one of the pieces is missing, it won't function.

"You made that bolt happen?" he asks.

"*We,*" she corrects. "We killed Mary. We brought her back." Madeline pats Father Johnstone on the leg, attempting to put him at ease. She says, "Look, I know that probably wasn't your finest moment back there, but believe me, it was completely necessary. If I had told you what we were about to do you never would have gone along with it."

"Let you kill my dog?" he asks incredulously. "No, I certainly would *not* have gone along with it."

"*We* killed her," she corrects him again. "But like I said, it was completely necessary. I couldn't have just told you. You would have thought I was crazy or something."

"I'm not totally convinced that you *aren't*," the pastor snips.

"Don't be pissy, Johnstone. I could zap you right now if I wanted," Madeline says. The pastor recoils in his seat slightly, clutching Mary even tighter as Madeline glares at him, eventually letting her mouth break into a smile. She gives him a playful slap on the leg and says, "Honey, I'm kidding. Relax."

Father Johnstone sighs, allowing his body to ease off the passenger side door. He can see the intersection of Route 9 and Main in the distance now. The gravel of the road begins shifting to a more compact substance, granting the tires and undercarriage a reprieve from the beating of rocks and pebbles. Madeline eases off the gas, allowing the Challenger to coast along. She gives her left hand another shake and flex, balling it into a fist and releasing, gritting her teeth.

"You're hurt?" the pastor asks.

"Rusty," she answers, switching on the turn signal as the Main Street sign draws closer. Madeline admits to the pastor, "I'm a little out of practice."

"You mean you've done that before?" he asks.

"There were a lot of things I used to do, Johnstone. Not all of them were good."

Madeline turns at the intersection, getting back on the worn blacktop of Main and heads towards the town, back to Pratt where discontent awaits. Father Johnstone remembers their faces, the disgust. Public opinion dropped so low that he very nearly left, and so the return home is bittersweet. It's familiar but not at all welcoming. He fears something worse may have happened to his home during this most recent absence, an even higher degree of vandalism or maybe arson, but he takes comfort in the fact that he has Mary and the Challenger. If worse came to worst, Father Johnstone could still escape from Pratt. He could still get out moderately unscathed, but Madeline won't let it happen.

"You've got that scared-bunny look in your eye again," she

observes. "Ready to take off at the first sign of trouble." The Challenger cruises at an even 20mph, bystanders stopping and staring at the vehicle that Father Johnstone is notorious for hiding away in his garage.

"It's never been this bad before," he says, staring out the window while Mary noses his chin, offering a few consoling licks. "Towns like this…when the people turn, it's hard to get them back in your favor. Forgiveness isn't their strong suit, no matter how much you preach it."

"Well, what if I told you this isn't completely your fault?" Madeline offers. "Your recent behavior, I mean."

"You finally taking responsibility?" the pastor asks, leering at Madeline from his side of the car. "Is this where you tell me that you've been giving me something along the line of what you gave Mrs. Tiller?"

"Actually, no," she says. "And I thought you would have figured out by now that Magda's silence is the only thing keeping this town from lynching you."

"You don't find your methods unethical?" he asks.

"It's not so black and white. Sometimes a little wrong corrects a larger one." She explains, "It's called doing damage control."

"You can't go around and play with people's heads like that, Madeline. It's not fair," the pastor says, despite the part of himself that's relieved by keeping his recent incident at the church under wraps. Madeline has a point: if the town knew, he'd probably be beaten to a pulp or worse by now.

"I take it you've been having trouble sleeping, right? Nightmares? Mood swings?" Madeline says, taking a right at the intersection and heading back towards the pastor's residence. "That sound familiar?"

"You're changing the subject again," he says, "but yes, as a matter of fact, I have."

"Then I'd be more worried about someone playing with *your* mind," she says.

Madeline pushes the button of the garage door opener, easing the Challenger up the incline of the driveway. From what the pastor can tell, no new damage has been done to the house. Madeline pulls into the garage, placing the vehicle in park and killing the engine. She pushes the garage door opener again, and the three occupants sit and listen to the slates of door rolling shakily along the track, afternoon light steadily dimming on the power tools and spare auto parts. Then darkness, and Madeline says, "We're gonna need a shovel."

She takes the keys out of the ignition, stowing them in her jacket pocket and heading inside the house. Father Johnstone does the same, dumping Mary to the ground once they pass the threshold. He comes to find Madeline standing before the fireplace in the living room, finger tapping thoughtfully to her lip. "And we'll need some of this firewood, too. And lighter fluid, if you've got it."

"Wait a minute, what's going on?" Father Johnstone asks.

"Trust me, just go with it," she says, walking out of the living room to the kitchen. She peels away the lace window curtain on the back door, yelling out over her shoulder, "And find us some matches or something."

"Honestly, considering what just happened out in the fields," the pastor says, tailing Madeline to the kitchen, "I don't know if I'm really inclined to 'just go with it.' Something bad always seems to happen."

Madeline turns, points. "Your nose." She grabs a washcloth draped on the kitchen faucet, tossing it underhand to the pastor. He presses it to his nostrils, soaking up the blood and feeling the beginning splinters of a migraine behind his eyes. Madeline approaches him, explaining, "That keeps happening because there's something here that's not supposed to be, and the longer you're around it, the worse it's going to get. Understand?"

Father Johnstone maintains the pressure of the washcloth, giving Madeline a nod. "You know what's doing this to me, then?" he asks, the question slightly muffled by the contents wet rag curtaining his mouth.

Madeline takes the cloth away from him, damp with blood and old water. She whistles out towards the living room and the two of them can hear Mary's little paws running towards them, nails clicking on the linoleum of the kitchen. Madeline kneels down, offering the washcloth to Mary for inspection, saying, "Find that for me." She stands up and gives the cloth back to the pastor, then opens the back door where Mary bolts out and begins circling the yard, little coal nose flexing just above the ground. Madeline says, "You think you're sick but you're not. Not in a traditional sense, anyway. That's why Dr. Keller can't find anything wrong with you." Madeline goes over to the kitchen counter where a stack of old napkins is sitting. She picks them up and hands them to the pastor, which he puts to his face to stifle the blood flow. "That's the beauty of it. If you can't diagnose something, you can't cure it." She motions to the backyard, at the rusted tin shed in the shaded back corner, asking, "Shovel?"

Father Johnstone nods, another wave of migraine flushing to the front of his skull, boiling behind his eyes. He follows Madeline out to the yard where Mary is standing still, legs quivering slightly with her nose to the ground. She barks and circles the spot, seemingly having found whatever she was supposed to look for.

Madeline walks out to Mary, squatting down and giving her a little pat on the head for her efforts. She tells the pastor, "C'mere and look at this."

Father Johnstone stands over it, a circular area in the grass that's about the size of a frisbee in diameter. He kneels down to make a closer observation, the headache spiking, pounding enough to get his teeth to grit. "It's…yellow," he says, remarking on the color of the blades of grass. There's so many dead spots in the yard, wilted patches that have shriveled under Mary's urine, that Father Johnstone has made a habit of turning a blind eye to his shoddy landscaping. He hardly notices them anymore, writing it off to collateral damage of owning a dog.

Madeline takes a fistful of the grass, ripping it out and presenting it to the pastor's nose. "Smell this," she says. Father Johnstone tentatively removes the bloody napkins away from his face, taking a couple test snorts to see if the bleeding has ceased. He inadvertently inhales the scent, the stench. It's sulfuric, like wet rot. Another spike of migraine erupts and the pastor turns his face away, pressing the napkins against his nostrils again, breathing blood and old French fry grease. Madeline says, "Get the stuff to make a fire. I'll get the shovel and start digging."

"The shed's locked. You'll need the key."

Madeline waves him off. "I'm pretty good with locks. Go ahead."

The two go their separate ways: Madeline to the rear corner of the yard where the shed is, the pastor heads back inside. He trashes the soiled napkins, splashing some water on his face from the sink to wash off the blood, snorting again. The flow seems to have stopped for the time being. Father Johnstone gets the items Madeline requested: a few wedges of mesquite from the stack near the fireplace, and then he pockets the box of wood matches off the mantle. Another wave of headache blisters beyond his eyes and inside his eardrums, causing him to clutch the wall, but only for a moment. He knows he has to fight through it. Be strong. It's his best shot at feeling normal again, if what Madeline is saying is true. He makes his way back to the kitchen, opening a cabinet on the bottom that contains a handle of lighter fluid, bundling everything in his arms like he's carrying an infant. Father Johnstone heads back out into the yard to find Madeline already splitting earth with the spade, breaking the relatively thin seal that maintained the stench. The yard reeks now.

"Should have had you gotten me a painter's mask," she says. "Smells like rotten shit over here."

The pastor lays the items down a few feet away from the dig site, noticing the color of dirt underneath the grass is a very dark brown, almost black. It looks like granulated coal, the stink intensifying as Madeline shovels. He leans over a bit, squinting, and there appears to be some kind of fluid rising through the soil, bubbling slightly. "What is it?" he asks.

"Probably a lot of things," she says, taking another scoop of dirt and dumping it off to the side, forming a small pile. "The ingredients aren't going to mean anything to you, but this is a very nasty version of what you've already seen with Mrs. Tiller. Slower, but more potent." Madeline quickly adds, "And before you even ask—no, I didn't put this here."

Another wave of migraine sweeps, a churn of nausea—it's either from the smell, or his regular symptoms are back in force. Father Johnstone covers his mouth, breathing consciously through his mouth and his mouth alone, attempting not to taunt his gag reflex. He can still taste it, the rot in the air, but he manages to ask Madeline, "Whatever you're digging up—you're saying that's what has been making me feel this way?"

"Yep." She dumps another shovel's worth of mud off to the side, a light sheen of perspiration building on her forehead. She says, "And you're not technically sick, Johnstone. You're cursed." Another scoop gets added to the pile and Father Johnstone stares at her, hand still tightly cupped over his nasal passages. He doesn't know what to make of the diagnosis, and Madeline picks up on this, venturing, "I take it by the furrowed brow you're confused by what I just said."

He nods, migraine turning to hot fever, sweating profusely. Despite doing nothing more than standing in one place, the pastor is perspiring even harder than Madeline, who appears to have finally struck something in the earth, something dead and corroded. Something meant specifically for him.

Madeline waves the pastor over with a finger, saying, "A curse is like poison, composed of many ingredients. It kills the grass and deadens any soil surrounding it, turning it to this stuff," she motions to the pile of black muck. "It festers and rots, and then it spreads like cancer to whatever is in the vicinity. And guess who sleeps less than twenty feet away from here," she says, referring to the main bedroom on the rear of the house. Father Johnstone, however, is still hung up on the terminology.

How odd, the pastor thinks, that Madeline would use the word 'curse,' as if anything so archaic could realistically exist, not to mention in his own backyard. And how strange that Madeline refers to this bundle of dead meat, this rotting mammal corpse buried in his backyard as 'ingredients.' All he can see is what may or may not be the top portion of a possum, half-submerged in muck. Sunken eyes and not a thread of fur left. Mud and fluids coat the muscle tissue, stain its teeth.

"If left unchecked, this thing gets inside of you," Madeline says. "Makes you think the way it wants you to think. You can try and resist it, but it always wins eventually." She grabs the wedges of mesquite and begins sticking them in the hole, taking care not to touch the mammal corpse or the muddy walls surrounding it. The logs are pushed down so they're making a point, almost like the framework of a teepee. Madeline says, "I knew what was going on with you at the bake-off because I had seen it before."

The pastor remembers those words: *"See you on the other side, Johnstone."*

"And I knew it wouldn't kill you because it's not meant to do that," she says, pressing down on the wood wedges so they're firmly in place, making a canopy.

Madeline takes the canister of lighter fluid, pops the cap, and gives the wedges a liberal soaking. It does little to combat the sulfur and corpse smell, and Father Johnstone also suspects that wood and generic lighter fluid won't be enough to stay lit in a pit of muck and animal remains.

He asks, "What is it meant to do?"

"Control you." Madeline squirts a couple more torrents of

lighter fluid on the logs, explaining, "You are the leader of the flock. If the shepherd is compromised, you compromise all that he has authority over." A hand slides down into her jacket pocket, removing a coil of white twine about ten feet long. She bunches it in her palm, soaking it in the remainder of the lighter fluid. Madeline cups her hand, containing the twine and fluid to a small pool. She says, "Word has it you've been out of sorts lately...been losing your temper and giving careless advice. But that's only a precursor to what Mrs. Tiller saw you doing in the church." Madeline places one end of the twine at the top of the log wedges, pinching it in the teepee's apex. She starts to uncoil the twine, backing away from the muck pit, almost like she's unraveling a fuse while the pastor watches her. The flush of shame almost overwhelms the migraine and the fever burning his brow. Almost.

"You have been compromised, Johnstone," Madeline says, lying belly-down on the grass with one end of the fuse pinched between her fingers. She gives the spot next to her a little pat, indicating that Father Johnstone should follow in suit. He walks over, remembering the dream, the bed and the candles, and how Madeline would smooth her hand over the sheets. Beckoning for his company. She says, "The best way to hurt a man of God isn't to destroy him, it's destroying his credibility. Sour the flock against him. Kill their faith."

It's certainly working, the pastor thinks. He's witnessed this much in the way Pratt looks at him, the way it openly hates and vandalizes his home, and it's only a matter of time before they take it that one final step. Violence, he thinks. This will all end in violence, a tale that will make the Mason Hollis affair look trivial by comparison. Father Johnstone is on the verge of learning first-hand just how far Pratt's *wrath* can extend.

The pastor lies next to Madeline in the grass, hand clamped over his nostrils like a gas mask. He feels Mary hop over his lower back, snuggling between their two bodies and using

Madeline's jacket for cover. Father Johnstone asks, "Why would someone want to do that?"

"The same reason most people do anything," she says. "Power." Madeline presents the end tip of the wet twine, pinched between her thumb and forefinger. She says, "Light that for me."

Father Johnstone retrieves the box of wood matches from his pocket, curious as to if a fuse is even necessary. Madeline seems intent on keeping her distance and staying low to the ground though, holding the twine steady as the pastor strikes a match. A flame blooms, slowly creeping along the path of the line, snaking through the blades of grass. It inches towards the pit, leaving a trail of char in its wake.

"Is there a reason we're lying down in the grass like this?" the pastor asks.

"Because I'm not exactly sure what's going to happen," Madeline says, eyeing the flame that's about halfway between them and the pit. "I only know about curse-breaking in theory. I've never actually done it."

Again, the usage of the word 'curse' rings suspect to the pastor. 'Curse' as in: the opposite of prayer. An action in which you wish ill upon a person, either poor health or loss of crop or mortal peril. This is an ancient term that is only referred to in scriptures—not in the modern day. However, the pastor can't turn a blind eye to recent events regarding his health and behavior. He can't deny that he very much is exhibiting the symptoms of a man blighted by something nefarious and unnatural, a condition that not even Dr. Keller can detect. It's exactly as Madeline said, "If you can't diagnose something, you can't cure it."

"How do you know about curses?" he asks.

"Think about what you've seen."

A recipe in which the person who ingests it becomes subject to influence and suggestion; lightning without traditional source or warning; random death, and then death overturned. A man of the cloth who suddenly wanders off the Divine path after thirty-some-odd years of serving in the Lord's favor, tempted and broken by *lust*. Then the flock sours, just as Madeline said because she's seen this before. She understands power, the type of power that Father Johnstone has chosen not to recognize as a real threat due to its outlandish nature. Despite their presence in the scriptures, curses are an obsolete device not meant to be taken literally. They are story-fodder and scare tactic. They're not real.

"Curses are the anti-prayer," Madeline says. "Just like you can request the gift of good health or fortune, there's also a flipside to that."

The flame burns along the twine, less than a foot away from the pit of muck and wood and lighter fluid. Father Johnstone's head pounds, nose clogged with hot blood and sweating so badly it encapsulates his eyes, stinging them. He burns with fever and flu, aches with hot sickness. It's the Pratt bake-off all over again.

"If you have the right ingredients, the right components," Madeline says, "almost anything is possible."

With the flame crawling along the twine towards the mesquite wedges, it finally adds up. Ingredients, Madeline said. Components that are used to make miracles, manufacture curses. One who is condemned in the Good Book for casting spells and being a spiritist.

'Anyone who does these things is detestable to the Lord,' it says.

"Witchcraft is what's responsible for your condition, Johnstone," Madeline reveals, eyes watching the flame crawl into the pit, nearing the mesquite wedges soaked in lighter fluid. "It's the reason this town is in danger, and if you want to save it, you're going to have to bend those beliefs of yours. You're going to have to accept that it's more than just God at work here."

And before Father Johnstone has a chance to react, gather a

coherent thought, or even blink—that's when the flame touches the pit.

That's when the pastor starts to believe.

On the Road with Billy Burke, Truck Stop Preacher

"I want you to pray for your health and the well-being of your kin...your wives and parents and kids. Pray that the Lord allow you to provide for them: food, shelter, warmth, and love. Pray He keeps you on the Divine path, and let you not fall to the temptation of meth hookers and strippers with shaved cooters. If you take a tab of ecstasy, pray to Him that you don't wind up breaking into someone's home so you can rub your pecker on their shag carpet. We are men alone on the road, voyaging across the country with little else to count on but ourselves. Let the Lord be the company you keep—not some Puerto Rican escort named Charlo. It may make all the difference between getting home safe and having sores crop up on your pecker. You know why sores are red? Do you? The goddamn Devil, that's why. Red is shade of the beast, and the beast lives in the saliva and cunt of every lot lizard and meth hooker you come across. Their shitters, too. The Good Book says to be wary of a dirty shitter. Now, I see a lot of men here with tattoos. Well, I'll tell you this: AIDS and herpes is the tattoo the Devil needles into your skin and your blood. Ain't no removing it. That shit sticks with you forever...even in the afterlife, and the last thing you want is to arrive at the pearly gates with a cold sore on your lip. So stay on the Lord's side. Ask that he keep you out of the bad cooch. For you married men that need to get back out on the road, you can get on your way. I'll say a prayer for you. Everyone else, we're all going to Candy's Playhouse on 17th Street. We're going to practice keeping the Lord in our heart while there's a big ol' set of titties in our faces. Ol' Billy Burke here believes in a practical approach. I surely do. You know what...fuck it— married guys, you come along with us!"

The Sheriff

"I'm glad we're getting this chance to talk," Madeline says, handing over an old mop bucket that still smells of bleach and industrial cleaners. Father Johnstone notices grime looping the interior as he takes it, fingers clamping firmly on either side. Knuckles turn white. He proceeds to vomit and spit, hacking up black fluid in the middle of the kitchen. Not blood. Something thicker and foreign, originating from his chest just below the sternum. He can taste the sulfur as it passes over his tongue. Rot scalds his nostrils. The bottom of the bucket begins to pool with fluid, staining the beige plastic like house paint.

Madeline sits down next to the pastor on the floor, bare knees kissing the old-fashioned linoleum. She smoothes her right hand over the pastor's back, patting him, saying, "That's going to get a little worse before it gets better, I imagine."

They were in the back yard only a moment ago, waiting for the flame inching along the twine to touch the contents of the pit: lighter fluid, mesquite logs, animal carcass, and a myriad of other 'ingredients,' as Madeline referred to them. Ingredients to manufacture a curse, one that wears its target down: affecting their mood and temperament, compromising their judgment. The recipient suffers night terrors too real to be written off as dreams. They experience blackout spells and lapses in memory. For the better part of two weeks, Father Johnstone had felt these effects intensify to the degree of barely being able to function, then past that. He wound up in the care of Dr. Keller, unable to decode the origins of this supposed illness and its culminating bleeding episode at the Pratt bake-off, but that was the intention. Curses, as Madeline explained, can't be medically detected or diagnosed. That's the beauty of them. It's why they're so dangerous.

"When a curse is broken," Madeline says, "the body begins the process of purging it from its system...kind of like food poisoning." She gives the pastor another pat on the back and more fluid comes out of his nose, his tear ducts, a small amount through the ear canal that crawls down his jaw line and neck. It stains the collar of his shirt. She tells him, "And you've had this thing festering in you for a while now—so hate to break it to you, but you and that bucket are going to be pals for a bit."

Another wave of fluid charges its way up the pastor's esophagus, boiling the back of his throat and splattering at the bottom of the bucket. His insides pinch and cramp. Lungs collapse. He spits. Hacks and spits, asking between heaves, "How...long?"

"Not sure," Madeline says. "Never seen this side of it, but it's gotta run out sometime." She stands up and moves to the cabinets, opening them one at a time. She finds glasses and tumblers, chipped coffee mugs. Another contains the pastor's modest dining set he picked up at Mrs. Daltry's garage sale some years ago, lined with a floral and vine pattern that she deemed as "too fussy." Madeline shuts the doors on these items and continues searching, asking, "Isn't there something you'd normally do in this situation?"

Father Johnstone ejects more fluid. Vomits. The vomit carves skin out of his throat like fingernail scratches. Pale slivers of flesh float over the surface. He can barely catch enough time to breathe let alone attempt an answer, so he winds up shaking his head to communicate his lack of perception. The question doesn't make sense to him.

Madeline opens a cabinet on the bottom row, two over from where she found the bucket under the sink. She pulls out his old aluminum teakettle, reminding him, "You'd pray, right? For your health and all that?" Father Johnstone hears her pry open the top of the kettle at the hinge, followed by another couple of cabinets being explored. He looks up just long enough to see Madeline raiding the spice shelf, talking over her shoulder, saying, "And what is prayer if not the conscious application of faith? It is the directive. It is the formal appeal for that which we cannot do on our own."

The pastor hears Mary's nails clicking on the linoleum, getting closer as he retches into the bucket again. It wasn't that long ago that she was lying still on the ground, charred and smoldering. Fur turned to ash, organs cooked inside of her. She was as dead as dead can get, and yet through prayer, or perhaps by the hand of God Himself, Mary was brought back to him. Divine power returned her to this world, healthy and alive. Madeline Paige, however, would have the pastor believe otherwise, that this was the result of witchcraft. And although he's witnessed acts to corroborate her claim, thirty-odd years of devotion to the Lord and His Word challenge otherwise. Old habits die hard, as they say, even if those habits have no definitive proof to back them up.

Into the teakettle, Madeline sprinkles in thyme, sage, a pinch of cinnamon. She grabs the canister of fennel and drops three seeds in, all to the tune of Father Johnstone coughing liquid rot into the bucket. His hands brace tightly to the rim, fingernails spattered in black. Mary wanders over and gives her owner an affectionate lick on the knuckle while Madeline adds more ingredients: honey and cane sugar and a sprig of grass that she plucks out of her hair. A spoonful of vanilla extract.

She says, "A prayer isn't that much different than an incantation, when you think about it. They can be used for good, or in your case, they can be used to hurt and control people." Madeline turns away from the spice cabinet, peeking over her shoulder, telling him, "You're almost out of bay leaves, by the way."

Father Johnstone heaves into the bucket again, the fluid standing about an inch high and bubbling, stinking of rot. His fever begins to slip, skin cooling, he's granted a few moments of reprieve from purging. He looks up to see Madeline tossing in a few teabags of Earl Grey into the kettle, and then adding water from the faucet to the mix. She turns on one of the gas burners and places the kettle on it, telling the pastor, "But prayer without direction, without power, equates to nothing. They're just words. It's why some people die of cancer and some go into remission."

Father Johnstone considers that theory. He's lost members of the flock to illness, to the versions of death in which Dr. Keller gave them so many months or weeks to live based on calculation and medical trends. The patient prayed, and the pastor prayed with them and their families, but it always ended the way Dr. Keller predicted. Death always came to pass, no matter how often they reached out to God. It didn't matter. Everyone's efforts seem wasted, not to mention the spiritual depletion one experiences in the presence of hope unfounded. Then Father Johnstone would give his spiel about how they passed on comfortably, in the care of friends and family and loved ones. "They're in a better place now," he'd say, but this always came off patronizing after all the emotional investment to keep this person alive. Heaven seemed like a consolation prize.

"Ever wonder about that, Johnstone? Why some people get better and others don't?" Madeline asks. "You ever wonder why faith—especially when you really need it to work in your favor, is so unreliable?" She soaks a nearby hand towel in cold tap water, bringing it to the pastor and pressing it firmly to his forehead. Cool water cascades over his cheekbones, nose, and lips, briefly muting the fever. He gags again, lungs punching upward. Another dollop of black careens over the gashes in his throat, chewing on his gums and lips, but Madeline is still composed, still nursing him. She says, "The answer, the truth, is that a prayer is only as good as the person doing it—and until today, you never had it right. Ever." Madeline drags the cloth down the pastor's face, across his lips and chin, mopping up the fluid. She tells him, "That's the first thing you need to accept: that your relationship with God isn't what you thought. And if you don't believe me, think back on all the things you've prayed for— for both yourself and for others. Think about that, and then do the math on how much of it was actually granted."

Even the most modest requests, the commonplace, the paltry favors of continued health and strength to lead the flock—even those were met with the occasional spout of illness, self-doubt, challenges of spiritual and personal nature that proved disruptive. As a man of the cloth, one would assume the Lord would grant these simple graces in order to further enable his preaching of the Word. As Madeline said though, there was a lacking in consistency. Even when he believed to have the Devil in his blood and was on the verge of losing himself, no Divine presence descended. In fact, his condition worsened—that is, until Madeline Paige intervened.

"Do you remember what I said about praying?" Madeline asks. "All the components have to be there."

Like the Challenger, every piece is essential. Distributor, radiator, pistons and spark plugs—without these, optimal functionality isn't possible. Missing pieces yield incomplete results.

"Both faith and Craft work on a formula," Madeline says. "The difference is that some of the ingredients aren't tangible. They're open to interpretation, like how much a man loves his dog." She caresses the pastor's face while giving Mary an appraising look. Madeline says, "Love can make a person very powerful if they know how to use it."

Father Johnstone feels another wave of sick surge upward, washing over his tonsils and lips. The fluid is thinner now, diluted to the point where it looks more like Travis Durphy's chaw spit than molasses. Madeline wipes the area below his mouth with the damp cloth, flipping it over and pressing the clean side to his forehead again. She gives the pastor an encouraging smile when he looks up from the bucket, blotting his forehead. The kettle begins its shrill whistle, and Madeline tells him, "Keep that on your forehead. We're gonna have company soon."

Father Johnstone accepts the cloth, patting down either side of his face and watching Madeline move back to the stove where she turns the burner off. He asks, "Who's coming?" but his throat is so raw it's nearly inaudible. The dying screech of the kettle overpowers him, and he ends up having to repeat himself after the noise has subsided. "Who's coming?" he asks again, a little louder this time.

"You've got a curse smoldering in your back yard, and it's made the whole area smell like rotten eggs and smoke," Madeline says, removing a ceramic mug from one of the cabinets and placing it on the kitchen counter. She puts a coffee filter inside the mug and begins pouring the contents of kettle onto the paper, slowly so it doesn't overflow. "If logic dictates anything around here," Madeline says, "I would imagine someone has already called the cops and they'll be stopping by shortly to check things out."

She's right, the pastor thinks, and a flaming pit of animal remains in his back yard is the exact kind of attention he doesn't need right now. Sheriff Morgan, like the majority of Pratt, doesn't take kindly to abnormality in his town, and a burning curse on the property of the local preacher is about as abnormal as it gets. Even if the sheriff doesn't figure out the true depths of what's happening, Father Johnstone's reputation can only be further tarnished by this. It will only reaffirm what people are whispering about him in every corner of the town.

Madeline, on the other hand, doesn't appear to be worried in the least. Her fingers pinch down on either side of the coffee filter, allowing the kettle water to strain through, leaving behind soft fennel seeds and various other remnants from the spice cabinet. The aroma cuts through the rotten smell that has all but taken over in the kitchen, replacing it with a pleasant robustness. "You look worried," she observes.

Father Johnstone nods curtly. There's no point in hiding it or attempting to lie. "Sheriff Morgan isn't exactly a friend," he says, still hoarse in the throat. He spits another rope of brown into the bucket, explaining, "He thinks man's law is above God's law. Doesn't do well with people questioning his authority."

Madeline tosses the coffee filter in the trash bin, asking, "And you think he'll what—arrest you? For a little fire in your yard?"

"If he wants," the pastor says. He coughs a few times, spitting into the bucket again. "I don't put it past him."

Outside, the distinct sound of a car door is heard shutting, to which Mary begins barking, bouncing off her front paws and running a couple tight circles on the kitchen floor. Madeline hands the mug of tea to Father Johnstone, telling him, "Drink this," and even though the pastor knows that any sort of food or beverage coming from Madeline may have side-effects (he can't help but remember Mrs. Tiller), the aftertaste of rot in his mouth is unbearable. Teeth and gums feel chalky and sore, stained from fluid now contained in the mop bucket. He brings the mug to his lips, sipping the tea and feeling the sulfur flavor dissolve from his taste buds. Steam assails his nostrils, cleaning them of rot and burn, almost as if he were inhaling pure menthol.

"I want you to sit there and finish that while I take care of this," Madeline says, lowering her hand into the waste bucket. She dips her forefinger into the black liquid, soaking the print and then bringing it to her lips where she applies it, still warm from the pastor's insides. Her finger smoothes the fluid over her bottom lip, painting it a shade of syrup brown. Madeline rubs one over the other, spreading the fluid over her mouth like cosmetics. She tells the pastor, "Don't say a word."

A series of knocks—pounding rattles the front door in its frame. Madeline exits the kitchen with Mary at her heels, barking yet again. The pastor drinks quietly on the kitchen linoleum, ears tuned to the living room where he hears the door creak open and the distinct drawl of Sheriff Morgan saying, "Afternoon, Miss Paige."

"Afternoon, Sheriff," Madeline chirps, as if she's happy to see him. "And to what do we owe the pleasure?"

"Oh, I think you know," he says. "Think you know exactly why I'm here. Got the whole goddamn neighborhood calling about that smell, telling me the ol' preacher and Maddy Paige are starting fires and the like," he says, almost relishing the moment. He tongues the toothpick in his mouth, shifting it side to side. "Ain't legal, of course. Law's the law. Might have to issue a citation or two. Probably going to eat into all that tip money you've been makin' at the diner."

"I see," Madeline says, non-argumentative. Non-combative. She doesn't give him a lick of sass to work with. Father Johnstone can hear the smile in her voice, a warm campfire smile beams at the grizzled sheriff as the pastor sits in the kitchen, quietly drinking the tea. Silent, just as Madeline instructed.

"'Course, this ain't *your* property," the sheriff points out. "Everyone know Maddy Paige lives in that fine house o'er by the daisy hill. Damn fine house," he says. "And who's to say that you ain't headin' back o'er there right now, hmm?"

"Nothing standing between me and home but the law," Madeline says playfully, and Father Johnstone can hear Mary give a disapproving growl. Surely she wouldn't leave, he thinks. She can't.

"You a damn quick learner, Maddy Paige," he chuckles. "Cute and clever girl—that's right...ain't nothin' standing between you and home...but *the law,* and right now the law thinks you wasn't really here, y'know, being an accessory and the like," he shifts the toothpick in his mouth again. "So tell me...before you get on home, where might that ol' wily preacher be? He ain't hidin', is he?"

"Not at all, Sheriff," Madeline says, almost flirtingly. "I'm afraid poor Father Johnstone breathed too much of the smoke and he took ill. He's most definitely still here."

"Damn shame," sheriff says, clearly pleased. "Damn shame, indeed. First, the poor feller's getting sick at his little church

party and now he got the smoke lung to boot? Mighty unfortunate," he says, but he doesn't sound sympathetic in the least.
Quite the opposite, in fact. He continues on, adding, "Law don't
take sick days, though. Sure you can understand that, right,
Maddy? Not like we can start cuttin' criminals loose for coughin'
fits, y'know."

Father Johnstone swallows his tea, fuming at that word: the
word "criminal." For years, an unspoken truce has existed
between the pastor and the sheriff, if only to keep the peace and
maintain a state of normality in Pratt. As much as Sheriff Morgan
resents Father Johnstone for holding power over the flock (or
whatever ill-contrived reasoning), he's always maintained a
respectable distance, almost as if he was waiting for him to step
out of line. A pillar can't go after another pillar without just cause,
and now that Father Johnstone had fallen out of favor with the
town, he had it.

"Indeed, yes," Madeline says. "Can't be too soft, can we? One
day it's an illegal fire pit and the next day you've got houses
burning down, right?"

"Escalation, Mad," the sheriff says with a nod. "That's what
we call it. Got to weed out the undesirables before they influence
the rest of the folk. Could tell you some stories, I surely could."
He puts a foot onto the threshold, the toe of his cowboy boot
breaching the doorway. Mary gives a little growl of warning that
he ignores. "For now though, why don't you go ahead and run
along home? I'll have a little chat with the pastor...get this all
sorted out. Ain't no need for you to be here."

"But you won't hurt him...will you, Sheriff?" Madeline asks,
contriving deep concern and feigning vulnerability. The sheriff
doesn't know her well enough to pick up on it. "You promise you
won't be too stern?"

"Well, y'know, I guess we'll just see," he says, non-committal.
"If he works with me, I'll work with him. Like I said...law's the
law, and I run a tight ship 'round here."

"That you do, Sheriff. And I just love a man that makes me feel safe…protected," Madeline says, her voice dropping to more of a whisper. It's so low the pastor can barely make out the last sentence. A few seconds pass by, and then a few more. It's silent, and Sheriff Morgan isn't responding. Not verbally, anyway. There's a sharp breath, the sound of lips mingling. Deep kissing. The pastor can hear it over Mary's curious grunt. Then another few seconds of silence before Madeline says in a less-girlish tone, "Kitchen! Now! Move it, redneck!"

The front door slams shut, and Father Johnstone hears the sound of rushed footsteps nearing the kitchen to the tune of Mary snarling, nipping at Sheriff Morgan's pant leg. He steps onto the linoleum looking catatonic, face smoothed over his normal expression of wrinkled disdain. Madeline pushes him along, her hand gripping the back of his neck and escorting him to one of the empty wooden chairs at the kitchen table. She says, "This guy's mouth tastes worse than what's in that bucket." And then to sheriff, sternly, she orders, "Sit. Now."

The pastor observes Sheriff Morgan in the chair, emotionally neutral with vacant eyes, much like Mrs. Tiller was in the hospital. He looks at the black fluid in the bucket, to Madeline, asking, "What did you do?"

"I took control of the situation," she says, pulling out a chair for herself at the table. Madeline sits down, crossing one leg over the other, sighing. "Did you not hear any of that in there? The guy had it in for you."

"No, I heard," the pastor says. "I just—"

"He wanted me to leave so he could beat the shit out of you," she interjects.

"Well," Father Johnstone frowns. "He didn't *exactly* say all that."

"He didn't have to." Madeline takes a handkerchief out of her pocket and wipes her lips off, scraping it against the sides of her mouth. "It's not what you say; it's how you say it. I thought you would have picked up on that by now." She turns to her left, asking the sheriff, "I'm not wrong, am I, Kip? You were going to beat the shit out of him, right?"

"Oh, yes ma'am, Miss Paige," Sheriff Morgan says, nodding concurrently. "Yes, indeed. Was fixin' to take a few of them pearly whites out with ol' Shelby here." His hand fondles the butt of his pistol, and Father Johnstone inches back on the floor, unsure as to whether or not he'll actually use it. Sheriff Morgan smiles at the pastor all yellow teeth, stroking the gun with the tips of his fingers. Mary positions herself between the two of them, snarling at the sheriff.

"Relax. He's harmless. Can't hurt a fly unless I tell him to," Madeline says, more to the pastor than Mary, although she too seems to calm down. Her haunches ease slightly, lips uncoil. The sheriff continues to smile, continues to stroke the gun with great affection, almost *lustfully*. He stares at Father Johnstone, knowing he's supposed to hurt him, to punish him. The desire is there, but he's been rendered immobile. He's being held back, being contained, and he doesn't like it.

"He's fighting," the pastor says.

"He won't win," Madeline says. "Stuff is too strong."

"That?" Father Johnstone looks at the bucket, the fluid.

"Yes," she says. "It's potent. Stronger than what you saw with Magda."

"It doesn't affect you?"

"No," she says. "I'm using it. It's not using me."

"What are you going to do with him?" the pastor asks, staring at the sheriff fondling his gun, still smiling like he's got an invisible coat hanger stretching his mouth apart.

"Well, you're smart. What would Johnstone do?" Madeline asks. "You know what his intentions were now. Go ahead and take point on this one."

"I wouldn't hurt him, if that's what you're asking," he says.

"No, of course not. You're better than that," Madeline smirks.

She looks at the sheriff thoughtfully, mischief flashing across her eyes. "We could have him hurt himself," she says enticingly.

"No, I don't want that either," the pastor says. The sheriff's fingers are still drumming the butt of the gun, trying to grip it. He fondles the handle, getting closer and closer to wielding it, and the smile becomes even more pronounced. Broader. At any moment, he could pull the gun out of its holster and shoot. One shot, point blank, right between the eyes. Father Johnstone says, "I want him to stop doing that," motioning to the sheriff's hand on the gun, his fingers.

"Kip, keep your mitts off the gun," Madeline says, and the sheriff's hand locks, shuttering at the wrist. His arm slowly moves away from the handle, resting in his lap. "And wipe the Joker grin off your face. It's creepy."

The corners of Sheriff Morgan's mouth pull down, making him appear more like his normal disgruntled self, all except for the eyes. He's livid. He knows what's happening to him and can't do anything to stop it.

"So we can get him to do what? Anything?" the pastor asks.

"Probably. I don't know. I've never used something like this before," Madeline says, leaning over to get face-to-face with the sheriff. She looks into his eyes, using her thumb to pull down on the lower lids. First the left, then right, she turns to the pastor and tells him, "Oh yeah, he's pretty pissed off in there."

Then the sheriff's radio chirps from his belt. Dispatch asks, "Sheriff, what's your twenty?"

"Kip, radio back that everything's fine here," Madeline says, leaning back in her seat and crossing her legs again. "Tell them it looks like some kids have been vandalizing the property and you've got it all under control."

Sheriff Morgan unclips the radio from his belt, bringing it to his mouth and thumbing down the button on the side. "Katy, I'm still at the preacher's place. Everything's...f-fine," he says, stammering slightly. "Looks like...some kids been givin' him…trouble." He releases the radio's button, clipping it back on the belt.

"Hmm, well that sounded terrible," Madeline says. "Kip, you trying to fight me off in there?"

"Oh yes, ma'am, Maddy Paige," the sheriff says, his smile returning. "If it were up to me right now, well I think I'd fuck that pretty lil' mouth of yours while ol' preacher here sat and watched. We'd have a real nice time, you an' me."

"Is that right?" Madeline coos. "And what if I said no?"

"Well, I s'pect you'd be havin' a short conversation with ol' Shelby here," the sheriff says. "And she don't have to say much to get her point across, if you know what I mean. People that don't wan' talk to the law usually end up talkin' to Shelby." His smile gets a little larger. "You wan' talk to Shelby, Miss Paige? I can bring 'er out…if ya let me," he suggests, hand drifting over to the gun, hovering, but not touching.

"No, how about we just keep those hands off of Shelby for now," Madeline says, and the sheriff abides, begrudgingly so.

It's different with him than Mrs. Tiller, the pastor notices. Mrs. Tiller was gentle and subdued, completely conquered emotionally-speaking. Sheriff Morgan, however, is clearly attempting to rebel. He knows he's stuck, being controlled, and it doesn't agree with him. Much the way Father Johnstone resisted the effects of the curse, so too does the sheriff.

"So what now, Johnstone?" Madeline asks.

The pastor stands up, legs shaking somewhat from the effort. He slugs the remainder of the tea Madeline made, lukewarm but still pleasant to the palate. The taste of rot seems to have vanished, but the smell in the kitchen is enough to make the walls peel. He places both the mug and bucket on the kitchen counter, staring at the sheriff and considering what to do, if anything. As shepherd of the flock, the pastor has led, but only to the extent that he gives advice and preaches the Lord's Word. Never though, has he controlled a person. Not like this—not in the way in which he can have Madeline make this man do whatever he wishes. He could just as easily make the sheriff leave his home as he could pull out ol' Shelby and eat a bullet. It's an overwhelming power, one that gives justification as to why people with supernatural abilities were so ill-regarded in the scriptures. They had a power that wasn't fully understood, and was therefore feared and rejected. Pratt would react no differently. Just as Father Johnstone anticipated violent reprisals for his diversity in behavior, so too would Madeline Paige. A modern-day witch hunt: the entire town looking for the two of them with their torches and pitchforks and shotguns. At the very least, Father Johnstone thinks, he can remove one part of the equation, the immediate threat that Sheriff Morgan seems so eager to wield.

"I want his gun," the pastor says.

"Ah, good choice," Madeline says. "Kip, hand Shelby over to Father Johnstone."

"Don't wan' to hand Shelby over," the sheriff says, although his hand is already drifting over to his hip, fingers wrapping around the silver handle and pulling the weapon from its holster. He extends his arm forward, weapon in-hand, saying through gritted teeth, "No fucking faggot preacher is gonna touch Shelby. No goddamn way."

Father Johnstone takes the gun by the barrel, prying it out of the sheriff's grip before he has a chance to put a finger on the trigger. Sheriff Morgan squirms in his seat, attempting to get up but his legs won't cooperate. Knees shake. He stares at the pastor hatefully, cursing still. Cursing and blaspheming. Father Johnstone looks at the gun, at Shelby, laid out over his two palms: a Colt .45, all silver. The sheriff has obviously been taking good care of his firearm, which gleams polished under the kitchen lights.

"How does it work, Mad?" the pastor asks, staring at the gun in his hands, admiring the weight and craftsmanship. The power.

It's the first time he's ever held one. "In a way that I'd understand," he adds. "Laymen's terms."

"Point and shoot," she says. "But I don't use guns."

"No. That," he points at the bucket with Shelby. "Curses. Witchcraft." Father Johnstone almost winces saying these words out loud. "How does all this work?"

"That's kind of a loaded question, Johnstone."

"Loaded how?"

"Because you're asking me to explain something you don't want to believe, even after seeing it for yourself," she says.

"Humor me," he presses.

"Well, there's faith, there's science, and then there's the in-between," she says, pausing a moment to see if there's any disagreement from Father Johnstone. He nods for her to go on. She says, "It's the gray area, the fringe between the two. A harmony." Madeline sighs, standing up and approaching the pastor who is still looking at the gun. She lifts it from his palms, saying, "To the untrained eye, this is nothing more than metal and gunpowder. For someone like me it's more than that. I can feel the intangibles. Hatred. *Wrath*." Madeline Paige looks at the pastor with those campfire eyes, braving a smile, "My skill set lies in knowing how to manipulate the intangibles."

"How am I supposed to buy that, Mad?" the pastor asks.

"The same way you buy your relationship with God, I'd expect," Madeline counters. "You can't see Him. You can't see electricity or air or magnetism or radio waves. You can't see love, but you accept these things."

"I suppose I do," he says, a tone of skepticism in his voice. He's still having trouble subscribing to Madeline's ideas, despite all that he's seen so far. A part of him still believes there's a perfectly reasonable explanation for everything, even if that explanation meant he were mentally or physically unwell. It would be easier to swallow than Madeline being able to manipulate intangibles, as she puts it.

"Ingredients, Johnstone. Everything is ingredients," she says. "For cooking, for praying, and yes, even for spell-casting."

"And what ingredients are those?" the pastor asks, pointing yet again at the bucket of black fluid, now simmering on his kitchen counter. Still smelling of rot and sulfur. "This man just handed me over his most prized possession, so it—what? Makes the person have no will of their own?"

"Hey, Kip, the pastor wants to know if you have no will of your own right now," Madeline says. "You want to take this one?"

"Oh yes, ma'am, everything in me wants to get up out of this chair and beat the ever-lovin' shit out the two of ya," Sheriff Morgan says, still squirming in his seat, teeth gritted and knees quavering. His arms are braced at either side, trying to push off the seat of the chair but unable to. "All I was gon' do was smack around ol' preacher, but now that he done and put his filthy mitts on Shelby…oh…he's gon' be dead man 'fore he know it. I gon' make it slow, too. Nice and slow so he know he done wrong."

"But you can't get up, can you, Kip?" Madeline teases. "I mean, we're both standing right here. What's stopping you?"

"Maddy Paige threw herself at the law, all kissin' on me like the whore everyone says she is," the sheriff says, grinning, as if he's recalling the moment fondly. "Whore got inside my head and the like…can't move under my own accord. Want to. But can't." The smile broadens, getting wider, and he says, "Only a matter of time, though. Matter of time."

Madeline turns back to the pastor, "Certain parts of the brain regulate certain things: heart rate, breathing, sensation, motor skills. Like anything though, they can be manipulated. You can plant thoughts or alter the person's personality. You can make them forget how to move."

"How come that never happened to me?"

Madeline says, "With a curse, like the one outside, it builds slow. It takes some time for the effects to manifest, like cancer. The stuff in the bucket, though—that's concentrated," she explains. "It's hitting his system directly. Make sense so far?"

"I guess."

"The bad news is that his body is already trying to process it and get rid of it," Madeline explains. "It'll wear off eventually."

"Yes, it will, Maddy Paige," the sheriff says, grinning. "An' then the law gonna come find you and ol' preacher. Gonna teach both you cunts a lil' lesson for what you did to me an' Shelby. Only a matter of time." He chuckles, straining in the chair. "Matter of time."

"How long?" the pastor asks.

"Hours? Days?" Madeline shrugs, glancing at the sheriff again. "Dunno."

"Can you give him more?" Father Johnstone almost feels guilty asking this, but after hearing all of Sheriff Morgan's threats, he's able to look past it. It's the lesser of two evils.

"In theory, yes, we could," Madeline says. "But we run the risk of him going into a coma or having a bleeding episode like you did at the bake-off. Not that I'd care but you probably do." She pauses a moment, offering, "We could always cuff him in the basement."

"No, the police know he's here. This is the first place they'd check," Father Johnstone says. "Even if that wasn't an issue, I couldn't do that to the man. It's not..." he trails off.

"What? Christian?"

"Not right. We're better than that, Madeline."

"This guy is a liability, Johnstone."

"Kip, are you seriously going to try to kill me first chance you get?" the pastor asks, ignoring Madeline. He walks over to the sheriff who is still sitting in the chair, fuming. "Do you honestly have that much *wrath* in you?"

"Don't need to talk to no faggot preacher," he answers.

"Kip, answer," the pastor tries again.

"Fuck yourself," he chuckles. "Maybe give Shelby back an' I'll consider it."

Father Johnstone turns to Madeline. "Why isn't he answering me? Isn't he supposed to do whatever we ask?"

"No," she says. "Just me."

"Why just you?"

"For the same reason I can't baptize or marry people. You have to be ordained," she says.

"So you're saying that he'll only answer to you and only follow your orders?" Father Johnstone asks. He doesn't want to hold the sheriff hostage, but he also doesn't want to cut him loose only to have him come right back. As Madeline said, he's a liability, and one that seems keen on taking the both of them down, especially after this incident. "Just you, right?" he confirms.

"Technically, no," she says. "The other one could do it, too."

"Other one?"

"I told you, I didn't plant that curse," Madeline reminds him. "That means there's someone else out there…someone like me." She hands Shelby back to the pastor, moving to the kitchen window where the curse continues to smolder gray, misting the back yard in sulfur. The tin shed in the rear of the yard isn't even visible anymore through the fog. Madeline stares into the void, shaking her head slightly. She sighs deeply, hands braced on the kitchen counter, saying, "This is usually the part where I run away."

"You mean you've seen this before?"

"Yes," she nods.

"Then what's stopping you?" the pastor asks. Unlike most people, Madeline hasn't been in Pratt for very long. She's not a lifer, the 'born here, die here' type, as Sheriff Morgan or Dr. Keller would say. All things considered, she has no real obligation to the town. She doesn't owe these people anything. "What makes this time any different?"

"Because I have something I didn't have before…something that makes me believe we stand a fighting chance."

"That stuff?" Father Johnstone nods towards the bucket, the curse fluid.

"No, silly," Madeline turns around, campfire smile and eyes just as warm. She puts her forefinger to the pastor's chest, touching him gently. "You," she says. "This time I've got you."

Las Vegas, NV

Sasha didn't make it.

Although we did fornicate to the point of climax, she made it clear that it was against her will—on both verbal and physical levels. She screamed the agreed-upon safe-word at me numerous times before reverting to the traditional protests of "no" and "stop" and "don't." Sasha did everything within her power to suspend vaginal penetration upon seeing the progression of my affliction, however, she was easily overtaken. A well-placed blow to the temple reduced her to a state of unconsciousness, allowing me to finish with relative quiet. My orgasm, however, was weak, accompanied by a displeasing sting that subdued all joy. It's been years since I've experienced orgasm at full capacity, not long after being exiled from my home, to be exact.

"You're going to help me, Father Latimer," I say.

I've changed my name again. I've changed locations again, moving from the Bellagio to the Four Seasons where I've booked three suites, the first of which is strictly a living space. Its only usage is for eating, sleeping, and relaxation. There is a device on the outer patio referred to as a 'hot tub' that I find extremely therapeutic. I'll often spend many hours there, marinating in several gallons of Holy water and the various wooden crucifixes that float on the surface. The intent is it serves as a heal tank of sorts.

"And yet, the infection worsens," I explain to the priest, citing the numerous ways I've applied the powers of Christ and His ability to heal all ailments, whether they be through tribute or prayer or ordainment. "My sickness spreads, Father," I say. "Despite the Lord being involved."

The priest shakes his head. Blood leaks down from his mouth to his chin, dripping in faint slaps against his robes. "You don't...that's not how it works," he struggles.

"Then explain it to me," I say.

The second suite is for storage and study. Multiple editions and versions of the Bible fill the living room, some of them used for forging tools while others are simply read. Herbs, plants, and spores fill the kitchen cabinets. For the most part, these are procured at the food and ingredient outlets known as 'grocery stores.' Organs—both human and animal—are preserved in glass jars and kept in the refrigerator. Sometimes I experiment, like with that of Desiree's infected vaginal cavity. The labia was carefully extracted with a sharp knife, seasoned with garlic and onion powder, marinated, then dehydrated using an electric oven. The flesh achieved a jerky-like texture that could be used for sustenance or an ingredient to a larger compound. My ability to fashion compounds was compromised some time ago.

The priest says, "You're taking it...much too literally." Blood continues to leak from the corner of his mouth, the gash in his lip. I sample it, attempting to discern the difference between his blood and that of a normal non-Divine individual. There isn't any from what I can tell. "And you have no...real faith," he says through labored breaths. "You're damned."

Father Latimer and I are in the third suite, the one in which practical application is exercised: fornication of both the traditional and faith-based varieties, human sacrifice, extended periods of worship, harvesting, theoretical application, and, if necessary, torture. I've had the priest bound to a hotel chair for many hours, taking samples of blood, hair, urine, perspiration, fingernails, and so on. If I ask him a question and don't receive the desired response, I either break a bone or deliver a blow to the face. This is why Father Latimer's ability to communicate has been encumbered: he keeps lying, which forces me to keep hitting him.

He claims I'm 'damned.' I break another bone in his hand.

He says I've misunderstood the message of Christ. I tenderize his face.

I ask Father Latimer why the Lord hasn't delivered him from me if, in fact, he truly is one of His chosen servants. "Why don't you make this easy and tell me what I want to know?" I ask. "Why do my methods continue to fail?"

I've told Father Latimer about all of it: the Christian lingerie and pious role-play. He knows about the vigil candles and gallons of Holy water I've procured for the sake of healing, sterilization, and prevention of disease. I've explained how pages of The Good Book were stapled into the whore Sasha and her skin was coated in Divine wax. Her eyes were covered in the leather and boarding of the Bible.

"Nothing works," I tell him. "I remain sick and those around me become sick themselves."

"The Lord..." Father Latimer says, "...He'd never condone... this...these whores."

"But I'm saving them," I counter. "I'm giving them the Lord's protection."

He shakes his head, spits blood. "They must accept Him... themselves. In their hearts. They must have...faith." Father Latimer spits again, waiting for another blow to the face, another broken bone or cut of the flesh. The intangibles, the ability to feel the priest's emotions, they indicate he believes his own answer. He's not lying, or at least he doesn't believe himself to be, so I decide to switch tactics.

According to their rules, Father Latimer is not allowed to indulge in what are known as 'impure thoughts,' which mostly refer to the act of fornication/sexual fantasy, however, this may also apply to violence, jealously, or greed. As a representative of God, he must adhere to the Divine path, never wandering in a spiritual, physical, or mental sense. To compromise that might further my education, and so I turn on the device known as the 'television' and access the hotel's on-demand service. Menu items consist of various pornographic films—movies featuring actors and actresses that are documented during the act of fornication. Admittedly, this is one of my favorite aspects of the modern world.

I tell Father Latimer, "If you climax, I'll allow you to leave. I won't hurt you anymore."

The priest weighs his morality against his personal safety, remembering the vows he took under the Lord God. I can feel this. I can feel him reaching out to his deity and requesting permission to indulge. A compromise. *Verbally, however, he says nothing.*

"*I'm going to assist you,*" *I tell him.*

The video plays. I fast-forward through the opening titles until I arrive at the first scene: a tan, platinum-blonde female receiving oral sex from her male counterpart. Her vaginal cavity is spread wide, glistening, and enlarged to the size of a dinner plate by the high-definition viewing device. She is performing oral sex upon another male who is standing over her. She moans convincingly, as do the male actors on-screen.

"*Climax,*" *I say.* "*Do what I ask and make peace with your God after.*"

My hands unfasten the black trousers of Father Latimer. Much to my delight, his genitalia has already begun to flush with blood. He's becoming firm, despite himself, and then I apply a liquid referred to as 'lubricant' to facilitate the current endeavor. In my hand, the organ becomes highly slick as if covered in animal fat.

Father Latimer says, "*Stop...please.*" *Blood flushes in his cheeks, as if to indicate a level of embarrassment or bashfulness. Intangibly-speaking though, I can sense his enjoyment. The pleasure of sensation that he's denied himself for years—possibly even decades. He begins to forget his vows and his God, instead, focusing on the blonde female being doubly penetrated: vaginally and orally. She moans, begs to be penetrated harder. I massage the priest firmly, stimulating the prostate and the cluster of nerves on the underside of the penis just beneath the head with my thumb. The process is a short one due to his low tolerance for indulgence. It literally takes less than three minutes before Father Latimer climaxes in a thick burst of chunky seminal fluid, which I immediately collect and store for later. I also taste some. Like his blood, this fluid too bears no discernable difference from that of the common man.*

Father Latimer sighs. He breathes deeply, clearing his throat, and the shame begins to swell in his spirit. Indulgence replaced by regret; I can feel this, too. "*You're damned,*" *he says.* "*A monster.*"

The Cooking Station

Madeline cooks.

She turns the knob on the oven to 350 degrees, preheating it while she removes various ingredients from the cupboards. Side by side, she starts lining up canisters containing flour, sugar, and baking powder. The canisters are wooden and well worn, almost antique-looking, not unlike the majority of the things in Madeline's home. Father Johnstone can only spot two or three declarations of youth in the form of fashion magazines, flavored lip gloss, and a few junk-food wrappers discarded to the coffee table. Other than that, this is still very much the home Josephine Paige resided in, right up until her death.

"I still say this is going to bite us in the ass," Madeline says, measuring and combining ingredients into a large mixing bowl. She stirs them with a wooden spoon until they're dispersed evenly, then adds ¼ cup of milk. "At the very least we should have kept the gun."

"We did the right thing," Father Johnstone says. "Try to have faith in that."

Madeline adds ¾ cup of warm coffee, a tablespoon of Kahlua, stirring again. She says, "Oh no, don't you play the F-card on me. You didn't even know how to pray right until today." Madeline stirs, whipping the spoon through the mixture to get the lumps out. She adds butter and sugar, reminding him, "If sheriff creepy man comes back, there's not going to be much I can do to stop him. Despite what you've seen so far, I'm not bulletproof."

He should be passing through the fields by now, the pastor thinks. Sheriff Morgan will drive through those thick golden pastures, blurring by them for what seems like forever. First, on the ashy gravel back roads, but he'll eventually reach the smooth track of the interstate. Miles and miles of blacktop and wheat and nothing much beyond that. Gas stations and farm houses can be found every few miles, a truck stop restaurant here and there. Sheriff Morgan's exile from Pratt was not willing, but rather, instructed.

"You'll get in your car and drive west," Madeline told him. "When the car runs out of gas, you are to get out and keep walking. You'll walk until you can't walk anymore."

According to the pastor, this was the best way to remove the sheriff from the equation without killing him or cuffing him to a radiator. It seemed fair, a high road compared to the many low avenues he could have taken, especially when considering all the threats made against himself and Madeline. He even gave Shelby back as a sign of good will, but not before doing his due diligence as a man of the cloth.

"I forgive you and will pray for your safety," he said. "Remember that when you come back. Remember that I'm not your enemy."

This was an olive branch. An opportunity for two pillars to mend the fence, so to speak, but Sheriff Morgan wasn't having it. His acrimony towards the pastor remained as consistent as ever. That much was made clear.

"Shelby and me...we'll be back real soon, preacher," he said, the grin coming back, yellow teeth overlapping like a basket of French fries. The sheriff said, "Gonna make you watch while I stick ol' Shelby up Maddy Paige's cunt. Maybe even fire off a round or two. Wouldn't be the first gal Shelby poked. You just wait," he said. "Only a matter of time."

In the kitchen, Madeline adds eggs to the bowl, beating them in with a whisk and staring the pastor down while she churns. She shakes her head, clearly vexed about adding another loose end to an ever-growing litany of loose ends. Pratt knows too much for its own good. Secrets are getting out, and it's so much worse than the rumors of a pastor gone rogue. If they knew even half of what Father Johnstone did, their reactions would far exceed the casual vandalism his home has suffered thus far. As

Mrs. Tiller said, the town doesn't react well to change or abnormality. What they don't know is that it's already here, hiding in plain sight at their renowned diner and mingling at social events. Madeline Paige has been here for months, sharing her desserts and hosting late-night wine tastings on her front porch, infiltrating the town.

Madeline says, "Would you be a doll and hand me that black book over there on the middle shelf?" She points at it with the whisk, ticking left-to-right as it drips, counting to herself. "Seventh one over towards the middle there—yep, your finger is on it."

Father Johnstone removes the volume. The spine and cover are all black, frayed at the corners, unlabeled. He places it on the kitchen counter in front of Madeline's cooking station, rotating it on its back.

"Book of Shadows?" the pastor guesses. To even say these words makes him feel silly.

Madeline stops stirring. She scoffs, shaking her head. "We really need to get you up to speed on things." She sets down the mixing bowl with the whisk still in it, handle-deep in cake batter. Madeline licks her fingers, cleaning them of batter and random dustings of flour. "Let's clear up some rumors right away." She opens the book, and Father Johnstone can hear the leather of the spine creak on itself. Her fingers slide one page over the other, too thick and durable to be run-of-the-mill paper. They're sepia-toned and stained, covered in symbols, pictographs, and measurements. Most of it, Father Johnstone notices, isn't written in English, and the handwriting seems to vary from page to page.

"First of all, there's no end-all be-all master spell book the same way there's no one Bible," Madeline says. "We're just as fragmented as you guys are."

"What do you mean by that? Fragmented?" he asks.

"Christians," she says, adding another egg to the bowl and

whisking again. "Catholics, Baptists, Methodists, Lutherans and Presbyterians. Protestants. Everyone has their book and their beliefs, and everyone thinks they have it right." Madeline swipes her finger through the bowl, bringing it to her mouth and sucking the batter off. "Everyone has their own translation that they're certain is the master key to their faith."

"And you're saying—what?" the pastor asks. "Everyone has it wrong?" He can't help but suspect that Madeline is, in fact, calling his own faith into question. He's heard this argument before; it doesn't wash. Not being universally right doesn't mean everyone is automatically false. "That's fool's logic," he says.

"No, I'm merely stating that the more options there are the more people tend to disagree. That's all, Johnstone." Madeline checks the book again, adding another pinch of sugar and two shakes of cinnamon. She whisks those into the batter, adding, "It's not an issue of correct or incorrect. It's what feels right, not what *is* right. A lot of bullshit could have been avoided if people were more accepting of other beliefs."

The Thirty Years' War and The Crusades. Protestants killing Catholics. Christians killing Islamics. Every soldier armed themselves believing they were either killing in God's name or were about to join Him in the afterlife. Gallons of bloodshed, all in the name of thy Lord and Savior. Father Johnstone has perused these scourges of history many times, however, this isn't what Madeline is referring to. Not exactly.

"It's a little bit better now. People are more tolerant, even if that tolerance is with a sense of reluctance." Madeline adds what smells like espresso powder into the mixture. She churns the whisk through it again, five times clockwise, three times counter-clockwise. "That courtesy isn't extended to people like me. It's why it's best to stay under the radar...act normal. Otherwise, people panic and that's when the torches and pitchforks come out." She turns the page with her free hand, checking her instructions, which appear to be in Latin if the pastor isn't mistaken.

"When an established belief meets a conflicting idea, it can be the makings of a perfect storm. I've seen it happen before and it's not pretty."

As the Good Book says, all power comes from either God or Satan. Father Johnstone has always subscribed to this, and by extension, the flock. All flocks. They've been instructed to believe that someone like Madeline is to be rejected, feared, and destroyed. Despite her good intentions, she acts not in the Lord's name, and therefore, in the name of evil. She's categorized as a threat by technicality, but more so by what she can do that others can't. Aversion to the strange and abnormal existed way before the town of Pratt and its residents.

Father Johnstone can recall a passage, one that's as concise as it is disdainful from the book of Exodus: *'Thou shalt not suffer a witch to live.'*

For all intents and purposes, Madeline Paige is fighting a span of bad press that goes back many centuries. Ages of slander, rumor, and gossipmongering. She can't escape it, no matter where she goes.

"I've been to a lot of places...traveled the world," Madeline says. "And if it's one thing that's consistent, it's that people are severely lacking in empathy. It's not that they don't understand — they just don't want to."

When Father Johnstone had his bleeding episode at the Pratt bake-off, none of the flock reached out. They didn't investigate or ask questions about his condition. Nobody wanted the real story, probably because they were terrified of what they'd find. It was so much easier for them to make the assumption that he was tainted and damned, that he was a harbinger of disease. And he can't really fault them for that. For a time, he himself believed to have the Devil in his blood. But perhaps this was his own fault, he thinks. Perhaps if he had trained Pratt to understand evil as opposed to fearing it, everyone would have been better off. A little more empathetic. As Madeline so eloquently put it, he could have avoided a lot of bullshit.

"I prayed the Lord restore my health and nothing came," Father Johnstone concedes. "Dr. Keller was no help, either."

Madeline removes a baking tin from one of the lower cabinets, placing it on the counter with a clang that stirs Mary who was napping on the living room couch. "Your point?" she asks.

"It would make me a hypocrite to turn my back on you or deny you empathy. And leaving town would make me a deserter and a coward."

"Even though your so-called flock has deserted you first?" she crosses.

"*Especially* then," he replies with a nod.

"You've become quite pious since we knocked that curse out of you," Madeline observes. She greases the indentations of the baking pan, applying a coating of what looks like fat or lard to the surface with a small spatula. "Forgiving the sheriff and cutting him loose, defending the flock that turned against you. You sure this is how you wanna play it?"

"It feels right."

"But you'll compromise by the end of this. Eventually," Madeline says. "You can't play by the rules forever when the other side isn't."

Then Madeline picks up the canister, a stainless-steel Thermos that she took from Father Johnstone's kitchen. He traditionally used it to transport cocoa or hot cider with him from his home to the church, mostly to keep warm on brisk days. Or he'd bring some to share with Mrs. Tiller while she mulled over paperwork. Now it holds something else, the curse fluid, still warm from the pastor's interior. It fumes of rot and sulfur. Madeline begins pouring it into the cake batter, a spaghetti-thin stream that she applies over the top. It rests on the surface, bubbling and alive, dissolving into the mixture as she stirs it with the whisk again. She screws the Thermos top back on and the smell tapers off, overpowered by aromas of cinnamon and coffee.

"I used to travel with a faith healer," Madeline says. "Now, the thing you need to know about faith healers is that most of them are complete frauds. They move from town to town, put on a little show, and leave with their pockets full of cash. A decent racket, if you know how to play it." She turns a page in her book, takes a moment to review the instructions and continues on, saying, "So this guy, Pastor Terry Bradford—who's a total bullshit artist, by the way—he and I go on the road together. It's a good situation. I'm going from town to town healing cancer, healing bone disease, curing cripples. People are getting out of their wheelchairs and walking. We're doing this all over the country. Pastor Bradford shows up and puts on his little show, just like normal—the difference being that we're now doing what he was only pretending to do."

"And what did he think of that?" Father Johnstone interrupts, curious as to how his reaction compared to his own.

"He said he didn't need to know the Colonel's recipe as long as he kept getting the chicken," she recalls. "I suspect he felt better *not* knowing."

"Ignorance is bliss."

"Exactly," Madeline says. "So one day we end up in this town called Grandfield in Oklahoma. Probably not even 1,000 people there. Total shithole. Pastor Bradford keeps saying how we're going to retire millionaires if we keep this up." Madeline pauses, sighs. "Only problem was that he had been to Grandfield before. Years ago before I signed on. They remembered how this guy swindled them and they were pissed…surrounded us with their shotguns and whatnot. So what do you think Pastor Bradford did?"

Father Johnstone shrugs.

"No guesses?" she asks.

"I don't know. Apologized?"

"Pastor Bradford pulled out a pistol from his coat, put it to my head and told them that he was going to put a bullet in my brain if they didn't back off. He didn't offer up the thousands of dollars we had or anything like that. He offered me up to save his own skin." Madeline gives the mixture a final whisk and begins pouring globs of cake batter into the pan, using the wooden spoon to aid it. "A man of God using a young girl as a bullet shield. That's a compromise, Johnstone. That's the kind of thing that happens when you get backed into a corner."

"I wouldn't do that," the pastor says. "I couldn't."

"Y'know, I thought that about Pastor Bradford, too, but like I told you...I can feel the intangibles. I know the difference between a man bluffing his way out of a sticky situation and someone so afraid they'll kill if they need to," she says. "His *greed* outweighed my life."

"So what'd you do?" the pastor asks.

"I handled the situation," Madeline says gravely, pouring the remainder of the batter into the muffin tin. She takes it and places it on the middle rack of the oven, setting a nearby egg timer for fifteen minutes. It ticks quietly as Madeline puts away the baking materials, capping the sugar and flour. The salt and espresso powder are returned to their rightful cabinet. She says, "If your faith fails...if Sheriff Morgan comes back and puts a gun to my head—or worse, tries to hike up my skirt so he can use me as a holster...what then? What are you going to do? Because it's more than just the two of us at stake here," she reminds him. "And this town is getting closer to finding out what's really happening."

At first Father Johnstone thinks she's referring to what's been going on with him lately: the curse and all the symptoms that came with it. His behavior has been out of the ordinary, and that's exactly the kind of thing that gets the rumor mill churning in a place like Pratt. People talk, they speculate. Most of those speculations turn out to be false, but that doesn't matter. It adds up to a bad reputation and being put under the microscope. Word starts going around that the resident voice of God in town has been turned, which isn't exactly untrue. This is when Madeline hands over yesterday's edition of *The Pratt Tribune*.

"Seen this yet?" she asks.

Father Johnstone has been so distracted by everything going on that he ceased reading the paper some days ago. He would skim the front page headline and occasionally check the local announcements for upcoming weddings and the obituaries, more out of habit than anything. Beyond that, he has paid the local news very little mind, and even discontinued his attempts at the daily crossword puzzle. To even try it, he thought, would frustrate him further, what with his uneven temperament and all.

The article Madeline points out is headlined: **Pesticide Has Odd Effect on Insect Life**

Beneath it is a picture of a grasshopper in the palm of someone's hand. Its top section is normal. The tip of its abdomen, however, is broken off in a familiar way. Cracked, as if the insect was completely dehydrated of any bodily fluid. Ash dusts the farmer's hand, streaking his palm with powder and shell fragments.

"They think it was chemically induced," Madeline says. "You remember the daisy hill, yes? The bees?" The pastor nods. He reads the article, skimming and seeing words like 'unexplained' and 'phenomena.' The journalist reports that specimens are being sent off for testing, that Pratt will be reaching out to other farm communities that are using the same pesticide strain.

"You said this was going to happen to the entire town," the pastor recalls. "What is it exactly?"

"A curse," Madeline says. "The kind we can't just dig up and incinerate, unfortunately."

"Then how do we stop it?"

"We find the person responsible. The other one," she says. "The problem with that though is this person isn't going to stroll down the street *High Noon* style and expose themselves," she explains. "We've been trained all our lives to stay under the radar, so it's a different kind of warfare. It's sneakier."

"So you're saying we have to draw this person out?" Father Johnstone asks, uneasy about the idea of instigating a fight.

"Normally, yes, but that would be unwise at this point."

"Why's that?"

Madeline frowns. "Simply put: we're not ready. You're just coming to grips with all this and I'm out of practice."

Father Johnstone notices Madeline flex her left hand again, rubbing the tips of her fingers over the circular burn mark on her palm that she acquired this morning. She's doubting herself, her ability, and for the first time since she's moved to Pratt she looks legitimately afraid. That confident young woman from the big city has regressed to something else, a state of apprehension. Father Johnstone watches her flip through the black book, leafing through so fast that the smell of mold radiates off the pages. The pastor sees numerals, measurements, ingredients in a multitude of languages: German, Romanian, and Chinese. Another one in Spanish. Most of the pages are ancient-looking, brown and chapped at the edges. Some are burnt or have odd stains which have caused the ink to bleed, smearing the lettering until it's almost illegible.

"The other one out there," Madeline says, "I'm not going to lie—they know what they're doing."

"You do too, though," Father Johnstone says, and although he has no frame of reference as to what he's talking about, he hopes Madeline is simply being modest in regards to her own abilities. She's the same way with her cooking, he recalls. Always in need of encouragement.

"I still make mistakes," she says, raising her palm so the pastor can see it. The burn is pink, wet-looking, with black scorch marks peppering the fringe of it. Heart and life-lines that would normally streak across her palm have been flash-fried, erased smooth. Madeline says, "This is what happens when you lose focus. You remember what I said about prayer? How all the parts had to be there?"

He nods. "Like the car," the pastor says.

"Well, I was missing something…and I paid for it," she says.

"Missing what?" he asks.

"It's the same thing as praying for something you don't really want," she says. "It's not going to go right. It can backfire." Madeline sighs. "I never wanted to see Mary hurt."

"Then why do it?"

"Because you needed to see it," she says. "Because real prayer is benevolent and raw, and you needed to know what that felt like…even though it meant taking the thing you love most away." She looks at Mary, curled up on the couch and snoring softly. "I just hope you feel the same about this town, because that's what's at stake."

"Sheriff Morgan and a few other bad apples notwithstanding, there are good people here," the pastor says, hoping that Madeline can at least somewhat agree with this point after the time she's spent here. "But the flock is fickle, as you know," he adds. "They panic easily."

Father Johnstone can't help but think about the murmurs probably already circulating around Pratt regarding the insects. People will swap opinions in the local bars like Lou's or the Tap Room over on 3rd, trying to remain optimistic at first, but that'll quickly decline. When they can't find any explanation for how a grasshopper turns to dust and ash, they'll begin to stir. Anxiety will set in. They'll say this is the first sign of things to come, the beginning of something much worse. An event they can't control. A plague, spreading upon the town and its people until they fold.

"You need to regain their trust," Madeline says. "Lead them again."

"Why me?" With his public approval having drastically declined, this idea sounds impossible to the pastor. He certainly couldn't reveal that he was cursed; it would get him lynched for sure, and they wouldn't even need Sheriff Morgan to do it.

"You're honestly not getting it?" Madeline asks.

"Getting what?"

"You're a pillar, Johnstone. You've been the shepherd of Pratt for over thirty years," she reminds him. "It only makes sense that they'd go after the person with the most influence."

"I think you're mistaken," the pastor says.

"It's *exactly* what I'd do," Madeline says. "If it were me, and if I was trying to hurt this place, you'd be the first person I'd compromise."

"And why not someone like Sheriff Morgan?" the pastor asks. "Someone with real power? The gun and the badge and all that."

"Because there's a difference between respecting someone out of obligation and doing so genuinely," she says. "The town doesn't love him; they're afraid of him. And for good reason, he's a sick asshole. You don't even want to know what I felt when I held that gun of his."

"The intangibles?" the pastor asks, still unsure how this part of Madeline's talents operate. "Maybe I should know."

"You really don't."

"I can take it," he presses, looking to Mary, still asleep. Calm. Alive. She breathes, torso expanding...contracting. "I've seen worse," he says.

"All the threats...what he'd do to us—to me, all that...he's done it before. Use your imagination on that one," she says, frowning in disgust. "Sending him away only delayed a very big problem. He'll come back, and he'll come back knowing what I did to him. We should have kept him."

"I refuse to hold hostages, Madeline. I won't compromise. Not like that," the pastor says. "I don't doubt that Sheriff Morgan has more than his fair share of misdeeds, but it's my job to offer second chances. He is a man of Pratt. It's my belief that if it comes down to settling the score with me and doing what's right for the town, he'll come through."

"But just in case that fails—and I very much think it will," Madeline says, "you need to get the flock back. That'll be your job at the sermon tomorrow."

Father Johnstone still can't recall the exactitudes of his last sermon, the one in which he openly questioned Christ and his miracles: 'The Feeding of 5,000.' The curse has all but stricken it from his memory, but he can still remember their faces. He remembers that moment on the church lawn, burning of fever and bleeding, the people crowding around him—not out of concern, but horror. Fear of him and disease and the Devil. A fear that has multiplied through the course of whisper and gossip. Although he has since recovered, it won't matter to them. Pratt still very much believes him to be compromised and unfit to lead.

"They won't come," he says.

"No, they will," Madeline says. "But only to see if you fail. They want to confirm the rumors."

"Hmm, well that's comforting."

"You *won't* fail," Madeline says, sliding her left hand across the kitchen counter. She places it on Father Johnstone's, gently patting it. "I guarantee you won't."

"How? Got enough of these to feed the whole town?" the pastor asks, motioning towards the oven, the cupcakes laced with curse fluid. "Were you just going to hand them out as people filed into the pews? Convince them to like me again?"

"No," she says. "It has to be under their own accord. Genuine and not temporary." Madeline smirks, mischief flashing across her eyes again. "Funny thing about what people choose to believe and not believe, though...all it takes is a little proof and you've got them in the palm of your hand. So that's what we'll do, Johnstone. We'll give them proof."

"And what kind of proof will I be providing at this sermon?" Father Johnstone asks, with a hint of skepticism.

"I was thinking something along the lines of a miracle," she says.

"You mean a spell, right?" he tries to correct her. "More witch-craft?"

"There's a fine line between the two, Johnstone, and I think it's time you learned the difference," Madeline says. "And I'll apologize to you in advance."

"For what?" the pastor asks.

"I've been going through my aunt's books since I got here, brushing up on my skills." She taps the black book with her forefinger. "Your episode at the bake-off...that might have been partly my fault."

Procédé IV: L'empoisonnement de Rêve

The female will require a tall mirror (mirroir), preferably propped against a wall for logistical purposes, and one elongated vegetable (légume). For best results, use a zucchini, squash, or cucumber. A banana or plantain for instance may be used due to their organic nature (caractère), however, is not practical as they tend to break and split. The material (matériaux) should be pliable yet firm, and washed of all earthly matter to avoid impurities entering the body. Coat the reflective surface of the mirror with the blood (sang) of the male. Application should be done using a brush composed of horse or goat hair and tree wood. There is no need to kill the animal for the harvesting of this particular material, however, the brush should be hand-forged by the female (reference: forging of tools). A store-bought or previously-owned brush will not yield the same effects and could contaminate the process. Once the mirror has been appropriately coated, the female may position herself in front of it on a bed of dry hay (foins). The female should then proceed to pleasure herself in front of the mirror using the vegetable. If done correctly, the labia will begin to flush and thicken with blood and she'll experience a tingling sensation in her genitalia (organes génitaux). During this part of the process, the female should envision only the male in question; doing otherwise may result harmful consequences for either or both parties. Insertion of the vegetable is recommended, although not necessary as long as full climax (point culminant) takes place in that of the female. It's possible that upon climax that the female will ejaculate a clear, water-like fluid. In the event that this happens, the female should attempt to bottle and store this fluid for later use (reference: storage methods). After climax, the female must say the Divine Prayer while looking into the mirror. Half the vegetable must be immediately ingested (ingéré) by the female; the other half should be placed in the center of the pile of hay. Set the pile of hay aflame, taking care not to prematurely extinguish (anéantir) it. Once the fire has died out, the female should take the charred half of the vegetable and add it to either a stew or other hearty dish for the male to consume.

The Craft

The egg timer buzzes on the kitchen counter. Madeline grabs it, twisting the knob slightly clockwise until it goes silent. "It's time you learned how this works," she says, slipping on a nearby mitt. She opens the oven door, retrieving the muffin tin off the middle rack, which now blooms six golden brown cupcakes. They radiate the scent of cocoa and cinnamon, effectively covering the sulfur smell that was once present. Father Johnstone would be tempted to indulge in one if it weren't for his intimate knowledge of the ingredients—specifically, the curse fluid. He recalls purging it from his system, the pain, a memoir of the incident written to the tune of cuts and gashes in his throat.

Madeline places the baking tin on the kitchen counter and removes the mitt. "Alchemy," she says. "You familiar with that term?"

The pastor nods. "It's like chemistry." Beyond the basic concept though, he knows next to nothing about the subject. In a place like Pratt, not a lot of stock was put into this particular area of academia.

"Chemistry that doesn't adhere to scientific law," Madeline says. "Any law, for that matter."

Father Johnstone is reminded of what he's seen so far in regards to Mrs. Tiller and Sheriff Morgan: instant, unmitigated control; the ability to rewrite memory, to bend a person to suggestion, even if they vehemently disagree with it. He's never seen or heard of anything like it—in the medical field or otherwise.

"It's how the terms black arts and sorcery originally came into use," Madeline says. "When the effects of something couldn't be explained through science—what passed for science, anyway—it was automatically categorized as evil."

"By the church?" Father Johnstone assumes.

She nods. "Despite themselves, priests are very *prideful* individuals. They don't like having their faith challenged, and I suppose it's easy to write something off as 'the Devil's work' when someone is able to do the thing you're not. This, for example," Madeline says, turning a few pages in the black spell book. She slides her fingers under the words *veritas serum*, explaining, "This is a truth formula, an organic composition that manipulates higher cognitive function." From the opposite side of the counter, Father Johnstone attempts to read the script, the listing of ingredients corresponding with numerical amounts. *Piscis oleum (x7), volucri pinnam (x3), pomum granum (x4).* It's all in Latin.

Madeline says, "A lie isn't automated. If someone is asked a question they don't want to give an honest response to, the brain needs a moment to make the necessary adjustment. What this does," she says, "is it inhibits the ability to make that particular adjustment."

From Leviticus, Father Johnstone recalls the passage: *'Do not lie. Do not deceive one another.'* What Madeline speaks of is the idea of removing deception from the table, a world free of falsehood. Truth that can be brewed and bottled and slipped into a drink.

"You can imagine this pissed off the clergy," Madeline says. "According to them, you should be honest because that's what God wants, not due to force or unnatural manipulation. They viewed Craft as a cheat," she says. "If you can circumvent a system and its values, you're threatening it by extension."

Elements brought on by command, death overturned, free will restricted; these are the events Father Johnstone has witnessed which he previously believed only God was capable of. These are the acts of Divine power, a power based on faith in the Lord and his Holy Word, and Madeline Paige is living proof that it's not exclusive. With the right ingredients and a certain know-how, you can manufacture supremacy.

"This is a spell that removes memory," Madeline says. She

turns a couple pages in the book, translating the next header, which is in Greek. Her lips move silently, sounding out the word to herself. "Sleep spell," she says. Father Johnstone watches her turn another page. A human diagram is meticulously sketched out, circles radiating from either hand like pond ripples. Madeline says, "This one teaches you how to amplify the naturally occurring magnetic fields in the body, also known as: biomagnetism."

From one of the drawers, she retrieves a small fork and places it on the counter. She extends her arm out to the pastor palm-up, the silverware on display in her hand. Madeline says, "I've been practicing this one a little. Started out with coins and worked my way up." The fork shivers, rocking a few times on Madeline's palm before it begins to rise slowly—first, at the handle where the weight is minimal. It tilts until it's balanced vertically on the tines, then it rises a centimeter or so. Floating. Pivoting deliberately. Father Johnstone reaches out to grab it, pinching the neck of the handle between his thumb and forefinger. He can feel resistance, an invisible pull that's stronger than the utensil's natural weight. It's encompassed by something, a field, making it seem as though the fork's gravity is central to the spot above Madeline's palm. She says, "Go ahead and take it," relinquishing her control over the object. The pastor holds the fork in his hand, examining it for something foreign, an indication of sleight of hand, but all appears to be normal.

"How do you do that?" he asks.

"It's a relationship," Madeline says. "It's understanding the attributes and properties of what's around us, whether it's a fork, a redwood tree, or a house fly. Everything has its own signature." She closes the book, walking it over to the large shelf and placing it back in its spot. The pastor can't determine any discernable method to their organization since none of them are labeled. Not unless the occasional symbol counts. Stars and Roman numerals are embossed on some of the spines. Madeline pulls another volume from the shelving and brings it over to the kitchen counter.

"So these are all spell books?" the pastor asks.

"Spell books, historical texts, journal entries," Madeline says, opening the volume so that she and the pastor are able to view the pages. Much like the previous book, this one also varies in print size and language. "A collection of stories, theory, and accounts."

"You mean in lieu of the Bible?" the pastor asks, and although he's a man of the cloth and remains loyal to his post, the question does come off a bit insensitive.

Madeline snickers, though. She's had this debate before. "Tell me something, Johnstone, if you had been given the Torah, or the Koran, or some of the L. Ron Hubbard bullshit when you were a kid...if someone handed you that *instead* of the Bible, would you really know the difference? Do you really think you'd still be preaching here in Pratt?" Glaring at him, she says, "You are what you were born into."

"God wanted me to be born a Christian," Father Johnstone responds sagely.

"No, honey, you were born, and *then* you were taught what God and Christianity were," Madeline counters. "It's not intrinsic. You didn't come into the world knowing what religion was the same way you didn't know how to cook ribs or change the oil in your car. All things, even faith, have a learning curve."

"You're including yourself in that then?" Father Johnstone asks, attempting to even the plain.

Madeline holds her left hand out, flipping it over palm-up so the scald mark glistens under the kitchen lights. "Still learning." She smirks, glaring at the pastor.

Through the scriptures it is learned that the Creator is infallible, but as Father Johnstone has explained many times to the flock, He, in all His wisdom, had the foresight to know man would by no means be perfect. "Think of sin as an opportunity," he's always told them. "Either to repent or for the Devil to lure you down his path."

Madeline Paige, on the other hand, is not afforded the luxury of forgiveness. "We don't get the same loopholes you do. We're given the tools and the instructions, and if we make a mistake, we pay for it," she says, rolling the fingers on her left hand again. Flexing it. Minute clicks and cracks sound off from her knuckles. "Craft is a faith and a relationship, but it's also a skill. It takes practice."

"And despite all I've seen you do so far, you maintain you're out of practice?" the pastor asks.

"When you're trying not to draw attention to yourself, you tend to get rusty in the process," she says. "That, and I've had nothing new to learn up until recently."

"You mean when your aunt passed?" The pastor's assuming she's referring to the assembly of volumes on the book shelf, which number around seventy or so. "This collection became yours?"

"These aren't the kind of things you want to lug all over the country," Madeline says. "My aunt, as you probably know, kept mostly to herself. She liked her quiet life and her daisy hill. She liked to bake."

Just like Madeline, Josephine was never one of the flock, despite any peer pressure she received from her local sewing circles or Father Johnstone himself. She was, however, an accomplished pastry chef, and even managed a few wins at the Pratt bake-off during her time in town. Other than that, she was a bit of a recluse.

"Aunt Josie had no interest in power or finding out how far she could go. She knew what a mistake could cost her so she never put herself in a position to make any. Craft for her was a casual relationship at best," Madeline says, frowning slightly, flexing her hand again. "When she got these, I imagine they went up on the shelf and were never touched again. Too afraid, more than likely. I'm probably the first person to read these in years." She turns a few pages in the volume, arriving at one headed with the word: *mixtura*. "I need to come clean on a couple things."

The pastor nods, knowing he's probably not ready for whatever she's about to tell him.

"I've been using the diner to practice," Madeline reveals. She pauses a moment to see what kind of reaction this gets from the pastor, expecting a paternal lecture of sorts. Or at the very least, a frown of disappointment. Father Johnstone has done this for years though, and if it's one thing he's learned in that time, it's that when someone is in the middle of a confession—especially one of this magnitude—it's best to let them finish.

"When you do this, it's best not to test it on yourself, so I got the job at the Presto to have some people to feed spells to. Nothing crazy, mind you," she interjects on herself, thinking Father Johnstone would assume the worst after what he's seen. "Simple things, within my experience."

"Like what?" Using residents of Pratt as guinea pigs notwithstanding, the pastor has heard nothing but good things about the Presto Diner since Madeline's employ began. If she's done anything wrong or had a spell backfire, it certainly hasn't come to mainstream attention.

"Well, I needed money…for clothes and materials and whatnot," she says. "So I may have cut a generosity spell into the pancake batter to help with tips." Madeline grits her teeth, somewhat ashamed to finally admit this to another person. "And the grain plant workers always looked pissed off and grumpy, so I started blending their morning coffee with a euphoria compound."

"Is that all?"

"And I was tired of old man Clevenger coming in drunk and passing out at the counter, so I cast a sobriety charm on his eggs. That one never worked well on him, though," she says. "I also may have put a little something into Mrs. Becker's iced tea...y'know...to make her less of a bitch to people."

"Anything else?" he presses.

"A few. A lot, actually," she edits herself. "But I never abused it, Johnstone—I want you to know that...and I've had more than my fair share of chances. Sheriff Morgan is a regular. Can't tell you how many times I almost poisoned that asshole."

"And why didn't you?" Not too long ago, Madeline was advocating he be chained to a radiator and held as a prisoner.

"It's a slippery slope," she says. "You play with dark things and before you know it, you can't stop. You begin to turn to it because it's easy. Then it becomes a habit."

In his thirty-some-odd years in Pratt, he's lost the occasional member of the flock to the soft options: to drink and drugs, to adultery and *lust*. A moment of weakness can easily turn into a lifetime.

"Craft is about harmony, and hurting someone—even a sick fuck like the sheriff—it can throw that harmony out of whack," Madeline says. She looks down at the book again. "This section talks a little bit about that, about harmony. It was written by a witch named Vivian de Bello, a theorist from the early 1800s." Her finger taps the header. "*Mixtura*, which is Latin for mixture, was something she warned against, citing that two spells working concurrently would have adverse effects," Madeline says, translating a portion from the middle of the page. "That, in turn, throws the individual harmony of both spells off. Make sense so far?"

"I suppose," the pastor nods.

"That curse buried in your yard should have hit you differently," Madeline says. "You saw what it did to the sheriff. That should have been you, only more intense."

She alluded to this already in the case of the truth serum, debilitating that which allows a person to act under their own accord. In Father's Johnstone's case though, it wasn't like this, erring more towards illness.

"It was meant to turn you into a puppet," she says. "And I know the damage has been done, what with you questioning God and all during your sermon, but I daresay it could have been much worse."

"You said were partly responsible for this earlier," Father Johnstone says. "What exactly did you mean by that?"

"You know…mixing," she says meekly, chewing her lower lip. "Lemon bars, cookies, cobblers."

"You cast on me?" The pastor asks, anger slipping into the words, but Madeline's prepared—has been prepared for some time now.

She inches back somewhat, explaining, "Technically, yes. I did. But that's also the thing that saved you."

"I almost died, Madeline. I almost bled to death in front of the whole town!" he shouts, which jerks Mary awake on the couch. She peers at the two of them, growling before allowing her head to lull back on the pillow, exhausted. Father Johnstone remembers what happened earlier today, what he almost lost. He softens. "I'm upset," he says. "The last couple of weeks have been—"

"—Shitty?" Madeline cuts in. "I know. I'm sorry."

"Are you?" he asks. "Because I'm not so sure."

"I came to town with very little on my agenda but to keep my head down and teach myself a few things," she says. "And when you're moving around and hiding as much I have, you tend to lose touch with people." Madeline sighs. "Yes, I cast on you. It was before…" she trails off, rethinking her words. "I'm different now. It's not going to happen again."

"What did you cast on me?"

"Something I thought would help," Madeline says. Vague.

"And what help did I need?" he asks. It was only recently that the symptoms of the curse intensified, but Madeline has been soliciting her desserts to him for many months. God only knows what they were supposed to do. "I was fine up until recently."

"Right. 'Fine,'" Madeline nods. "The man who builds a car instead of a relationship...who has a dog instead of a child. Leader of the flock but no real friends. No one you can be yourself around." She stares unapologetically. "You've been alone your whole life. And you can say that it's part of the job and that you're okay with it, but I know you're not."

As much as he doesn't want to admit it, she's right. She's right about everything. Every part of it, and although he's always known this on some level or another, it's quite another matter to have someone else address it so directly.

"Do you know why all the ladies in town are constantly coming to you, begging you to try their desserts and their casseroles and all that?" she asks. "Do you really think it's because they're trying to get an edge in some little cooking contest?"

It never occurred to him that an after-hours visit from a flock member with a pie or tray of seven-layer dip could be viewed as anything other than platonic. He always assumed they were playing strategy or overzealous for a win.

"It's because it's hard to see a good man alone," Madeline says. "You are the shepherd, the guiding light in Pratt, but you're still a man that has nothing and no one. You'll get older and retire from your post, and then you'll die alone. For a woman, that's damn hard to watch, even if it's self-imposed." She sighs, folding the pastor's hand into her own. Madeline stares at him with the campfire eyes. "I cast on you. When I gave you those desserts, I was trying to make you feel less alone. That's all."

The pastor purses his lips, saying nothing.

"I imposed. I shouldn't have done it," Madeline says. "But the rub is that you'd be just like the sheriff had I not. You understand that now, right?"

He nods. He believes her. And he believes she's remorseful for her actions, despite it resulting in the lesser of two evils. Waking up in the care of Dr. Keller at the hospital after a three-day coma was never something he wanted to experience, but better that than the alternative. Sheriff Morgan's probably halfway across the state by now, all under the unnatural commands of Madeline Paige. God only knows what this other person intended the pastor to do. If it was merely to ruin his reputation and shake up the town, then in that regard, they were successful. What Father Johnstone fears is that it's not over yet for him. As Madeline said, if it was her that wanted to hurt the town and its people, the pastor would be her primary objective. Without God, without the direction of the guiding light, Pratt is enervated.

"You said earlier that I'm the most likely target," Father Johnstone says. "How does someone stand to gain from that?"

"How do you think?" she asks rhetorically. "It's about power. It's about taking away the control you had over something and making it their own."

"You're referring to the flock?"

"I am," she says. "These people come to be led, to be guided through life. Nothing shakes a person's faith more than a pastor or priest gone rogue. It reminds them the system is fallible." Madeline pauses, a look of chagrin crossing her face. She tells him, "The Catholic church has been dealing with it for years. You hear about it all the time: how some little kid gets molested and all that happens to the priest is a transfer. It's because the clergy knows it wasn't really their fault."

"You mean they're aware of people like you?" the pastor asks, but it comes out slanderous, as if Madeline's a part of the scandal. "People that can do what you do?"

"What you have to understand is that some people—people like me," she says. "Some of them take that Bible shit just as seriously as you do. All the talk about how we shouldn't be allowed to live and we're agents of evil and all that—they're retaliating. It's payback," Madeline explains. "Sometimes a molestation case is just some sick asshole touching a kid. Other times it isn't."

"A curse," Father Johnstone says.

"Right. And they have no way to detect which is which," Madeline reminds him. "So they give them the benefit of the doubt and move across the country. Still doesn't change the fact that it gives the church a bad name."

The relationship between pastor and parish can be a shaky one. The flock is cultivated and trained, taught how to follow the Lord's Word and refrain from sin. With the right leadership, they will follow to the ends of the earth. One mistake though, and all is compromised. Bedlam ensues. All hope is lost.

"Why do you care if the church gets a bad name?" Father Johnstone asks. "You're not a part of it."

"I'm not against it though, either," she says. "This isn't my war, Johnstone. I'm not going to go after an institution over some shit that was written centuries ago. It has nothing to do with me."

"Are you saying it has something to do with me?" the pastor asks.

"I'm saying that whoever did this to you isn't going to stop until they get what they came here for," Madeline says. "They buried that thing in your yard to break you down and control you, and they put a lot of thought into it. We just undid a lot of hard work by incinerating it."

"Why wouldn't they just cut their losses and leave then?" he asks. "I mean, as little as I know about this, it sounds like the operation was botched."

"No," she says. "You don't get it. It's a relationship."

"You're saying I know this person." He looks at her doubtfully. It's difficult for the pastor to pinpoint just which resident of Pratt is capable of this.

"No, I'm saying *they* know *you*," Madeline specifies. "They know your weaknesses, your fears, and more personal information than you're probably comfortable with. They know the exact timeframe in which to go into your backyard and dig a three-foot hole without anyone noticing," she says, an eyebrow cocking. "A curse isn't just a bunch of random shit thrown together and calling it good; it's a bond, an investment. It's the process of polluting you with their own self."

It wasn't simply a matter of not being able to sleep or not feeling like himself. The pastor's spirit, his soul, it felt poisoned. And what an opportune moment that would be for someone else to step in: to influence, to instruct him on what to do.

"Now that it's broken, they'll seek another means," Madeline says. "Another way to hurt you. And they're not going to be subtle about it anymore."

Father Johnstone doesn't like the sound of that. It was bad enough when his assailant kept their distance. "So what do we do?" he asks.

"We get your flock back. We turn the tide back to you," Madeline says with confidence. "And I'll be by your side the entire time, walking you through it."

"At the sermon tomorrow, you mean?"

"Correct," she nods. "And hey, not to put any undue pressure on you, but if we don't nail this thing tomorrow, it'll be the last sermon you ever do."

On the Road with Billy Burke, Truck Stop Preacher

"There's a gay bar down the street from here. Now what comes to mind when you think of gay bars? I'll tell you: a bunch of sweaty young men rubbin' their peckers and fingering each others' shitters—that's what. They're dancing to that crazy techno music and playing grab-ass with each other—kissing on each other...one guy jerkin' another guy off until he squirts a hot load on his forehead in the bathroom. Lord as my witness, these guys are taking piles of dick butter and using it to style their fucking hair. I seen it! Now, you may be asking yourself, 'What the hell was ol' Billy doing in a fag bar?' Well, I wasn't sucking on no dicks, I can tell you that. I was scouting...formulating the attack, as it were. See, you lot here, you drive by it...you curse it under your breath and ignore it, but ol' Billy here, he ain't afraid to get his hands dirty. Let it be known, Billy Burke will step into the Devil's den if that's what needs doin'. And make no mistake, it does need doin', gentlemen. If they're going to ignore the Lord and His Word, then we gotta bring the Word to them. We gotta get our hands dirty. This is Divine intervention, my friends! Now how are we gon' do it? What's that, Frank? Huh? No! No, we're not gonna beat the snot outta them. We're not hate-crimers. We're better than that. No...what the Lord is telling me—He's telling me that Chet and Donny need to bring their wives to Tootsie's tonight...and...and He's saying you need to bang their fine asses right there on the dance floor. As for the rest of us, we will provide protection in the form of a human barrier prayer circle...keeping out Satan's homoerotic influence. What's that, Frank? Yes. Yes, you can drink and pray. We all will. First round's on ol' Billy Burke."

The Last Sermon

Father Johnstone's guts twist—not due to illness or unnatural manipulation, but from nerves. Pure and simple anxiety, the kind he hasn't felt since his twenties when he first took the helm as pastor of Pratt. He was inexperienced, but found this could be compensated for with enthusiasm and an unmitigated passion for the Lord. It was something the prior pastor, Father Hilliard, had lost some time before through no fault of his own. At eighty-one-years-old, he could hardly get through a reading without becoming winded, and patrons were often lulled to sleep by his brittle voice or the void of silence beyond the fifth row of pews in which his words couldn't carry. Their patience had grown so thin that when Father Johnstone finally took the helm, it was as if he breathed new life into their faith, if only by the trivial virtue of being young and easily heard.

"That new preacher got a real chip on his shoulder," they used to say. "Got somethin' to prove, that one."

His inaugural sermons were a tad on the clunky side, but refreshing in that they had discarded that feeling of stale routine Father Hilliard had accustomed the congregation to. Their new shepherd had no beaten path nor any established order. It was a rebuilding year, and so they rediscovered the Lord in a sense with Father Johnstone, through his sermons and his zeal for the Good Book that many described as 'infectious' and 'captivating.' None of them ever knew how terrified he was on the inside, always afraid they wouldn't accept him as a suitable replacement.

It is today—a burgeoning spring afternoon—that the pastor is reminded of the sermons from his former youth: the panging nerves and a pre-game nausea that has compelled him to vomit not once, but twice. The pressure to win back the flock, despite Madeline's assurances that all will be well, has proven too great for his system.

"They've seen the cracks and now they're waiting for you to fall apart," Madeline said that morning. "They'll arrive in droves to see you fail."

Indeed, much of the casually devout are coming out of the woodwork today. Mr. and Mrs. Larkin haven't been to church since last Christmas for the annual midnight mass ceremony. Others, like Luke Hagen and Bob Orson, haven't shown their faces for many years. Father Johnstone can't remember the last time he's seen such a turnout, and yet, their arrival is predicated on disaster. Each face is either laced with disgust or a sort of twisted fascination, like an audience watching a man strapped to an electric chair. They're counting down the seconds to when the switch will be thrown and the fireworks begin. They want to see the pillar break.

"But you won't fail," Madeline said. "In fact, you'll inspire. You've been reading to them from the same book for over thirty years, instructing them on how to keep to the Divine path. It's time you rewarded them for their devotion."

Father Johnstone meanders about the front of the church, watching as the pews steadily fill with the residents of Pratt. Two hundred, then about fifty more that have to stand or lean against the walls of the church. Sometimes the pastor will say 'hello' to a familiar face, a regular of the flock, but these are returned with a haphazard nod or empty salutation. No one smiles. No one shakes his hand, still offended by his outbreak of blood at the Pratt bake-off. They're not afraid anymore. It's since shifted over to abhorrence.

Meanwhile, Madeline ushers certain members to the front row of the church, most of the escorted being elderly and hard of sight. Sick and old and weak. It's an unspoken rule that the decrepit are allotted prime audience space, and today is no exception. Ms. Doakes, who hasn't walked in some years, sits flaccid as Madeline pushes her along in her wheelchair. The campfire eyes rest upon the pastor, and with that, a smile just as warm.

Madeline mouths to him, "Relax."

The pastor notices Travis Durphy holding the hand of his wife, a despondent Mr. and Mrs. Fairfax, and Helena Wright who is sitting stoically in the ninth row. Her hair is tied back with a red ribbon, and Father Johnstone wonders if that's supposed to mean something, if she's inviting him into her life one final time.

Madeline approaches the pastor, whispering to him, "Just like we practiced last night. Don't over-think it."

His eyes survey the crowd again, spotting Dr. Keller at the back of the church, cleaning prescription glasses with a pocket handkerchief. Another irregular entering the fold. And not even two feet away from him, Mrs. Tiller is accompanied by Deputy Clarke, opting for the tan uniform and badge instead of plain clothes. Mrs. Tiller turns to the deputy, whispering something to him that the pastor can only assume isn't favorable. They appear to have an agenda beyond simply seeing whether or not the pastor will crumble or have another medical outburst. Even if today's events go according to plan, the pastor fears he may be leaving the church premises in a squad car.

"Don't worry about them," Madeline says. "Just do what we talked about and the rest will take care of itself."

The crowd is restless—close to three hundred people crammed ass-to-ankles in the pews, pushed up against the walls and support columns of the church. They're murmuring, gossiping with no regard for tact or secrecy. Sometimes the pastor can hear his own name being said, along with something to the effect of: 'Can't wait to see what this asshole got to say for himself.'

And then from another section of the church: 'He better not try and tell me my Lord was some trickster again. Either he give up a dag-gum apology or get the hell out of Dodge.'

Madeline snaps her fingers. "Focus," she says. "Take control. I'll be nearby when you're ready." She turns to take a seat in the front-left pew, right near the aisle, which is no longer a clear path down the center of the room. It's overflowing with people who couldn't find seats or showed up long after the perimeter had been filled, angry and waiting for answers. Waiting for an explanation. The pastor stands poised, allowing the din of the room to shrink, smaller and smaller until only a few random whispers can be heard. Then nothing. Silence. Silence and the occasional creaking of pews as people adjust within their close quarters. Father Johnstone looks in the eyes of his oppressors, telling them what they already know.

"The Lord's house swells with *wrath* today," he says.

It was at the behest of Madeline that he address this: the elephant in the room. *"When an angry mob shows up to your doorstep,"* she said, *"the last thing you wanna do is play dumb."*

"You've heard rumors," he says. "You believe me to have fallen out of favor with the Lord, that I'm damned and no longer fit to lead. This is what's been going around town, if I'm not mistaken."

The gallery shouts in agreement, a voice, a man's voice from the middle of the crowd shouting, "You got that right, preacher!" They tense, seething.

"And you believe that I am evil," he presses on. "That I should be dealt with, hung, strung up and shot, yes? Battered, beaten, made an example of? This is why you're here today, right?" And once again, the crowd agrees, cheering, raising their fists. They edge a little bit closer, ready to accept the invitation the pastor is so willingly extending to them.

"Over thirty years here, and just like that, you'd break my neck and burn me alive. Is that what I'm hearing?" the pastor asks. "Have I fallen out of favor with you *that* quickly? Have I sunk into the same league as Mason Hollis?"

A hush falls over the crowd, be it ever so brief. They remember Mason, the stories, the rumors of what had happened to him. And even though it's been years since his residency in the town abruptly ended, the mere mention of his name still inspires a certain disquiet amongst the assembled. Pratt is reminded that they've done this before, but their vengeance and paranoia outweighs their logic. They won't let an old wound distract them from the current blight on the town.

"Ya done fucked up, preacher!" Mr. Landry, one of the local mechanics yells. He points a finger at Father Johnstone, still stained with dead motor oil and engine grit. "Got the goddamn Devil in ya and we all seen it!"

From the head of the church, he notices the distinct glisten of metal from different parts of the room. Most of them are oversized cowboy belt buckles, like the ones Danger Durphy used to wear back in his bull riding days. Some of these objects are bladed. Knives, a pistol here and there. They're either being held discreetly or concealed within a small jacket. And Deputy Clarke isn't going to do anything to stop it. His loyalty has always been to Pratt and Sheriff Morgan's brand of law.

"You believe that I am unfit to preach the Lord's Word, and you have arrived to deliver punishment in His own house," the pastor says, taking note of the mob inching a little bit closer. "But you forget that you don't speak for the Lord. In fact, I'm more in his favor now than I've ever been."

Father Johnstone signals to Madeline, who promptly stands and positions herself behind Ms. Doakes' wheelchair. She pushes her so that she's stationed at the front of the center aisle, facing outward to the crowd of people, the flock and the malevolent alike. They pause, holding steady and wondering just what exactly the pastor is playing at by bringing out ol' crippled Ms. Doakes to the center stage. Seems wrong, they think. He's just pestering that poor woman. He's going to hurt her or defile her in some way.

Father Johnstone says, "I believe you all know Ms. Doakes." Knobby knees like misshapen fruit are pressed together, extending downward to slippered feet in rusted stirrups.

Bernadette Doakes is plopped in the chair like a sack of old spuds, head slung lazily to one side. She's been wheelchair-bound for the last seven years. Dead weight just waiting to have her number called; everyone knows that.

"She will walk today," the pastor announces to the crowd, drawing guffaws and a few more scattered jeers. He maintains his sentiment, as impossible as it may sound, telling them once more, "By the power of Christ, she *will* walk."

Father Johnstone says this. He says it with conviction, just as Madeline instructed him to. *"Tricks are for magicians,"* she said that morning. *"So whatever we do, it has to be real. It has to be so convincing that there's no room for debate."*

The pastor squats down next to old Ms. Doakes, hand resting on her shoulder. He tilts his head forward, resting it on her forearm with his eyes closed, ready to pray. He prays for Madeline to come through, to save him from thy neighbors and enemies. As she told him last night, this is one part of the equation, the formula.

"Faith is an ingredient like love is an ingredient like flour and water and sugar are ingredients. Some of these you can keep in your kitchen cupboard," she said. *"Others, you have to draw from people."*

Madeline stands behind Ms. Doakes, one hand resting upon the nape of her neck, the other on the shoulder of Father Johnstone. The pastor's head rests upon the stale arm of the woman in the wheelchair, completing the triangle: the source, the conduit, and the recipient.

"It's where the term 'faith healing' comes from," Madeline explained. *"If a pastor came to town and made your cancer go away or restored your sight, more than likely it wasn't God that did that. It was someone like me."*

In these instances, the man of the cloth served as a battery of sorts. That's why the practice of faith healing was so frowned upon: it was the partnership of conflicting ideals, and therefore, couldn't be officially sanctioned in the eyes of the church as it was deemed 'impure' and 'blasphemous.'

"The clergy spurned us for having an ability and knowledge they didn't," Madeline told him, sometimes citing specific examples from her spell books, although they usually were in another language. Father Johnstone was thankful for the regular usage of diagrams and schematics, as they were the saving grace in spelling out the concepts he couldn't read for himself. He learned about elemental summoning, alchemy, and anatomical manipulation. He learned that witches were called in to treat cancerous tumors before civilization really knew what cancer was. Hippocrates discovered it and gave it a name, but it'd be another five centuries before a witch would successfully cure it.

"We remedied disease, we quenched droughts and harvested the properties of the earth for food and medicine," Madeline said. *"And for these acts, we were hunted, stoned, burned at the stake, and slandered in every ancient text."*

Today, in the First Church of Pratt, something happens that this town hasn't seen in a very long time: movement from Ms. Doakes' lower half. A twitch. They stare at the pastor in awe, still on bended knee at her side, eyes closed. All the while, Madeline stands mute in the background, healing, repairing nerves and deteriorated bone. She directs blood flow to the lower extremities and nurses atrophied muscle tissue. According to her, this is the space where faith and science meet, that little in-between gray area she mentioned.

"That's where miracles are made," Madeline said.

Ms. Doakes curls her toes inside her old house slippers, flexing her foot and testing the integrity of her ankles. The silence of the audience breaks, peppered with murmurs and chatter that the pastor takes as a sign of the plan's success. He moves in front of the wheelchair, carefully folding the stirrups of the wheelchair back so Ms. Doakes' legs are unencumbered. She places one foot down on the church flooring, then the next. She motions for Madeline and the pastor to help her to her feet, waving her arms.

Her head is upright and alert, traced with a smile the town had long forgotten. Father Johnstone and Madeline take an elbow on either side, assisting Ms. Doakes to her feet. They bring her upright until she's standing. Standing and smiling, looking down at her own slippers.

The pastor asks, "How do you feel, Bernadette?"

She turns her head, smiling stained false teeth. "Tall," she says. Her head gently dips forward, thanking him. Ms. Doakes walks down the aisle, splitting the crowd. She heads toward that place she played as a young girl, that part of town so beautiful is was like walking inside a painting. Slowly, steadily, she walks out of the church to the daisy hill.

"The first one always quiets the doubters," Madeline said that morning. *"You'd be surprised how quickly one little run-of-the-mill miracle can get people to shut the hell up."*

As it happens, the pastor isn't surprised at all. Like much of the attending crowd, he too can't help but stare at Ms. Doakes, pacing along heel-to-toe through the arched entryway in her stained gown and house slippers. Jaws go slack as they watch one of their resident cripples stride by as if she had never used a wheelchair in her life, smiling all the while.

"Don't get caught up," Madeline whispers to the pastor. "You need to keep going."

Yet again, Madeline pulls her next miracle from the galley of the church, another afflicted individual stationed in the front row. She plays the part of the assistant, folding Mr. Gibson's hand into her own and escorting him to the head of the church. As she's doing this, Father Johnstone pushes Ms. Doakes' wheelchair stage-right where it careens into a cluster of grain plant workers and farm hands.

"We're far from done," Father Johnstone says, recapturing the attention of those still lingering over this first miracle. "Some of you came here looking for a show, so we're going to make sure you get what you came here for." He waves over the next candidate, saying, "Madeline, place Mr. Gibson next to me, if you'd be so kind. I feel the Lord may be able to help him with his little problem."

Just as the Bible makes mention of witchcraft and sorcery, so too does the inverse relationship exist between texts. *"We've been writing about the clergy and the distinct power they possess for centuries,"* Madeline explained last night, citing a section of one of her books written in French, entitled: *rupture malédiction norme.*

"What this section tells us," she said, *"is that men of the cloth have the ability to infuse materials with special properties. As it happens, the best way to break a curse is to incinerate it by way of Holy fire—your lighter fluid and firewood, to be specific."*

Extenuating on the 'everything is ingredients' premise that Madeline often referenced, it appeared that faith was no exception. It could be used to heal, to summon the elements, and to either combat or combine with Craft, depending on the scenario. Some priests and pastors formed alliances and became faith healers; others subscribed to the idea that witches were intolerable and needed to be exterminated, becoming aggressors.

From Leviticus, the pastor recalls: *'A man or woman who is a medium or spiritist among you must be put to death. You are to stone them; their blood will be on their own heads.'*

This is the slander that Madeline spoke of. Permission to commit genocide, to murder, all for the sake of eliminating any potential threat they might pose. People read those words and they followed them to the letter. No alliances were to be made. No helping hand extended. Only a rare few members of the clergy ignored what was written in the Good Book, deciding it was best to see for themselves why witches were regarded with such umbrage.

"Through harmony and cooperation," Madeline told the pastor, *"we can be more together than we ever were apart, and I think it's time Pratt saw a little of that."*

Mr. Gibson is another one of the town's hard cases, another

piece of dead weight on the community. "He's just milking that disability money till he croaks," Mrs. Sugarman candidly remarked once. Everyone in town knows he's a blinder than a bat on a mug of moonshine, but only Dr. Keller refers to his condition by its formal term: *Retinoblastoma*; a form of eye cancer.

Jimmy Gibson has lived in Pratt for thirty-nine years; he hasn't seen the town in over three decades. Not with his eyes, anyway. He lost those before all of his baby teeth fell out, but some say he knows the town better than anyone, tapping left-right-left-right on the cracked sidewalks with an old cane. He counts to himself, just like his mama taught him. "Takes two-hundred and forty-seven paces to get from my house to the Presto," he said. "Seven paces from the front door to my favorite booth where the sun hits my face."

Kids in Pratt sometimes stop Mr. Gibson on the street, asking him how far the gas station or the daisy hill is in paces from their current location. Rarely is off by more than one or two steps. Other kids—the ones in their teens with too much time on their hands—they'll follow Mr. Gibson, shouting out random numbers in an attempt to confuse him and throw his count off. It never works, though. "Know this town better than most folks know the back of their own hand," he tells people. Finger tapping one of his temples, he says, "Best map of Pratt is right up here."

Inside the church, Father Johnstone addresses the audience again, telling them, "Mr. Gibson will see the sun today. He'll see the daisy hill and the spring sky and every single one of your faces." He says, "Today is the last day that he'll ever need to count his steps," and unlike his last proclamation regarding Ms. Doakes and her ability to walk, there are no scoffs of disbelief this time. No one laughs. The anger and *wrathful* intent that originally brought them to the church has since shifted to fascination, to hope.

"The more you do this with me, the easier it's going to get. The

relationship gets stronger with practice," Madeline said. *"Just do what comes naturally based on what you know."*

Father Johnstone is positioned face-to-face with Mr. Gibson, his eyes milked over white and foggy, ghosts swimming over the corneas. He studies them, regarding their filth, their unclean nature, leaning to Mr. Gibson's ear, the pastor says, "This is going to feel a bit weird, Jim." He leans back, aiming his mouth slightly upwards, and spits. Father Johnstone spits into Jimmy Gibson's left eye, and then again into the right, massaging the fluid into the ocular tissue with his thumbs. Audience members gasp, offended by what their shepherd has just done.

Madeline plays the supportive assistant, a hand on the hip of each man, connecting them. She cleanses the cancer cells, washing away the damage using the sanctified fluids of the pastor. She restores light and depth-perception, color and hue distinction. The spit is an ingredient like vanilla extract is an ingredient like beryllium, magnesium, and arsenic are ingredients. Yet again, the pastor and the witch are right there in the middle, that little gray area between faith and science where cripples walk and Mr. Gibson begins to regain his sight.

"How do you feel, Jim?"

"Honestly?" Mr. Gibson says. "I feel like you just spit in my face." He pauses slightly, lips pursed until he can't hold it any longer. Jimmy Gibson laughs, slapping the pastor on the shoulder like an old friend and bringing him into an embrace. Arms wrap around so tight Father Johnstone's ribs bend. Madeline looks on, smiling.

"Faith is more than showing up at to a certain place and reading certain passages," she said that morning. *"It's more than following the rules. It's a relationship...with people. It's something Jesus had with his followers and now you need to have it, too."*

As Mr. Gibson walks through the center aisle, the mood in the room shifts over once more. Their anger has been quelled, fists unclenched and expressions soft. Heads turn, following the once-sightless Jimmy Gibson, smiling, looking at the sun beams pouring through the stained glass windows of the church. He takes in their faces, of both the flock and the mob, nodding at them in turn. No walking stick or counting required, Mr. Gibson exits the First Church of Pratt to rediscover what a spring day looks like, if the grass is as green as he remembers it being from when he was just a boy.

"The relationship you have with these people will make you capable of great things," Madeline said. *"But you must maintain absolute honesty and candor. That means no secrets, Johnstone. No reservations. Their faith in you has to be pure."*

After two miracles, the audience is primed. Although they're not aware of Madeline's covert involvement regarding the actual process, in their eyes, the pastor has done his due diligence. Despite any initial doubts or rumors, he's convinced them that he truly is in the Lord's favor, and this much can be seen by the looks on their faces. Optimism and awe. Inspiration, just as Madeline foretold that morning over breakfast. Whispers mist over the galley of this newly revealed power, how Father Johnstone must be closer to the Lord than he's ever been. Then he speaks once more.

"I've sinned," he says.

Murmurs flood the audience, once again recalling all those nasty stories they heard about the pastor, how the Devil got a hold of him, got inside his soul. Blackened him, twisted him to the absolute worst of himself.

As Mr. Buelle so eloquently put it earlier in the week, "Lucifer done took that man's spirit and wiped his wet, red ass with it. Men don't bleed like that. Unnatural, it was."

Father Johnstone stands at the head of the church, hand held high, beckoning for the flock's silence and the mob's momentary cooperation. He shouts, "I've sinned, and I've hurt people close to me." His eyes fall on Mrs. Tiller, who gives him a definitive nod at this admission. So too does Mr. and Mrs. Fairfax and

Helena Wright. Travis Durphy fans his cowboy hat up and down at the people around him, aiding his pastor in obtaining a level of quiet so his voice can be heard.

"Like most of you, I strayed off the path," Father Johnstone says, connecting with select members of the flock: the adulterers and those who covet. He looks at them, and they know they're no better. "I lost my way, I've seen my share of temptation, but I've since consulted the Lord. I sought His forgiveness and His sanction, and I'm back a better man now."

Part of the gallery cheers with approval hearing that last proclamation. A few scattered shouts of "Amen!" trickle out, easing the pastor's original swell of nerves. He's making headway, winning them back just as Madeline said he would. *The first miracle gets their attention,*" she told him that morning. *"The second removes the possibility that what you're doing is a fluke."*

There was never any talk about a third miracle, but the pastor couldn't help but think that Madeline was holding something back intentionally. Ms. Doakes' and Mr. Gibson's exploits notwithstanding, the spectacle of the sermon doesn't feel complete. Something's missing. A singular ingredient is all that stands from completely turning the tide back in his favor, and whether it's another phenomenon or prayer or apology, the pastor is uncertain.

He says, "Some of you came here looking for vengeance. You entered the Lord's house with motives of anger, believing that it was upon you to exercise God's *wrath* in His stead." Father Johnstone points this out, noticing certain individuals tilt their head down in shame or look away. "And I forgive you," he says. "Fear compels us to act irrationally, but this is the instance in which we should seek God, as I have."

Father Johnstone stands at the helm with Madeline just behind him, hanging back idly, hands folded in front of her and listening to the sermon. The two of them notice movement in the crowd, a man making his way forth from the back of the church.

Just loud enough so only the pastor can hear, Madeline very distinctly says a word to him, a warning of sorts. At first it sounds like a curse, but it's not, he realizes. She's saying the word 'fork.'

Father Johnstone says, "We should seek peace. We should seek harmony *together*."

The church is calm, hanging on the pastor's every word—all except for the man. One man continues to cut through the crowd gathered in the center aisle, pushing people aside and cursing at them for not making way. Father Johnstone hears Madeline shuffle forward slightly, saying the word yet again. "Fork," she hisses.

"I will not tolerate vengeance nor *wrath*," the pastor says. "I will not allow the Lord's house to become a poisonous place for those who wish to walk the righteous path with me."

The pastor can see the man's face finally: grizzled and chapped, slightly red in the cheeks from what most of the town describes as 'a constant booze binge.' Old man Clevenger is making his way to the helm, pushing people with a sense of sobriety that's unlike him. There's no stagger in his movements or drunken eyes. His jaw has reeled in from its usual slacked position. He looks focused.

The pastor says, "Violence will be the end of us."

Old man Clevenger emerges from the crowd, a pistol drawn. He's grinning, holding the gun level and aiming at Father Johnstone's chest, his heart.

"I'll always find you," he says.

Madeline rushes up behind the pastor just before the hammer of the pistol drops and the gallery screams in panic, saying the word one more time. "Fork," she says, pressing herself against his back, using him like a shield. Fingers clip around the pastor's wrist as the hammer drops, igniting the powder.

A bullet is heading their way.

The third miracle.

Las Vegas, NV

I go Catholic for a stint.

There are a few places of worship on Cathedral Way, which is just off South Las Vegas Blvd. Western religion, I'm realizing, is just as much a financial institution as the hotel and casino business. The 'down on his luck' degenerate gambler sits next to the family of five which sits next to the reformed whore. Under the eyes of God, they're all equal. They're all a source of tribute to the Lord and the church, a monetary offering known as a 'tithe.' It's the only city in which casino chips appearing in the collection plate is considered normal.

Although there's no specific usage of the words 'gambler' or 'gambling' in any of the religious texts that I've studied, I suspect that the source of my income would be deemed impious considering the method in which it's procured. I have an ability. I've been using said ability to extort the individuals known as 'dealers' for the past several months. Players too. I can tell when they're lying to me, can smell the oils in their skin change and feel their eyes dilate when they attempt to 'bluff,' as it's referred to. The casino staff that watches over these games suspect that I'm using a rudimentary mathematical system of cheating known as 'counting cards,' however, this couldn't be further from the truth. My skill set lies in being able to read people, and if I so choose, exploit them. I've been exploiting a lot of people throughout my time here in Las Vegas: the casinos, the whores, the hotel staff, and the various clergymen I seek out for answers, and so far the answers haven't been clear.

"Bless me Father for I have sinned," I recite.

The man across from me is old, nearing his twilight years. I've done my due diligence by restraining him in the most humane way I could fathom, a couple pairs of handcuffs that bind him to the arms of the chair. He's bound but not in pain. Father Latimer didn't receive such comfortable treatment.

"This isn't how it's typically done," he says, tugging at one of the

handcuffs to test its durability. They're forged out of steel, and although they were bought at Frederick's of Hollywood, I made sure to boil them in Holy water to cleanse them of any sexual impurities.

"I seek absolution," I explain, burping. All around the basement are filing cabinets, old décor and dusty paintings, office supplies. Cases of wine. Cases of wafers. The blood and body of Christ. I've been eating and drinking them in turns, waiting for the first man of the cloth to come down the stairs. "Your assistance would be invaluable to me," I say, holding back the next flux of air in my throat.

After having imbibed three full bottles of Christ blood and four boxes of His body, the pain of my genital sores and the urethral sting have muted significantly. Physically, there has been no change. The dermis remains infected and raw, but I can feel His strength pulsing through me, restoring health. My vitality heightens with every bottle and box of Him I consume.

"You will refrain from harming me," the priest says. "You will let me go. Those are my conditions." Unlike the others, this one does not fear death. In fact, he looks forward to the next stage of non-existence known as 'the afterlife.' It's not bravery that allows him to speak to me this way. He simply isn't threatened.

"And what of the tithe?" I ask, taking another drink.

"You wish to pay a tithe?" He seems surprised by the offer, but I confirm this with a stern nod. "It's one-tenth of your earnings," he says.

From my jacket pocket, I pull out a variety of casino chips (red, black, and midnight blue). They're made of clay and a myriad of other ingredients to keep them durable; I feel this just by touching them, the intangibles. "Open your hand," I say, and in the clergyman's palm I place $200,000 in tokens that he may exchange for cash at Caesar's. Bony fingers wrap around them. Tight. Not a drop of greed in his fragile little body. He won't keep a single chip for himself.

The priest nods and I begin.

I confess my sins, telling him about all the various whores—both in regards to the endeavor and those purchased out of sheer indulgence.

Sometimes my gratification was limited to fornication and that alone; other times I proceeded to experiment on them after reaching sufficient climax. If death came to pass, it was never achieved out of malice, but rather, a test taken too far. An accident. When I want to understand something, I explain to him, I have a tendency to push the individual to their absolute threshold.

"I'm currently pushing faith," I say. "I've heard so much about what it can do...miracles, even...and now I wish to see that for myself. Rules have been broken in the process."

I tell him about my various undertakings involving Christian lingerie and pious role-play, the candles and the Holy water and the Good Book itself. They are used to protect me, to protect others, and yet I'm haunted by a string of failures. Disease spreads and I'm no closer to understanding the Lord and how His power functions, even when utilizing Divine materials and their by-products, such as the seminal fluid of Father Latimer. There's an honest attempt on my part to convey the logic I'm using, although it quickly becomes obvious that I'm confusing him, offending his sensibilities. Yet again, the clergy doesn't understand the concept of wielding Divine power in a practical sense.

"You speak of faith as if it's a skill," he says.

Alchemy, which is the knowledge of elements, concentrates on the composition and transformation of different components. Faith is little more than a spiritual form of that. It is an aptitude, a competence to be learned, practiced, and mastered. Biblical texts confirm this much. I've read it. I've even seen it on late-night television: clergymen healing members of their flock.

"A disabled individual approached the stage. The priest then proceeded speak in Divine tongues before delivering a swift blow to this person's skull," I say. "They fell out of their mobile chair device... stood...and regained the ability to walk under their own accord. The priest then praised the Lord God for his ability. So explain how that's not a skill."

The priest looks down, shakes his head, sighing. I attempt to read him but the over-indulgence of Christ blood clouds me. Intangibles blur.

"It's falsehood," he says. "A trick. A show. That's not real faith, understand? Whether you're absolved or not, that is something that can't be taught."

"Perhaps you're the one who's deficient," I say. Anger swells. I can feel the sores burn again, the sting at the tip of my urethra. Nothing is going to plan. I've wasted my time.

"You may release me now." The priest begins tugging on his restraints, even going as far as to attempt to pull his hand through the cuff. Suddenly, he becomes overtly eager to distance himself from me. I can feel that, his disgust. He keeps pulling on the cuff, coiling his empty hand in order to slide it through the metal loop.

"No," I say.

What happens next I credit to pure instinct. In reaction to his attempted escape, I reach out to tighten the cuff, however, I remain in a seated position due to my level of intoxication. It simply slips my mind that I need to stand and physically walk over. Instead, my arm extends, homing in on the metal around his wrist. I can feel it, the difference in composition compared to the surrounding air, its organic make-up. I feel it in my fingers. Consciously, I don't even mean it to happen, but the cuff contracts. Without me even touching it, the metal loop closes, causing him to scream. It cuts through this skin, applying pressure to the tendons. Blood seeps down the metal of the restraint, dripping onto the arm of the chair.

After so many months in Las Vegas and countless trials ending in failure, I finally realize what I've been missing. The hunt can resume. I can go looking for her again.

My Madeline.

The Pawns

"How did you do it?"

This is the first question Deputy Clarke asks the pastor, which may or may not be part of an official interrogation. He doesn't say: "Are you okay?" or "Would you like to press charges?" He wants to know the trick, the secret to how Father Johnstone walked out of the church without a gaping hole in his body.

"Cos you know what I think, preacher?" the deputy asks, taking a pull on a Marlboro. He blows the smoke across the desk, cocooning the pastor who's seated opposite. "I think you're full of shit. You may have them fooled," he points at one of the windows with his cigarette, indicating beyond the wall, the people of Pratt, "not me, though. Not by damn sight."

"Am I under arrest, James?"

"It's Deputy while the badge is on, preacher," he says smugly. "And no, you're not under arrest. But I can think of a few reasons. Being uncooperative comes to mind, and we don't want to start off on the wrong foot, now do we?" he muses, pulling on the cigarette again. "So why don't you make this easy and tell me how you did it."

At the last possible moment, it kicked in just what exactly Madeline meant when she said the word 'fork.' He remembered that moment in the kitchen, a piece of silverware hovering just above her palm, rotating slowly. Even when he went to grab it, there was a force preventing him from removing it, as if it was stuck in mid-air. 'Biomagnetism,' Madeline called it. With her ability, she could amplify naturally occurring magnetic fields in the body, thus, controlling metallic objects to a certain degree.

"How do you stop a bullet, preacher?" Deputy Clarke asks, leaning closer, exhaling another cloud of smoke. "Don't even think about lying to me."

Years ago, Father Johnstone had some long overdue dental

work done. It wasn't as bad as he initially thought it was going to be: a couple fillings and an under-the-gum cleaning that left his mouth sore for the next three days. No root canals or bridge work, thankfully. He'd forgotten all about it up until this morning when old man Clevenger fired that bullet. The memory of it came rushing back when he felt the silver in his teeth move. Splinters of metal spiked and rattled inside his molars, singing in pain as Madeline sent out a wave of magnetic force.

Deputy Clarke places a bullet on the table, sealed in a tiny plastic bag marked: *Property of Pratt County Police Department.* Besides a little char from the firing process, the round remains mostly unspoiled, silver with a stunted copper head.

"This here should be crunched in," the deputy says, fingering the tip of the bullet through the plastic. He picks it up, displaying it to Father Johnstone. "Or inside your chest," he adds. "Any theories?"

This is his way of saying: '*I know you know, so let's not bullshit each other.*'

He remembers feeling ice shoot through his fillings, the metal on his belt buckle pouncing forward as Madeline Paige cuffed his wrist and squeezed so hard the tendons ached. The bullet from old man Clevenger's pistol slowed, easing to a standstill before dropping to the church floor with a hard tap. Then a riot broke out, but not the one everyone in Pratt had originally conspired. Father Johnstone had not been lynched or beaten or dragged behind old model Ford pick-up trucks. No one assaulted him. Not a drop of spit was launched his way. Instead, it was old man Clevenger who inherited the rage of mob and the flock—first, by disarming him, then the beating ensued, incited by an assembly of grain plant workers, laborers, and generally vengeful people. Along with the bullet, three teeth were collected and put into evidence bags.

"A man tried to kill me today," Father Johnstone says. "He fired upon me in my own church, and yet, it feels as if you're blaming me."

"Right," the deputy snickers. "Play the victim card. That's good. I like that."

"Am I allowed to inquire as to the current location of my assailant, Deputy?"

"Where the hell you think?" he says. "Hospital. Dr. Keller's got him in a room, locked up and cuffed to a bed. Man his age can't take a beating like that."

"But I should be able to take a bullet?" the pastor snipes.

"Don't sass me, preacher. Just because you healed a couple cripples today ain't making me forget what a piece of shit you are. Ol' Magda Tiller done hinted at it," the deputy says, pulling on the Marlboro again. Once again, Father Johnstone feels the smoke lick his eyes, stinging, but he doesn't blink. He doesn't take the bait regarding Magda and what she may or may not remember about her visit in the hospital. Deputy Clarke says, "She told me there was something not right about you. And now you can *do* things, huh? Stop bullets? I'm inclined to believe her."

"I'm guided by higher powers," Father Johnstone says sagely, although usually it's more specific. Usually he says 'the Lord' or 'God.' Not this time. "Crack a Bible if you want to understand how I can do what I do."

"Now that's a crock'a shit you can feed to someone who ain't had lunch." Deputy Clarke takes one more pull off the Marlboro before stumping it out in a nearby ashtray. Years of cinder scorch the glass, crusting it black. A thick husk of coal. Another ingredient that Madeline could probably use. *Envy*, ash, magnetism— these are all ingredients. "I just wonder...if I pulled out my own pistol here," he says, a grin spreading over his face. "I'm wondering if you could do it again."

Father Johnstone smiles back, brave, watching Deputy Clarke finger the handle of his pistol not totally unlike the sheriff. It's the toy he never got the play with, forbidden fruit. He's tempted to pull it out, to point it right at the pastor's face, maybe even press the barrel against his cheek. Press it real hard until it leaves an impression in the skin. He wants to. He wants to watch him squirm in the chair a little, doing that thing where the target brings their hands up to protect their face. Like that would help. Fucking bullet would tear through those old fingers like hot dog meat, the deputy thinks. Shards of knuckle and phalanx showering the office, and blood—it'd take forever to clean up the mess.

"There's plenty I could do. *And* the town," the pastor reminds him. "Pratt can hold its own when it needs to. Like today," he says, throwing the deputy a combative look. "Impressive how they took down old man Clevenger on such short notice, don't you think? Basically did your job for you."

"Oh, I do the job fine, preacher. Don't worry about lil' ol' me," he says. "Let's just hope you can repeat your little trick should the occasion arise. I'd expect you'll have to…sooner or later." He smirks again.

"Then I pray the Lord allow me the strength to rise to the occasion again," the pastor says coolly. "And I pray the responsibility of serving and protecting our town doesn't prove to be too much of a chore in the absence of Sheriff Morgan."

"Yeah, I bet you do," Deputy Clarke says cynically, glaring at the pastor. "And after your little show today, I find it a tad peculiar our good sheriff would decide to skip town after paying your home a visit. Don't you?"

"Yes. Quite."

"He hasn't been in contact…not even picking up his radio, but don't worry yourself too much about that. I've been on the phones," the deputy says. "Told law enforcement in the surrounding counties to keep an eye out for his cruiser. Only a matter of time, I think."

Father Johnstone is oddly reminded of the sheriff uttering these words himself: *"Only a matter of time."* It feels that way to him, as if this is all counting down to something. The curse, the insects, the miracles—they're all adding up to an event, a composition. These too are ingredients, Madeline would tell him.

"He'll turn up," the deputy says. "He may have drove himself out but I'm not convinced he was completely behind the wheel, if you know what I mean."

Years of the sheriff's bitterness have been passed down to his second-in-command, inciting suspicion at every turn. He's on to the pastor, but there's one aspect Father Johnstone can take comfort in; the deputy hasn't incarcerated or cuffed him yet. If that was a card he was holding, he'd have played it by now.

"I know you're up to something," the deputy says. "You and that Maddy Paige you've been spending so much time with. Word around town says you're more than friends. You and anyone willing to tip 20%," he chuckles.

"Are you asking me a question, Deputy?"

"Course not," he reclines back in his chair, relaxed. "You and her? Together? Fine woman like that ain't gonna give a ride to an old prick like you."

Father Johnstone feels his face flush, hot needles in the back of his neck. Anger—not at what the deputy is saying, but how he's addressing it. It's different with the sheriff; he's a pillar. Equal footing allows for the relationship to be strained, and at times, disrespectful. Deputy Clarke, on the other hand, is a stand in. He's temporary.

"Maddy needs a *young* man," the deputy says. "Like me."

Fire burns his ears and neck, watching the deputy chuckle, laugh. Father Johnstone shifts uncomfortably in his seat, the muscles in his back tightening. He's tense, knowing full well he's being taunted. Father Johnstone is being tested, but not by thy Lord and savior. Not by God. Deputy Clarke, as crass as he might be, is trying to do the thing the sheriff never could.

"She's probably one of them shavers, don't you think, preacher?" the deputy asks, grinning. "Bet there's not a single whisker on that biscuit. Maybe you could put in a good word for me? Or should I just pay her a visit myself?"

Anger mounts in the pastor's chest, his neck, but it lasts only as long as it takes for him to figure out the game. Deputy Clarke is goading him for reasons beyond simple intimidation or personal joy. He's looking for something specific, something the sheriff never got out of him: a reaction.

"Not really much that can stop me, now is there?" Deputy Clarke asks. He's looking for a heated response, something to bring Father Johnstone down to his level. "Certainly not you, preacher. Probably never had a fight in your life."

He doesn't want information. He doesn't care about what happened in the church today, miracle or otherwise. These issues were merely an appropriate reason to get the pastor down to the station for questioning, although their meeting has since devolved to a barrage of ridicule. Deputy Clarke would never deprive the sheriff of taking down the pastor, but he relishes the opportunity of 'playing with his food,' as they say.

When the father leaves the homestead, it is their next of kin that will find themselves drawn to their earthly possessions. In this case, Sheriff Morgan's unofficial claim on the pastor. The Good Book identifies this as coveting; it's yet another ingredient being tossed into the recipe that is Pratt's recent state of disquiet.

"And what do you plan on doing the next time someone steps out of the crowd ready to attack?" the deputy asks. "Cos you can't always count on one of your little miracles. Or the town, for that matter."

"I have faith that I can," the pastor says. He intentionally stands up from his chair slowly, so as not to give the deputy any reason to remove his pistol. A sudden movement is the last thing he wants to make, lest he be faced with another bullet coming at him from a much closer range than this morning. Deputy Clarke follows in suit, also rising to a standing position. Mixed emotions cross his face, mentally weighing the outcomes of allowing the pastor to leave the station versus containing him, if only for a while longer.

In the end, the deputy leaves Father Johnstone with an official warning, informing him, "I will be keeping an eye on you." He says, "You and the cunt."

"Then I pray, Deputy, that you don't miss anything more threatening while your attention is diverted," the pastor retorts. "You are the law in Pratt now, after all."

"That's right, preacher. Glad that's clear," Deputy Clarke nods. "And I think it's best you stay put until we get all this mess with old man Clevenger and the sheriff sorted out. Consider yourself lucky I'm letting you walk out at all."

Father Johnstone formally observes the deputy's sentiments with a nod, choosing not to respond to the final barb. Luck has nothing to do with it, he thinks. 'You treat a puppy like a mean bastard, you're gonna have one mean bastard of a dog on your hands,' folks say.

As the pastor exits the police station, he comes to realize that the exchange between himself and the deputy was the longest they've ever shared. Apart from the congenial nod or polite wave, their interactions have always been limited. Sending away the sheriff hasn't delayed a problem as Madeline originally thought; it's merely transferred it to another agent. Today's events at the church were indeed a success, but whatever the next part of the plan is, it won't be without a watchful presence as originally assumed. Deputy Clarke is aching to prove himself, and the letter of the law will factor in very little (if at all) in his quest to achieve that.

"Only a matter of time," he said.

Father Johnstone walks the streets of Pratt, stomach panging from all the recent excitement, not to mention the state of affairs regarding his last meal. Madeline's bacon and eggs are currently touring the town's sewage system instead of his guts, and so he's hoping now that the deed is over, he'll be able to keep down his chow. Something heavy, like a steak and a baked potato topped with sour cream. Buttered bread would hit the spot, too, but that may have gone to mold in his cupboards some time ago.

Over the course of the week's events, it wasn't just Father Johnstone's health and temperament that went to hell. Both his home and his flock were compromised, and in an abrupt fashion, no less. Vandalism and violence brushed against his existence, threatening his livelihood through methods he believed too archaic to exist beyond scripture. Madeline proved that assumption was wrong, that he had indeed been feeling the effects of a curse. Poison would slip into his mind and body, his dreams, and had it soaked in a little bit more, he might not even be walking the streets under his own accord. It is Madeline that saves, that guides. It is Madeline that is able to do more than he's ever been able to in over thirty years.

She comes into view as the pastor nears his home. Madeline stands on the cracked sidewalk just outside Father Johnstone's house, Mary saddled over one of her arms. Her floral print dress billows as the wind pushes dust and grime along the street. Figures are all over the property, working, toiling. Silver tins of paint and bags of mulch line the house. Ladders are leaned against the east face of the home, granting rooftop access. Four trucks are parked along the street, and from the within beds various men remove toolboxes and more buckets of paint. Brushes and power washers and plants in plastic housings.

Father Johnstone sidles Madeline and Mary, giving the latter a little scratch along the jaw. She grinds her face into his fingers affectionately, purring. "I take it your little meeting with the deputy went well, then?" Madeline asks.

"He seemed a little too eager to let me know he'll be keeping an eye on us," the pastor answers. "It's like the sheriff never left."

"I wouldn't worry about it. I've got my ways of keeping an eye on things, too," she says with a smirk. Madeline strokes Mary on the crown of her head, pushing back the caramel and ashen fur. "They came here after the sermon." She gestures towards the house, the men.

"On their own?" The pastor cocks a suspicious eyebrow.

"I wouldn't waste the good stuff on a little home repair," she says. "Consider it a bonus for putting on an exceptionally good performance today."

"It felt pretty real to me."

A couple of the guys on the rooftop offer the pastor a friendly wave, which he promptly returns. He smiles at them, unsure what Madeline meant by calling it 'a performance,' as if what they had just done was all for show. Mr. Gibson and Ms. Doakes had indeed left the church in a better state than which they had entered it. To imply it was fake does a disservice to them and the people it inspired.

"Despite what you believe, we did a good thing today," the pastor says.

"Some gestures are simply a way to send a message. Clevenger, for instance," she mentions. "It was a sloppy move. Tactless. Far too aggressive, but in this game we're all sharing the same pawns."

"You think he was sent?" Father Johnstone asks this, but he knows the answer the moment the words are uttered. Kurt Clevenger is a consummate lush, a blight on the town, yes, but definitely not the violent type. Even for him, charging into a church with a pistol is way out of character. Contrasting reputations and practices notwithstanding, Kurt Clevenger has always gotten along with everyone, and that includes the men of God.

"He'd be a likely candidate to be sent, yes," she says. "Old man Clevenger, the lush. The drunken fool. That is what you refer to as *sloth*, yes?"

"Correct," the pastor says.

"And is that not a deadly sin?"

"It is," he nods, suspecting she's building up to a point.

"And what is deadly sin, Johnstone? What's so dangerous about them exactly?" She asks this, not so much out of genuine inquiry, but more to see how the pastor fields it.

"They are the path to damnation," Father Johnstone says. "The gateway to hell."

Seven in total: *wrath, greed, sloth, pride, lust, envy,* and *gluttony.* To commit them is to disobey God, to oppose His will, and is sure to keep one from entering the Kingdom. This is what the pastor learned during his stint in seminary school, anyway. He's sure Madeline has other ideas about the subject, notions that adhere to a more radical system.

"They are more of a gateway to control," she says, giving Mary a couple scratches behind the ear. Madeline lowers her voice so as not to be overheard by any passing workers, stepping aside so her shoulder is touching that of the pastor. "In the 4th century our people came into contact with a man, a Christian monk by the name of Evagrius Ponticus. Greek. Highly intelligent for the time. Forward thinker."

"The name sounds familiar," the pastor thinks aloud.

"It's because he's the guy that got the ball rolling on the deadly sin concept, which at that point in time, was more or less just a list of bad thoughts he put down on paper," Madeline explains. "Vices, I guess you could say. And if you wanted to put it yet another way—"

"—Ingredients," the pastor says.

"Right," she nods. "Craft was still very much in its infancy, but there was a breakthrough when we started to figure out that the composition of a *lustful* individual was very different from that of someone who was happily married. They were vulnerabilities. These deadly sins, as they'd be referred to a couple centuries later, became the main elements in our periodic table, so to speak."

"To exploit, I take it," the pastor ventures.

"Imagine the clergy freaking out over every drunk or whore or *gluttonous* individual stuffing their face. The *greedy,* the vengeful...any one of them could have been a puppet, a weapon," Madeline says. "So imagine that going on for a few centuries: witches having priests attacked and their churches burned, and the clergy responding with secret executions and kidnappings and torture."

"Why secret?" the pastor asks.

"Because when you have a weak point, the last thing you want is for the people to see it. You've already seen firsthand how bad it can get...how quickly people can turn."

The pastor nods.

"Faith is a delicate system," Madeline says. "And certain individuals decided to use their knowledge of the Craft—not for betterment of the spirit or personal progression—but for war. Two beliefs trading blows, sniping at each other, and then in the late 1400s, what happens? The whole thing reaches a fever pitch and we got witch-hunts. Tens of thousands torched at the stake, and most of them weren't even guilty of anything."

"I remember reading about them," the pastor says, not knowing whether or not to offer empathy. Madeline is frowning, upset.

"Yeah, *your* history," she says critically. "There's two sides to every story. My aunt spent most of her life keeping part of the other half safe. How do you think this town would have reacted if they found out what she was?"

"Poorly, I imagine."

"And me?" she asks, turning away from the house and the workers. She looks at the pastor. "What do you think they'd do to me?"

"If you're lucky?" the pastor considers. "Exile. Kick you out of town. Tell you to never come back." He's seen this happen before on more than one occasion.

"And if I'm not so lucky?"

"They'd hurt you. Hurt you in a way you'd never forget." The pastor opts for brutal honesty. "You'd be beaten, raped, and tortured. They'd cut you up, let you scab over, and then they'd cut you up again. These are simple people, Mad. Simple and intolerant."

"And weak," Madeline adds. "It's the culture. I get it."

"What do you want me to say?" Father Johnstone gets a little short with her, still on edge from his meeting with the deputy. "That this is a bad community? That they don't deserve protection?"

"No," she shakes her head. "I'm merely pointing out how these people here working on your home, painting and re-shingling and fixing windows—not long ago they showed up with knives and pistols looking to turn you into a pincushion. They're fickle. Irresolute."

"They're sheltered," he counters. "The flock panics easily, and they're terrified of change."

"And the one that sent Clevenger out today knows that," Madeline says. "He knows how to bend these people, to get them to do what he wants, and unlike you or me, he doesn't care what happens. They're just pawns," she explains. "Sometimes you send one out to take a piece; other times it's so you can see how the other player will react. Doesn't matter how many he loses though. He'll make more."

He's reminded of what Madeline said: *"...you'll compromise by the end of this. Eventually. You can't play by the rules forever when the other side isn't."*

Father Johnstone could never actively use someone, not even an old drunk like Kurt Clevenger who's dying to be put out of his misery. That line seems too damning to cross, despite the recent danger he's found himself in. Kurt's actions at the church today bring up yet another issue that the pastor can't wrap his head around. Although his understanding of Craft and the mechanics of it are elementary, there's something that doesn't add up when taking into account all he's seen so far.

"When I was cursed, it came on slow," he says. "It took well over a week before it became unbearable and it started to really affect me. That doesn't seem to be the case with everyone else."

"You're a man of the cloth, Johnstone. You're not like everyone else." Madeline looks to the left, to the spot in the yard where the dogwood tree is planted. White blossoms soak in the afternoon sun. She points at it, saying, "Pretend that tree represents every person in Pratt: you, me, these workers. Everyone."

"Okay," the pastor nods.

"It starts with the trunk there, which extends into a limb, and then that extends into a branch," she says. "And then those branches keep extending until you get to the twigs at end there...so frail you could snap them with your fingers." Madeline pauses a moment, allowing the analogy to soak in. "It's the hierarchy system, and it's in almost everything: this town, the government, the Catholic church," she says.

Pope is above cardinal, which are both above archbishop. 'Pillar' is the informal term for 'person of great worth or impor- tance' that has endured over the years, a status that makes someone like the pastor a viable target.

"Clevenger is like one of those twigs," Madeline says. "Weak, pliable. It's not going to take a lot to break someone like that."

"You're saying I'm one of the main limbs, then," the pastor assumes.

"I'm saying you're the foundation," Madeline corrects him. "When a tree gets sick, it cracks, it decays. The leaves turn yellow and wilt, and the branches die. It's very much what happened to this town, because it wasn't just the flock that turned. It was nearly everyone."

Father Johnstone watches the men working on his home, painting, repairing. They spread mulch and plant flowers. These men, along with everyone else showed up at the church today, arrived angry and ready for some type retribution. They wanted blood.

"You are the pillar, Johnstone. The keystone, the main support," Madeline says. "Whether you want to accept it or not, you have the most influence. What happens to you is going to have a ripple effect on the entire town, flock or no."

Father Johnstone sighs. The gravity of his role in Pratt has gotten that much greater—not just as the shepherd, but as a protector.

"You said that the other side sometimes makes a play just to see how the other side will react," he says. "So what now? Are we to expect more of that?"

"He's tried cursing you, controlling you, turning the town against you," Madeline lists. "Shooting you didn't work either. He knows we're aware of him, but he maintains the advantage in that we don't know where he is. He's close though."

"You're saying he's in town somewhere?" Father Johnstone confirms. "Hiding out?"

"Oh, most definitely. Probably in one of the houses," she speculates.

"I'm not disagreeing with you here, but you know how this town feels about outsiders," the pastor says. "If there was someone new lurking around Pratt, we would have heard something by now."

"No, you *wouldn't* have, and that's the point. I told you, Johnstone, we're either hiding in plain sight or just plain hiding," Madeline says. "He's around here somewhere."

"Should we talk to Kurt perhaps?" he asks. "Maybe he knows something."

"I'd venture he knows too much," she says. "He let that much slip at the church today, right before he took a shot at you." Madeline pauses, frowning. "He always finds me."

"Who does?" the pastor asks. "Kurt?"

"No. Pollux," she says. "His name is Pollux."

חיים בעלי אילוף XI: תהליך

For this process the male (גבר) will need either: a horse (סוס), a ram (איל), or a bull (שור). Smaller animals, such as the feline (חתולי) or fox (שועל) may also be used. They will lack size and strength but possess a certain cunning that larger mammals (יונקים) do not. You should make your selection based on the desired attributes (תכונות). Gender (מין) of the animal is without significance, however, the individual performing the process must be male. To penetrate is to establish dominance (שליטה), and therefore, a female will not be able to do this. The male will first need to capture specified animal, however, it is of the utmost importance that this is done without harming or killing (הרג) it. Spears, arrows, or bladed objects should not be used. High level poisons (רעלים) should also be avoided. A sleeping draft is preferred, but it's important to keep in mind the dosage in ratio to the weight of the animal. Too much or not enough may have dangerous consequences, and killing an innocent beast (חיה) isn't without reprisals. Ideally, the animal should be laid on its left side facing the sun's origin (מקור) point in the east, legs bound together and muzzle secured. Garnish the beast in red rose (שושנה) petals, sage sticks, and the blood (דם) of its opposing gender; same species (מין). Sheep are the easiest to accomplish this with as they are traditionally found in flocks, however, this is a weak and stupid animal, and should be avoided. Unclean animals should also be avoided: pigs (חזירים), rats (חולדות), and dogs (כלבים). After the preparation stage is complete, the male may proceed to penetrate the animal while reciting the Divine Prayer of Dominance. The male must fornicate (לנאוף) with the animal until the point of climax. If climax is not achieved, then you have just partially fornicated with a wild animal for nothing. Upon orgasm, the seed (זרע) of the male must remain inside the beast and all bindings must be cut so that it may be set free. Effects of the process will transpire after three moon cycles (שלב). The seed will more than likely not manifest into offspring, however, in the event that a half-beast/half-human child (ילד) is born, it should immediately be killed and harvested.

Attempts to love (אהבה) or father it will be met with violence at the wrath *(זעם) of humans, which is the majority of the reason why the centaur race was unable to flourish.*

The Feri Tradition

"I'm going to be a little more transparent about what I know," Madeline says, sitting cross-legged on Father Johnstone's couch with Mary coiled in her lap. She strokes her head, combing the fur with short chewed nails, lulling her to sleep. To Father Johnstone, she discloses, "There are going to be points you disagree with or don't believe—"

"—That's been occurring quite a bit anyway," he interjects.

"However," she presses on. "You need to listen. Because if you don't listen, I can't help you. Or your town. Understand?"

Workers are still crawling all over the outside of the house, hammering nails and applying fresh paint. They're planting flowers in beds of woodchip mulch, trimming the perimeter of the foundation in spring colors, the kind that brighten a home's curb appeal. It's a soft din of thumping and swiping brushes against the composite siding, and although he hasn't said this out loud, the pastor feels protected having company around. Safe from harm, from this Pollux individual that Madeline refuses to speak of until she's had her say.

"I will listen, but on the condition I finally get some answers," he says. "No more half-truths. If people are going to shoot at me, I think I'm entitled to know who's behind it."

"Careful what you wish for, Johnstone." She smiles, testing the pastor. "You almost skipped town once already. I'd hate to scare you off."

"I'm not going anywhere," he says. "I want you to tell me about Pollux. Why is he here?"

"I can't. Not without putting him into context first," Madeline says.

"Why?"

"Because if I just told you outright that he's better at this than I am, that what we've seen so far is nothing compared to what he's capable of, and if we're being totally open right now, things will probably get a lot worse—if I told you all that, you'd probably want to leave, wouldn't you?"

"Yes," the pastor says. He remains seated though, waiting. He waits for her to speak.

"The Deschutes Forest, just outside Bend, Oregon," Madeline says. "That is where we'd learn about the Feri tradition."

Father Johnstone shakes his head. "Never heard of it."

"I'm not surprised," she says. "You're a man of the cloth, a Christian. I'm sure your interests in other cultures were sparse, what with you having it right and all." Madeline pauses, allowing her jab to sink in.

"Continue," the pastor says.

"I want you to imagine that tree again, the one that represented all the people of Pratt," Madeline requests, receiving a nod from the pastor. She says, "Think about it, but in terms of faith this time. Just as Western religion has a limb and its many branches of Christianity and Catholicism and the like, so too do we. There's hundreds of them, existing all over the world."

When Father Johnstone was shown the spell books, every page was in a different handwriting, a different language. Dutch, Mandarin, Russian, English. Sometimes the script was nothing but symbols or drawings. Other times: the universal language of numbers, or 'numerology,' as Madeline said. The pages varied in age and author and origin, however, were always bound by the their common thread of belief. It didn't make sense to the pastor. It would be like taking pages out of the Bible and the Quran and the Torah and blending them together, shuffling their history, their views on God.

"There are many covens and tribes, all with their own views on Craft and rituals—the difference being that we're not battling over who's right. We're not going to war over who God loves most," Madeline points out. "We learn, we share. It's the reason why you never see us fighting amongst each other."

"Excluding right now, you mean," the pastor observes, returning the favor for Madeline's previous comment.

"Fair point, but you only know about that because I told you," she says. "Think about if I hadn't stepped in."

The ripple effect: first, the pastor is compromised. Then it spreads to the flock.

"At a very early age, we go over every religious war, every massacre, every line of slander," Madeline says. "That way, when our parents tell us to not draw attention to ourselves, we know exactly why. We're aware the consequences. I know you think of the Bible as a guide, but I grew up viewing it as a warning."

The pastor could counter, of course. He could throw out numbers regarding the Holocaust and World War II and all those desert skirmishes in the Middle East for the sake of *pride* and oil, but it wouldn't matter. Religion maintains the number one spot for why one man kills another. With so much blood soaking the ground on both sides, the word 'victory' becomes open to interpretation.

"Treat faith like a competition and there's going to be casualties," Madeline says. "All of us seemed to comprehend this. In our little community outside of Bend, we knew bad things happened if you drew outside the lines. It's why learning to hide in plain sight was so important."

"I take it he didn't feel that way," the pastor ventures. "Pollux."

"We followed the rules for a good while," she says. "I was seven; he was nine. He and I would learn the Craft together…and then a bit more." Madeline pauses, but only briefly. "It was easy with him. He was motivated. Ambitious, and that sort of generalized over to me," she says, a smile emerging. "Cute too. Very good-looking. For me it was like going to summer camp and having the most handsome guy in the place take you under their wing. He practically walked me through my first cast. Nothing big, mind you." Madeline downplays it, but there's obviously a sentiment of meaning there. The pastor can tell. "I wasn't a natural at it like he was, but being with him felt right. So we spent much of our time together: learning about ingredients— both the tangible and intangible, how to communicate with the earth, with each other. We studied and read about the deity of the Feri. In our community, this was more or less the standard for children until they came of age: learning the basics."

Like Madeline, Father Johnstone was shown the ways of higher powers: the creation of the earth, miracles, stories of sacrifice. The difference, he realizes, is that the concept was always predicated on faith. Always faith, never proof.

"My education went on like that for a few years: absorbing all that I could about the Feri and its traditions and rituals," Madeline says. "Our faith was different in that it was more integrated into daily life. We didn't learn math and English to become accountants or teachers; we learned it to be able to practice Craft. There was no school or day jobs or anything like that," she explains. "Just our little unit secluded out in the woods, learning and sharing. Thirty-six people in all, each with a task that they did for the community."

A living situation that was more prevalent in older cultures, the pastor recalls. One person to chop wood, one person to hunt, another to strip and prepare game. Each individual had exactly one task they did at a high level of proficiency, and thusly, shared that gift with the rest of their village or tribe.

"That's how I learned to bake," Madeline says. "My mother and I would spend hours cooking loaves of oat bread or dinner rolls. Sometimes we'd make a couple of pies. Pollux would usually stop by on those days wanting a piece," she recalls, smiling. "His specialty was field dressing. He tagged along with the hunters, and if they killed a deer or an elk, he was the guy that harvested the meat, hide, and everything else. And anything we weren't eating or using to keep warm, we were using for Craft."

Antlers were ground to a fine powder. Intestines were used for spell casings. Hearts always got planted in the earth, an homage to the goddess for blessing their people. These standards and practices of the Feri could all be found in the repository maintained by Josephine Paige.

"Growing up in the forest was nice. Everyone knew everyone. It was a family-friendly environment," she says. "I guess you could say it was a little bit like Pratt, but without all the gossip and smalltown bullshit."

"No pillars?" the pastor asks.

"Well, that's kind of where the problem began. No one was in charge. There was no established leader," Madeline says. "The Feri tradition was transcribed and taught to a core group of followers in the 1940s, but there was nothing to the effect of a priest or pope or anything like that."

Father Johnstone can see the problem already. A flock without a shepherd, regardless of their beliefs, will eventually self-destruct. They'll lose their way as a group or begin to turn on each other.

"That system worked fine for a while," Madeline says. "But when we came of age, things got complicated."

"What do you mean by that? 'Came of age'?" he asks.

"Each denomination of Craft has different beliefs and practices. Different gods. Different specialties and different ways of casting," she says. "Voodoo, which was created in 18th-century France, employed the usage of dolls as a method of cursing. Asian witches had a penchant for animal kinship, utilizing foxes and snakes as familiars. Our coven, the Feri, concentrated on the sensual experience."

'The sensual experience' meaning: eroticism. It means experimenting with the body for the sake of itself, usually under the guise of some spiritual connection. A pagan granola-nut pansexual orgy where fidelity means nothing, nor the bonds of marriage. Empty, meaningless fornication.

"So sex, then?" the pastor confirms, already dismissing the idea. A large part of him doesn't even want to listen to her response.

Madeline senses this, but presses on, saying, "The human orgasm is subjective, but often equated with nirvana, a state of zen or pure bliss. It is a non-thinking euphoric clarity, the absolute, and to be able to achieve it indicated a transition into adulthood, according to our scriptures."

"All due respect, it's a bit radical for my tastes," the pastor says.

Madeline smiles, though, giving Mary a little scratch behind the ear. She's patient with him, almost as if she knew the conversation would take this turn. "Is it really any more ridiculous than deeming a thirteen-year-old boy a man at a Bar Mitzvah?" she asks. "Or a Quinceañera? Or an Aboriginal walkabout?"

"It's celebrating *lust*, Mad."

"Difference of customs, Johnstone. People may think eating a Jesus cracker with some Christ juice is totally normal, but I find it rather silly." She throws a look at the pastor in the vein of a warning, telling him: *'we could argue about this all day.'*

"Then I guess we disagree here," he concedes.

"And it probably won't be the last time that happens," Madeline says, although not in a combative way. "Look, I don't need you to endorse it, but if you want to understand, I need you to at least see my perspective on things."

Part of the problem is what Madeline's saying, of course. 'The sensual experience,' as he puts it. He doesn't agree with it. Refuses to. Over three decades of preaching against that sort of behavior has made him a steely advocate for fidelity and chaste behavior, and it appears that Madeline understands this much. At the very least, she can empathize with the difficulty that he's having with this particular subject matter. It's too crude, too obscene. It explains much of what he saw in his dreams when Pollux was inside his head. What Father Johnstone is having an issue with is deciding: were those thoughts put there? Or were they cultivated from an already existing impurity? Both avenues frighten him in their own right.

"Much in the way he showed me the basics of Craft and walked me through the various histories, Pollux escorted me through the coming-of-age process," Madeline says. She pauses a moment, considering her phrasing for what she's about to say. "You have to understand that this is what we grew up in. It was normal for us," she explains. "Sensuality wasn't about frivolity. It was a blessing, an homage to the higher powers."

There's no argument from Father Johnstone's side of the living room this time, only a slight shake of the head. He remains quiet, despite himself.

"The human orgasm, like cane sugar or bee nectar or tree bark, is also an ingredient," Madeline says. "And Pollux was especially keen on experimenting with it. Your curse, for instance..." she trails off.

She doesn't need to finish her sentence. In fact, the pastor takes it as a sign of respect that Madeline spared him 'the gory details,' as it were. The science behind the formula eludes him still, but he assumes it functions the way that prayer does. Specific wording with specific intent. Sometimes a regular element is ordained with higher properties, such as the water used at a baptism or the cinder crosses bestowed to the flock on Ash Wednesday.

The priest will say: "Remember that thou art dust, and to dust thou shalt return," at which point, the clergyman bestows the symbol of the Lord upon the faithful.

It is within the power of any man of the cloth to ordain normal materials with Divine purpose. Wine and water, although commonplace, become the blood of the Savior when blessed. Perhaps, the pastor thinks, that ability exists within other branches of faith.

"In our teenage years, our education expanded well beyond

most of the individuals in our community," Madeline says. "We could do things they couldn't, and Pollux resented them for that...as if they were holding him back. 'Weak and unskilled,' he called them. He changed when his ability began to catch up with his potential. His thoughts on the matter were that the most powerful should lead, and because I loved and adored him, I didn't disagree with the idea."

Madeline admits this to the pastor, her tone noticeably dropping. He's seen this before, usually with members of the flock who are confessing their mistakes, their crimes. It's guilt, not necessarily from something Madeline did, but her failure to act.

"So one day Pollux tells the hunters that he won't be going with them...says it's a waste of his time, and he's not exactly polite about it," she explains. "You can probably guess that this didn't go over well. There were a lot of whispers about respect and one's obligation to the community. He and I both knew what everybody was saying, but he didn't seem to mind. He spent the day harvesting ingredients and poring over some books. We made love that afternoon...several times, actually, and he collected the sweat from my neck afterwards. 'Part of a surprise' he hinted, and I was too damn smitten to think anything bad would happen.

"The hunters came back that evening empty-handed," Madeline says. "They had been coming back empty-handed a lot, only now Pollux was calling them on it. He sort of rubbed it in their faces with his little 'I told you so' moment...gave them shit. That was the first time in a while people witnessed anything remotely resembling an argument. It just never happened," she says. "Our whole 'us against the world' mentality kept us civil towards each other, right up until that point. That's when he stated that the group needed a leader...that it had needed one for some years because the system was flawed. In front of everyone, Pollux said he would prove that he was the person to fill that role.

"The next morning, there were eighteen deer in our camp. All dead," Madeline says. "No wounds. Not a scratch on them. You would have thought they were sleeping if it weren't for their bodies being cold." She shakes her head remembering this, frowning. "Eighteen deer, all of them keeled over at the most central spot of our little village. Nobody heard or saw a thing, but they didn't really need to. They knew," she says. "They knew who did it and what it meant."

"Pollux," the pastor says.

"He came out that morning and took credit for what he had done, saying that this was merely one way in which he could provide. All he needed was their allegiance," Madeline explains. "He would make sure the Feri were protected and accommodated, but they had to accept him as Consort to the Goddess."

Father Johnstone stops Madeline at this point, asking, "Consort to the Goddess?"

"To put it in your terms, it'd be like you announcing to Pratt that you're the Second Coming," she says. "So as you can imagine, his decree wasn't exactly well-received."

From the Book of Matthew, the pastor would recite during his sermons: *'Watch out for false prophets. They come to you in sheep's clothing, but inwardly they are ferocious wolves.'*

He'd warn the flock of those who claim to have been touched by the Divine or perform miracles. Odd, the pastor thinks, that he himself is guilty of this. To share that similarity with Pollux unnerves him.

"We have a rule when it comes to killing animals: you don't use Craft," Madeline says. "And you definitely don't do it out of malice or to prove a point like Pollux did. It is intangibly negative."

"Intangibly negative, meaning: doing something with the wrong intentions, yes?" the pastor confirms.

"Correct. When you kill or cut down a tree or cast, you're

entering into an unwritten contract of sorts," Madeline explains. "The intent ultimately defines the relationship, like when a woman marries for money over love."

Vows are said, rings are exchanged, but when marital bond is made under the premise of *greed*, it is a tarnished matrimony. This too, is a method of living in sin. It is no better than adultery or having a child out of wedlock. Motive defines action.

"The Feri would not follow," Madeline says. "Pollux had broken a cardinal rule, and he had done so out of rancor. 'A grudge-killing,' people were calling it. He introduced violence into their sheltered lifestyle of sensual experience, and they were upset about it. He was asked to leave, and I was forced to go with him."

"Forced how?" the pastor asks.

"What nobody recognized right away was that all eighteen of the deer were male," Madeline says. "So whatever he buried in the ground was both highly toxic but also extremely alluring. So alluring that they could smell it over great distances."

"Pheromones," the pastor puts it together.

Madeline nods gravely. "He told me he cut some of mine into the mix to lure them to the camp, and that made me partly responsible."

"But you didn't know."

"Doesn't matter," she shakes her head. "When you grow up in a culture where you're taught that everything is an ingredient, you're accountable for the ones you give away."

"I'm not sure I follow," the pastor says.

"If you come to me with a gun and I supply you with a bullet—according to our beliefs—that makes me partly to blame for whomever you shoot," she says. "Those eighteen deer...some of that blood was on my hands. So I said goodbye to my parents and everyone else. I was sad, of course. It killed me to see my mom cry, but I think it would have been worse if I had stayed behind," Madeline says. "Despite how everything played out with the community, I still loved him very much."

"How?" the pastor asks.

"I wrote it off to his ambition getting the best of him, and he kept reassuring me that the community had been holding us back," she says. "I was seventeen and impressionable, so I ate every line he fed me. I played right into his 'let's see what's out there' bullshit, and what we found was temptation and excess and this newfound liberty of escaping a sheltered life," she says. "We weren't stepping out totally blind, but years of scare tactics had made us wary of people. Our 'hiding in plain sight' training kicked in, so we stayed low for a while and refrained from openly using Craft. During the day we'd walk around the city and observe. At night, we'd sleep in the park. He and I would huddle together under a blanket, dirty and cold and famished from moving around all day on little food. Our outward appearance got to be so bad that most people thought we were homeless. It got to the point where we couldn't go into the library and grocery stores without getting shooed away. Everyone we passed in the streets just sneered at us. This is when Pollux said to me, 'We need to do a better job at blending in,' and I knew he wasn't talking about getting jobs and joining society. His ambitions were far too great for that. It's what led him to betray the Feri in the first place.

"Escorting me through the city the next morning, Pollux told me that we needed money," Madeline says. "He pointed at a coffee shop, a bank, the dry cleaners. He pointed at all these different businesses and explained to me that every person that worked there had a specific skill or product they exchanged for monetary compensation. They would then take that compensation and apply it back to the system. 'Currently, we're outside of the cycle,' he said. This is when Pollux decided it was time to apply my skills. Now what do you think he meant by that, Johnstone?"

There are two by the pastor's count: baking and Craft, but

only the former would be deemed by modern society as useful. Madeline has never made a cookie, cake, or pie that was anything short of pure bliss. Any grocery store or bakery would be lucky to have her. His gut, however, is telling him this isn't how the story plays out.

"Sex," Madeline answers her own question. "Pollux took me to a strange building with blacked-out windows and told me what happened inside. 'The men go in and buy sex,' he said. 'Never women, always men.' It was your run-of-the-mill pornography store. So take one guess at what he was thinking."

"He turned you into a prostitute?" the pastor asks.

"I didn't think of it that way. Not really," Madeline says. "Like he said, I had a skill, and men would pay for that skill to be used upon them."

"What about breach of commitment? Infidelity?"

"The Feri don't subscribe to that. Monogamy conflicts with the sensual experience, and disagrees with human nature," Madeline says. "Marriage is an archaic system. As I'm sure you know, not every member of your flock is what you'd call 'faithful.'"

She's correct, of course. The pastor has often dealt with couples who've struggled with their marital commitments. That doesn't make it right, though. A vow, regardless of the degree of difficulty it poses, is still a vow. They're not meant to be taken lightly.

"So Pollux and I stood outside the shop for a while, observing," Madeline continues her story. "All men, like he said. Some married; some not. They'd go in, and then a short time later they'd emerge with a purple plastic bag...sometimes with magazines, sometimes with a video or two," she says. "We only had a vague idea of what a sex movie really was due to our upbringing, but it was easy enough to piece together. We could feel the consistency in them...that certain want."

Lust. The want she refers to is *lust.*

"You exploited their weakness, then," the pastor states. He finds himself shaking his head, already knowing the next turn the story will take.

"Yes," she says, absent of any shame. She's remorseless. "A man pulled up in a car, and he was just like all the rest we'd seen. He'd go into that store and browse a little, letting his eyes dance over the covers: blonde girls with heavy makeup, mouths provocatively open, begging to be penetrated. Or maybe he wanted a redhead. Or a brunette. Or maybe he wanted a girl like me, warm and real and able to respond to his needs.

"We approached him, the two of us," Madeline says. "He was cautious at first, but only until he realized how young we were, and it was clear that we hadn't been eating well. The man stopped halfway between his car and the shop, unsure if he should keep walking or offer us help or tell us to 'get lost.' That's when Pollux said he'd like to offer my services in exchange for money. And just like that, too," Madeline says. "'Would you like to purchase sexual favors from my companion for money?' was his exact phrasing, and the man looked at me again, but not with the same pity he had only moments ago. It was the same expression he had when his eyes were locked onto the shop, but now they were aimed at me. Then he started asking questions.

"The first thing he wanted to know is if we were cops, but I think he knew this was a stupid question. We didn't even look old enough to enter the store he was about to go into, so he went to the more logical question, asking if I was legal," Madeline says. "Legal, meaning: the age of eighteen or older. Not legal in the sense the Feri defined it, which is what Pollux responded to with a resounding 'yes.' Yet again, this guy looked me over, only now he was mentally weighing how much was in his wallet against how much he was willing to shell out."

"He finally asked how much it was going to cost him, and this is where Pollux sort of lost me. He said he needed a $100 bill. 'Not two fifties, not five twenties,' he said. A $100 dollar bill. He was firm about that part of the transaction, and the man had it, but first he wanted to know what he was getting in return for his money. 'A hundred bucks for a dirty girl like that is pushing it,' he told Pollux, paying me very little mind. At that point, he stopped looking at me like a person. When you know you can buy someone, it's okay to objectify them," Madeline says.

It's yet another maxim of the story the pastor disagrees with, and has even preached about during his sermons, but he retains his silence for the time being. Madeline continues.

"Pollux said a half minute sounded like a suitable exchange, but then the man started laughing at him. He laughed, asking how the hell anything was supposed to happen in half a minute. 'I can barely get my zipper down in that amount of time,'" Madeline imitates his voice. It has a sort of hick-like twang to it. "Pollux corrected him though, explaining that the climax itself would last a half a minute; not the actual encounter. And the man looked me over one more time, doubtful. It started to feel like a scam to him, just like most of the things our kind are able to do that people don't believe," Madeline gives the pastor a knowing wink.

"Then he closed him. Pollux said that if it didn't last the full thirty he wouldn't have to pay, and that's all he needed to hear." Madeline pauses briefly, taking a moment to consider how she wants to phrase the next part. "I got in the car and did what was expected of me. I'm guessing the logistics of that aren't important to you." She intentionally keeps this part vague—not for her own benefit so much as the pastor's. She doesn't want to offend him if she can help it. "The man lost consciousness so I took the money from his wallet. A $100 bill, just as we had agreed upon. There was plenty more there, but I left it."

"Dare I ask *why* he was unconscious?" the pastor cuts in.

"Everyone has a threshold, Johnstone. Physical, mental, chemical," she lists off. "Heroin, which comes from the opium plant, is tricky in that it's very easy to overdose on. One milligram too much and your breathing and heart rate slow down, eventually stopping altogether, depriving your brain of oxygen. You either slip into a coma or just plain die, all because you had a fraction more than your body can handle," Madeline explains. "Regarding our gentleman in the car, his threshold was about ten seconds. I took him past that and he couldn't take it."

Madeline frowns, looking down at Mary in her lap. "I gave the money to Pollux. He said our lives were about to change. He said this with the same expression he had back in the forest when he borrowed my pheromones for his spell...like he was up to something," Madeline hints. "He wanted a high denomination bill because he had taught himself how to clone money."

"You mean forge it?" Father Johnstone asks.

"No, I literally mean clone it," she confirms. "The paper had the same linen to cotton ratio. It had the same watermark signatures and color shifting ink, same off-center portraits. Same serial numbers."

"Craft?" the pastor asks.

"Right. But he wouldn't share it with me. It was the first time he had done that...said it was best if I let him worry about it," she says. "But currency, just like any composition, is made up of ingredients. If you can reverse-engineer something, chances are, you can make it yourself."

"And how much money was he making?" the pastor asks.

"Too much to carry," Madeline says. "Pollux didn't trust banks nor did he have the necessary documentation to start an account, so he kept everything in a storage facility. Piles of it, Johnstone. I'm talking millions. For about a month we were broke and dirty and sleeping under playground equipment in the park. Within twenty-four hours of getting that first $100, we were in a four-star hotel and eating filet mignon in Egyptian cotton bathrobes. We bribed staff members to bring us champagne and vodka and a bunch of other things people our age weren't legally supposed to have," Madeline recalls with a smirk. "We looked like a couple of stupid rich kids. *Literally* stupid," she says, absent of any shame. "We asked the concierge so many dumb questions. I swear, that woman probably thought we were retarded. 'How does a phone work?' 'What's the difference between shampoo and conditioner?'" Madeline quotes. "'Why are people sneaking into our room and cleaning it?'"

It hits the pastor that perhaps that was part of the Feri's plan, to make its residents so scared and unready for the outside world that they'd be terrified at the thought of departure. He's watched this same phenomenon play out in Pratt nearly all of his life. People rarely leave, and if they do, they don't wander very far.

"The money gave us a pass on a lot of things. Neither one of us could drive at the time, so we hired chauffeurs. We didn't have the credentials to get on a commercial plane, so we flew private," Madeline says. "Pollux got sick of having to go to the concierge every time he had a question—and he had a lot of them, mind you...so he hired one. If he wasn't cloning more money or buying shit, he was asking this woman what a McRib was or how a traffic light worked. It went on like that for about a year: we'd travel, see the sights, and soak in the culture. In each new city, I would go shopping with one of our employees while Pollux filled up another storage facility with cash. He had a bunch of them scattered throughout the country: New York, Vegas, Dallas. There must have been at least thirty or so."

Madeline sighs. "Now think about it, Johnstone: two kids with infinite resources and virtually no restrictions. No rules. No one telling us to stop." She asks, "What do you think happened?"

The pastor could rattle off another misremembered Bible quote about how money is the root of all evil, an axiom he very much agrees with, despite its origins. Instead, he chooses to put it in Madeline's terms, telling her, "I think you went past the threshold."

"The superiority complex kicked in again and he started

buying people," Madeline says. "It wasn't just limo drivers and information assistants anymore. He started booking whores...usually four or five at a time," she says, noticeably distraught about this part. "He'd have them sent up to the room and fuck them, or he'd sit at the foot of the bed and shout things for them to do to each other while he watched, and I must admit, it made me angry. I had given up my livelihood and my family for him, and in return, I got to witness him degrade all these women in the same bed we slept in."

"I thought you said you didn't believe in infidelity," the pastor reminds her, but not in a spiteful way.

"Whores are one thing. Sex is sex. I can understand that part of it," Madeline says. "This was torture though, like watching a kid pick the legs off an insect." She goes silent for a moment, appraising Father Johnstone's own mental threshold for what he can take. Respecting his virtuous nature is important to her, but equally important is his understanding of what threatens the town. Fortunately, the pastor makes the decision for her.

"If there's more to it you can tell me." He prepares himself for the worst. Now more than ever, he needs to learn to endure. He can't be coddled anymore.

"A curling iron can heat up to over 400 degrees Fahrenheit," Madeline says. "That means it can start burning your skin before your central nervous system tells you there's any pain. Even one second of contact and you're looking at a nice little blister," she says. "More sensitive skin, like the inside of your mouth, for instance—it will burn so intensely that the body will lose consciousness as a defense mechanism in the event of prolonged exposure. So imagine my surprise when I walk into the bedroom and see Pollux holding this curling iron. One whore is passed out in the bed...two others are crying and squealing," Madeline says. "He's holding this thing, and there's all these little pieces of meat sticking to the metal. Smoking and cooking...it smelled like charred pork. And this poor fucking girl, her cervix and labia had third degree burns and she was oozing some kind of pink fluid onto the sheets. Pollux was laughing…blood smeared all over his mouth and coating his teeth. He tells the other two whores he'll toss a million on the bed if they'll go down on her, pointing at the space between her legs with the curling iron. It looked boiled."

Father Johnstone feels his guts tighten, twisting. He leans forward in the chair, clamping his eyes shut and trying to hold down the vomit.

"Well, you get it." Madeline spares him. "There was no limit, no accountability. He could treat people however he wanted without consequences, and he took every conceivable advantage of that. Their *greed*, Johnstone, allowed him the kind of control he had been craving," she says. "It brought out the worst in him…made him sick."

"Did you leave?" the pastor asks, assuming this is the next logical turn.

"Not yet. Not at that exact moment, no." Madeline frowns again. "I loved him, I'd known him for most of my life, and I wasn't ready to throw that away. There was an attempt on my part to convey that things had gotten out of hand, that we had all but turned our backs on the Feri and its traditions. Apparently, this was the wrong thing to say to him," she says with misgiving. "He snapped. Beat me up. Raped me, and not a soul stepped in to help. They didn't want to lose their meal ticket. That's how powerful *greed* can be."

Madeline says, "Hours later, I woke up in a different hotel room with seventeen stitches and a couple separated ribs. Broken nose. One of my eyes was swollen shut." A tear falls, sliding off her face into Mary's fur, still coiled in Madeline's lap below. "He hired a private doctor to come and patch me up. None of the other girls got that, so I guess I should consider myself lucky. The damage had been done, though. In our community out in the woods, we didn't really have any concept of sin, y'know. It wasn't like here," Madeline makes a small circular motion with her finger. "We had an understanding, and we thrived on the ideals of peace, community, and love. To go against that, to either murder or rape, brought darkness upon a person in a way that can't be reversed. They become damned in the eyes of the Goddess. Like your Christian diety, she also has a threshold for what she's willing to tolerate. She *too* can be vengeful," Madeline says. "In a faith predicated on the sensual experience, rape is blasphemous. I believe you would equate it with eternal sin."

Also known as the unforgiveable sin or the unpardonable sin, it is the instance in which one speaks blasphemy against Holy Spirit. They are, therefore, unable to be absolved and beyond repentance.

"What kind of reprisals does that entail?" he asks. "Hell?"

"Not in the way you're thinking of it, with the fire and brimstone. Not like that," Madeline says. "Our understanding is that the crimes you commit on earth are paid for on earth."

"You don't sound sure."

"Well, I'm not," she says. "After the incident in the hotel, I took off. I was done. No way was I sticking around to see what happened next."

"Back to the community?"

"No." Madeline shakes her head. "I knew I wouldn't be allowed back, plus, I didn't put it past Pollux to try and track me down. The last thing I wanted to do was lead him back to the people I cared about," she explains. "I limped out of Vegas broken and beat the hell up and got on a Greyhound. Didn't even know where it was going—I just needed to get away, y'know. So I rode on this thing for about a day or two, mostly just sleeping and trying to recover. I ended up in Kansas City and remembered that Pollux had one of his storage facilities there. Thought I'd be clever and break into it, but it was too late."

"What? He emptied it?" the pastor asks.

"Not exactly. Took me about three hours to pick that lock.

Magnetism is a bitch if you're not used to it," she says. "Tips of my fingers were numb and bleeding by the time I managed to pop the thing open."

"Probably worth the effort though."

"Would have been if it still contained any money," Madeline says. "When I opened that storage facility it was nothing but ash in there. Reeked of sulfur. The money had died, in a sense. This is when I knew there were consequences for what he had done. Now that he had fallen out of favor with the Goddess, his abilities had been compromised."

"Why not revoked completely?" the pastor asks.

"I imagine he discovered the same thing I did," she says. "After I found out the storage facility was a bust, I wandered out to the country. I felt safer in that environment. The problem was that I was still in bad shape. I was coughing up blood. Some nights I couldn't even sleep the pain in my ribs was so bad, and that's right around the time I came across my first faith healer," Madeline says, giving a small smile. "A priest and his assistant going from town to town, putting on a show. In this little vinyl tent filled with folding chairs, I watched them cure a kid with a bad kidney, a cripple, a burn victim. The priest performed his 'miracles' and the audience paid their money. Of course, I was the only one who saw the assistant for what she really was, and I noticed her eyes kept drifting towards me. It was like we knew each other even though we'd never met. She healed me, taught me about the branches and how they can work to compliment each other," Madeline says. "The same way there's multiple faiths, the same holds true for Craft. You can cross-pollinate, so to speak."

"How is that even possible, though?" the pastor asks.

"Faith, Johnstone. Faith is an extremely powerful ingredient," Madeline says. "It's why the flock has followed you all these years without an ounce of proof, and it's also why I've gone from levitating silverware to deflecting bullets. It's the reason I can fully revive things instead of just healing them." She sighs, smiles bravely. Madeline stares intently at the pastor, telling him, "You are the reason I haven't run off again."

"You mean from him?"

"Yes. He has a knack for finding me," she says. "Doesn't matter where. I go to a small town in Missouri, and two months later an EF5 tornado rips the town apart. I go to New York. Not even a few weeks go by and a hurricane hits."

Plagues, the pastor thinks.

"Droughts, landslides, earthquakes," Madeline ticks off on her fingers. "It took me a while to figure out, but when he comes, disaster comes along with him. People get hurt, they die, and I'm partly responsible for that."

"And it's happening again," the pastor says, remembering the bees, the moths. From dust they came; to dust they returned.

"I'm not running off this time though. I'm done with that." Madeline looks at the pastor expectantly, as if she's waiting for him to formally declare his alliance.

Sympathetic to her plight though he may be, Father Johnstone is thinking about himself at the moment. He nearly lost himself, and the flock found themselves in a state of disarray because of it. As much as he'd like to defer the problem and get Pratt back to the way it was, he can't have that hanging over his head. He can't allow Pollux to leave town only to repeat what he's done in a different location. As Madeline would say, that would make the pastor partly responsible.

"What can I do to help?" Father Johnstone asks.

Madeline bites her lips, smiles bashfully.

"I need a virgin," she says.

On the Road with Billy Burke, Truck Stop Preacher

"Keep the Lord in your mind and your heart. At all times—keep him the fuck in there. The Lord is your weapon, more powerful than any handgun, grenade, or nuke. If you are a fat disgusting fuck driving by a Wendy's—the Lord is what keeps you from ordering that Baconator. When some lot lizard is pounding on the door of your rig so she can suck your dick for a beer—the Lord gives you the strength to stick a boot in her face...and if that meth hooker gets up, you use the Lord to kick that crusty cunt right in her pie hole again. The Lord heals. He heals your gout and your shingles and anal fissures. He heals your anger. We've all got anger, don't we, gentlemen? You can pray all you want...don't mean some prick ain't gonna come along and drop a big ol' steamer in your life. When some cop pulls you over for some bullshit or the president fucks with your health care—that's just Satan taking a shit in his hand and throwing it at you...like a goddamn monkey. He's an animal. Only animals shit in their hands and chuck it. And how do we react to that? Are we supposed to just let the shit drip down our faces and turn the other cheek? There's a time for that. Ol' Billy Burke has done his fair share of walking away, I can assure you. But there's also another side to God...a vengeful side. We—as men that walk the Divine path—we need the Lord to tell us when that time is...and I just so happen to know. I've communed with the Lord...and He told me, 'Billy, you need to round up your flock, and you need to torch that mosque where all the terrorists plot against Uncle Sam on the magic carpets. Then you need to piss on the ashes. You and your boys need to show them America don't take no shit.' Those were His orders. Now, I don't know about you, but ol' Billy Burke don't pass up an opportunity to serve the Lord. So I ask you...any of you boys hauling some gas you can spare?"

The First Tribute

Anxiety mounts within Father Johnstone, the fear that another one of Pratt's residents will emerge from the shadows to finish the job that old man Clevenger couldn't. They could come from anywhere. At any time. They could strike him down on the very sidewalk he tours now. The pastor can finally relate to the paranoia that triggered all those witch-hunts of the past. It almost justifies why the clergy acted so irrationally. Madeline, of course, can sense the pastor's turmoil beyond his tense body language. It's one of her gifts.

"Nothing's going to happen. You can relax," she says covertly out the side of her mouth. Madeline smiles and offers a salutation to Mr. and Mrs. Bellow, who are currently drinking iced sweet tea out of jam jars on their porch. "Try to act normal," she whispers, waving off an invite to join the Bellows for a glass with an apologetic hand. "We'll take a rain check," she shouts up to them. Again, smiling. Pretending everything's fine. It's all part of hiding in plain sight.

"I *am* acting normal." The pastor keeps his head on a swivel, searching for another pistol or a sawed-off shotgun aimed his way. He checks over his shoulder to make sure they're not being followed, eyes darting to the blind spots, bushes, and dark corners—hiding places. "I'm trying," he amends.

"You've got the aura of an electric fence right now. Stop thinking everyone's going to shoot at you." Madeline pulls a sleeve up on her brown leather jacket, exposing an arm. Every strand is raised off the skin, saluting, as if it's just been massaged by a circus balloon. "See that? You're making my hair stand up."

"I'm not meaning to do it. Honestly." It's just like all those times the pastor's had to go to Dr. Keller for a flu shot: how the pain receptors would bunch up around the injection point like a beehive in his skin. His entire person is buzzing, sensing harm in every direction.

"It's broad daylight," Madeline says. "We're walking through a populated area and half the town is out enjoying the rest of the weekend." Yet again, Madeline gives a smile and wave, this time to William Hicks and his three boys who are playing horseshoes out on their front lawn. They briefly pause to acknowledge her, tipping their hats in turn. "No one is going to attack you under these circumstances, especially with Mary around."

Father Johnstone lets his eyes drift down to the little Yorkshire terrier taking the lead in front of them. Mary jogs along energetically, sometimes stopping to sniff plots of Bermuda grass or a nearby elm, as if she's checking for clues rather than a desirable spot to urinate.

"What's Mary got to do with anything?"

"Dogs have their own set of abilities," Madeline says. "You and I only have five scent receptors; Mary has over a hundred million. It's why she was able to sniff out that curse in your yard through all that dirt," she explains. "I'm having her scout the area for us. Believe me, if something's funny she's going to know long before we do, so relax, okay?"

The pastor walks along, attempting to follow Madeline's advice. "I'm still not sure why you don't want to check in with Kurt at the hospital. Seems like he might know something we could use."

"I guarantee you he doesn't. Even sober, that guy was of no use," she says. "And I'm not exactly keen on the idea of taking you back to the guy that tried to kill you."

"He wasn't responsible for his actions," the pastor reminds her. "You know that."

"Just like you weren't, Johnstone. I know. I get it," she says, slightly exasperated. "You're Mr. Morals, and that's really great and all, but the clock is ticking here. You need to focus on the larger problem."

Madeline warned him about this before, that there were going to be occasions in which the difficult choice would have to be made. As much as he doesn't want to, Father Johnstone is compromising, and he suspects it's not going to be the last time.

"I promise we'll sort everything out once this is over," Madeline says. "But right now we need to focus on Travis Durphy."

"I don't mean this to sound rude," Father Johnstone says. "But are you going to try to sleep with him? Because I really can't endorse that."

Madeline hasn't been entirely transparent with her plans thus far, vaguely citing how this 'needs to be done' and it's their 'best option.' Time constraints being what they are, the pair of them really can't afford to go on a virgin hunt around Pratt. All Madeline said was that Travis Durphy would be serving as 'a tribute.' Nothing more. She won't even share the contents of the satchel that's slung around her shoulder.

"No, Johnstone, I'm not gonna sleep with him. Geez!" Madeline groans. "I'm not into guys that chew, anyway. It's like kissing a wet cigarette. It's disgusting."

"Then what do you want with him?"

"I want what you want," she says, yet again, vague. "Look, if it makes you feel any better, we're not going to be breaking any of your little rules."

"They're not mine. They're God's," he says.

"You know what I meant," she waves him off. "Nothing is going to happen that you wouldn't be okay with."

Father Johnstone prays: for their safety. He asks the Lord to protect them from those that would wish them harm. Most of all, he prays neither he nor Mary ever have to endure another experience like the one out in the fields. May God spare them both having to go through that kind of pain again. May God spare Travis whatever trials he's about to endure.

"I can feel that, too," Madeline mentions, looking left to the pastor who's walking alongside her. She throws a knowing smirk his way.

"Feel what?"

"That Holy insurance policy you're taking out," Madeline says. "Don't worry. Travis is going to be fine."

Durphy Ranch—or 'Danger' Ranch, as it's informally known—lies on the outskirts of Pratt on a half acre of land, a ten-minute walk from Madeline's place out by the daisy hill. It consists of small barn, horse stable, and the main residence, which is a small three-bedroom. Its main attraction, however, is the makeshift bullring that Travis's father had built back when he was on the circuit. Heavy wood planks reinforced with steel framing. "Enough to hold ten of these angry bastards," he used to say. An entire summer was spent by himself and his crew of volunteers, usually on weekends under the skin-peeling heat. Once it was constructed though, Durphy Ranch became a resident hot spot for beer, barbeque, and best of all, bull riding.

Going to work on Monday mornings with cuts and bruises meant one of two things: either you got into a tussle *or* you got thrown off and ripped to shit by Brisket, the Durphy family bull (*God rest his soul*). Men wore those wounds like badges of honor, more proud of those than any tattoo or barroom bottle scars they'd acquired. Up until Danger died, Durphy ranch was the proverbial hot spot in town.

As the trio approach, Father Johnstone offers a wave to Travis, who is currently working on a lawnmower out in his driveway. He's glazed in sweat, wearing jeans splattered in white fence paint and an old undershirt with holes in it. A mixture of confusion and pleasant surprise cross his face, but Mary plays her part of the ambassador well. She sprints to Travis, licking his oil-stained fingers and bouncing on her hind legs happily. It seems to convey the message well enough that Madeleine and the pastor mean no harm.

Travis finds his feet, cleaning his hands off with an old rag. He says, "Quite the sermon today, preacher. Didn't know you had it in ya. Whole town's talkin' about it."

Father Johnstone is unsure how to respond. He decides to avoid the topic entirely, hoping that Travis will simply think he's being humble. "Have you met Madeline Paige?" he asks, making the introduction.

"Not formally, no," Travis says, displaying his hands. They're still caked in oil and motor grease. He fumbles with the rag a bit before tossing it on top of the mower. "I'd shake but I don't want to make a mess outta you."

"It's fine," she says, turning on that campfire smile, the warm eyes. "Our own fault for coming over unannounced, I'd say."

"Not a problem, Miss Paige," Travis says. "I think the missus has a new batch of cider whipped up if y'all are thirsty," he offers, looking to Madeline then the pastor, gauging their interest.

"I'm okay," the pastor politely declines. "Madeline?"

"Oh, me? No, I'm good," she shakes her head.

"Sure? It's really no trouble," Travis says. "But I dare say Heather might try to get a recipe or two outta ya, Miss Paige," he warns her with a smile. "I heard you're quite a talent in the kitchen."

"Oh, Mr. Durphy," Madeline laughs girlishly, bringing her palm—the burned one—to her chest. "You have no idea."

"Was looking forward to trying some of your dessert at the bake-off. Damn shame about what happened." He cranks his head off to the left to spit, wiping the chaw juice off his chin with a bare arm. "Heather and I, we prayed for you," he tells the pastor. "Looks like the Lord gave you a little more than your health back though, I suspect," he says, once again attempting to breach the subject of this morning. Travis and his wife were there; they witnessed the miracles for themselves. Now he's searching for the explanation.

"Indeed," the pastor says. "My situation has improved."

"You will understand if our good pastor isn't exactly talkative about the matter," Madeline interjects. "Rumor mills, Travis. It'd be a great disservice if people tried to turn this into some kind of scandal."

"I hear ya," Travis says. "Not into the gossip myself. Had a scandal or two of my own I've had to deal with."

He could be referring to a few things: his father gone too soon and the alcoholic widow he left behind, the weight of following in the footsteps of Danger, or perhaps all the salon talk about his little problem in the bedroom.

Tragedy and faded glory. Wasted potential. This what people think of when the Durphy name is mentioned, and Travis has lived with it most of his life. People aren't exactly chastising him and spitting on his boots, but he's smart enough to know when he's being talked about. Rumor thickens the air.

"So what brings the two of you out here?" Travis asks, launching another rope of chew spit to the gravel and dirt at his feet. Madeline flinches at the sight of it, repulsed. "Figured you'd be—I don't know—celebrating, I guess." It comes out sounding like a question.

"No, I'm afraid there won't be any of that just yet," Madeline says. "We're here on business."

"And what business might you have with me?" Travis asks, although he gives the pastor a shifty look, wondering if their confidentiality has been broken. "You thinkin' of casting another one of them miracles?"

It bothers the pastor hearing that word, even in a joking sense; the word 'casting.'

"No, Mr. Durphy," Madeline smiles, attempting to ease the tension. "We come to solicit your services, if you'd be so willing."

"You wantin' the ring?" Travis nods his head into the distance where Danger's bull-riding arena stands, which is now a liability of splintered wood and rusted metal. That hasn't stopped him from renting it out, though, mostly to kids in their late teens trying to make it out of Pratt the way Danger almost did. The Durphy name allows Travis to do this without Sheriff Morgan getting on his back about permits and the like.

"We're actually wanting you to judge," Madeline says, surprising both the pastor and Travis. "In light of Mrs. Tiller's health problems—you heard about it, of course, yes?"

"Yep." Travis nods.

"Well, I'm going to be helping out a bit," Madeline says. "Y'know, balancing the books and *hopefully*, should we get enough people again, organizing another bake-off," she explains. "Getting the food never seems to be the problem, though. It's the judges. Father Johnstone thinks it's best if he sits this one out, ain't that right?"

She's not helping out with the books nor are there any plans to arrange a bake-off, and considering the conversation they just had, the timing couldn't be worse for an event. Pratt is under a plague. He's seen that with his own eyes.

"There is a condition, though," Madeline says, not waiting for Father Johnstone's affirmation. A hand reaches inside the leather satchel she has around her torso, removing a small white take-out box with folds on the top. She peels it open, revealing a small dessert: a cupcake emanating cinnamon and cocoa, overtaking the smell of cow shit and dust hanging in the air. "We need to see if you can do the job," Madeline says to Travis mock-seriously before breaking into a smile. The campfire smile that no man can resist. She lifts the box upwards slightly, offering it to him. "Take a bite and tell me what you think."

It is the third time that Father Johnstone has seen Madeline do something of this nature. Mrs. Tiller was manipulated for the sake of keeping the pastor's name intact. 'A necessary evil,' she would say. Then there was Sheriff Morgan, the would-be assailant (and possible rapist) in hero's clothing. He'll be walking that lonely interstate road by now, blood and blister juice flooding his boots. Starving and dehydrated and wincing with every step.

Travis Durphy will be the third to experience the reticent

powers of Miss Madeline Paige. Oil-black fingers reach towards the take-out box, pinching off a sample of the dessert and placing it in his mouth. His jaw churns. Curse fluid enters his system, soaking into the bloodstream and swimming to his frontal lobe where it begins to go to work, altering chemicals and synaptic firing. It changes Travis Durphy's decision-making and behavior. It bends his emotions. His trepidation slips and he can't remember why he's eating, only that what he's consuming is good. He likes the flavor, the texture, how it makes him *not* feel and *not* think. For the first time in a while, Travis doesn't feel like the son of his father. He's beyond, outside himself.

"What are you doing to him?" Father Johnstone asks.

"*We,*" she corrects him. "I keep telling you this is a two-person gig."

"He looks brain-dead." Father Johnstone remarks on Travis's slack face, the glazed-over eyes staring off into the middle distance.

"Technically, he kinda is," Madeline says. "He's not thinking. Unlike the sheriff, he's not resisting it." To Travis, she says, "Feeling okay there?"

"Hmm, just peachy, Miss Paige…like I ain't got a care in the world," he says dreamily.

"See? Told you he'd be fine," Madeline says.

The pastor takes a moment to observe Travis, the facial expression he's currently wearing that's akin to a happy drunk. "So what are *we* doing here then?" he asks.

Madeline says, "We're here to finish the job you couldn't." She folds the tabs of the take-out box back up and stows it away in the leather satchel. "Paying tribute," she tells him. "You came to Father Johnstone with a problem recently, didn't you, Travis?"

"Yes ma'am, I sure did," he says, although the words come out slurred. Something's muffling him.

"Spit the chew out," Madeline says. "In fact, I don't ever want you to chew again. You got that, Travis? No more chew *ever*. It's gross."

"Yes ma'am, Miss Paige," Travis says. He hocks out the wad of dip, swiping his tongue in the space between his lip and bottom row of teeth, cleaning it out and spitting a final rope of yellow chaw juice. "Not gonna plug no more, ma'am. Never again."

"It's just that easy," Madeline says to the pastor. "We can make a sheriff give up his gun or have ol' Travis here kick his dipping habit cold turkey. We can even access memory and alter it, if we so choose. You can understand why the clergy were on edge about us," Madeline says. "Nobody likes having their decisions made for them."

"And are we choosing to do that with Travis?" the pastor asks. "Besides kicking bad habits."

"The same way we can remove lung cancer or arterial plaque, we can remove other things, too. Things that aren't tangible," she says, turning away from the pastor. "What happened when you came to Father Johnstone with your problem, Travis?"

"I told the preacher I wanna do my duty as a husband. Told him I need to consummate my marriage to make it right in the eyes of God and the church," Travis says. "He got cold on me. His soul went dark and he talked to me in a way I ain't ever heard."

Father Johnstone recalls his meeting with Travis, however, not this particular section of conversation to which he refers. It's blank, washed over by the thoughts of someone else.

"He told me I need to fuck my wife like the Devil himself was inside of him," Travis says. "Told me my daddy fucked all these women behind my mama's back...made them scream the Lord's name so loud they heard it up in heaven. He said I'd never be half of what Danger was until I did that, and he had a mean smile on him, the preacher did. Grinnin' like a coon over a fish carcass, Miss Paige."

"I don't remember any of that," Father Johnstone says.

"He's not capable of telling anything other than the truth right now," she says. "It came out of your mouth. That's all he knows.

Right, Travis?" she asks.

"Oh yes indeed, Miss Paige. Those are the words the preacher said—no mistakin' it," Travis declares, giving his head a little shake. "No mistakin' it *at all*," he says. "Then he told me that if I didn't screw my wife, someone else might just step in and do it for me. Hintin' at it like he was gonna do it himself. That's when I walked out."

Madeline turns to the pastor, bending towards his ear, she whispers, "Pollux."

Then Travis keeps talking, admitting, "I was gonna hurt you today, preacher. Had my knife in my pocket and everything. Was ready to cut you up for what you said."

Madeline finds this particular confession interesting, considering she didn't ask for it. She turns back to Travis, asking him, "And why didn't you hurt him?"

"That's a man of God, right there, Maddy Paige. Half the town is worried they ain't getting into heaven because of what they intended to do to him today, myself included."

"And the other half?" Madeline asks.

"Think he's a charlatan. A trickster," Travis says. "They say he's pulling the wool over our eyes somehow with his miracles. People want to know why ol' preacher here waited so long to help the cripples and such if he in so good with God."

It's just like the pastor has been preaching for years: *'beware of false prophets.'*

"There's something funny in the air," Travis says. "A disruption. People can feel it but they don't wanna say nothing about it. Too scared."

"And what do you know about fear, Travis?" Madeline asks.

"It consumes every bit of me, Miss Paige. I could never ride the bull like my pop wanted," Travis says. "Could never live up to what he was. I feel him lookin' down on me shaking his head like he wish he never had a son. All I did was wreck the name."

"Who put the idea in your head that you had to live up to

what your father was?"

"Preacher did," Travis says, tilting his head in Father Johnstone's direction. "He said that he lives on through me...that I carry the torch."

The pastor can see the big picture now: a child that sees his father killed right in front of him, left traumatized and fatherless. He latches on to the next best thing, told that he can follow in Danger's impossible footsteps. He's told he can defeat the very thing that truncated one parent's life and left the other a drunken mess. Travis was told the Durphy name depended on him, and he believed it. *Envious* of his father, driven by the *pride* of the name.

"You asked me why we're here, Johnstone, and now I'm going to tell you," Madeline says, shifting away from Travis and facing the pastor now. She sighs deeply, telling him, "We're here to fix this man. Granted, he's not crippled or blind or suffering from brain parasites, but he's broken just the same."

"And what can I do about it?" Father Johnstone asks. He knows the blame is being placed on him, even if she's not directly stating it.

"We'll clean house. The amygdale, which is part of the limbic system, is the primary component in processing emotion," Madeline says, extending her hand out towards the pastor. She places the other one on the face of Travis Durphy, palming his forehead like she's taking his temperature. "I'm going disable that part of the brain that overwhelms him with fear and anxiety, and you're going to help me do it."

"And why are we doing this?" the pastor asks.

"Hey Durphy," Madeline says, "Johnstone wants to know why he should help take the fear out of you. Got anything to say?"

"Cos I prayed for it, Miss Paige. Every night I pray the Lord come give me strength and make me the man everyone thinks I should be," Travis says. "I pray just like preacher tell me to, and nothing happens."

Madeline cocks an eyebrow at the pastor, wiggling the fingers on her still-extended hand. She says, "Grab on."

Father Johnstone does, folding his hand into Madeline's. It's warm, and he can feel that buzzing sensation again. His palm and fingers tingle hot, almost burning.

"Now pray," Madeline says, palm still pressed to Travis's forehead. She shuts her eyes and leans in close to him, preparing herself to go to work. "If we screw this up, you'll be burying another member of the Durphy family."

Las Vegas, NV

I had it wrong.

Every experiment involving Christian lingerie and church candles and the various excerpts and materials harvested from those religious texts — they were never going to work. No combination would yield the intended result. No whore would be spared my disease, nor would I ever be able to remedy it under my own accord. Prayer would fail. Confession would fail. As the clergyman stated, I had been viewing the faith incorrectly the entire time. It's not a skill, not exactly. It's a partnership.

"It's nice to meet you," I address the priest, a young Catholic man by the name of Father Wainwright. He's potent. I can tell. "My name is Pollux," I say.

I've gone by many names during my time in Las Vegas: Mr. Thomas, Mr. Ross, Mr. Smith. Changing identities was a means to justify the end of hiding in plain sight, blending in, but I have nothing to fear anymore. I'll be departing from this place they call 'Sin City' soon enough. The individuals running the sex trade have become wise to me, my reputation, and the rumors have spread well beyond Sasha and Desiree, as has the disease. 'Pure evil,' they refer to me as. 'A walking plague.' These men send their muscle to look for me at Caesar's. They go room-to-room at The Four Seasons and The Bellagio, bribing front desk clerks for information, banging on doors. My picture is printed off from security camera footage and distributed. Gigantic men study it, fold it up into quarters, and continue the search at Excalibur, Luxor, and Treasure Island. They carry guns now. After what happened with Desiree's personal detail, I'm now considered 'extremely dangerous.' Up until recently, they were only partially correct about that.

"I'm going to test your faith," I explain to Father Wainwright. He frowns in response; it can only be seen in wrinkles through the duct tape. After the third or fourth clergyman, I became tired of hearing them scream for help, hence, the tape.

Like the sex-trade workers and underbosses of Las Vegas, the hotel and casino staff have also become wary of me. They too have their own little print-outs and security footage. On the game floors I extort them for money. Exact amounts remain unclear, but it's definitely in the realm of several million. For a while they simply tried to win their money back, but no matter how many times they swapped decks or changed out the dealers, they failed to deduce my non-mathematical system of winning. This, along with the various reports and complaints about my behavior—both from guests and staff members—has severely tarnished my reputation in the city. 'The cheat,' they call me. 'The whore killer' and 'organ collector.' Even the lesser venues such as the Golden Nugget and Four Queens had me removed from the premises within minutes. Reading the intangibles aren't necessary at this point; the city is done with me. They want me captured, killed.

It's why Father Wainwright and I must continue the endeavor here: a shoddy hotel room which charges by the hour. No security cameras. No room service or on-call staff to cater to my whims. Sex permeates the air, as does the fumes of the marijuana plant and other chemical compounds. Harsher substances such as crack and methamphetamine. Their scent sticks to the walls, impregnates the ceiling and lighting fixtures. Father Wainwright and I notice this. The whore sprawled out on the bed does not.

"Heroin," I explain to him. "A formidable narcotic. We're going to see if we can get this poison out of her system."

I place one hand on the priest; the other I lay upon the whore. She is currently in the middle of what's referred to as 'an overdose,' the point in which the body's natural threshold for substance has been surpassed. Her body convulses, shakes. This was done intentionally.

"She's going to die if you don't help me," I say. "So focus. Pray. Otherwise, I'm going to leave you in the room with her corpse, understand? I'll knock you out and put you in bed with her. I imagine that'd hurt your reputation, yes?"

Father Wainwright doesn't nod or grunt in the affirmative, but I feel his comprehension, his desperation. I feel him reaching out to the

Lord for assistance, silently begging for help, and then the Lord reaches back. Warmth courses through his hand into me, then into the whore. It's channeled, refined, and not a moment later, manifesting at the entry point of the whore's arm. Narcotics and blood bead, growing larger until it's leaking down and around her arm and onto the stained comforter. Shaking lessens, then stops. The whore stabilizes and the many wounds of past indulgences heal to scars.

I break contact with the priest, checking the whore's breathing and heartbeat. Fingers press into her neck, gauging a healthy pulse. She's no longer slipping away, but she's not conscious, either. It's the fringe. The gray area. Death grazed her but couldn't hold on.

"You did well, Father Wainwright," I say, turning back to him in his chair next to the bed.

He's aged roughly thirty years in under a minute. Bones have gone stale, brittle like classroom chalk. Skin resembles notebook paper that's been crumpled and spread flat, in both texture and pallor. Father Wainwright is yet another in a short line of clergymen that this has happened to, a side-effect that can only be described as 'hyper-aging.' With the aid of these men, I am able to perform Craft, but it's not without cost. Either they forfeit years of their life during the cast, or the cast itself somehow backfires, usually in the form of intense pain in the extremity or a debilitating headache.

I peel the tape off the priest's mouth. He's not going to scream. Not when his vocal chords feel like wood for kindling. Father Wainwright smiles, tears building in glazed eyes. "I'm going home soon," he says in barely above a whisper.

As the light inside another man of the cloth dims, I realize that this is no longer an issue of personal skill or knowledge of Craft. It's now a task of finding the right person to be by my side, my equal. I've abducted enough of their kind to learn that much. If I wish to take my Madeline back, the individual I seek must correspond with my spirit and personal inclinations. He must be a willing advocate.

Laying my hand on that of Father Wainwright, I utilize the last of his earthly life to request a beacon, to give me guidance. A destination.

Unlike Madeline, there are no tracks to follow, no scent to lead me. The hunter cannot hunt the unknown, and so I must put my faith in the hands of the deity. A path must be provided by the Divine.

"Elk City," Father Wainwright says.

Those are his final words.

The Fire

Travis Durphy is fucking.

Inside his ranch-style home, high-pitched screams emit as Heather Durphy gets slammed by her husband in a way she never thought he was capable of. Almost violently. Bent over the kitchen counter, on the living room couch, against the wall where family photos shake loose and fall to the floor from all the pounding. Travis plugs her—fucks her, his prick stabs so deep it's practically in her guts. Heather feels what the gals at the salon call 'the good hurt,' when it's been so long since you've had a proper lay it's painful. Painful, yet gratifying. And so long overdue. Heather screams and groans, her mouth skip-repeating "Ohmygodohmygodohmygod" while her husband pummels her against the refrigerator, her entire body hot except for that one rosy cheek pancaked against the cool appliance. She's covered in sweat and motor oil. Travis didn't wash his hands or speak a word before jumping her bones, so now Heather's breasts and ass are covered in smudgy black handprints. Her hips reek of lawnmower grease. The Durphys have at each other—kissing, fucking, squeezing, biting, screaming, coming—they come at the same time in the master bedroom, the guest bedroom, that little space between the toilet and the shower. Travis injects hot white orgasm inside his wife, so much it creams out, leaking down her thighs while he's still pulsating. They fuck, come, fuck again. For hours the Durphys do this, regressing back to teenage years where energy is ample and foresight is lacking. They're living in the now, the moment. Within this typically quiet ranch-style home, sweat spots stain the walls and faux wood siding. Warm micro-puddles brand the couch cushions and bedding and the rust-colored shag carpet of the living room. And all along their bodies are scratches and cuts from fingernails or the sharp edges of the coffee table. Travis Durphy lifts up his wife against a wall, one ass cheek per palm, and pounds her—fucks her so hard the drywall gives and makes a torso-sized crater in the hallway. Then Heather gets on top, riding her husband on debris and paint chips, caking her knees in dust rubble. Sweat and hairspray trickle down her face, tracing along her cheekbones and jaw, dripping, smacking on Travis's chest. The Durphy's consume each other until their muscles ache and throats go hoarse, until they go past the threshold: sore, spent and exhausted, but happy.

"This is how we pay tribute," Madeline says, walking back from the outskirts of the Durphy's property to the main population of Pratt. Father Johnstone paces along at her side while Mary scouts on ahead, sniffing plumes of grass and random footprints left in the dirt. Her nose hovers over a bouquet of stomped-on dandelions, taking a few inquisitive snorts before she moves on to another area of interest.

"It wouldn't have killed you to be a little more upfront about your plans," the pastor says. He shakes his head slightly, unsure as to whether or not he should feel some sort of shame over what he just help Madeline achieve. One might even say his recent actions are that of a disloyal servant, a traitor to the good Lord and his faith.

"You really think I can't feel that remorse coming off you right now?" she asks. "I'm fighting decades of Christian programming here, Johnstone. You and I both know you wouldn't have gone along with it." Madeline drags her fingers along her forehead, swiping the hair out of her eyes and tucking it behind an ear. She says, "Trust me, in some scenarios, the less you know the better."

"That's the problem, Mad," he says. "I was there and I'm still not exactly sure what happened."

Madeline's palm was on Travis's head, her other hand interlocked with the pastor's. He prayed, begged the Lord to undo the damage he'd done to that boy so long ago. He asked Him to set things right. Then, not even a minute later, Travis's eyes shot open filled with purpose. Aggression. He said, "I need my wife," not even bothering to say goodbye. Travis turned on a boot heel, stormed inside his home and slammed the door behind him. That's right around the time the screaming started.

"We freed him, absolved his spirit," Madeline says. "I told you, there's more ways than one a man can be broken."

Father Johnstone extrapolates the idea. "I take it this was about your deity."

"Some people sing songs and praise Jesus for what they need. Our methods are a bit different." She says this in a cavalier fashion, as if the pastor should get it by now.

"I don't know if I can do this," he says. A threat.

Madeline stops in her tracks. "Did we break any of your rules, Johnstone?" she asks. "Did we not fix that man's problem?"

"I feel…" the pastor starts, pausing. His frustration keeps him from being able to form the right words. It's taking a bit of effort on his part to keep from scolding her. "Compromised," he says. "I feel like I'm compromising."

"It's culture shock," she says. "Just like at the church this morning. Just like everything else I've ever shown you."

"That's the problem, Mad, you keep showing me after the fact. You do whatever you feel like doing and clue me in later," he says, his voice raising.

Madeline sighs, screwing her mouth tight, thinking. She stares at the spot over the pastor's shoulder, into the distance where the daisy hill lies: a pile of popcorn. Bumblebees crack and crumble, taken away as dust on the breeze. She says, "You're the first one to have lasted this long."

"First what?"

"Pastor. Man of God," she says. "The others either got scared and ran off, or it wasn't a good fit. I've tried being upfront before, Johnstone. A few times…and just like my parents warned me, it backfired," Madeline says, frowning. "And now *you're* on edge, worried about every little blind spot we pass. Worried about another Clevenger coming at you. I'm not trying to piss you off;

I'm trying my best *not* to scare you away."

Father Johnstone's anger subsides. Ever since the incident with old man Clevenger at the church and the conversation with Madeline that followed, a sense of paranoia has loomed over the pastor that has yet to go away. As much as he'd prefer not to admit it, she has a point. Had Madeline been forthright with him about everything, he would probably be in the Challenger right now, driving along the interstate with Mary riding shotgun. Destination unknown, but it would be far away from Pratt—that's for sure. Like most people, he'd spend the trip counseling with the Lord and convincing himself none of it was real.

"What did you mean by others?" he asks her. "You said there were others that weren't the right fit. Have you done something like this before?

"Well, that's kind of—" Madeline is cut off, interrupted by Mary barking. She's bolting towards the two of them from the distance. Neither the pastor nor Madeline noticed her sneak off during their exchange, but they can see the problem already. A veil of gray is slipping skyward just beyond the daisy hill, getting thicker as the seconds go by. Madeline breaks into a run with the pastor trailing behind her. Even with the heeled boots and satchel weighing her down, she manages to move swiftly. "High ground," Madeline shouts over her shoulder, pointing at the peak of the daisy hill. She makes it to the bottom of the slope where the flowers bloom, scaling the incline. White petals and dust particles of dead bees kick up, and the pastor struggles, a stitch in his side that feels more like a knife. He can see the sky go dark as he follows Madeline, just a few paces behind her. She reaches the top of the hill and curses, screaming as Mary circles her feet, bounding through the flowers and barking at her owner to catch up. He reaches them, and Father Johnstone finally sees what Madeline is so upset about.

Fire.

Madeline's house lies under a blanket of flame, boiling the

paint and roof shingles until they bubble, turning to char. The smoke thickens to ash black and spreads, enough to taste it in the air on top of the daisy hill. Neighbors can be seen taking refuge on their porches, either gawking in horror or trying to make a call to the fire department on cordless phones. This is when Father Johnstone looks past Madeline's house, down the street to where Dan O'Brien and his crew should be arriving at any moment with a fire truck. Instead, two Ford F-150s are flipped over on their sides, creating a barricade. They're not damaged, the pastor notices. It's almost as if they were parked nose-to-nose and were somehow tipped ninety degrees. No vehicles will be accessing the street anytime soon.

Meanwhile, sections of Madeline's roof are collapsing, falling into the attic and spreading to the interior of the home. Paint and siding are stripped. Windows burn to brittle brown, shattering like candy. The fire chews on the support beams of the porch overhang, searing the wood, and this is when Father Johnstone instinctively grabs Madeline's hand. No words or forewarning. No plan.

On the peak of daisy hill some thirty feet above the town, Father Johnstone stands with Madeline Paige of the Feri tradition. Hand-in-hand, they bow their heads as Mary plants herself at their feet. The pastor prays, feeling that warmth flush through his extremity, a crackling tingle that feeds from him on to Madeline.

Then rain.

Not a cloud in the sky. Just rain pouring heavy over a one-block radius. A sun-shower so thick the flames of the house thin to steam in no time. It's a flash flood. A micro-typhoon. So much rain it washes the smoke out of the air and chokes every gutter. Enough rain to drown the flowerbeds and the sirens whaling from the fire truck in the distance. Even through the sheets of wet, Father Johnstone can make out Fire Chief O'Brien attempting to push the barricade of trucks so he can get through, a mostly futile enterprise.

Madeline finally cuts the downpour, taking a moment to assess the damage to her home, which is mostly black now. Sections are missing from the roof and the paint has been all but scorched off. Thankfully, this is the extent of it. Smoke damage aside, the interior should be mostly unharmed, but Father Johnstone has a feeling this won't be enough to console Madeline. She's crying, clearly upset about the attack. Both the pastor and Madeline know this wasn't an accident. It wasn't random bad luck.

Madeline points to the tract of land at the rear of her home, a small garden where she grows vegetables and herbs—probably for Craft purposes. Father Johnstone sees him, a frail-looking individual in black, running with a limp through the potatoes and muck, barely able to keep his balance. He's pale with patchy hair, making a dash towards a field of corn crop that lies roughly fifty yards away from Madeline's back door. Around his torso is a satchel not unlike Madeline's.

"That's not Pollux," she says. Madeline draws her left hand out, aiming it at the man in black who is now a mere ten feet away from the corn stalks. She squints one eye like she's stalking deer with a rifle, breathing slow, steady. Concentrating. Father Johnstone feels Madeline's fingers tighten their grip on him, tingling and buzzing, almost hurting. Her extended arm tenses, and the pastor realizes what she's doing only a moment before it happens.

Lightning.

Hot white splits the cloudless sky once more, the clap of thunder so loud it needles the pastor's eardrums. He instinctively releases Madeline's hand, clamping his palms over the sides of his head and watching the man in black fall forward into the stalks of corn. She missed. Madeline failed to make direct contact, and now he's getting away, escaping into a field of crop.

She says, "Mary, track him—"

"—*Excuse me?*" Father Johnstone cuts in, shouting over the ringing in his own ears. "You're not using her for that."

Madeline says, "Some asshole just torched my house and I want to find out who it was." She squats down, getting as close to eye-level as she can with Mary, telling her, "You'll track, you'll find that man, but you keep your distance." She says, "Track only, okay? And then you come find us and tell me where he went, got it?"

Mary nods. She bolts down the daisy hill, and Father Johnstone follows her with his eyes as she speeds down to the washed-out yards, past Madeline's home and through the water-logged vegetable and herb garden. At the edge of the corn crop she gives pause, taking a moment to pick up the scent of the man in black before she disappears from view, beginning the hunt. He prays for her safety. Father Johnstone demands the Lord return her in the exact condition in which she left.

"Thank you," Madeline says.

Father Johnstone nods, placing a finger in his ear and rattling it around, attempting to regain his hearing. As much as he doesn't want to admit it, tracking down the man in the fields is their best bet on finding a lead to Pollux. Mary can do that, but Father Johnstone no longer feels paranoia regarding his own safety. It's all out in there in the fields: Mary in unfamiliar territory tracking a stranger. He's most definitely not from Pratt. The pastor has been in this town long enough to know that the man in black isn't a resident. The limp and overall look of malnourishment is definitely something he'd remember, or perhaps this is a man who's undergone a great change of his own.

"She'll be okay," Madeline says, giving the pastor a comforting pat on the shoulder. "Mary's smart. Smarter than you probably realize. And look…" she says, bringing up her left hand into view. The palm is still seared and flecked with scorch marks, however, the condition is no worse than when she made the first lightning cast. "My aim was shit but at least I didn't blow my hand off."

Father Johnstone knows what she's really saying, that the tribute of Travis Durphy was indeed successful. It worked. The Goddess has bestowed additional strength upon her, amplifying Madeline's ability. This is the formula that Father Johnstone still hasn't come to grips with: sex equating to power. Not only in regards to morality, but the scientific logic behind it doesn't add up in his mind.

"You're confused," Madeline says, beginning the trek down the daisy hill, carefully sidestepping down the incline to ensure she doesn't lose her footing. She briefly turns to look back at the pastor, telling him, "That's okay. So were a lot of Israelites when the Red Sea parted for them. Even Moses wasn't exactly sure what the hell was going on."

"And what tribute did Moses have to pay to swing that?" Father Johnstone asks. "What did he sacrifice?"

"I imagine he did whatever it took to get the job done," she says, either missing or outright ignoring the pastor's austerity. "You learn a lot about yourself when you're backed into a corner."

It is the compromise, Father Johnstone thinks. This is what one learns when faced with a potential threat to their own person or the place they live. They will bend or break their own rules, turn against their maker, or in the pastor's case, form an alliance with someone who's been deemed 'impious' by The Good Book.

"I feel like we're already backed into one." Father Johnstone continues to ease down the slope of the daisy hill, the scent of smolder getting thicker as they near Madeline's home. It mixes with the smell of the rain. "You said this was a chess game. Now you've got people setting your house on fire," he says. "In broad daylight."

"Maybe it's the other way around," she says. "Maybe they're the ones that feel like they're trapped."

Madeline and the pastor reach the foot of the hill, immediately greeted by the head of Pratt's fire department, Dan O'Brien. Down the street, his truck remains parked by the blockade of Ford F-150's turned on their sides. A few of the neighborhood kids gather around it, pointing at the flashing lights on the roof of the vehicle. Pratt's fire-related incidents are few and far between, so seeing the truck with all its hoses and levers is a rare sight, as is the opportunity for Chief O'Brien to exercise any authority. Unlike Sheriff Morgan, he takes little joy in it.

"You know I can't let you go in there, Miss Paige," he says. "Not until we've had a look around and made sure it's safe."

"And you know that I'm going to go in there anyway, Mr. O'Brien, so I guess we're both ahead of the curve today." Madeline continues to walk briskly towards the home with the pastor in tow. "Besides, Father Johnstone will be looking after me, and I'm sure you've heard by now he walks in the Lord's favor."

"There could be structural damage, Miss. Paige. Hate to see a beam fall on your noggin just because you were too damn impatient to give us ten minutes to poke around," he says. "No offense, Father," he offers the pastor an apologetic look. "You could be walking into a deathtrap is all I'm trying to say."

"Then pray for our sake that that won't be the case," Madeline retorts.

Chief O'Brien places himself between Madeline and her home, taking a more stern approach. He says, "The hard way, then. You either stay the hell out or I'll radio the deputy…and word has it he's been itching to throw his weight around." He stares at her a moment, pleading with his eyes to not be forced to do this.

Madeline reaches back suddenly, clamping her hand around one of the pastor's wrists. She winks at one of the houses down the street, not far from where the chief's fire truck is parked. One corner of the Jergen's residence breaks out into flames, no bigger than a small campfire. It covers just enough area to cause the distraction Madeline needs. She points at it, telling Chief O'Brien,

"I think you're needed elsewhere right now."

He follows her finger to the Jergen's household, cursing. Chief O'Brien looks at Madeline, the fire, back to her, eyes squinting. Father Johnstone can tell he's putting together what just happened, but Madeline is walking again before the matter can be discussed. "Sorry about that," she says. "We really don't have time to be dealing with regulations at the moment."

"Did you have to set Mr. Jergen's house on fire?" the pastor asks.

"It's a baby fire, Johnstone. Let the chief have his moment," Madeline says. "Better he's down there than snooping around my place."

"Because he might see something?"

There's a particular weight the pastor puts on that word, the word 'something.' Spell books, strange historical texts, odd tools and ingredients for casting and Craft. God only knows what else Madeline might have lying around. Father Johnstone hasn't exactly seen much beyond the kitchen and the living room.

"We could be walking into a deathtrap," Madeline says, pacing through her own waterlogged yard with sloshing footsteps. "Not the structural kind. Like, there could be something set up in there for us," she warns. "Best we look around first, yes?"

Father Johnstone prays that this is not the case. He prays that no threat is lying in wait for them, that the home isn't rigged to collapse. He prays, and when he does so, feels the Lord communicate back to him that all will be fine for now. Not in words; a feeling. The two of them ascend the stairs of the porch and arrive at the front door, which is now scorched dark, paint either seared away or in a frozen state of boil from when it was extinguished.

Madeline positions a hand inches away from the deadbolt, fingers clenched like she's holding an invisible baseball in a fork grip. She turns at the wrist, twisting in a jerking motion to the left. Father Johnstone can hear the metal of the lock being shifted within the wood, unlocking the door without key or contact. She's using magnetism.

"You didn't touch me that time," he says. Madeline turns, looking at the pastor. She leans in close, inspecting his face, not saying anything. He tells her, "Normally you grab me before you do something like that."

"What color are your eyes?" she asks.

"Huh?"

"Your eyes," she repeats. "What color are they supposed to be?"

"Blue. What to you mean 'supposed to be'?"

Madeline reaches into the leather satchel, fishing around a moment before she pulls out a silver compact. She opens it, bringing the mirrored portion into the pastor's sightline.

"They're brown," he says. "Why are they brown?"

Madeline shakes her head, frowning. She ignores the question, turning the knob of the door and entering her home. A wave of moist smolder hits them, causing the pastor's eyes to water. Char is in the air. It's thick, so overwhelming Father Johnstone can taste it on the back of his tongue. It reminds him of the sulfur smell from his backyard, the curse.

"You didn't answer me," the pastor says, watching Madeline investigate. Besides the wet sulfur smell the home is mostly intact, although no longer fit for habitation. Not unless Madeline can live with the smell of wet char and the random breezes sweeping through the empty windowpanes.

"He took one." Madeline is at the shelf that holds the many volumes of spell books and historical texts. She plants herself on the wet carpet, leaning in close to read the spines. Madeline checks the sequence of the preceding volumes to determine which one is missing. "Book XVIII, Johnstone. Do you have any idea what's in Book XVIII?" She asks this desperately.

"No," he says, short. "Why is my appearance changing?"

Madeline stands up, her knees and boots glistening from rain water. She makes her way over to the kitchen, taking a quick peek at the counter space to verify her suspicions. "The muffins are gone and so is the Thermos containing the remainder of the curse fluid. Are we still worried about your eyes?"

"That's what I'm asking," the pastor says. "Should I be?"

"The question was rhetorical," Madeline says. She leans against one of the walls, sighing. Spring wind pushes against the house, mixing the smolder with the scent of rain and the flowers on the daisy hill. The wooden framework creaks, a few pieces of roof debris breaking off and hitting the attic floor. "I was wrong, Johnstone."

"About what?"

Madeline stands up, smoothing out her dress. She looks disheveled, tired. "We're the ones being backed into the corner," she says. "There's a reason my Aunt Josie was the one to look over these books, and it's because she never had any intention on using them."

In all her years in Pratt, Josephine Paige never did a single thing to draw attention to herself in a negative way. Nothing was ever said about her to indicate she was 'odd' or 'strange.' If that were the case, the town would have filtered her out long ago. She was quiet and kept mostly to herself, which is probably why she fit in so well. If people knew what she was hiding in her home, the mob would have burned her house down years ago.

"There is Craft far more dangerous than what you've seen so far," Madeline says. "And I just helped weaponize the other side with it."

"You couldn't have known someone was going to break in and set your house on fire." Father Johnstone's old habits kick in, attempting to console the inconsolable. The difference is he can't spout off his go-to lines regarding the Lord and how He is in control. He can't tell Madeline that God has a plan and that she should just let life happen as He would will it.

She snickers, looking at him, the new eyes. "I can feel you

wanting to counsel me," Madeline says. "You want to tell me it's going to be okay but you don't want to lie."

"Yes," he says.

"I *did* know that someone could come here," she says. "It's always been a possibility. I just assumed they wouldn't. It's too brazen. It's not how we do things. We're not the type to go around committing arson."

"I suspect they took advantage of your assumption," the pastor says. "As you said: 'You can't play by the rules forever when the other side isn't'."

Quoting Madeline Paige—it shouldn't feel so natural, the pastor thinks. It really shouldn't, but the words flow out of him organically, much like when he reads from The Good Book. It makes sense to him.

"Come outside with me, Johnstone," Madeline says. There's a good two- or three-second pause before she reveals in a cryptic manner, "It's about to happen." Madeline takes the pastor by the hand, walking him through the entryway of her home, beyond the scent of sulfur and burnt paint. Spring air offers relief as Madeline leads Father Johnstone back to that place: the pile of popcorn. They look at the daisy hill together as Chief O'Brien waters the flames of the Jergen's household down the way. Children look on with their parents standing by, gossiping amongst each other about random fires and freak rainstorms. They exchange theories on how those two Fords ended up on their sides in the middle of the street, none the wiser to what's about to transpire.

"What did you want to show me?" Father Johnstone asks.

"You may have noticed the books are in different languages," Madeline says, ignoring the question. She has a habit of doing this, the pastor's noticed. It usually means what she's telling him takes precedence over what he wants to know.

"I really had no idea what I was looking at," he admits. Spanish, Greek, Chinese, Russian—he couldn't make sense out of any of it.

"That's more or less the point. It's a security measure," she says. "The volumes were compiled that way to complicate the translation process…just in case they fell into the wrong hands." Madeline explains, "Unlike the Bible, these books aren't meant to be read by a wide audience."

Beyond the hill, the sun dips lower and lower, a shadow stretching down the street. Madeline pulls Father Johnstone along, bringing him to the foot of the hill where the daisies begin to sprout. They slope all the way up to the top, which is a good twenty-five feet above street level.

"I've been translating them ever since I got here. Translating and practicing," she says. "Book XVIII, however, is not written in any language you'd know."

Madeline leans over, picking a nearby fragment of a bee off a flower petal. She examines it—what's left of it: the head, half a thorax, a couple legs and one shattered wing. Her fingers pinch down, crushing the remains to wet ash and wiping them off on her dress. Father Johnstone notices that the petals of the daisies are beginning to brown at the tips, wilting slowly. Grass fades to saffron.

"When you fall out of favor with the Goddess like Pollux did, you are marked. A curse follows you wherever you go," she says. "You can't run from it. You can't stop it. One way or another, everything around you is destroyed."

Brown fades over every petal, reaching out to the yellow buds of the daisies. They shrivel and wilt, drying at the stem until the weight of the flower is too much. One by one, thousands of daisies snap or bow into rotten yellow grass. Father Johnstone watches, remembering what Madeline said about all the places she had been before, and ultimately, how she left them. The tornadoes of Joplin and the hurricane of New York, the earthquakes and droughts and coastal floods. For Pratt, Pollux brings about a plague.

"Some books talk about how to amass and control power, how to pay homage to your god," Madeline says. "Others, like Book XVIII, talk about how to overthrow them...to become one yourself. In theory, anyway."

The sun sets on Pratt and everything dies: every flowerbed and blade of grass. Life drains out of the trees, the bushes; their leaves wilt, molt, turn to dust. Rainwater absorbs into the earth, a once-rich soil that is drying, hardening. Father Johnstone watches the daisy hill petrify until it cracks, and he begins to pray. He prays the Lord save them from this sickness in the earth. He prays God intervene and defend Pratt from evil men.

"No, Johnstone. Not this time," Madeline says, giving his hand a comforting squeeze. "I can feel what you're doing and — unfortunately — we can't simply will this situation away."

"Then what do we do?" he asks.

Still gripping the pastor's hand, Madeline leads him so they are facing away from the hill, looking down the street to where Chief O'Brien is stationed. Red lights flash on top of the fire truck as local residents mill about, still talking and gossiping. Mr. Jergen's silhouette crosses the muck that used to be his lawn; he attempts to survey the damage to his home in the fading light of day. It's not nearly as bad as Madeline's, which is virtually unlivable now. She stares at the trucks, the Ford F-150s laid nose-to-nose on their sides creating a blockade to her street.

Madeline reaches out, straining, trying to pull them towards her. Father Johnstone can feel this. The fillings in his teeth quake as Madeline attempts to move over four tons of vehicle towards them. Slowly, they pivot, the pair of them opening like French doors, disturbing the local residents gathered about the Jergen's household. Metacarpals swell out the top of Madeline's hand from the effort, pulling thousands of pounds of metal from an entire block away. She relents, releasing her grip on the pastor and breathing hard. Blood trickles from her nose and there's a sheen of sweat glazing her brow. Madeline leans over at the waist, bracing herself on her knees, panting. Bleeding. A light current of blood flows down her lips and chin, dripping to the dead ground beneath her feet.

"I think we're going to need another tribute," she says.

Işlem XXVIII: özü toplama

The female (kadin) will need at least three males for this next process. It's preferable that she has more: seven is an ideal number, but anything past eleven and the female runs the risk of drowning, being overpowered, or raped to death (ölüm). Sound judgment will need to be exercised when determining the number of males (erkek), although higher risk yields higher reward (ödüllendirmek). The female must first guard her skin, either using animal venom (zehir) or fish toxin (toksin) over a layer of rose oil. Wood paste may also be used, however, this gives the female a skin texture that the male(s) might find unappealing. If the female fears that her anus or vagina (vajina) may be violated, she should occupy them with the leaves of poison sumac or ocotillo spines (refer to: defensive plants). The protective elements (elemanlari) may be stuffed into a sac of thin animal hide and inserted into their respective cavities within the female. She may also choose to sew up her orifices, however, this will likely leave scarring and the male can simply cut the stitching. Earth-based protection (koruma) is best. After preparation, the female should say the Divine Prayer of Safety before attempting the process. She should have a hollowed-out bovine horn that has been blessed (refer to: sanctifying tools) and a blessed blade for further protection. The female will then lure the males into her bedroom chamber, clarifying that she will pleasure them orally and/or by hand, not anally or vaginally. It's recommended that she pretend to be a whore (fahişe), and for this purpose, she may wear the garb of a whore. If the whores of the region are distinguished by specific markings, it's recommended she feign those, too. The female will sit on her knees in the circle of men, starting with the one closest to where the moon (ay) rises and then moving clockwise. She will use her mouth to stimulate the penis of the man, alternating with her hand in a stroking motion to bring them to climax in turn. The process will be exhaustive and arduous, and no male should leave until they have climaxed. All seeds should be collected in the bovine horn (boynuz) and stored collec-

tively (refer to: storage methods). The higher combination of seeds will yield better results, exemplified by the health, physical strength, and dexterity (maharet) of the male(s). After all males have climaxed and the seeds have been stored, the female should immediately purify herself (refer to: purification methods). No attempt to harvest should be made.

The Second Tribute; The Second Sign

At Larpe's Pond, the disease hasn't spread. Not yet.

"It will though," Madeline says, "Just give it time."

Much like the daisy hill, the grass will yellow and blanch, turning to dust. The trees will dry out and petrify. Even the pond itself will spoil, making it uninhabitable for the many bluegill and carp that live there. The plague has intensified, a second wave of ill effects that poisons the land itself.

"When you start to see fish floating dead at the surface, that's when you'll know the water has officially soured," Madeline says. "Everything here—all of it," her hand motions to the pond, the trees, the bushes, "it will cease being part of the circle of life, retrograding to dust. A sickness. Cancer of the earth," she says.

Like every grasshopper, fruit fly, and black beetle, the land will harden and die. Trees will no longer produce oxygen. Water will be incapable of accommodating plant and marine life.

'Remember that thou art dust, and to dust thou shalt return,' the pastor recalls. He takes it in one last time: the mossy scent of the pond and the sound of leaves rustling overhead. Under his boots, the grass is so soft and lush you don't even need a blanket to lie on it. Couples utilized it in the afternoons, sharing cheap gas station wine and the shade of the trees. Talking and kissing. Numerous burgeoning lovebirds of Pratt spent their inaugural dates this way, but that era is coming to an end. Only the locust tree will reveal what this place once was. All those initials and hearts chronicle the moments in which true love and commitment existed, even if it's since wilted away. Like a tombstone, the locust tree will continue to tell the story.

"A bullfrog can be harvested for useful materials in regards to healing and restorative spells. Poison sumac, as strange as it sounds, has properties that can relieve migraines," Madeline says. "We operate within a system of ingredients and alchemy, so what happens when all this dries up and dies?"

Madeline pulls a clump of dandelions out of the ground, which drip soft dirt from their roots. She sniffs the bundle, then proceeds to discard all but one of the flowers. The bud is rubbed vigorously against the top of her hand like an eraser, staining it yellow, and she sniffs again.

"All this will be gone by morning," Madeline surmises. "The crop, too. Corn, wheat...everything."

"I thought you said you needed to pay another tribute," Father Johnstone says. Now that he's seen the damage that's being done to Pratt, the idea no longer seems impractical or one of sacrilege. Desperation outweighs his morality.

"We are," she says. Madeline whips around to the locust tree sitting on the edge of Larpe's Pond, dragging her fingers down many inscriptions and carvings: initials and multi-cornered hearts. "You may think you're looking at a moment in time or an empty promise, but these are contracts," Madeline explains. "A covenant."

Travis Durphy had been wed for some time without the crucial act of consummating the relationship. In a sense, Madeline assisted the church, although to justify her own ends of assuming power. It is the 'gray area' that she's often warned him about: bending rules for the greater good.

Madeline touches the inscriptions, sometimes placing her entire hand over an area and pressing her weight against it. Her eyes close and she concentrates, breathing deliberately. "They are stories," she says. "Penned in pocketknives, screwdrivers, sharp rocks. I can feel each one of them in that moment...like a time capsule."

From the leather satchel, Madeline pulls out a small blade, no longer than a #2 pencil. For a moment, Father Johnstone believes that she's about to carve her own initials on the locust tree. Instead, she introduces the edge of it to the palm of her right hand, applying enough pressure to puncture the skin. Blood trickles from the slit; it looks black under the low light of evening. She presses her hand to the tree, allowing the blood to stain the shaved bark and lettering, soaking into the fibers. A signature.

"Now you," she says, motioning for the pastor to come a bit closer. Madeline takes the pastor's left hand into her own, cradling it. Sticky blood blotches his knuckles and the tops of his fingers. The edge of the knife is pressed against his palm, right across what is known as the heart line. She says, "This is an older form of Craft. The blood serves as a pledge to the two individuals we're about to reunite."

Madeline presses the blade into the pastor's palm, applying enough pressure to split the skin. It weeps, blood pooling in his hand to the size of a dime, then quarter. Letters on the locust tree are stained from Madeline's blood, glistening. The inscription reads: *RF + JS*

"Tonight, we enter into a contract of our own," Madeline says, guiding the pastor's dripping palm to the still-wet initials. "We commit to them the same way they committed to each other."

Father Johnstone allows his hand to be pressed onto the tree, his blood mixing with that of Madeline's—they cover the memory. He contemplates the initials, flipping through his mental Rolodex of Pratt and trying to recall a name. There's too many, though, and the range of dates is decades wide. Unlike Madeline, he isn't able to feel the intangibles.

"Don't worry, you'll know who it is soon," she says. "We're going over there right now."

Not a moment later, Father Johnstone finds himself in the passenger seat of the Challenger with Madeline at the helm. Even with the threat of being randomly tipped over like the Ford F-150s on her street, Madeline said that it wasn't practical to walk all the way to the pond on foot.

"It's also fairly difficult to flip a car that's in motion," she said. "I wouldn't worry about it."

Even with these reassurances, the pastor remains ill at ease, expecting the Challenger to randomly fishtail or careen into a ditch. The engine block could catch fire or the tires could explode just as they're rounding a particularly unsafe piece of road. If Father Johnstone has learned anything by now, it's that the fear of getting caught, being publicly exposed to the people of Pratt— it no longer matters. The attacks are more tawdry now, aggressive. Madeline's home being torched in front of an audience proved that much to him.

"You're going all electric fence on me again. You need to relax," Madeline says. "I can feel you in my fucking teeth."

"How are you doing that?"

"You've counseled these people," she says. "In your church. You brought them into your office and tried to give them advice...about their marriage or their sins or their relationship with God," Madeline says, eyes never leaving the road. More blood on the steering wheel; it glistens like oil under the moonlight. "These people come to you with a problem, but they never really come out and say what it is, do they? They never flat out tell you: 'I'm sick of my wife' or 'I'm afraid of what will happen if I drink again.' They need someone like you to dig it out of them," Madeline says. "Someone who can sense these things, the intangibles, the feeling in the air."

Half the time, Father Johnstone knows a fledging couple is on their way to a divorce before they know it themselves. He can spot a cheating spouse a mile away. All the angry and violent have a distinct temperament about them, something beyond simple facial cues and body language. For three decades, he's honed this skill: excavating the fault, the dirty secret. Their contrition. He digs it out of them, isolates the problem, and through the good Word of the Lord, curbs their behavior back to the Divine path.

"I feel these things, too," Madeline says. "In objects, like Sheriff Morgan's gun. These items develop a history and personality based on how they're used."

"You could barely hold it," the pastor recalls. "Looked like you were about to be sick."

"He's a twisted individual, Johnstone. More than you know," she says. "When I took Shelby, I didn't just see what he had used it for—I saw the intentions behind it. Takes a certain kind of person to enjoy bringing harm upon someone. It's the exact quality that Pollux would look for in a Secondary."

Father Johnstone looks over from the passenger seat. 'Secondary' is a term Madeline hasn't mentioned before.

"It's the nomenclature we use for someone like you working with someone like me," she says.

"Wait...are you saying that the man running out of your house—"

"Yes," Madeline cuts in. "The man in black with the limp—he's like you," she says. "Well, not *exactly* like you, but he's being utilized in the same way."

As Father Johnstone understands it, he—or more accurately, his faith—it serves as the power source. It is what Madeline draws upon to cure cancer and manipulate metal and even overturn death. He is the battery. Without him in the equation, Madeline's abilities are limited.

"You're putting it together now, aren't you, Johnstone?" Madeline says, driving a steady 25mph into the town. "You're wondering how a man like yourself could work with a man like Pollux, what with all the rules and everything?"

"Well, technically, *I'm* not even supposed to be working with you."

As the Good Book says: 'Thou shalt not suffer a witch to live.'

"But your heart's in the right place. You're trying to save a town," Madeline counters. "What you need to remember is that belief isn't static."

"What do you mean by that?" he asks.

"I've been out there. I've seen groups holding signs on street corners that say 'God Hates Fags' and 'Pray For More Dead

Soldiers.' I've seen kids brainwashed into thinking their Lord created AIDS to wipe out gays and minorities," Madeline says. "These are hate groups, obviously, but in their mind they think they're serving God. When they read the Bible, this is their interpretation."

"I've heard of them," Father Johnstone says. "Hatemongers. They protest military funerals and whatnot."

"And as skewed as it might be, my belief is that Pollux has found a man like that...someone more aligned with his own radical disposition," she explains. Madeline pauses for a moment, looking over to the pastor and giving him a small smile. "It's the reason I can feel you so clearly. We're harmonized, in a sense."

"And what about those that weren't 'a good fit'?"

"All things can go sour," she says. "Even this." Madeline puts her right hand on top of the pastor's, the one with the slit in it. The bleeding has since been staunched, clotted over with crust and tree grime. "If you believe that God has a plan, though...that there's some grand design all plotted out ahead of time and we're just game pieces following the path—if that's what you believe, then this will end at the exact moment it's supposed to."

Father Johnstone thinks about that, sighing heavily. This is indeed what he used to believe, what he preached in his sermons: that God is in control. There's a blueprint. "Even if you don't understand it," he used to say, "just take comfort in the fact that there is one. Even when things go wrong under the duress of tragedy, there's a reason behind it." He used to believe that; now he's not so sure.

"You're uncertain. Conflicted," Madeline says. "And that's okay. All it means is you're more willing to be open-minded."

"As opposed to having it all figured out like I thought I did," the pastor adds sourly. He drags his thumb across the slit in his palm that Madeline administered. It doesn't even hurt.

"Your faith makes you capable of great things, Johnstone. You brought a woman out of her wheelchair, brought sight to the blind," Madeline reminds him. "Travis Durphy's marriage stands a chance because of you. Regardless of the actual method, you should take *pride* in these things."

"I thought this was a two-man operation," the pastor corrects her. "Isn't that what you keep saying?"

Madeline smiles. "Now you're getting it."

The Challenger cruises the main roads of Pratt at low speeds, passing dead grass beneath the sparse streetlights. Moths that would normally be bouncing off the glass are dead on the ground, ash to spoiled earth. Mrs. Yates picks through what used to be her flower garden, flashlight in-hand with water can and seed packets by her side. She appears to be crying as she plucks dead-yellow orchids and snapdragons from dry soil plots. Roots slide out all too easily, molting like the hair of a chemo patient. Father Johnstone witnesses other residents diagnosing their trees and bushes, either attempting in vain to nurse them back to health or mourning their apparent loss. Only he and Madeline could reveal the true extent of what's happening. Only they can stop it, and it is under this pretense that Father Johnstone discovers the compromise he's able to tolerate: if Madeline Paige and her abilities can bring Pratt back from this state, then he will bend for her. Father Johnstone won't stray from the core teachings of The Good Book, however, he must adapt to a modern evil that it never prepared him for. When the other side isn't playing by any inherent sense of rules, then he too must forgo some of his own.

"Look in there." Madeline brings the Challenger to a stop and puts it in park. She points to Father Johnstone's left, through the passenger-side window to the little blue house. The shades of 324 Berry St. are drawn shut so that all the pastor can see are two silhouettes embracing in the living room, familiar outlines he's seen many times before.

The pastor turns to Madeline. "This is the Fairfax's place," he says. His eyes shift back to their home, one shadow holding another.

RF + JS, he remembers. Before Jean was Mrs. Fairfax, the unhappiest woman in Pratt, her last name was Selwyn. It was before Father Johnstone had officially assumed his role as leader of the flock. Richard and Jean were one of those young couples that wasted their days lounging upon the grass banks of Larpe's Pond, back when their love and passion was at its apex.

"They're in that moment right now, Johnstone. Pure bliss," she says. "Just enjoying each other. Sometimes we forget how to do that. We get caught up in the petty little everyday things like leaving the toilet seat up or not bringing the car back with a full tank of gas in it."

These trivial arguments are what brought the Fairfax's to a constant state of being at odds, either bickering or outright screaming at each other. Didn't matter what; Father Johnstone has heard reports on a wide range of disputes, from tracking mud into the house to not tipping enough on breakfast at the Presto. These small predicaments clouded the larger nature of their marriage, ultimately, tarnishing it.

"And now at look them," Madeline says. "Not a care in the world. No animosity. No tension. It's like when they first met all over again. They haven't the slightest concern for the ground rotting beneath their feet, no regard for their town being on its deathbed." Father Johnstone turns back to Madeline, a startled look flashing through his new brown eyes. "Don't worry," she amends. "What we've done here will pay its dividends later on."

"Because they have sex," the pastor says. "Tribute or no, the act seems self-indulgent."

"Because they love," she corrects him. "It's not really about what they're doing, but why. The intent," Madeline says, starting the engine of the Challenger. "In the end, the intent is every-thing."

It is intent, Father Johnstone muses, that brings about the flock. They file into the pews, get down on the prayer bars when told, rise when told, repeat the passages he commands they repeat. Every Sunday, the pastor watches the residents of Pratt come before him and go through the motions, but not always with the same motivations. Any one prayer can be recited with a multitude of reasons, either inspired by their love of God or their fear of eternal damnation. They pray to fit into the social structure that is Pratt's religious mold. As Madeline said, intent defines action.

This is when he notices the red ribbon tied around the mailbox post of the widow Wright, the signal indicating she's in need of his help. He sees this, and by extension, Madeline sees it too. She hits the brakes on the Challenger, slamming him forward so hard the seatbelt cuts into this collarbone.

"You all right?" she asks. "You're spiking again."

Father Johnstone takes a beat, rubbing his shoulder and remembering his last encounter with Helena Wright. It was a blatant misstep to say the least, but he knows it wasn't purely his fault. Under the resolve of Pollux, a sliver of *lust* manifested in the worst way possible. He indulged in a member of his congregation, or perhaps it was the other way around.

"You're a shame storm right now. What the hell is wrong with you?" Madeline asks. "Does that ribbon mean something?"

"An invite," he says. "But after my last visit, I'm not so sure I trust myself. Or her."

"It takes two to tango, Johnstone," Madeline says. She puts the Challenger in park, killing the headlights and the engine. "No worries, though. You and I both know you weren't completely behind the wheel last time you saw her."

"Mad, you've gotta cut that out." Father Johnstone shakes his head.

"Can't help it," she says. "What's funny is that you've been brought up believing that God has more or less the same unfettered access...but you probably never batted an eye over it, huh?"

"It's different when it's a person," he says. "People shouldn't be able to do that."

"Then tell me more about the ribbon...in your own words," she says. "Communicate with me."

"Helena—Mrs. Wright, I should say...she does that when she needs me. To talk about her husband," Father Johnstone says. "At least, up until recently, that's how it was. Now I don't know."

"Because of what happened the last time," Madeline says. "The dynamic has changed. I get it."

Father Johnstone shrugs sheepishly, mildly embarrassed he's even having this discussion. He remembers what the widow Wright accused him of saying, that he referred to her not as Helena, but as Madeline. It makes sense considering it was Pollux that prompted that moment of weakness. It makes sense, but that doesn't necessarily mean it's the truth.

"We should check on her," Madeline suggests.

"I don't think it's a good idea if you come with me. I think it'd upset her," the pastor says.

Madeline shakes her head. "No, she's not okay." She looks at the house, back to the pastor. "Something's wrong in there."

"This is Mrs. Wright we're talking about. There's *always* something wrong in there," Father Johnstone says, immediately realizing how insensitive this sounds. "She never really got over losing her husband is all. Never learned how to be alone."

"No, I mean she's hurt," Madeline says. This time though, she doesn't wait for the pastor to respond. She disembarks from the Challenger, slamming the door behind her using magnetism instead of her hand. Madeline approaches the Wright household almost jogging, and Father Johnstone is right behind her, that feeling of paranoia coming right back. He checks left, checks right as the two of them cross the yard of dead dirt and yellowed grass. Father Johnstone checks the stark bushes and naked trees, seeing nothing but twisted frames and shadowy fingers of deceased wood.

"Mad, we can't just go barging in there," he hisses.

She doesn't listen. Madeline doesn't even feign the courtesy of polite entry, opting to open the front door of the Wright home in her own fashion. Her right hand draws upon the deadbolt before she pulls her arm sharply back, ripping it from the wood of the frame and creating a gaping hole in entryway. Metal trimmed with splinters hover, held mid-air by Madeline. Her hand makes a little sweeping motion, tossing the deadbolt over to what used to be Mrs. Wright's flower garden of begonias and hydrangeas.

"It's like I'm in one of those hotel rooms again." Madeline walks into the home of Helena Wright at a brisk pace, passing the empty living room of wilting candles and charred incense. Father Johnstone follows her, taking note of the sickly sweet aroma in the air like burnt sugar. "The air," she says. "There's anguish in it. You could tell these girls had never been more scared of anything in their life."

On the kitchen counter right next to the ceramic salt-and-pepper shakers, the pastor sees a small plate. The plate holds the remaining crumbs of a dessert and its baking paper. Madeline notices it too, bringing her nose to it, sniffing.

"Cocoa, cinnamon," she says. "Sulfur."

Madeline takes a left into a small hallway and now they can hear something, the sound of whining. A series of cold whimpers. They move closer to it, following the audio down the small hallway that leads to Mrs. Wright's bedroom, the door slightly cracked. Lights off.

"I'm warning you now," Madeline whispers, turning to look at the pastor over her shoulder. Every hair on her neck and arms is standing at full attention. "When I open that door," she says, "you're not going to like what you see in there."

She takes the pastor's hand, interlocking her fingers with his. Madeline pushes the door open slowly, the creak of the hinges overlapping the sobs. It becomes clear that they were supposed to see this.

Pollux's name is all over it.

On the Road with Billy Burke, Truck Stop Preacher

"The Lord's prayer can be aggressive...even hateful. If you've got hate in your heart, that's fine. Let that hate out. Best to let it out to the Lord than on your wife or someone you care about in a moment of weakness. Ol' Billy Burke has done more than his fair share of hate-prayin'. Oh yeah, I've wished pain and anguish upon those who've wronged me. And it ain't about wrath. *It's about what's right...what's fair. I see a few of you that don't look too sure about what ol' Billy is saying. Seems a bit mean-spirited, don't it? A preacher down on his knees wishin' disease and cancer on his enemies. Praying for a slow death. Not exactly pious behavior, is it? Well let ol' Billy put it to you this way...the Lord supports your ill will towards the Devil, and the Devil is who I pray against. I'm not talking your run-of-the-mill lot lizards and meth hookers. I'm talking about these young men that are shooting up elementary schools and movie theaters...killin' just cos they can. Killing kids, killing families. They get a gun and start pumping rounds into anything that moves because someone called them a faggot one too many times. Then these shits get to sit in a little box as their punishment while your tax dollars keep them warm and fed. That sound right to you? No sir...don't sound right to ol' Billy, either. It's shit is what it sounds like. So I consult with the Man upstairs about these men...tellin' the Lord, 'Make them hurt. Make them suffer. Let them be raped and beaten and broke for the rest of their shit lives. Let cancer eat their peckers right off. Take my anger and the anger of this country, and funnel it right into their shitters, Lord. Then toss 'em on down to Hell where they can burn for eternity.' It's okay to have anger, gentlemen. We all have it. And with the help of the Lord, ol' Billy Burke is going to help you do something constructive with it."*

The House Call

Blood.

Blood everywhere.

While Father Johnstone tends to Mrs. Wright, Madeline is walking the perimeter of the bedroom and reading the walls. Symbols that look neither Latin nor Greek nor Arabic. Madeline studies them, her lips moving as if she's dictating the words to herself. Meanwhile, Mrs. Wright is shivering, quaking, fists balled tight and clutching the hem of her slip. What's left of it, anyway. She's covered in blood and shredded silk, eyes wide but not looking at anything in particular. Irises ticking left-right-left-right.

Father Johnstone snaps his fingers once, twice. He says, "Helena," waving a hand in front of her sightline. He says, "Are you okay?" and Madeline turns away from the wall, shooting him a look like: *Does she* look *okay? Does any of this look okay?*

On the walls, the symbols are finger-painted on top of old floral print paper that's peeling at certain places along the ceiling and baseboards. Blood arcs and glyphs, blood passages that are thin at some points and littered with chunky clots at others. Madeline attempts to read these, moving from one wall to the next, tracking them with an index finger.

She turns to Father Johnstone after a moment, looking over to where he's sitting on the bed next to Mrs. Wright. "Not good," she says vaguely.

"Mad, she needs help. Look at her." Yet again, Father Johnstone tries to elicit a response, snapping his fingers next to Helen's ears this time. Ears crusted over with splashes of blood. He asks, "Can you do anything?"

"I have no soil. No flora nor any herbs or fruit seeds," she says. "I have no animal horn or a single drop of fresh spring water. There's no ingredients left to work with," Madeline reminds him. "The land is dead. Dead land means no Craft."

"I've seen you cure cancer with nothing," the pastor says.

"She doesn't have cancer. She's not blind or crippled or suffering from spinal injury, Johnstone. She's not 'normal person' sick. I mean, what do you think all this shit is?" Madeline motions around the room, the symbols. Characters drawn in blood that are neither Japanese nor Russian nor French. All four walls are covered in them, the inside of bedroom door and the mahogany nightstand.

"What is all that?" he asks.

"Not really sure. It reads like gibberish." Madeline looks at the walls again, trying to find a pattern or some clue to decipher the blood script. One symbol looks like a pitchfork with a halo around it; another symbol looks like the number '8' overlapping a plus sign. "I assume it's a curse of some sort. That's the vibe I'm getting," she says.

Mrs. Wright continues to shiver, tremble. Tears well up and spill down the side of her face, carving a path through the sticky red splashed onto her temples. Blood gives the room a stale meat odor, and that mingles with the stench of urine coming from the mattress. Father Johnstone touches Mrs. Wright, palm to forehead—she's freezing. From head to toe, her skin is milk pale and goose-pimpled. Father Johnstone finds himself looking at her body, her neck, shoulders, and extremities. There's not a scratch on her.

"You have no idea how this feels." Madeline looks around the room, shaking her head. Her cheeks flush and a tear falls from her eye that she immediately wipes away. "No idea. Poor woman would eat a bullet right now if that was an option."

Helena fidgets, twitches. She curls her fingers into her own palm so tight the nails pierce the skin. Whimpering—sobbing continues. Mrs. Wright opens her mouth, tongue spilling over her lower lip, gagging. Fluid can be heard churning in her throat and she coughs up black mucus that spatters on cotton sheets.

Sulfuric rot enters the air and Father Johnstone looks at the walls—unable to read the message or whatever it's supposed to say—but he knows it's wrong, knows it shouldn't be there. He prays he could scour it from the surface, prays the Lord cleanse this home, and that's when Madeline finally makes a suggestion.

"Grab her shoulders," she says, moving to the foot of the bed. Madeline flinches when she makes contact with Helena's skin, hissing, "Good God, this chick is freezing." She bundles Mrs. Wright's ankles under her armpit, clamping down and using her arms to support the weight of her lower half. Father Johnstone and Madeline go through the process of moving the body off the bed with no aid from Mrs. Wright, still shivering and convulsing, cold and bloody and crying. "The couch in the living room," Madeline says. She struggles to keep up her end of the body, constantly having to readjust so Mrs. Wright's ankles don't slip. It's like she's carrying one too many logs of firewood—the kind that are slick with blood and won't stop moving. Sometimes they kick.

They eventually make it to the couch and lay Mrs. Wright down as gently as possible, blanketing her with a nearby quilt. Neither expect this to do much in the way of keeping her warm. It's more of a token response as is the pastor's attempt to get some sort of reaction by snapping his fingers, asking if she can hear him. He asks Mrs. Wright, "Can you speak?"

She says nothing. Oil creeps out of her mouth and onto the couch cushions. Fluid leaks from her nose, her eyes. Moving her from the bed seems to have dislodged this in her system, and the pastor wonders if this was the right thing to do.

"You need to get Dr. Keller on the phone and have him meet us over at your place." From the kitchen, Madeline takes the cordless off the charging cradle and hands it over to Father Johnstone. She briefly checks out Mrs. Wright who is still shivering, telling the pastor, "And he needs to be discreet."

"What *exactly* am I supposed to say to him? That she's

cursed?" he asked. "Because I don't see that going over well."

"He's like you, Johnstone," she says. "If you say it's a medical emergency he'll come. He's not going to try to think of an excuse to get out of it."

"No, I get that part of it," Father Johnstone says to Madeline who walks out of sight, into the bathroom. He can hear cabinets open and closing, pill bottles swan-diving from their respective ledges and banging around the sink beneath them. "The problem is I think he's going to ask questions," he says, voice raised so it carries to the bathroom. "Y'know, questions that are going to make this secret little thing we've got going on not so secret anymore."

Madeline reenters the living room holding a candle and can of hair spray, telling the pastor, "There's really no secret anymore. It's all out there now, and people are going to start piecing it together." On the coffee table, she sets down the can of Aqua Net and the candle, which has only been used a moderate amount. From her pocket, she takes out a Bic lighter and sets the candle aflame before telling the pastor, "Bless these, then call. Be snappy about it." She checks on Mrs. Wright, still shivering under the quilt, mumbling nonsense, eyes wide and spilling tears. "Little lady over there doesn't look too good."

"Bless these?" Father Johnstone looks at the candle, the hairspray, back to Madeline.

"Yes," she says. "Pretend her life depends on it if that helps you."

The pastor looks at the candle again, the hairspray. He remembers the Holy pyre made out of his firewood in his back yard, ignited by matches, lighter fluid, and a string fuse. According to Madeline, these common items take on a different meaning when they belong to a man of the cloth. Their intangible nature is blessed in the eyes of God. As she said, it's how juice and crackers become the body and blood of Christ.

"And what do you plan on doing with these?" He knows the

answer before Madeline even says it.

"Set fire to the room, of course."

Father Johnstone nods approvingly.

"Bless these objects," he says. "In the name of the Father, the Son, and the Holy Spirit, and give Madeline sanction as she uses them for the destruction of words that make this house and the spirit of Helena Wright unclean." His fingers draw upwards, a few inches down, right, then left, forming a cross. "Amen," he says. Madeline takes the candle and hair spray as Father Johnstone dials Dr. Keller, yelling out to her as she exits the room, "Be thorough."

Mrs. Wright quakes, lead-colored veins branch up her neck and past the curvature of her jaw. They extend and darken as the pastor holds the phone to his ear, waiting for Dr. Keller to pick up his end. He presses the back of his hand to Helena's cheek and it's somehow even colder than it was only moments ago.

Meanwhile, Madeline torches the bedroom of the widow Wright. Starting low at the baseboards, she shoots hairspray through the candle flame and fans the bottom fringes of the wallpaper. Flames creep upwards, eating old glue and tiny pink and blue representations of flowers. Blood symbols blacken, char, deform to ash with a crackle. Madeline starts another wall, setting down the spray and the candle to wrap a nightshirt around the bottom portion of her face like a mask. Smoke is filling the room, crawling along the ceiling and moving throughout the house.

Father Johnstone is on the phone with Dr. Keller in the living room, telling him, "You know I wouldn't be calling you at this time of night unless the circumstances warranted it, David. You know that."

"Yes, but you're not giving me a lot to go off of here. I can bring my kit but that might not be enough," Dr. Keller says on the other end. "You said she's cold?"

"Freezing," the pastor stipulates.

From the hallway, the smoke detector sirens loud enough for Dr. Keller to hear on the other end of the line.

"Another fire, preach?"

Madeline reenters the living room at a run, gasping for clean air. She coughs hoarsely, keeling over and saying, "We need…to go…now," panting between words. Madeline bolts out the front door, sucking down fresh air.

Father Johnstone can smell the smoke entering the living room area, the warmth of the house intensifying. "I'd bring oxygen, if you've got it handy." He approaches the living room window and peels back the curtains to see if Madeline is okay. The lights of the Challenger flick on, cutting through the dark.

"I'll come but if there's nothing I can do, I'm bringing her in. You have to know that," Dr. Keller says. "I can't risk someone's life for the sake of discretion."

Helena starts hacking up fluid, black blood. Father Johnstone peels himself away from the window to check on her, and she's shivering, crying on the couch. Her lips are moving now, forming words, but they're impossible to make out over the sound of the smoke detector and Madeline honking the horn of the Challenger in the front yard.

"Fine, David—meet me in five minutes," Father Johnstone says. He hangs up. Patting Helena on the back, he tells her soothingly, "We're getting you out, okay? I called Dr. Keller." But it's as if she doesn't hear him, still attempting to communicate her own message. Her lungs and throat are choked with fluid, obstructing her breathing, her speech. She can barely hear anything through the congestion in her ears and the whining of the smoke detector.

Outside, the sound of the Challenger's suspension being mistreated makes a loud crunching noise as Madeline jumps the curb, parking the vehicle in the front of Mrs. Wright's yard. Headlights pour through the living room window, illuminating the smoke that's creeping through the residence. Madeline gets out of the car and runs back into the home, her breathing almost normal again.

"Well, that ought to get the neighbors talking," the pastor says.

"They'll have bigger problems to worry about soon enough," Madeline says. "You take the legs this time. I don't want her kicking me." She hooks her arms under Mrs. Wright's, clamping her hands on the back of her neck. It almost looks like a wrestling hold, only a bit more disgusting with the blood and various fluids leaking out everywhere. "What'd Keller say?" Madeline asks.

"He's en route." The pastor bundles Helena's legs together under an arm and lifts. Cold perspiration and blood soak into his shirt, black fluid as thick as syrup. As Madeline forewarned, Mrs. Wright isn't exactly cooperating. Her legs randomly spring outward making it hard to hold onto them, so he chokes up, wrapping her knees and clamping down hard. "David sounds apprehensive about the whole thing."

"You're calling him in the middle of the night from a burning building," she says, straining to keep Mrs. Wright's torso elevated as they clear the threshold. "I should've taken the legs. This end's heavier."

A moderate amount of squirming aside, Madeline and Father Johnstone manage to move the body to the Challenger, opting to lay her down in the confines of the backseat for the sake of space. She's still shivering, still hacking up spurts of black fluid onto the interior. Sulfur overwhelms the scent of Armor All and pine air freshener, filling the vehicle with its stench as the outlines of neighbors watching from their windows can now be seen, either due to the fire or the sound of the Challenger hopping the curb.

"We should have called the fire department," Father Johnstone says. "Whole damn house is gonna burn down now."

"Like I said: bigger problems," Madeline repeats. She does a quick check on the rearview mirror before peeling out in reverse, abusing the suspension again as the Challenger hops off the curb. Another violent clang for the neighbors to hear. She shifts into drive and heads back towards Father Johnstone's place, asking him, "Because you know what happens next, don't you?"

"With what, specifically?"

"This place," she points out the window, the barren yards and petrified insect life hidden by dark. Bald trees turning grayer by the hour, depleting in earth tones to shades more akin to granite. "It gets worse," Madeline tells him. "The insects and the land are the start, but then it begins to affect the birds and the squirrels. Dogs," she says, turning to look at the pastor for a moment. "All your food, your produce and all the grain at the plant will have begun to sour. I pity anyone who eats it. And then you know what's next?"

"Us," the pastor says.

Madeline nods, taking the next corner going over 45mph on cracked asphalt. The tires barely hold and Mrs. Wright is sliding around the backseat, still hacking, sobbing. A streetlight catches the side of her face and the veins in her cheeks have subsided somewhat, much to Father Johnstone's relief. He prays for her health. He prays her soul not be tarnished.

"There's two ways about this," Madeline says. "Either these people need to jump ship or they're going to get sick and die like the rest of the town."

"And what about stopping it?" the pastor asks.

"That's on our shoulders, Johnstone."

"It's possible, right?"

"It's going to be our burden to bear," she says, sidestepping the question. "Because when these people come out of their homes tomorrow…when they realize the land is dead and the water has soured and everything around them is cursed—it's going to be you they come to. They're going to come to you, Johnstone, and they're going to want another miracle," Madeline says. "Even the non-flock will change their tune about you.

That's how desperate they'll get."

"And what am I supposed to do when that happens?" he asks.

"What any man of God would do: make them believe," she says. "That is your job, after all."

Madeline pulls the Challenger into Father Johnstone's driveway, which is now covered in crude chalk drawings wishing him well. Pastel blue and pink thank-you notes and Easter yellow crucifixes. Flower arrangements lie upon the front porch. They're dead, of course, but the crisp petals and hardened stems make his stomach drop with a peculiar sense of guilt. It is not Deputy Clarke nor the mayor the people of Pratt will reach out to; they'll seek out the pastor, and they'll expect a solution, Divine or otherwise.

"It's starting already," he says.

Mrs. Wright's breathing amplifies under the silence, fluid glugging with every breath. Her respiratory system is flooded with the stuff, and it brings back a few memories the pastor wishes he could forget about his own experience. It was like breathing soy sauce, he remembers, but with more of an acidic quality to it. Mrs. Wright is still shivering and coughing in the backseat, seemingly unaware of where she is or who she's with. This is when Dr. Keller pulls up in his late-model sedan, a silver Honda. He parks in the street, getting out of the car and rushing up the pastor's driveway with a handled black case. "How is she?"

"About the same, I think," Father Johnstone answers. "Maybe a little better."

Dr. Keller removes a flashlight pen from his jacket pocket, clicking it on and shining it in the backseat where Mrs. Wright is curled up and shaking, coughing up wet black. The sweat seems to have thinned out, but her body glistens with blood. Nostrils twist when the sulfuric smell finally hits him; he flinches, turns to the pastor and says, "That's not from smoke."

Father Johnstone nods. "You are correct."

Dr. Keller shines his light in the backseat one more time, glancing over Mrs. Wright and attempting to devise some sort of pre-diagnosis. He'd like to ask more questions: where the blood came from and how long she's been in this state. The issue is that it's late, it's dark, and he's standing in the driveway of a pastor who's got a half-naked woman in the back of his car. It's the exact thing Deputy Clarke has been looking for. If he were to drive by right now, no amount of testimony from Dr. Keller would keep the two of them out of cuffs.

"I guess I'm an accomplice now." Dr. Keller takes a breath, holding it as he reaches into the backset of the Challenger. The sulfur smell remains strong, and black fluid and blood shine opaquely on the black leather, much to the pastor's displeasure. The two men carry Helena's body into the house. Madeline assists with front door and tends to Dr. Keller's medical kit.

"Get her a bucket," she says. "That's what she *really* needs right now."

Father Johnstone and Dr. Keller lay Helena down on the couch, positioning her on her side just in case she vomits again. Helena maintains a wide-eyed stare at no particular object, tears streaming freely with gravity. Hair is soaked from sweat, flecked with pebble-sized clots of blood. Lips continue to move silently when she's not hacking into the bucket that Father Johnstone has brought her from the kitchen.

"You two certainly seem calm under the circumstances," Dr. Keller says.

Neither the pastor nor Madeline respond. Father Johnstone takes a seat in one of the nearby chairs, sighing heavily. He's exhausted. Madeline dumps out the doctor's kit like a bucket of toys, spilling medical scissors, cotton swabs, and a myriad of silver instruments.

"We could say the same about you, Keller." Madeline sets a small bottle of disinfecting gel on the coffee table. Next to that: a Tylenol 3 tablet in foil wrap and a roll of gauze. "You ever see someone bleeding tar out of their head like that? Or is this the second time?"

Dr. Keller doesn't respond—not immediately, anyway. He shines his flashlight into Helena's right eye, then her left. Another wave of fluid can be heard churning in her neck, and so he halts the examination, backing away as another torrent of rot spills from her mouth. Helena shivers, cries; the doctor removes his blazer and drapes it over her.

"Kurt Clevenger is dead," Dr. Keller says. He clicks off the flashlight pen, pocketing it in wrinkled trousers that were laid crumpled on the floor when he got the call. His dress shirt is in the same condition, but now blood and black fluid blemish the sleeves. He says, "Word has it our fair deputy is itching to question you again—and yes, Miss Paige, this is the second time."

"And I imagine you examined it, yes?" Madeline asks the doctor as she makes her way over to Father Johnstone who is sitting in his chair. She takes his wounded hand with the slice across the palm and begins to mend it. First, by applying a generous amount of disinfectant. The cut stings but he doesn't wince. "Lemme guess," Madeline says. "Inconclusive?"

"As a matter of fact, it was, Miss Paige," Dr. Keller confirms. "And it makes me wonder how a simple waitress would know that...amongst other things."

"Oh? Like what?" Madeline asks innocently, wrapping the pastor's hand. After the third revolution she cuts it with the medical scissors, using a gauze clip to secure it.

"I examined Bernadette Doakes and Jimmy Gibson myself, ran the tests and confirmed the results. I've even had them back for follow-ups over the years," Dr. Keller says. "They were what they've always been: a cripple and a blind man. Then you show up, Miss Paige."

Madeline nods, smiles. "That's right, I show up. And?"

Dr. Keller stares at her grimly. "What are you?"

She doesn't appear to be offended by the question. In fact,

Madeline welcomes this turn in the conversation. "What do you think I am, doc?"

"Honestly?" Dr. Keller smirks. "I think you're the thing he's *pretending* to be." He motions to Father Johnstone who is sitting in the chair, testing the integrity of the bandages by flexing his hand. "The figurative 'man behind the curtain'," he says. "I think it's very strange what's been going on with the Presto and Magda Tiller and the bake-off...and these so-called 'miracles,' as people have been referring to them," he says with a fair amount of skepticism. "It's not in my nature to believe that, but I can't explain it, either."

"Go on." Madeline gives a little nod.

Father Johnstone doesn't speak, remembering how this was all explained to him some time ago: *"There's faith, there's science, and then there's the in-between. It's the gray area, the fringe between the two."* When one can't explain something medically nor put any stock in faith, the gray area is all that's left.

"And now the land is dying. People are getting sick in a way I've never seen and can't explain, and that includes the preacher here," Dr. Keller says, disheartened. "You're the common denominator, Miss Paige."

"Yes," she says. "Common denominator. Quite right."

Dr. Keller takes in the two of them: Madeline and the pastor. They're a tad worse for wear, dirty, running on fumes. Father Johnstone has bags under his eyes like grocery sacks. Brown eyes; Dr. Keller can't remember if this is right or not. Nevertheless, this is a look that has become commonplace as of late, ever since he began his association with Madeline. It's as if her arrival marked the beginning of the town's renaissance affair, a period in which Pratt's people soured right along with the land itself.

"But you're not the reason for what's happening out there," Dr. Keller says. In his heart, he knows the two people in front of him aren't responsible for Pratt's recent deterioration. "If I had to guess," he says, "I'd say you had a bit of trouble follow you to our fair town, Miss Paige. Pratt may not be aware, but I know the difference between a girl looking to escape the big city life for calmer pastures and a girl in hiding. Makes me wonder though what a girl like you would be hiding from," Dr. Keller muses. "Or *who*."

"Indeed, Dr. Keller," Madeline says. "Who *does* a girl like me run from?"

"Someone like yourself, I'd imagine," Dr. Keller says. "An individual who can also do what can't be explained by men like me."

Helena Wright's throat churns again, spitting up more black fluid onto the couch and the bucket next to it. She's pale, sweating, but when Dr. Keller presses his fingers to her leg, it's slightly warmer than it was when they first moved her inside. Old man Clevenger—despite the doctor's best efforts—he never went into any sort of remission. Mrs. Wright appears to be ridding the substance from her system. With Kurt, it's as if it augmented inside of him until his body couldn't handle the overflow. It leaked out his nostrils, his tear ducts and mouth. Every word he spoke was laced with that rotten-egg stench. He was pissing and shitting the stuff towards the end. Two of his nurses lost their lunch over the smell, and his head RN kept asking whether or not they should call in outside help, if Mr. Clevenger was contagious.

"Kurt's death was slow, painful," Dr. Keller says. "That poor man lost his mind right in front of me...handcuffed to a bed and bleeding that stuff out of every hole in his body." Dr. Keller pauses, taking a moment to get his bearings. "He kept saying a name."

"And what name might that be?" Madeline casually prompts, but she already knows. Both she and Father Johnstone are well aware of the other variant lurking around town. According to Dr. Keller, the pastor said the name himself while he was unconscious in Pratt Medical. Three days lost, all because of him: Pollux.

"Miss Paige, it is my belief that the two of you are on the right side of things," Dr. Keller says. "I can't say for sure who you're hiding from, but if you're familiar with Mason Hollis like the rest of us are, I'd say that'd be a damn good reason."

Father Johnstone leans forward in the chair slightly, brow furrowed. "What does *he* have to do with any of this?"

"That's the name he kept repeating," Dr. Keller says. "Doesn't make a lick of sense, but I think Kurt was trying to tell me he's back."

"Of course it doesn't make sense. Mason's been dead for years," the pastor says.

"Did you see a body? Was there a funeral?" Dr. Keller asks rhetorically. "You know as well as I do that story has been through the rumor mill so many times it's lost all credibility," he reminds him. "Mason Hollis is a ghost story now, and the only guy that can tell you what really happened is the sheriff. Good luck finding him, though."

Madeline and the pastor exchange a knowing look. During that moment, he notices that the hairs are standing up on Madeline's arms again. He's spiking, worried yet again how Sheriff Morgan could arrive in Pratt at any moment. The plague would be but a mere distraction in his efforts to find the two individuals that sent him away, out into exile against his will. Sheriff Morgan will return with pure *wrath* in his heart, supplementing his current infamy with another tall tale of smalltown justice.

"Morgan sure picked a helluva time to skip town," Dr. Keller says. "With everything that's been going on lately and that hothead deputy of his just aching to throw his weight around, I don't have a good feeling about the coming days. Could get ugly." He turns to Helena who's still shivering under his coat on the couch. He presses two of his fingers to her leg, giving a little nod. The cold is slowly retreating from her skin.

Madeline smiles, but just barely. Helena's recovery notwithstanding, there's still the larger issue of Pratt becoming a ghost town to deal with. People will either begin to starve or take sick. Perhaps not in a way where they're coughing up fluids and bleeding out of every hole in their bodies, but something more to the effect of what's happening to the earth and water. They too will sour, deteriorate. Cancer of the flesh, cancer of the blood. Like the trees, bones will dry to a brittle chalk. Hair, skin, and organs—all these things, they'll deform to ash and flake away.

Dr. Keller can't fix it.

No Craft can be made to stop it.

Only by cutting it off at the source will it end.

This is when Madeline feels a fourth presence in the nearby proximity—something not nearly pronounced as Father Johnstone's anxiety or Dr. Keller's state of turmoil over how much he doesn't know. It's smaller, more subtle, not complex enough to be human. Madeline feels it coming from just beyond the front door: scared by the unfamiliarity of these new surroundings, but brave. Obedient.

"Mary's back," Madeline says.

Las Vegas, NV

My departure from Las Vegas isn't without challenges.

At McCarren International I'm on the no-fly list. Fortunately, this is information I was able to ascertain before physically stepping foot onto the property. Now that I'm ready to leave, it's paramount that my exit be as discreet as humanly possible—not only to avoid those who may be looking for me—but to ensure I'm not followed, either. The adage of 'what happens in Vegas stays in Vegas' isn't always true, especially when you've extorted several million dollars from their casinos, tortured their whores, and killed numerous religious figures, regardless of whether or not it was intentional. Las Vegas regales in its celebration of lust and greed, but should one push it past the threshold as I have, Sin City has a well-developed sense of wrath to contend with.

My face continues to circulate around the city, and so I forgo any attempt to travel by air—both commercial and private avenues. Trains and buses are also a risk; it's likely my pursuers will attempt to apprehend me before I can board. 'The word is out' about me, as they say. My past transgressions in Vegas haven't been forgotten, and my current ones have brought the city's hostility to a fever pitch. There's a bounty on my head now, and without an adequate Secondary, my ability to defend myself operates on a thin margin. Evasion will only carry me so far. Although the lights and general disquiet of Las Vegas have provided sufficient cover, I am but one man in a region of hungry predators. Changing locations and names is of little consequence. They are armed; they know my face.

They've heard the stories, and just like any classic game of telephone, these tales have become marred with rumor and embellishment. I've transcended into urban legend, a ghost story the older whores relay to their younger contemporaries in terrifying excerpts: the whore I cooked with a device known as a 'curling iron,' the whore I bit, chewed, and digested when she requested I 'eat her out,' another few whores that climaxed so hard they defecated in the bed, then a few more *that were physically beaten out of sheer boredom or my resentment for Madeline having left me (and in a state of damnation, no less). The 'Christian fetish' as they call it went so much further than ordained lingerie and candles. It wasn't always so cosmetic and polite. Sometimes I'd brand them with the symbol of the savior using tempered metals, or I'd carve into their backs using the sharpened crucifix I had fashioned. Applying the aptitude of taxidermy, I stuffed the vaginal cavity of one whore with pages of the Old Testament, allowing poisoned seminal fluids to soak into the paper. It was yet another ill-fated attempt at prevention. Alas, the disease spread as does the story.*

'Doesn't matter if you're a casino owner, a nickel whore, or a priest,' they say. 'He's an enemy to everyone. He needs to be stopped. Permanently.'

Exile is no longer an option. There is no apology, no monetary figure that will quell their anger. Through the course of the endeavor, I've abused their system, that unwritten rule denoting the function of the whore: fornication, companionship, and a supplement of self-worth. They are borrowed property, and therefore, to be returned in the same condition in which they arrived—not abused and poisoned as I have done repeatedly for the past many months. I've tainted the well, and I'm not exactly sure with what.

Roughly 70% of my genitalia is a dark bruise color, almost black; the remaining surface area consists of splits and weeping wounds. Yellow fluid sponges from my pores. Amber crust scabs over the tip of my urethra. Vacating the bladder has become such a painful affair that I've taken to avoiding it, sometimes as much two or three days at a time. I abstain from the act until my torso aches and can no longer endure, usually indulging a bottle of Christ blood to dim the impending sting. It's never enough. Urine is a honey-brown color, rife with infection, and stinks of rot so potently the impulse to vomit can't be controlled. I scream. I sweat, hand braced against the nearest wall. Sharp, boiling fluid bursts through the crust and scalds the toilet, poisons it just like all those whores. They too have spread this virus, and it continues to circulate once vacationing men return to their wives and domestic partners.

What they say is true: I am a walking plague.

Unfortunately, the application of Craft is not a viable option. Not yet. Even if the correct materials were available to me, I lack their itemization and the procedure on how to combine them. It will have to wait until I have access to the depository of books again, currently being watched by Josephine Paige in the town of Pratt. Thus far, I've kept my distance. Startling her would be unwise at this point, especially when she's in the favor of the Goddess and I'm not. That tide will turn soon. There are many thresholds left to cross, many paths to explore.

The immediate one lies east of here.

My Divine path leads to Elk City.

The Ally

Mary crosses the threshold of the front doorway, fur flecked with bits of stale corn stalk and petrified wheat seed. Prints of grime stain the carpet of the living room as she paces in, adding to the discharge of black fluid from Helena Wright. Father Johnstone doesn't mind; all that matters is she's back. Mary's home and safe now. Despite Pratt being impaired and the countless other threats lying in wait, Mary's return allows Father Johnstone to forget about that for the time being. He lifts her up, holds her close as she licks his face. She smells like grime and old ashtray, but the pastor burrows his nose into Mary's neck regardless, sighing deeply. Then Madeline brings him back to reality.

"Mary tracked the man from the fire," she says. "So we should think about leaving soon. The three of us." Madeline turns to Dr. Keller who is still seated by a slowly recovering Mrs. Wright. "You'll tend to her...keep her breathing, make sure she doesn't choke to death," she orders. "See if you can get her talking."

"Madeline, she *just* got back," the pastor says, clutching Mary closer to his body. She's exhausted, breathing shallow. Her coal black nose feels like ice against his cheek and he doesn't want to let her go again, let alone endanger her. "Can you give her a minute?"

"We don't have a lot of those to spare," she says.

"You can't just have her tell us where to go?" the pastor asks. He knows he's reaching. If that was an option, he'd like to think Madeline would have offered it.

"It doesn't work like that, Johnstone. She doesn't know the difference between north and south. She can't write down an address for us," Madeline explains. "Sorry, but she has to come with us."

"Pardon me, Miss Paige, but are you saying you can communicate with that dog?" Dr. Keller asks.

"Yes," she says, short. Madeline presses on, explaining, "To her that trail is like an invisible rope. She can't tell you where it ends or where it's going. All she can do is follow it," she says. "And we'll just have to go where she takes us."

"So we're supposed to follow her with no idea of what we're walking into," Father Johnstone says.

"Correct," Madeline says. "But if it makes you feel any better, they won't know we're coming."

"What unnerves me is that he can flip over a two-ton truck," Father Johnstone says. "In addition to whatever else he's capable of."

"Then pray we don't wind up in a parking lot." Madeline stares him down; he's scared. She can feel it in every hair on her arms and neck, as if they're being static-shocked.

"Wait. You two know the person that flipped over those trucks?" Dr. Keller cuts in.

"Yes," Madeline says. Again, short. "C'mon, Johnstone, you knew it was going to come to this eventually."

"Would this person have anything to do with Helena and Kurt's condition?" Dr. Keller asks.

Madeline finally turns around to face him. "Yes, as a matter of fact."

"And you're going to track this person down armed with nothing but your wits?" Dr. Keller asks, scoffing. "That sound like any kind of a *plan* to you, Miss Paige? Even I know you don't walk into a fight unprepared."

"It's complicated," Madeline counters weakly. She looks at the pastor, back to the doctor, unsure as to how much she wants to tell him.

"Then uncomplicate it for me," he says.

Father Johnstone sighs. "She's right, David. It's complicated."

"Complexity I can handle," Dr. Keller says. "But if you assume this to be an issue of me not believing you, then I'll say this: for thirty years, I've never seen you do anything remotely remarkable, Pastor. You've led the flock well, but I'd hardly call that out of the ordinary," he says. "Now you're performing miracles and healing people I know full well can't be healed. So I ask myself, 'What's changed the last thirty years? What's the new variable?'" he ponders aloud. "When I ask what you are, Miss Paige, I'm doing so with the understanding that you aren't exactly like our pastor here, and you aren't exactly like me. Make sense? I'm allowing you to admit that you might not be like the rest of us." Dr. Keller pauses a moment, smiling at one corner of his mouth. "My singular regret about your aunt's passing is that the rest of this town never knew how truly gifted she was, and I never discovered the extent of that gift. She too was a complicated woman, if you know what I mean."

"What did she tell you?" Madeline asks.

"She told me that I had cancer, Miss Paige," Dr. Keller says. "Lung cancer. Never smoked a cigarette in my life, but ol' Josie came out of the blue and said that I had it and that I didn't have much time left. There I was, going about my day, rifling through produce at the market and she laid that on me. I thought she was a kook, to be honest. Never showed any symptoms," he says. "But I did the X-rays anyway. It was there. Stage III," he says, frowning slightly. "I handled it about as poorly as anyone could. You're basically dead at Stage III. The cancer is already beyond your lungs, spreading into your lymph nodes and the rest of the body. I had a decision to make: either keep quiet about it or break the news and let the town begin the process of bringing in the next in line. Help out with the transition and the like. Josie reached out before I could do that, said she had something for me that might help."

Craft, Father Johnstone determines: the place between religion and medicine, the gray area in which a miracle can be boiled down to formula and ingredients. In the end, everything is ingredients: prayer, emotion, and even cancer cells. Cancer of the lungs, cancer of the earth.

"At three in the morning on a Tuesday, I drove over to her place by the daisy hill per her request. Whole town was asleep," Dr. Keller says. "Didn't want any witnesses or neighbors peeping out their windows, I guess. Josie said she wanted people knowing she was helping me just as much as I wanted them to know about the cancer eating me up. Discretion, right?" He gives Helena's leg a little pat. She's no longer coughing or struggling to breathe, seemingly in a state of comfortable rest. "We know what happens to people in this town who are considered strange, don't we?"

Dr. Keller pauses, allowing that question to sink in. Like the land and the water, people too can sour quickly.

"Josie sat me down in front of a platter," Dr. Keller says. "On top of it was a rabbit ripped open at the belly, stuffed with herbs and powders and whatever else. This thing is smoldering and kicking up fumes, stinking like embalming fluid and sweet perfume—she tells me to breathe it in. Any other time, I would have walked out of that house and never looked in her direction again. But I knew what was inside me, knew my time and options were short. I was just desperate enough to try anything, so I did as she asked. Inhaled that stuff until I couldn't take it anymore. Sucked it down until I was puking in her toilet," Dr. Keller says. "Felt like my lungs were being twisted like a dishrag. And Josie, she was knelt down on the bathroom floor next to me, patting me on the back and telling me not to make a big fuss about this later on...said I'd never understand anyway, so don't come back asking a bunch of questions about how this and that worked. Some things are just too complicated to be explained, she told me."

Dr. Keller stares at Madeline. "I'm sitting here because your aunt made it so, Miss Paige. You can feel free to confirm or deny what she was—that's up to you. Either way, I consider myself in her debt and think she'd want me to help you. So beyond looking after Helena here, how may I be of help?" he asks. "Or is it still too complicated?"

Madeline smiles. "What can you offer, Dr. Keller?"

"Tools of the trade, Miss Paige," he reaches over to his medical kit, removing a leather case about the size of a paperback novel. He unzips it along the edges, unfolding the two sides to reveal an assortment of surgical instruments: scalpels and lancets. They're unscuffed and bright, almost as if they've never been used. "Stainless steel, sharp as all hell," Dr. Keller says, removing one from the case and displaying it. "No pesky wooden or plastic handles to get in your way, if you know what I mean. Take it," he says.

Madeline reaches out with her hand, fingers aiming towards the handle of the instrument. Dr. Keller, however, retracts from her. "Problem?" she asks.

"Take it the *other* way." He gives Madeline a knowing smirk, one in which she returns. She takes a couple steps back and extends her arm towards the scalpel, zoning in, plucking it from his fingers. The object glides through the air, landing gently in her palm. "Magnetic manipulation. Impressive, Miss Paige," he says.

"Anything else?" Madeline holsters the scalpel in her jacket pocket.

This time Dr. Keller does not reach for his medical bag, but instead, the blazer draped over Helena Wright who appears to have stopped shivering completely. From the inner breast pocket he pulls out another leather case, although this one is much smaller than the last, about the size of a men's billfold. He unzips this one along the edges and displays the contents: one syringe capped with a plastic sheathe. "Etorphine," Dr. Keller says. "Also known as M99. Should knock out anyone needing it."

"Beats making something from scratch." Madeline takes the syringe and places it in her own inner breast pocket, plunger-side up. In the absence of Craft, modern medicine appears to be the next best thing that can be weaponized. "And what about my partner here?" she nods towards Father Johnstone who suddenly becomes sheepish at the idea of carrying a weapon.

"Can never go wrong with a gun," Dr. Keller shrugs.

"I don't own one," he says. Madeline throws him a look. He can practically hear her thinking, *'See, I told you we should have kept Shelby.'*

"I've got a shotgun with some rock salt shells in my trunk," Dr. Keller says. "You can borrow that for now."

"A little hardcore for a doctor," Madeline says.

Dr. Keller grins. "Right to bear arms is practically the eleventh commandment around here, Miss Paige. You've lived here long enough to know that."

Father Johnstone would prefer not to shoot anyone if he can help it, even those who'd wish harm upon him. He prays his hand won't be forced, prays Madeline's abilities serve Pratt and its people as the Lord would see fit.

"Let's head out." Father Johnstone sets Mary back down on the living room floor. She sniffs in the direction of Helena Wright, clearly offended by the odor of rot and stale blood.

Dr. Keller exits the home with Father Johnstone, Madeline, and Mary close behind. The four of them walk out to the late-model sedan parked in the street, yellow grass breaking down to particles. Barren trees waving their limbs with the wind, and sometimes snapping off completely when their integrity gives way. Dr. Keller pops open the trunk, revealing an old tackle box, some random medical supplies, a spare tire, and as promised, a long-barreled shotgun with cherry-red shells scattered about the interior. Father Johnstone reaches in, grabbing shells and placing them in his shirt pockets and jeans.

Meanwhile, Dr. Keller picks up the gun and loads it with a couple shells, cocking it closed. He hands it over, explaining to the pastor, "Point and shoot. Easy peasy. Won't kill anyone, but it'll put them down quick."

Father Johnstone holds the gun in his hands, attempting to

acclimate himself to its weight and architecture. Forged steel and wooden stock that's been sanded and stained—ingredients to make parts, and parts that compose a weapon. The pastor is put at ease, no longer defenseless or dependent on forces he doesn't completely comprehend. "Thank you, David," he says.

"My phone." Dr. Keller retrieves a small Nokia from his front pocket, handing it over to Madeline who slides it into an unoccupied space within her jacket. "I'll stick around here with Mrs. Wright," he stresses. "You call when you get wherever you're going."

Father Johnstone nods. He shakes Dr. Keller's hand, telling him, "Thanks again, David."

"You're welcome. Good luck out there," he says. "And don't forget to call."

"We won't." Madeline squats down, addressing Mary now, she says, "I know you're tired, but I need you to take us to the man you found. The man from the fire. Can you do that?"

Mary sighs, tilting her head slightly down. She sniffs the air before walking east at a slow jog, and the pastor and the witch follow closely behind. They follow her into that dark unknown, hunting that which would hunt them.

Procedeu XLIII: Renaştere

The following process is based upon Divine theory (teorie), and has not yet been successfully executed (executat), although it's been reported that many have attempted it in vain (zadar). Absolute purity (puritate) of intention is required—not to be confused with momentary desperation (disperare) or infatuation (dragoste nebună), renewed, manufactured, or otherwise. Divine connection (conexiune) must be established prior to the death (moarte) of the primary (primordial). The deceased female (femeie) should be stripped nude and laid face-up upon a bed of roses (trandafiri) and thorns (spini). Blood (sânge) will discharge from the wounds (răni), soaking into the earth (pământ), thus communicating directly to the Divine God (zeu) that her mortal shell has expired (expirat). Rosebuds will also collect blood essence for a later step in the process. No attempt to purify (purifica) the female corpse should be made, nor should the mortal body be altered or modified in concurrence with vanity (vanitate) or for self-indulgent reasons. The male must be a sub-primary. No common male (masculine) is capable of executing this process, therefore, it should not be attempted. Adverse effects (repercusiune) would instantly manifest in the form of death or physical decimation, even if their intentions are pure. Only a sub-primary will have the requirements necessary for execution, and even then, the chances of success are low to non-existent. The male will need to begin the process within a half moon (Lună) cycle of the female's mortal body expiring. He will lie upon her, also nude, and penetrate the vaginal cavity with Divine purpose and a refined sense of will while reciting the Prayer of Revival (Renaştere). Thorns will also puncture the physical body of the man, and his blood will also soak into the earth and rosebuds, mixing with that of the primary. Upon climax (punct culminant), the sub-primary will need to pluck seven (şapte) of the rosebuds from their stems, stuffing them into the vaginal cavity of the female in order to contain the life (viaţă) seed. This should initiate the *revival process, and if done correctly, will bring the female about in due course. However, it should be reiterated that no successful attempt has been made, and the most likely outcome is death, decimation (spiritual and/or physical), or a permanent dream (vis) state in which the sub-primary is forever tortured* (torturat) *by an anti-Divine presence, which is said to be worse than death. If the sub-primary should attempt this process, then they should establish a third-party executioner that is spiritually unbiased as an exit* (ieşire) *clause.*

The Party

The trio has been walking for close to an hour now, well beyond
Father Johnstone's quiet residential area with its modest homes
of under 1,000 square feet. Every yard is blanketed in strands of
lemon chiffon that used to be plots of heavy grass. Decomposing
flowers bow in arid beds, arcing in defeat. Dead ground. Dead
air. Everything rots at an accelerated pace.

"How much longer?" Father Johnstone asks.

"Not sure. All we can do is follow until she stops," Madeline
says, lowering her eyes down to Mary who is walking briskly in
the middle of the street.

"No." Father Johnstone shakes his head. "I meant Pratt. How
long?"

At the market, white and blue mold spots every tomato and
strawberry. Apples and pears are browned within their storage
crates. Even the cider has deformed to a sweet sludge, more like
sand than liquid. Everything sours or rots or depletes. It all dies,
and so it's only a matter of time before the people follow in suit.

"Won't be long," Madeline says. "You taste that? The air?"

"It's bitter," he says. "Like orange peel."

"That's the oxygen being replaced with something else," she
says. "Eventually, it won't even be breathable."

Mary pauses in the middle of the street, the coal-black nose
inspecting the air. She releases a small cough as she lumbers on,
nails clicking on the pavement at a much slower pace than when
they left the house. Father Johnstone doesn't need to consult
Madeline to know that she's on the brink of exhaustion. They've
practically crossed the entire town on foot, having started on the
eastern side where the pastor's house is. They're now nearing the
western fringe where only a few of Pratt's more upscale homes
remain, one of those being Dr. Keller's. Beyond that, it's nothing
but fields of brittle crop and gravel. Acre upon acre of diseased

ground that reeks of corrosion.

"You're worried," Madeline says.

"Yes." Father Johnstone slings the shotgun over his shoulder, letting the cool barrel rest against the side of his neck. For the first twenty minutes or so of the trip, he was concerned about being seen walking the streets of Pratt so brazenly with a firearm in-hand. He realizes now, this is the least of anyone's worries.

"Not about the town, though," she says. "Or yourself. This is a fear you tried to forget."

"That's one way of putting it."

"Then put it another," she says.

"As pastor you tend to preach certain virtues, hitting some harder than others such as forgiveness and refraining from temptation," he says. "'Hate the sin; love the sinner.' I've told the flock on many occasions that there'd be times when the Lord tests them, pushes them past their own threshold. I thought I led the flock well, but Mason Hollis changed all that," Father Johnstone says. "He showed me what this town is capable of when the circumstances become dire."

"You mean the Graybel girl?" Madeline confirms.

He nods. "They acted—not with the Lord in their heart—but with pure unmitigated *wrath*. They let hate dictate their actions. To deal with a monster, they became monsters themselves. And when it was all said and done, we got stories...stories about what he did to little Betty and the reprisals he paid...stories I don't even want to repeat."

"I've heard a few," Madeline says.

"Have you ever seen Betty?"

She shakes her head. "Can't say that I have."

"There's a reason for that. When something happens in this town, these people like to wipe away any reminders," the pastor says. "You saw how quickly this town came after me. That's the culture we're living in. Even though little Betty did nothing wrong, everyone looks at her like she's an eyesore. Like she's some kind of scar they want to buffer out. Raped and molested, and yet, she's the one that's cooped up in her own home, hiding out like a prisoner."

"I would think that sort of injustice would make you angry," Madeline says.

"It does." Father Johnstone nods, briefly scanning the ground for Mary who continues to trot along a few yards ahead. They're passing Dr. Keller's home at the moment: a three-bed, two-and-half bath ranch style so immaculate with its smoke white paint and cherry shutters, it completely detracts from the travesty of his lost lawn and infirm flowers.

"Then what are you afraid of?" Madeline asks.

"I've compromised. My fear is that if I encountered Mason Hollis, he could do to me what he did to this town," the pastor says.

"Fear is an ingredient, Johnstone," Madeline says. "As is your morality…as is the inadequacy I feel in you each time you remember you're carrying a loaded gun. Certain individuals are counting on your reluctance as a weakness." She gives her head a little shake. "I don't want you to forget yourself, but I don't want you to forget what we're doing out here either."

"We're following a trail to God knows what," he says.

"Not exactly." Madeline stops. She nods at Mary who is stationed at the center of the cul-de-sac, legs quivering from fatigue. Her head turns to Father Johnstone and Madeline, back to the house in front of her, growling. "Mary says this is it." Madeline pulls the scalpel out of her pocket, her forefinger bridging over it like a splint. She nods to the white house numbered 1811, asking, "Who lives there, Johnstone?"

At the center of the cul-de-sac, Mary eyes the estate of Mayor Andrew Farnsworth, who is currently celebrating his fourteenth year in office. And although the length of occupation may seem suspect, politics functions much like the law in Pratt, and is subject to its own jurisdictional rules and the personal whims of those who govern. People like Dr. Keller and the pastor had to earn their designation of 'pillar.' For Mayor Farnsworth, it was a position acquired through purchase.

'Boon money,' the pastor has heard it called. Money that wasn't earned, but handed over as part of an ancestral inheritance. Instead of starting a business or investing in a corporation, he assumed control of Pratt—viewing the population more like employees than friends and neighbors. They are part of the industry, a workforce, and Mayor Farnsworth has never been one to 'mingle with the help,' as they say. He and his third wife, Cady, tend to keep to their own kind, the other well-to-do living at Waterstone's end.

"Hm, well I guess that makes sense," Madeline says.

"What makes sense?" Father Johnstone asks.

"The mayor," she says. "Makes sense he'd come here."

"I never said anything about him."

"You didn't have to," she says. Madeline clicks her tongue, crouching down in the middle of the cul-de-sac. Mary paces over, breathing shallow, tongue hanging out and panting. "We're going to the house. If you see anybody coming, you have to warn us, okay?" Madeline says, giving her a little scratch under her chin. A tuft of fur breaks off from her jaw and drifts to the dead ground. "Go on," she says. Mary takes off at a jog, her gait uneven and labored. She weakly hops the curb that separates the cul-de-sac from dead ground. Brown grass breaks as she runs through it. Father Johnstone and Madeline watch her veer off to the left of the Farnsworth household, disappearing into shadow.

"She's not up to this," the pastor says, shaking his head, remorseful. The air tastes significantly worse than it did two blocks ago, a more pronounced bitterness. "It's killing her, isn't it?"

"Keep that gun ready." She ignores the question, marching toward the home with the pastor following close behind. Madeline pauses at the curb, looking right then left, saying,

"We'll check the windows first."

She follows the path that Mary cleared in the front yard, boots kicking up dust and debris that looks like compost. Father Johnstone has trouble breathing, gagging quietly on the stench of sour earth. Dead earth. Air laced with mold and poison. He prays for Mary, prays she doesn't see a single person out where the streetlights don't touch. He prays the good Lord provide safe passage. Father Johnstone prays, and Madeline feels every one of them.

"It's okay. Relax," she whispers to him. At the side of the house, pressed against white siding, Madeline brings her lips to his ear, telling him, "We stay quiet. We listen and play this smart, okay?" She pulls back, her cheek brushing his. Madeline feels him spiking, nerves shot. Father Johnstone's hands shake with adrenaline, fear. Anxiety. It's making her skin cook, so Madeline does the only thing she can to ease the tension.

She leans in, letting her breath mix with his, then pressure applies as Madeline kisses him. She kisses him gently, lovingly, and he lets it happen, lets all his worry and angst soak into her. He allows himself to have the moment because it could very well be the last time, and then Madeline pulls away. Slowly. She stares at him in the dark.

"Why?" he asks.

"Because now you're not thinking about being caught or killed," she says. "I need you calm." Madeline hooks a finger inside the waistline of the pastor's jeans, pulling him along the side of the house. "Now follow. Quiet."

They approach the first window, Madeline careful to duck her head under the sliver of light slicing through the curtains. She eases her back against the house and places two fingers to the corner of the glass. Father Johnstone waits, giving a quick check behind him and off to the left where it's nothing but dark dead yard and a few crumbling oak trees. Madeline removes her fingers away from the glass, motioning for the pastor to keep following.

She repeats this process at the second window, then the third: stopping, touching the pane and listening through her fingers. Madeline will wait a moment, shaking her head as if there's nothing suspect happening within these rooms, but the pastor thinks otherwise. He can hear noises in each one, can see bodies moving through the cracks in burgundy curtains. There's definitely something of interest happening in these rooms, but before the pastor can voice it, Madeline turns to him, mouth to his ear, saying, "I hear it, too. Tributes."

A ritual, the method in which homage is paid to the Goddess, Madeline explained. Father Johnstone would like to believe that Mayor Farnsworth is too respectable of a man to allow this to happen under his roof, but it's not beyond possibility. Farnsworth has never been one of the flock, has remarried twice over to women many years his junior. Word around Pratt is he's terribly unfaithful.

Madeline peeks around the corner of the house, making certain that no one is standing guard by the back entrance with a shotgun of their own. The rear deck of the Farnsworth household is sizeable, and the floodlights fixated on the back of the home illuminate it well. Too well to sneak around without being seen, but Madeline eases onto the wooden planking anyway with Father Johnstone close behind her. The cedar two-by-fours haven't gone completely rotten yet, but they're on their way. Splits and soft spots are emerging already, making it more like walking on a very hard Styrofoam as opposed to wood.

Father Johnstone thought the plague would only extend to the elements: the soil and foliage, the water and wildlife. Now he realizes it won't stop there. Homes will gradually weaken and crumble. Cars will be devoured by rust. Whether or not he and Madeline will live to see it remains to be told, but it's happening already. Pratt is dying. Fading fast.

Madeline scoots along the back wall of the house, nearing the sliding glass door that separates the cedar deck from the main living space inside the house. Light filters through sheer curtains, glowing less harshly than the high-powered LEDs over the frame. Father Johnstone trails along, always mindful to check behind them and beyond the cones of halogen. He holds the shotgun firmly, ready to fire at the first sign of movement.

"Our guy is in there," Madeline says, peering through the edge of the sliding glass door. There's an inch or so of space that the curtain doesn't cover, allowing her to look inside. She reaches back with her non-scalpel hand, tugging on Father Johnstone's shirt cuff to bring him over. "Look," she tells him.

Father Johnstone sees Mrs. Farnsworth pushed up against an antique credenza, completely nude except for a pair of flesh-toned pumps. Mr. Neilson is between her legs, pumping her, oatmeal-textured buttocks flexing with every thrust. The furniture shakes violently as he penetrates her, framed family portraits wiggling, falling flat. A symbol is drawn on both their foreheads.

"They've been marked," Madeline says, picking up on the pastor's inquiry. "Like cattle."

He sees Mr. and Mrs. Aames, Deputy Clarke and his wife, the Halstons, however, none of them are paired up with their spouses. Each is with a foreign partner, fornicating upon a couch, against a mini bar, on the living room rug. All of them have that same marking swabbed upon them, the same blood. The same vacant look in their eye, as if they're miles away from themselves.

"Now look at the back table there." Madeline drapes her chin on the pastor's shoulder, her mouth in his ear again. "See anything familiar?"

A silver serving tray is stationed near the back wall, surrounded by bottles of red wine and dark liquor, glasses and flutes at varying stages of emptiness. Soft morsels of cake populate the tray, no larger than a standard crouton. Most of them have already been consumed.

"They've been eating my curse," Madeline says. "They're not themselves right now. Just like what happened to you…at the church," she whispers, eliciting a spike of shame in the pastor. He desecrated the Lord's House, stained the floors with *lust*. "It's not their fault," she says. "No one is to blame but him."

Then the man emerges from a hallway near the back of the room, the man from the fire at Madeline's home. Father Johnstone remembers the patches of baldness spotting his scalp, although it appears to be more severe now. Only a few wispy strands remain. He's still wearing the black cassock and pants, a clerical uniform sans the white inner collar enveloping the neck. Mud and grass stains streak the fabric, as if he's been sleeping outdoors for weeks. Even at this meager distance, Father Johnstone doesn't recognize him as a man of Pratt or otherwise. The face is grizzled, chapped. Sickly pale like a cancer patient. Eyes are gaunt, receding into the socket as if they can't wait for death.

He approaches Cady Farnsworth and Mr. Nielson, now having concluded their affair upon the credenza. A wedding photo of Cady and the mayor has fallen to the floor, spreading cracked glass over their smiles. Mr. Nielson steps away her, already wilting at the waist. He walks out of the room as the man in black squats down between Cady's legs, readying a small receptacle. His fingers pry her vagina apart and Father Johnstone witnesses what appears to be her pushing, straining to eject the semen of Mr. Nielson into a stone bowl. Her abdominal muscles tense from the effort. The semen sputters unevenly, chunky, a few sprays of urine unintentionally hitting the bowl and the shoulder of the man in black, adding to the mud and grass stains already embedded in the uniform. He doesn't seem to mind. Like everyone else within the room, he too seems miles away from himself.

"A harvest," Madeline says. "They're collecting ingredients."

"For what?" the pastor asks.

Madeline shrugs, the leather of her jacket wrinkling at the shoulders. "I don't know, but they're gathering a lot of them."

The man in black sticks his forefinger inside Cady Farnsworth, straight upon entry, but then he curls it like a hook to excavate more fluid into the bowl. Dirty fingers with soil from the fields under his nails. He repeats this a few more times while Cady continues to push, the inner labia spread wide like a yawn. Slick pink organ discharging fluid. It's clear with only the occasional white morsel flowing into the bowl. The man in black stands up, uttering something to Cady that neither the pastor nor Madeline can hear. She remains on the credenza while the rest of the room continues to philander — to fuck. Slack faces and dead eyes. They don't even appear to be enjoying it. Father Johnstone determines it isn't *lust* he's witnessing, but rather, a forgery of the act.

"We cross when his back is turned," Madeline says. "The rest of them are too out of it to see anything."

The pastor watches the cleric survey the room, checking couples with the bowl ready in his hands. Ready to collect tribute, to collect ingredients. Deputy Clarke climaxes joylessly, immediately reaching for his pistol lying in the holster on a nearby tabletop. He removes it, inserting the barrel of the firearm into the vaginal canal of Mrs. Halston who begins to push. The man in black sees this, hurrying over to assist, but Mrs. Halston is spilling everywhere, and the fluid is leaking into the bullet chamber where it will be difficult to harvest. He takes the pistol from the deputy, shaking it over the bowl, and this is when Father Johnstone feels Madeline give a firm push.

"Now," she hisses.

They cross the stretch of window separating them from the party. It takes only about a second. Madeline checks to make sure none of them noticed, and it's just as it was: people fornicating, the man in black shaking Deputy Clarke's pistol over the stone bowl. With his back turned to them, she finally notices a searing in the fabric of the cleric's shoulder. Wounds scabbed over with dry blood. Madeline was able to hit him with lightning, but not directly. The burn on his shoulder was the result of being grazed.

"As you probably guessed, that's his Secondary in there," Madeline says.

The battery, the power source, the counterpoint to Father Johnstone. Same function with differing usages. The pastor is tempted to storm into the room, gun aimed and level upon the cleric. He'd fire and it'd be over. He could end this calamity, put Pratt back on the Divine path. Begin the healing.

"No." Madeline puts a hand on his shoulder. "We play it smart. We check all the angles before we attack."

She heads towards the opposite end of the deck, passing two more sets of windows with bodies writhing inside. Father Johnstone follows, catching glimpses of skin, shreds of sex through the burgundy curtains. He can't make out any of them, but the motion is familiar. Madeline doesn't even bother touching the windowpanes this time, instead, proceeding to the wooden staircase that leads to the widow's walk on the second level. Between wine tastings with friends or shopping trips, Cady Farnsworth used to sit up there for hours, either reading magazines or painting her nails. Gusts of wind would blow in from the east and all those beautiful crops would wave with it, almost like liquid.

Madeline sticks the scalpel into the handrail of the staircase, testing it, turning to Father Johnstone and whispering, "Careful. It's not going to hold for much longer."

The two of them ascend, conscious to keep their feet towards the end of the stairs where it's reinforced instead of the middle. There's plenty of give, the pastor notices. Each step is like walking on a gymnasium mat. The cedar compresses, leaving heel and boot-print impressions, but the two of them make it to the top without incident. Under the floodlight of the widow's walk, Madeline and the pastor see Cady's padded lounge chair, a small side table with a bottle of nail polish resting upon it. No people.

The two of them edge toward the door with an already-tarnishing brass knob. Windows are on either side, curtained, but not closed. One of them is cracked about an inch, allowing the conversation within the room to seep out to the widow's walk. Yet again, Father Johnstone is conscious of holding a shotgun that he may soon have to use, but that's when Madeline touches his hand, mouthing, "Relax. It's okay."

They level their ears to the crack in the window, eavesdropping. From within the room, the mayor says, "Town's never taken well to outsiders."

"I'm not an outsider," a second voice responds. The tone is dulcet, almost raspy. "I'm from everywhere." He pauses to the take a drink, the heel of the glass clunking gently on wood countertop. He sighs, continuing, "Besides, what these people think is of no consequence. They're sheep."

"Well, I've never stated it *that* bluntly," Mayor Farnsworth says. "But a town can't run without people. No people, no industry. No economy."

"Oh, the people will stay," the second man assures him. "They're too stupid to leave. Most of them are praying the situation resolves itself when they should be packing. Being set in your ways can prove to be hazardous in times like these."

"*Will* the situation resolve itself?" the mayor asks.

"Oh, you don't need to worry about that. I'll hold up my end of the deal," the second man replies.

"You make a bold claim, Mr. Pollux."

Madeline looks at Father Johnstone, nodding gravely. She pulls one of her jacket sleeves up, exposing an arm flecked with raised hairs. The pastor's spiking again, nerves returning. Anxiety. She mouths to him, "Relax," hand reaching over and landing on his, cradling it. Her thumb smoothes over his knuckles and the bandage. "It's okay." He nods, sighs softly. Pressure eases in his chest and shoulders. He prays for safety, prays they not be discovered.

"My demands are just as bold," Pollux says. "Pratt is done. No industry, no economy, as you said. It's a money pit. But more importantly, you've lost respect in this town."

"Is that so?" the mayor argues. He's none to pleased to hear this.

"It is. Because when they wake up tomorrow…when they walk out of their homes and everything around them is dead and the air tastes like rat poison—it's *not* going to be you they turn to," Pollux says. "They'll flock to this Father Johnstone you've been telling me about."

Upon hearing his name, the pastor emits another spike—this one powerful enough to crack and peel the paint off the house. The cedar of the widow's walk shivers beneath the two of them, threatening to give way.

"A goddamn charlatan is more like it!" Mayor Farnsworth says heatedly. "The audacity of that man, thinking he can go over my head."

"Mmm, yes, I've heard."

"For thirty years he's been as docile as a dead horse," the mayor says. "Now I'm hearing about 'miracles' and an entire slew of other rumors. Revolting things, Mr. Pollux, as I'm sure you're aware. It's not a good look for this town."

"Oh, I'm well aware of that. In fact, I daresay I'm more intimate with the situation than you are," Pollux says. "And that's why you're going to allow me free rein to handle the situation as I see fit."

"Within reason, of course," the mayor says.

"Have you seen what's become of your town?" Pollux asks. "I'd say the state of affairs in Pratt has become strikingly *un*reasonable."

"As are your demands," the mayor says. "Your associate…he won't go over well here. Father Johnstone has swayed the people with his little performance. He's got their allegiance."

"My associate will be fine. Curing a few debilitated is one thing. Curing a town is another," he says. "People here…they're fickle, I've learned. Simple. They like their routine. And if it's one thing simple people absolutely loathe it's complexity…makes them forget themselves, like this situation you've got on your hands," Pollux says. "Loyalty is always the first thing to go. When you're starving…when you're sick and tar is boiling in your lungs—you'll take aid from just about anybody."

Mayor Farnsworth clears his throat, unsettled. "Where might your associate be now?"

"Keeping an eye on things. I know you can't feel them but we've got company lingering about," Pollux says.

Father Johnstone spikes. Madeline can feel it in her teeth this time, like the nerves are being squeezed with pliers. She backs against the wall of the house, skin on fire. She can barely hold the scalpel. The pastor shakes, holding the gun tight to his chest as paint molts from the house and cedar strains beneath him. He can't move. Can barely breathe.

"We've got two little mice sneaking around," Pollux says. "And what do mice do? They stay very quiet and very still, and they watch you from the cracks."

In the distance, Mary is barking. She's staggering through what used to be the cornfields, barking as if someone has a hand around her throat. Father Johnstone looks to Madeline, hoping she'll know what to do next or have some sort of a plan, but she's shivering, nose bleeding.

"Stop," she whispers. "Please."

"And you let them watch, mayor. You let them think they're safe," Pollux says. "You let them think they're nice and hidden, and that's when you spring the trap."

From just above the floodlight, something swings across the spectrum—an object long enough to clear the distance between the roof and Madeline's face. She's hit in the cheek by some blunt object, knocking a few teeth loose. Blood gushes and careens around her mouth, onto the window and wall. Instinctively, the pastor fires above him—not aiming—shooting at God knows what. Rock salt shatters the lights and the widow's walk goes dark. It's quiet for a moment. Quiet, except for Mary struggling to warn her owner and the sound of shifting weight on the roof shingles above. The pastor wants to run out to her, wants to pick her up and escape, but his cowardice of what lurks above prevents him.

So he prays. Father Johnstone prays and the Lord has nothing for him.

The cedar begins to crack, splitting like a sheet of ice under his feet. He presses his body against the wall, quiet, just like a little mouse. A helpless little mouse praying and hoping not to be caught.

"You can come on in, if you'd like, preacher," Pollux says. "Join the party."

He waits a moment for the pastor to answer, but there's no response, no reasonable way he can be faced in the pastor's mind. Not without Madeline, that is. He prays for her to wake up. Prays the impact didn't kill her.

"No? You sure?" Pollux offers one more time, but again, no answer. "Have it your way."

Not a moment later, an object hits the flooring of the widow's walk originating from the roof, too light in weight to damage it any further. It takes a couple seconds for Father Johnstone to realize it's hissing, emitting something into the surrounding air. It tastes pungent, and burns. He begins to cough, choke. His throat closes and he can't breathe, can't see anything because his eyes are burning and tearing up.

Father Johnstone staggers away from the wall, onto a section of the planking with less support. The cedar of the widow's walk finally gives under his weight, breaking like Styrofoam. He falls through. Father Johnstone falls, and Pratt's salvation falls with him.

On the Road with Billy Burke, Truck Stop Preacher

"Been on the road a long time now. Long, long time. Can barely remember the place I used to call home. It's almost as if it's been burned right outta ol' Billy's mind. Don't really matter because as long as I got the Lord in my heart, I'm right where I need to be. We all are. We got the road. We got each other. I've witnessed many of you come of age in your faith, and I'm mighty proud of that. You give me hope that the world ain't gonna fall into the hands of the faggots, sand-niggers, and undesirables. When the Devil come at ya, I know you boys will do the right thing and punch him right in the fucking pie hole. Your bond with the Lord is strong now; you're strong. These clueless assholes kneeling down on the prayer bars to give the Lord a hummer are just going through the motions. They're scared...trying to take out an insurance policy for the afterlife. Their faith is passive and weak. They'd rather scrub the floors of the Lord's Kingdom than fight alongside Him. I see a lot of brawlers in this room...got the cuts on your knuckles to prove it, too, don't ya? Taken a few licks dishin' out the Good Word. Well, I've got my scars, too, boys. I'm proud of them. Proud of every goddamn one of them. Ol' Billy here...he's inclined to add a few more to the collection before the winter ends."

The Chairs

...hours later.

Father Johnstone wakes up in a room he doesn't recognize, body aching and the burn of what feels like a large gash sweeping across his forehead. Another sears the side of his neck. Sweat pours into the wounds where the cedar of the widow's walk bit into his skin, stinging him to a state of consciousness.

"You gotta keep this stuff warm or it's worthless," a man speaks low from the corner, almost too quiet to hear. "That's the trick."

Father Johnstone is disoriented, seated in a metal folding chair like the ones he keeps in storage at the church. Not seated by choice, though. Duct tape is wrapped around his ankles, binding him to the front legs. Many more lengths encompass the torso, from his stomach to his sternum — he's held firmly to the backing of the chair. It makes it difficult to breathe, and the air he *can* take is rotten like old meat, testing his gag reflex. His wrists are taped together above his lap, hands purple and peppered with various splinters and cuts. The gauze dressing on his palm remains, although it's now soiled with a rust-colored patch. It needs to be changed.

"No warmth, no life," the man says.

Light pouring through the living room windows obscures his face, but the pastor can more or less see what he's doing, even through the haze of residual tear gas coating his eyes that faintly burns. The man dips what looks to be a short-handled brush, coating thin bristles in some kind of liquid before applying it to a paper surface. He paints across it methodically, slowly.

"You don't appreciate life until you have it threatened, preacher."

This is neither Pollux nor the cleric that attempted to burn down Madeline's home. He's got a full head of hair with a lean, healthy build. His voice is a bit craggy, containing a hint of Midwestern twang that almost makes him sound local. Perhaps not from Pratt specifically, but one of the surrounding towns.

"Who are you?" Father Johnstone asks. His throat is raw, almost as if it's been charred by vomit. It's uncomfortable to speak.

The man chuckles at the question, dipping the brush into the bowl again and painting. Small careful strokes are used to apply the liquid on the page, glazing it in a thin coat. "Your friend is comin' round."

He points a finger past Father Johnstone. Sitting roughly five feet to his left is Madeline, also bound to a metal folding chair. Shades of eggplant and strawberry-red label the point where she was hit in the face. Dry blood crusts her lips, traveling all the way down to her collarbones. She spits and then immediately winces from the effort. Father Johnstone can only assume the inside of her mouth was split open by her own teeth.

"You okay?" he asks her.

Madeline sighs, eyes closed. Closed tight. She shakes her head, then gives a little wiggle of her arms to test the integrity of the tape. She can't even push her own elbows off her ribcage.

"You were hit," the pastor says.

"Figured." Madeline spits blood again. It's the same shade of brown as old motor oil. She connects eyes with Father Johnstone a moment before noticing the man in the corner, still toiling away: dipping the brush, painting, repeating. She nods towards the man, looking at the pastor as if to ask, 'Who's that?'

Father Johnstone attempts to raise his shoulders, failing to shrug because of the tape. He doesn't know the man. He doesn't recognize the room they're in or the dead tract of land beyond the dirty windows. Outside, he can see tiny lumps of animal twitching on the ground, but his vision is too blurry to make out what exactly.

"Birds," Madeline says, testing the tape around her ankles

now. It also holds.

Those last moments flash through the pastor's mind: trapped on the widow's walk with Pollux on one side and another man waiting on the roof, clutching onto the shotgun with no idea what to do. Mary was barking, trying to warn the two of them to get away. To escape. He doesn't want to assume the worst, but the pastor can't help but think Mary spent her last breaths out in those dark dead fields, trying to save the only family she's ever known.

"It progresses," the man says, still swiping that brush over the paper. Sunlight continues to obscure his features. He's seen in outlines of gold. "*Insecta* first, then *Rodentia* and *Aves*," the man says. "Proceeding to larger *animalia*. They, too, return to ash and dust. That's what he tells me."

From the next room over, Madeline and Father Johnstone hear the sound of two sets of footsteps. One is staggered but supportive; the other is intermittent, laced with the distinct sound of boots dragging over old flooring. After a moment, Pollux passes through the entryway with the cleric holding on to him, a slender arm wrapped around his neck. Tufts of thinning hair that he had the previous night have since molted away, leaving his scalp bald with the exception of a few random sores and lacerations. He's weak, can barely open his eyes let alone walk. Pollux escorts him to the corner, shrugging him off. He doesn't look how the pastor imagined he would, an assumption made having been acquainted with him through actions rather than conversation. Pollux is handsome, young, but there's an exhaustion in his face that makes him appear strung out, as if he hasn't slept in years. He lets the cleric's body slide down the wall where he winds up crumpled on the floor, breathing shallowly. Twitching. Dying.

Father Johnstone prays for deliverance. He prays with every desperate fiber in his soul the Lord strike this man down and return Pratt to its former self.

"I can feel that," Pollux says. He breaks into a small grin, not offended. Seemingly pleased, if the pastor didn't know any better. "You know what's interesting about prayer, Father Johnstone?" he starts. "If I tell a congregation I'm praying for someone to develop lung cancer or a brain tumor or to get in a fatal car accident, people get all bent out of shape like I'm approaching religion the wrong way," he says. "But if I tell them it's directed at a man that bombed a movie theater or shot up an elementary school—suddenly, it's okay. That's the compelling thing that I've noticed while traveling around: that deep down at the core of their being, people want their God to be as vengeful as they are."

"Let us go," Madeline says.

"And *speaking* of vengeful, I'd try to get comfortable because you're not going anywhere for a while," Pollux says. "Or have you not yet realized how you ended up in that chair?"

"You mean the part where you had me hit in the face with a baseball bat?" she says.

"Sledgehammer. Rubber head. Couldn't have you blocking it and running off again, could I?"

Madeline leans forward, sneering. "Maybe you need to stop chasing me."

"Oh, but I have," he says. "Why do you think I had your house set on fire? For fun?" Pollux glares at Madeline. She doesn't reply. "I needed to get your attention…give that mutt of his something to track. And you followed, just like I knew you would. You came right to me." Pollux pauses thoughtfully before looking over to Father Johnstone. "Your friend had been snooping around though, Pastor. Last night's harvest was important and I didn't need Dr. Keller ruining it. He needed to be kept busy. So I gave him something to do…something he wouldn't feel comfortable leaving unattended after the untimely passing of Mr. Clevenger."

"Helena," the pastor says.

Pollux nods. "The doctor's tried calling a few times," he says, removing the cell phone from his pocket, displaying it for the two of them before setting it down on top of the nearby desk. "And I know you don't feel things the way we do," he briefly glances in Madeline's direction, "but those ribbons Helena put out for you, the pure *lust* and want dripping off of them…exquisite. She made for a good harvest. Lured our guests right in. A bit old for *my* tastes, but I think you would have found her cunt adequate enough." He smiles, and the pastor feels a flush of anger course through his neck and face. Pure gall. He wants out of the chair, wants to level the shotgun to Pollux's chest and rectify his mistake, and he can feel this. They both can.

"He's pushing your buttons," Madeline warns him.

"We just know each other too well, don't we? Or at least I thought we did," Pollux amends. "You remember our last day among the Feri, don't you?"

"I remember you breaking the rules and getting us kicked out," she says. "And I remember having to say goodbye to my family and everything I've ever known because of your ego." The blood from her cheek fills up the gutters of her mouth again. She spits, telling him, "That's what I remember."

"I remember the hunt," he says. "I remember being out there in the forest for hours…cold, hungry. We would follow hoof tracks and urine marks and trees that had been horned like a trail that might never end. It was inefficient, to say the least." Pollux sighs, he smiles. "That's when I realized we could bring the hunt to us. All you need to do is put the scent out and wait."

"What you did was for spectacle and nothing more," she says. "You weren't providing; you were showing off."

"Maybe." Pollux gives a non-committal nod of the head, taking a few paces across the room. He briefly checks on the cleric wheezing in the corner. "It worked on you, though. You came right to me. You put yourself exactly where I wanted you."

"Yeah, you said that already," Madeline retorts.

He scoffs. "You don't even know, do you?"

"Know what?"

Pollux stands over Madeline, leaning over to bring his face closer to hers. He brushes the hair out of her eyes with a finger, slowly, savoring her skin. "Odd, that a woman your aunt's age would die for no apparent reason, isn't it?" He pauses, allowing Madeline to soak this in. "Even more odd that she'd leave everything to you."

When Josephine Paige died, there was no mention of foul play or anything to indicate that she passed on before her time. Most of the women and wives referred back to what Father Johnstone told them: that God has a plan for everyone. They didn't need to understand. 'Just take comfort that He is in control. There is a path, and if you follow his Word, you'll be with Him in the Kingdom.'

Madeline frowns, apparently, more upset with herself than she is with Pollux. Father Johnstone can almost hear her thinking, *I should have known. I should have been more careful.*

"How?" she asks.

Pollux nods. "I was kind about it, if that makes any difference. She didn't even know it was happening. It was easy."

"But you denied her the proper burial," Madeline says, much to the chagrin of Father Johnstone. He presided over Josephine's proceedings himself, so he has no idea what she means by this claim. He lowered her into the ground, he prayed, and those that attended the service mourned in her honor.

"I didn't need another loose end to tie up. She was bait, and I treated her as such," Pollux says. "Besides, those traditions aren't mine anymore." He looks at Father Johnstone, brow furrowing. He smiles and turns back to Madeline, "Your Secondary has no idea what we're talking about. You really don't tell him anything, do you?"

"He knows enough," she says lamely.

"I highly doubt that. If Clevenger were still alive, he could report in person on your unsavory methods of harvesting," he says. "My scouts saw more than you'd care to know and this town smells it on you. Your reputation precedes you."

"As does yours. Can't go anywhere without it all turning to shit," she says. "Your friend in the corner there is learning that firsthand."

Pollux makes his way over to the cleric, standing over him, clicking his tongue a couple times. "Such a waste." He turns to Father Johnstone, telling him, "Picked this one up in Barnes. You remember Barnes, don't you? Same place you bought that Challenger you love so much. I'm sure you haven't forgotten." He squats down next to the cleric, picking up one of his arms so that it's above the shoulder. It drops dead weight when he lets go, slapping hard against the floor. "I'm afraid I put too many miles on this one."

"He doesn't need to hear this," Madeline says, referring to the pastor.

"See, when the Primary and the Secondary aren't a good fit," Pollux says, ignoring Madeline's interruption, "you're going to see some side-effects. Could be any number of things: exploding white blood cells, cancer, brain tumors. Unfortunate things happen when you try and force it."

"Stop it! I'm warning you," Madeline tries again, firmer this time. She's bucking in her seat now in an attempt to shake the chair loose at the screws.

"Excuse me one moment," Pollux says, giving the pastor a smile. He makes his way towards Madeline, bending at the waist so that his face is inches away from hers. "If you think you can bolt lightning through here to try and fry us all, you might consider that you and your friend are strapped to metal chairs."

Madeline smirks before launching a torrent of blood and spit in his face. Pollux smiles back, licking the cleft of his upper lip and tasting it. He thumbs his nose and tongues the print clean, apparently pleased.

"You and that fucking mouth of yours. I missed it," he says. "Does it miss me?"

She doesn't answer. Madeline breaks eye contact, staring off to where the sun is pouring through the windows.

"Silent treatment, eh? I can work with that." Pollux snaps his left hand out, clamping down on Madeline's face. He digs his fingers into the spot where she was hit, nails digging through the bruise like it's old fruit. She starts to scream. Madeline screams as the gash on the inside of her mouth grinds against loose teeth, fresh blood cascading down her chin. She's so loud the pastor's eardrums rattle. The pastor interjects, yelling at him to stop. He screams at Pollux to let her go, but he knows the gesture is futile. He won't stop, won't relent. Not until he feels like it.

"Open," he says.

"*Frrrruk you!*" Her words are muffled by blood and palm.

Pollux pulls the scalpel out of his jacket pocket, the one that Dr. Keller gave her in the event she ran into trouble. He places the edge of it so close to her eye it's flirting with the lashes.

"Want to see if you can push this away before I stick you with it?" Pollux says.

Madeline doesn't respond, doesn't blink. Tears run down her face and Pollux digs his fingers into the wound again—hard enough to elicit another scream. He slips the scalpel between the rows of teeth and pushes the blade against the roof of her mouth. Already, the pastor can see fresh blood trickling down the handle and rolling over Pollux's fingers. He pries down on the interior of her mouth, pushing until Madeline can no longer tilt her head back any further. Veins in her neck pop and strain. Blood from her cheek and the roof of her mouth accumulates in the back of her throat, eventually making it so each breath geysers onto Pollux's knuckles in splashes.

Father Johnstone prays he yields. He prays for the Lord to send them a miracle.

Pollux sprinkles something into her mouth with his left hand.

Not a powder. They look more like food crumbs, if the pastor isn't mistaken.

"Little taste of your own work," he says.

Pollux straddles Madeline, very nearly sitting down in her lap. He removes the scalpel from her mouth and pushes on her jaw so it closes, clamping down hard.

"Swallow," he says.

Madeline groans, chin tilted up and strong hands cutting her breathing. Pollux grazes the blade of the scalpel against her good cheek, eliciting a sharp yelp.

"I'm going to cut off your air now. You're not going to be able to breathe, so that blood building in your throat is going to become a bit of a choking hazard," he says. "You ever choke on your own blood before? They say it's the only thing worse than drowning. They say sometimes the taste of it becomes so overwhelming the person will vomit in their own mouth. I wonder what you'll do."

Madeline groans. Screams through teeth.

Pollux pinches down on her nostrils.

"Swallow or I'm going to field dress your friend here, just like back home. I'll harvest him for parts and then splay what's left of him up in the fucking streets. He can cook out in the goddamn sun for all I care. You follow?" he asks. "I'll skip the burial. No casket. No prayer. You know what happens to people like him when they're denied that. He'll get to watch what I do to this town from limbo. That what you want?"

After about three seconds, the definitive sound of fluid churning through Madeline's throat can be heard. Her neck gulps down the blood, the saliva, and whatever foreign substance Pollux sprinkled into her mouth. Hands are removed from her face, immediately followed by Madeline panting—panting hard. It's strained through the tape constricting her torso, cutting into her breathing. She spits, curses at him.

Pollux walks back over to Father Johnstone, removing a

handkerchief from one of his pockets. He proceeds to clean the blade and handle, polishing it. "As I was saying, the Primary—her," he points at Madeline, "and the Secondary—you," he nods to the pastor. "That's a relationship based on many different factors. You're a car guy though, right? So you know what happens when you put in the wrong parts under the hood."

Either it won't run efficiently or it won't run at all. Peak performance will never be reached. Father Johnstone nods. He knows what this is building towards.

"You get the right pairing together...there's a lot of potential there," Pollux says. "Like this instrument, for example: I touch it and I know your friend Dr. Keller has had possession of it for many years, but it's never left the case. There's no history. So I come along and I give it one. I give it a reason to exist and I give it purpose. I bring out its potential." Pollux motions to the cleric in the corner of the room. "That gentleman there. He was a lot like you used to be: alone and unfulfilled...just sort of going through the motions. Then I came along and I brought out his potential."

Father Johnstone lets his eyes fall on the man. He's pale. Feeble. Fingers look like white sticks about to break. "He's dying," the pastor says.

"We all are," he says. "As soon as we're born. Doesn't have to be that way, though. You've read about it. You've seen it for yourself."

Mary. Mary came back. She was dead, and then just as quickly, alive again. He prays for her, prays she got away safe and can breathe clean air again.

"My associate and I are working on something." Pollux nods to the man in the corner, still toiling away at the desk: dipping the brush, applying the glaze to the page, repeating. Even when Madeline had a scalpel splitting the roof of her mouth, the man couldn't be bothered to look. "We'd like to bring you in. You could do a lot more with us," Pollux offers enticingly. "Reach your potential."

"I don't see that happening," the pastor says.

"You sure about that?" He asks this, but not in a threatening way. It almost sounds as if he's genuinely concerned for his wellbeing. "Maybe you should consider why you're even in this situation."

Father Johnstone looks at Madeline. She's crying, struggling against whatever is coursing through her system, fading away as the miles between herself and reality expand.

"You're taped up, cut to shit, and exhausted. You're helpless. And it's all because of her," Pollux says, leaning his face towards the pastor. "Do you agree, Madeline? Do you admit this is your fault?" he asks her.

She strains, grunts, trying to contain the words. "Y-yes."

"Maybe you didn't know it, but you're changing already. Blood type, iris pigmentation." Pollux thumbs down one of the Father Johnstone's lower eyelids, examining. "I took the liberty of reading your charts while paying a visit to Mr. Clevenger. It's already underway. Look at your fingerprints."

Father Johnstone tilts his eyes down, twisting his hands outward against the grain of the tape. Lack of circulation has turned his fingers purple, but the padding remains discernible. In all honesty, the pastor has never familiarized himself with this piece of himself, but he knows what a fingerprint is supposed to look like: a swirl pattern, a circular maze. However, what he's looking at doesn't match the traditional model. Wavy grooves span across from left-to-right, uncoiled, in a state of transition. He spikes and Madeline is too far gone to feel it.

"You're O negative because she is, Johnstone. The more you facilitate her, the more you change," he says. "Every trait, from your eyes to your teeth." Pollux smoothes his thumb over the pastor's. "You're already losing yourself. You have to know that," he stresses. "Madeline did. You knew this was happening to him, didn't you?" he addresses her.

"Yes," she says. The response comes easier this time.

"It starts like that, and before you know it, you're losing your hair. You feel sick," Pollux says. "You can't sleep. Can't eat. Not because you don't want to. Your physical self becomes so thrown out of whack it ceases to function normally. You dry out and decompose, and then eventually, you end up like him." Pollux nods off to the corner where the cleric lies still, just barely breathing. He's a little more than a shell of himself.

Pollux takes the now-cleaned scalpel and begins sawing away at the gauze wrapped about the pastor's hand, cutting it loose. "Madeline has never been particularly good at taking care of her things...more of a 'shoot first, ask questions never' kind of gal." Father Johnstone looks at his hand, the one that Madeline sliced and placed against the locust tree at Larpe's pond. The wound is turning green, spoiling around the edges of crusted blood. "This is infected," Pollux says. "You're going to lose this hand if I don't fix this. Would you like me to fix it?"

He waits. Pollux waits for the pastor to give him permission to go to work on him, examining that tinge of pear green spreading on his skin. It's souring, just like the water and the locust tree and all those once-golden fields. Father Johnstone sighs, nods. He swallows his *pride* and Pollux caresses his thumb over the gash...once...twice. It's warm. Scab granules loosen and crumble to the flooring. The green regresses to flesh color. When he's done, there's little more than a muted scar to remember it by.

"As you can see, it's within my ability to still perform Craft," Pollux says. "But I'm damned, as you'd say. I have a disease. When she and I get too close, it intensifies. In the most terrible ways you can imagine."

Earthquakes, floods, hurricanes. Now, a plague.

"A lot of innocent people have been hurt over this. Many more are on the fringe," Pollux cranes his head to the window, the light. "They're all out there looking for you right now. I've seen them." He turns back, smiling at the pastor like an old friend.

"Hundreds of people getting sicker by the minute, scared, and they still haven't jumped ship yet. It's because they believe in you. They wait for their preacher to perform another miracle."

"But you and I both know that's not what it really is," Father Johnstone says. "It doesn't adhere to the Divine path. Not really."

"Oh, but it does," he says. "See, I'm a man of history. I think it's important to know where we came from. You and I are supposed to be able to coexist, believe it or not."

At this point, the man in the corner lifts his eyes away from the book, telling Pollux, "He won't listen. A true man of the cloth, that one. Always has been." He dips his brush back into the bowl again, coating it and applying the glaze to the paper. His voice, the pastor thinks—he's heard it before but it's since changed. Like Father Johnstone, he's not himself anymore.

"My associate is correct. You won't believe it coming from me." Pollux eyes the pastor who remains taped tight to the chair. He looks at him, through him. "My actions have made you leery. There's no trust. Madeline, though," he looks at her, gently swaying back and forth in the chair like a drunk. Blood leaks from the corners of her mouth, dripping off her chin and slapping the band of duct tape wrapping her torso. "You'll believe her, won't you? You've seen how this curse works already and you know she won't be able to lie."

"I'll be skeptical, regardless," Father Johnstone says.

"I have a talent for turning skeptics, Pastor." Pollux resumes standing position, walking over to Madeline, he says, "Clear your mouth out." She ejects a spray a blood, then another—this one much smaller in scale. "Now open," he demands. Unlike the last time he made this request, Madeline doesn't resist. She obediently widens the space between rows of teeth so that Pollux can have a look inside. He leans in, leveling an eye to her oral cavity and examining the various wounds within. With his left hand, he takes hold of her wounded cheek, slipping a thumb on the interior skin and gripping it like a Frisbee. Two fingers from his right hand are placed on the roof of her mouth, settling on the cut from the scalpel. Once again, Father Johnstone witnesses him make that same caressing motion, gently rubbing Madeline's face and mouth. Shades of bruise slowly regress to maroon, then red, returning to her normal healthy pallor.

"Are you sufficiently healed?" he asks. Pollux wipes the excess blood and saliva off against his pants.

"Yes," she says. The answer is short, concise, lacking personality or any of Madeline's normal distinction. More mechanical. It's Mrs. Tiller all over again.

"Are you ready to answer questions?"

"You know that I don't have a choice," she says.

"Tell me about the first time you met Father Johnstone," Pollux says. "Be thorough."

"It was my first day in Pratt. After I finished filling out the paperwork regarding my aunt's estate, he was summoned by the local clerk's office to escort me to her burial plot. He was a kind and accommodating man. Father Johnstone walked with me to the cemetery and stood as I evaluated the earth for impurity. I sensed none. His loneliness, however, was palpable. Father Johnstone, like many potential Secondaries, compensates for his lack of relationships with *animalia* companionship in the form of a Yorkshire terrier, restorative projects in the form of a 1970s model Dodge Challenger, and involving himself in the problems of others to feign the sensation of marital and intimate affiliations. He was aching for connection. I felt that. We went to the Presto Diner and I engaged in conversation with him, attempting to ascertain as to whether or not he knew what Josephine Paige really was. He appeared ignorant to it. Father Johnstone was more concerned with my comfort, and his sentiment towards me often wavered between surrogate daughter and young lover. That intrigued me. He possessed many of the qualities that a Primary looks for in a potential Secondary."

"See?" Pollux says to Father Johnstone. "First day in town

and she was already sizing you up for use." He turns back to Madeline, asking, "What made you decide to stay in Pratt?"

"Convenience," she says. "I had a house and a potential Secondary land in my lap. I had an extended collection of volumes at my disposal. The isolation of the town promised a relatively safe location for practice and its residents made for a sufficient harvesting and testing pool."

"That's how you lure 'em in, Pastor," Pollux says. He turns back to Madeline, "And what did you harvest?"

Madeline lists off: "Hair, blood, skin, fingernail clippings, saliva, teeth, seminal fluid of the male, menstrual blood of the female, urine and fecal matter—both genders."

"No organs?"

"Not human," Madeline says. "*Animalia* only."

"I see," Pollux says. "And how did you come to harvest these ingredients?"

"Varying methods," Madeline says. She frowns. It's reminiscent of Sheriff Morgan, how he attempted to resist answering the questions he didn't want to.

"I'll be blunt: how many men have you fucked in this town?" Pollux asks, checking over to Father Johnstone, smirking.

"Fifty-six," she says. No shame or regret. Just a flat admission that makes the pastor's heart sink in his chest.

"And how many of them were married?"

"Forty-two," she says.

"That's a whore right there," Pollux says to the pastor. "That's your ally."

He remembers walking into the Presto Diner, either to pick up Madeline's newest round of treats or merely to check in on her. If it was one thing that stuck out about those meetings besides her natural allure, it was the reaction to everyone else seated amongst the various booths and stools, the glaring. They always looked at the pastor as if he was infringing upon their turf, like he had some ulterior motive that a man of the cloth shouldn't have for a young girl like that. The reality is that her status as the town whore was well known, but the idea that she'd give an old geezer like a preacher a roll in the hay—that was simply too far.

"Ask her why," Father Johnstone croaks.

"Excuse me?" Pollux appears caught off-guard by the imposition.

"If she's a whore, then I'd like to know why she does it," he says.

"Because a whore can never be satiated, Johnstone. It is a disease of the spirit. You know that."

"I'd like to hear her answer," he presses. "Ask."

Pollux pauses, nodding his head slightly. Father Johnstone can tell this is not the direction he wants to take the interrogation. The facts are damning, yes, but their reasoning may hold redeeming qualities. "Madeline," he says, "why did you sleep with all those men?" The question comes out strained.

"To harvest so that I may advance my knowledge of the Craft, both practically and theologically based on the volumes of texts I had inherited," she says. "If I was confronted again, I wanted to be prepared."

Father Johnstone nods his head. He's comforted by this answer.

"And are you prepared, Madeline?" Pollux asks.

"Considering all factors and variables, I surmise a 51% chance of beating you in combat," she says.

"All factors and variables? That include you and your Secondary being taped up to chairs?" he asks.

"Yes," she says. "My Secondary and I are powerful. We're in the favor of the Goddess while hubris leads you to believe you can overthrow her."

"So you know what he's doing?" Pollux asks, referring to the man in the corner.

"He is applying the living seminal fluid and blood of your tributes in order to make the text materialize for translation,"

Madeline says.

"And you know what volume it is, don't you? You know what it does."

"Book XVIII is an ancient text that denotes the ascension to godhood—specifically, overtaking a deity by becoming one," Madeline says. "You believe this will negate the curse on you, but these are desperate measures. Failure is likely."

"I'm willing to risk it." Pollux addresses Father Johnstone, "I take it she's never told you about the Book of Shadows before, has she?"

"No," Father Johnstone answers, feeling foolish. He doesn't know what to believe anymore.

"And what of Christ?" he asks.

The pastor shakes his head. Yet again, he feels grossly uninformed.

"Well then," Pollux smiles, looking at the pastor with sheer delight. "You're in for a treat." To Madeline, he says, "Tell him the story about his Lord and Savior...the one that we know. The real one."

Madeline recites, "The Virgin Mary was impregnated by a celestial force by God's own design. Despite the controversy surrounding His conception, He was born to great acclaim and wielded power that none had ever seen before...power even He didn't truly comprehend in His youth. However, He would learn over time, becoming proficient in the arenas of: alchemy, elemental manipulation, organic healing, and annulment of death. Most of these occurrences would be omitted from all Christian-based texts with the exception of a select few."

Water into wine, the feeding of 5,000, and His walk on the Sea of Galilee. These are the traditional acts of the Lord in which Father Johnstone and the flock have become familiar with over the years. He's preached them for as long as he's been at the helm. *"An example of His sovereignty,"* he used to say.

"His life would be edited in the histories, skipping from His teen years to His thirties…the era in which fear and loyalty surrounded Him equally. His superiority made Him different from His fellow man, and by extension, an outcast. Christ would disappear into the desert for forty days, during which time, He instructed His disciples on the ways of what we now recognize as Craft. They learned how to combine herbs and plant life for medicinal purposes. He taught them to communicate with and harvest *animalia*. In the' isolation of the desert, Christ trained these men on how to conjure large bodies of water and bring about rainstorms and lightning. They could manipulate the elements and bend natural law. It would be documented, composing part of what we now recognize as the Book of Shadows.

"Upon their return from the desert," Madeline continues, "the disciples would quickly realize that in the absence of Christ, their power was greatly depleted. They could no longer perform the abilities that they had been taught to full capacity. Rainstorms cast for crop turned out to be little more than drizzle; lakes for livestock to drink grew no larger than puddles. Words spoken to *animalia* fell upon deaf ears. The disciples sought Christ to enlighten them on their recent complication, and He said, 'In the absence of the Divine, you'll lack Divine power.'

"And so was introduced the concept of the Secondary, a man of faith who lived for no other reason than to serve the Lord and God. He could also serve as a power source for those trained in the ways of Craft, although these pairings were not always successful. The clergy resented the disciples for their God-like ability and capacity to perform miracle, an ability that they themselves lacked. The disciples found cooperation with the clergy problematic and wrought with struggle, especially in instances of selfish indulgence. Pairings often resulted in rapid degradation of the clergyman and disturbance of the spirit. Casts would often backfire. Only rarely did the partnership between Primary and Secondary yield fruitful results, when ideals aligned and intentions were mutual."

Father Johnstone glances at the cleric writhing in the corner, dying. He becomes thinner and weaker by the moment, whereas the pastor remains strong, vital. His blood and certain aspects of his appearance may have changed, but the effects have not become debilitating.

"Failed partnerships between the clergy and those skilled in Craft would eventually lead to a rift between the two parties, and so the monikers of 'witch,' 'sorcerer,' and 'occultist' would be coined in order to identify an enemy that shall not be suffered to live, and that propaganda would be spread for the next many centuries in the scriptures…the cause of much war and mistrust.

"The Book of Shadows," Madeline says, "details the actual history of Christ and His teachings. It is the missing gap that was omitted in biblical text, namely, the fact that Jesus Christ was the first witch and was ultimately responsible for causing an underground power struggle that spanned many centuries."

Pollux nods, satisfied. He takes a beat before telling the pastor, "I understand that's a lot to take in. You've been living most of your life based on partial information, and that's disheartening. I get that," he says, although there's no pity in his voice. "She could have told you this before but she found it appropriate to keep you in the dark. Now you know where you came from, though."

"What do you want from me?" Father Johnstone asks, seething with anger. He wants to hurt this man, craves to inflict harm upon him, but the binding holds. He's helpless.

"I want you to help set things right," he says. "I want you to remember the part of what she said…how the relationship between Primary and Secondary will only work when ideals aligned and intentions were mutual," Pollux recites. "Between the three of us, I think we may have accomplished that balance."

Father Johnstone almost catches himself laughing. He shakes his head, saying, "She'll never work with you. *Ever.* She despises you."

"Not her. Him." Pollux looks over his left shoulder, to the man guised by sunlight working on the translation. He continues to dip the brush and glaze the pages methodically, that is, until he's summoned over. "Found him while I was on the road. Pastor Burke here, like me, was also exiled from his home. Had to reinvent himself...find his calling."

The man sets down his tools, assuming a standing position from the chair and walking out into the light. He stands next to Pollux, wearing the standard clerical uniform. Father Johnstone can't help but notice the scars branching above the collar, reaching up all the way up to his ears and jaw. They look like burn wounds.

"I offered to remove these," Pollux says, touching the man's neck gently with his finger. "Told him I could repair his vocal cords, too. They'd been cooked inside his throat some time ago, but he refused me...said it was important to remember what happened and where he came from."

Father Johnstone looks at the man's face: gaunt and withered, yet familiar. He's been trying to forget it for years.

"He's home now," Pollux says. "Mason Hollis is finally home."

Elk City, OK

I escape from Las Vegas.

The majority of my fortune and possessions are left behind in the many high-end suites I never bother checking out of. Detectives will spend the next many weeks collecting and labeling articles of clothing, the preserved organs, and various religious paraphernalia. They'll take photographs and dust the walls for prints, shaking their heads in shame and commenting on what a 'sick fuck' I must have been. 'This one's gonna fry for sure.' Interviews will be conducted and samples will be gathered: blood, hair, fingernails, seminal fluid. Much like forging a spell, they'll combine all of these elements to formulate a case and track my prior and present whereabouts.

The hardship is that I don't exist on paper. My documentation is either falsified or stolen, and therefore, can offer no insight. Any 'clue' they gather and analyze will lead to a path to nowhere, and so it is with great liberty that I depart the city, silent and unobserved. One piece of luggage is in my possession containing: two changes of clothes (a suit and civilian wear), two editions of the Bible, a bottle of Christ blood, one box of Christ's body, one plastic bag of dehydrated labia, the sharpened crucifix, assorted toiletries, bottled water, and $1,800,000 in bundled cash.

I purchase a late model Ford SUV from a local, offering him an additional $20,000 for his discretion. Greed *compels him to accept, outweighing any suspicions or the sinking feeling that he's seen my face before — perhaps on the television or a large billboard overlooking the strip. I'm gone before his inquiry becomes verbal.*

I disappear from Vegas and never return.

* * *

There is an Elk City in Kansas, and yet two more in the states of Idaho and West Virginia. My Secondary, however, is in Oklahoma. I know this. It is dictated by Divine power, instilling a natural pull in direction not unlike certain species of animalia: birds that fly south for the winter or the great sea turtle migration. I'm compelled eastward, arriving roughly sixteen hours later on a Sunday, God's day.

It is the day in which I come upon Pastor Billy Burke during his sermon, which is conducted in a structure resembling a large shed. It holds roughly forty people. Despite its less-than-pious appearance, I'm drawn to it, to the man shouting at the helm within. They call him 'the truck stop preacher.' 'A blue collar man of God.' He travels from town to town to spread the Lord's true gospel, a version in which sin is to be understood—not feared and avoided at all costs.

"I see fornicators in this room!" he says. "Drunks, meth-heads, masturbators, and liars! I'm in the company of men that paid some poor gal $10 to bust a squirt in their mouth! And you know what?" he asks. "I understand. That's why you're with me instead of some virgin whitebred fuck, right?"

And these men—these hard-as-nails truckers and day laborers— they nod, cheer, praise Billy Burke, shouting, "Amen!"

"Just how in the hell is some man who's never had a lick of cunt in his life supposed to tell you how to abstain? How's a man who's never indulged in sin supposed to understand it?" he asks. "Read about it? The news? Do you really think they get it?"

"Fuck no they don't, Billy!" one of them yells from the right side of the shack.

"You want to stay on the Divine path," pastor Burke says, "You gotta know what's outside the lines."

* * *

Billy Burke concludes his sermon.

It is a sermon he's performed many times in a multitude of locales.

The flock files out of the oversized shack beaten, exhausted, emotionally broken and rebuilt. Reborn, even. This is not the routine service of: kneel, pray, stand, recite, sing, repeat. Pastor Burke has not become victim to apathy. He is a man that pushes his endeavor to the threshold, the absolute. He is like me. I linger at the back of the shed until the audience dissipates, watching him count money on a metal folding chair.

"You're not from here," he says, shuffling through fives and tens. Money that could have been snapped shut into the G-string of a stripper or traded for drugs. It'll be used for gasoline, food, and lodging so Pastor Burke can keep going, keep spreading the gospel. He pockets the money, standing and taking me in. "You're quite a ways from home, if I had to guess."

"As are you," I say. The shed is clear now. It's easier to read him, the intangibles.

"I have no home," the pastor says. "I travel and the Lord travels with me. That is my path."

"And where does that path lead next?" I ask.

"Not sure just yet." He gives a non-committal shrug, scratching the side of his neck. A nervous habit, if I didn't know any better. Like me, this man travels alone and prefers not to have his future whereabouts questioned. I'm making him uneasy.

"You ever been to a place called Pratt?"

The pastor's blood goes cold. Billy spikes so hard the hair raises on my arms and the back of my neck. I can feel him in my teeth, my chest. A static, a charge, something I've never experienced with the other men of the cloth.

He pulls a pistol from the back of his waistline, cocking it. Billy points the gun at me, saying, "You've got about ten seconds."

My head tilts, reading him. "You're from there," I say. "And you have...a history."

"Seven," he says.

"It's why you're here...on the road...alone."

"Five," he says, aiming the barrel at my heart.

"They did that to you." I point at his wrinkled neck then draw down to his torso. Skin itches, aches of bad memory. It haunts his dreams.

"Two." Billy's arm shakes.

"I can help," I say, arm extended.

"No. You can't," he says. "Zero."

Billy pulls the trigger.

* * *

At Hog Trough on South Main St., Pastor Billy Burke feasts upon pork ribs, BBQ baked beans, and neon-yellow potato salad that I'm afraid might upset his stomach if he has too much. He swathes a piece of sandwich bread through the sauce, indulging in yet another hunk of slow-cooked pig's flesh. He chews, swallows, picking up a foggy gray tumbler of root beer and washes it down.

"No one ever knew much about Josephine Paige," he says. "Kept to herself mostly. Not exactly a social butterfly, if you know what I mean."

"The majority of my kind isn't," I tell him. I've told him more than I've ever told anyone and yet he remains seated, calm, unafraid. I don't conflict with his faith or ideals—I improve upon them. "Josephine was never particularly talkative."

Billy licks the sauce off his fingers, nodding, "Hiding in plain sight, as you say." He grabs a small stack of tan napkins from the tin dispenser, cleaning off his fingers and the corners of his mouth. "Been doing a little of that myself."

"I know," I say.

"And what else do you know, Mr. Pollux?" he asks, smiling. "Besides how to stop a slug mid-air?"

Billy fired the gun and I reacted. Nothing more. This, however, illustrated to the both of us exactly what's possible when we're together. We can accomplish far more as a pair than we ever could separately; I explained this the best way I could, by example.

"I know that if you come back with me, you'll never have to be afraid of anything ever again. You'll never be alone," I tell him. Billy nods, scratching at an area on his chest. "I can even get rid of that, if you'd like." My finger motions to his chest, the scar tissue.

"No. That stays," he says, giving a shake of the head, sighing. "It's

important to know where you came from."

I smile, nodding. *"I happen to agree, Mr. Burke."*

"Mason," he says. *"Call me Mason."*

* * *

"Don't you find it odd?" Mason asks, sometime later.

We are on the road. We have an accord, he and I: that we will help each other get what the other man wants. That is, after all, what a partnership is based upon. It's harmony. Balance.

"I believe, as you do, that the gods work in mysterious—sometimes coincidental—ways," I answer. *"You call it fate, I believe."*

Mason and I, we have business in Pratt. A great task lies ahead of us, and we have much to learn if this is to be a successful venture. Our first order of business, of course, is Josephine Paige. She will be our lure, our beacon for Madeline to follow. I imagine she'll jump at the chance to call somewhere home again, especially if she receives the added incentive of the Feri's collection. Prior attempts to hunt her down have resulted in disaster. This time, she will come to us, and we'll remain at a safe distance until the time is right.

"Tell me more about this Father Johnstone," I say.

"You wish to use him?" A twinge of jealously courses through Mason's veins.

"I wish to take him out of play," I explain. *"Do you know what happens when a town like that becomes leaderless and without God?"*

"I know exactly what happens," Mason says, letting his shoulders ease back into the seat. He smiles, saying, *"It tears itself apart."*

"So what do you know about Father Johnstone, then?"

"He's alone. He's unloved. He's afraid of his past," Mason says. *"In his own little way, he's also hiding in plain sight."*

"How would you break him, Mason?" I ask, curious as to what his thoughts are on the matter. Although he's yet to learn about Craft and its numerous capabilities, I do enjoy hearing the pedestrian side of warfare.

"I would show him that part of himself he doesn't want to see," Mason says. He scratches his neck again, plotting, planning, scheming. "I'd show him the worst...turn him. Make him compromise. Let him walk with the Devil and see how he likes it."

The Reunion

"It's good to see you again, Jairy," Mason says.

Years have passed since he last saw him, the pastor thinks, and it wasn't at the abduction. He wasn't there for that, although he's often heard of others claiming they were (and lying about it) for the sake of invoking credibility into their campfire tale. Father Johnstone never testified to be present when Sheriff Morgan and his mob pulled Mason Hollis from his home, clawing at his own lawn before he was stuffed into the back of a police cruiser. Most people agree the last they saw of him was his own fist beating against a bulletproof window, face bloodied up courtesy of Shelby. What happened after that, only God knows. That still falls into the category of urban legend. The scars, Father Johnstone realizes, are quite real. They make his neck look like it's coated in old candle wax, folding unevenly at odd angles whenever he speaks.

Mason refers to the pastor as Jairy. No one has called him that in over three decades.

"I was in the church," Mason says. "The day the town showed up ready to beat you bloody and drag you out into the streets. Mr. Pollux has taught me quite a bit about hiding in plain sight. Everyone was so intent on hurting you it's like I was invisible. Or perhaps I've changed *that* much."

He is no longer pale or lanky, no longer easy prey. The Mason Hollis that stands before the pastor is someone else now, a stronger version resembling a young Danger Durphy, the same poise and build. Those dainty little fingers that caressed the nude body of Betty Graybel are chapped and tan, well worn from life on the road. He's been getting his hands dirty.

"How did it feel, Jairy?" he asks. "What was it like to have them turn on you so quickly for something that wasn't even your fault?"

"You're comparing the two of us," Father Johnstone says. "Even for you, that's a stretch."

"It's a sickness, Jairy. I think you know the feeling," Mason says. "I think you know what it's like to have someone so deeply ingrained in yourself that you're compelled to act." He scratches the side of his neck. Folded scar tissue goes taut, almost appearing normal except for the varying skin tones. "I've faced my past. You, on the other hand, continue to run from it. You deny yourself, Jairy."

Father Johnstone is spiking. When he looks over at Madeline the hair on her forearms is raised off the skin. Miniscule bolts of static shock mingle above the tissue, and he prays. The pastor prays for her to break free of the spell, prays the Lord release these restraints and deliver them from evil.

"We're not so different," Mason says, but this offends the pastor to such a degree he forgets his fear. He forgets he's bound to a chair and completely helpless.

"We're *completely* different," Father Johntone says. "You're a degenerate, Mason. You dishonor that uniform."

"He's angry," Pollux observes with an amused grin. "He wants to hurt you...wants to take another pass at you with that shotgun, I suspect."

"You think you know pain, Jairy?" Mason leans forward, placing his mouth to the pastor's ear. He licks the side of his face and Father Johnstone cringes, groans, twists within the tape trying to shake loose. "I'll educate you," he says, standing upright. Mason's fingers unfasten the top four buttons of his shirt, revealing cooked skin behind the black curtain. Large pits and craters populate his chest from burns that never healed right, never received the proper care Dr. Keller could have given them.

"In the front of your parietal lobe...right about here," Mason sticks his pointer finger into the flesh of pastor's forehead, "that's where your sensory cortex lies. So when I touch you, Jairy—

that's the part of your brain that lets you feel me. That's the part that let little Betty Graybel feel me...my fingers...moving deeper inside of her until I was practically in her guts." Mason closes his eyes, sighing deeply. He relishes the memory. "I'll be seein' her again later. Her and my ol' pal, Sheriff Morgan. I'm going to make him watch while I finish the job. See, that's real pain. That's the kind of pain that can't be dished out with a blade or a gun." Mason smiles. "Oh, don't get me wrong, I'll set his body on fire like he did me. No mistaking that, but real pain...the worst, the absolute—it happens when you break a man's soul. Break his spirit."

Father Johnstone spikes harder, and Madeline starts to convulse in her chair, back arching. Blood leaks from her ears, mouth, and nose, but none see it. Pollux and Mason are too busy playing with their food, and the pastor prays. Through seething anger, he prays to the Lord he won't break under torment, won't have his spirit shattered.

"Does it disgust you, Jairy? Does it twist your stomach?" Mason slaps the pastor across the face. He grabs him by the jaw, giving him a little shake to get his attention. "I am as God made me, yes? How did He make you?"

Mason smiles at him. He's enjoying the control, the power. Father Johnstone doesn't need to feel the intangibles to confirm this. It's written all over Mason's face.

"Your father left while you were still in the womb, and your mother was a drunken illiterate who couldn't even spell the name right on the birth certificate," Mason speaks low. "And then she abandoned you...which was probably for the best."

It's an old wound. Not many people in Pratt even know about it, and those that do respect Father Johnstone enough not to bring it up, because it's not gossip. It's a bereaved reminder of where their pastor came from: a boy that never knew his father, that can't remember his mother. Both their whereabouts unknown. Considering his genesis, to throw himself under the Lord and His teachings wasn't just logical, it was easy. It was the escape from himself, a path to greener pastures where a devout life bloomed from shame.

"Absentee father, drunken dumb whore of a mother," Mason says. "No wonder you hid behind the cloth."

"As you hide now?" the pastor says.

"Exactly," Mason says, giving an affirming nod. "Because we're the same. We seek sanctuary from ourselves."

Father Johnstone shakes his head. "I'm not like you."

"I disagree. I've seen what you're capable of...seen you fuck Miss Paige there." Mason gives his temple a couple taps, winking. "Been inside your head a little. You're confused, too. Don't know if you want to bounce that girl on your knee or fuck her brains out, so you can drop the pious act." Mason paces over to Madeline, still convulsing in the chair. She's moaning, bleeding out dark fluid from every orifice. "She *is* beautiful." He swabs some of the blood away with his thumb, tasting it. Mason spits. "You could have her, y'know. We don't mind sharing. It's only the Graybel girl and the sheriff I want for myself. That's all. I ain't *greedy*."

If Father Johnstone knows anything about Pratt, Betty is holed up at home with her parents, breathing soured air while the debate ensues on whether or not to get the hell out of Dodge. Either that, or it's as Pollux said: like the rest of the town, they too wait for another one of the pastor's miracles. They wait to be delivered from evil.

"Miss Paige is needed for a certain ritual at the behest of my associate," Mason says.

"You can play with the leftovers after we're done, Johnstone," Pollux chimes in. "Won't be much left though."

"We'll leave it up to you as to whether or not to put her out of her misery. You can be the one to decide if this brain-dead little cunt is worth holding on to," Mason says. "That'll be your pain. That, and being exposed to the town for the fraud that you are.

'A false prophet,' I believe you call it. That'll sit nicely with them."

"Unless you'd care to join us," Pollux offers. "But I sense otherwise. That *pride* of yours…it compromises your logic."

"That's fixable." Mason positions himself so that he's standing right beside the pastor, his burn wounds at eye-level. He says, "Make him see."

Pollux places his left hand on Mason's forehead; his right hand is place on that of Father Johnstone's. A channel. A conduit. He is the wire that connects the two of them.

…it's cool. The air is clean and breathable again. Father Johnstone is lying upon a bed of lush grass, cowering under the figures standing above him: Sheriff Morgan, Tuck Graybel, and Travis Durphy. He's done something wrong, something that he couldn't control—but wrong, just the same. His body aches. He's got an eye nearly swollen shut, and there are multiple gashes on his face from Sheriff Morgan pummeling him with that damn gun of his. Shelby, as he refers to her. She's got blood all over her grip, more blood seeping into the bullet chamber. Father Johnstone hopes it causes a misfire. He begs for mercy. The sheriff chuckles, laughs. Tuck Graybel tells him he doesn't want a dead body on his conscience. He says that the fun has gone on long enough to which Travis nods meekly in the middle distance. There's no blood on his hands, no malice in his gaze. He's a reluctant spectator at best. Ol' Travis is about to lose his supper in the dirt, Tuck says, attempting to dissuade Morgan from going too far. No surprise there, the sheriff replies. Not half the man his father was. Doesn't have it in 'em to get his hands a little dirty. Danger Durphy would have killed this man twice over by now. Travis, the sheriff says, why don't you make yourself useful and grab my pack in the front seat? He follows the order. Travis stalks off through the high grass, heading towards a couple of red taillights of the parked cruiser. Tuck's rig has its high beams shining on the patch of grass Father Johnstone sits upon, still cowering. Shaking. He doesn't know if they'll hang him, beat him, or worse. He doesn't know, and that uncertainty scares the hell out of him. Scares him like the trip over. Sheriff Morgan dragged him kicking and screaming out of his own home and stuffed him into the back of the cruiser, but they didn't go to the station. Law's too good for you, Morgan said. You won't learn nothin' in a cell. He drove right by it and kept on, out into the unknown, the fields. Father Johnstone knows the only thing out there is crop and dirt with the occasional machine doing its diligence. I ain't the law out here, the sheriff told him. I'm much worse. I'll teach you a thing or two about touching little girls.

Travis comes back from the cruiser, a small pack in-hand. Clevenger's moonshine, the sheriff says. Take it out. And Travis does. The liquor and bottle are clear, reflecting off the truck's high beams. Sheriff Morgan pops the cork for him, placing it inside his pocket. He says, have a swig of that…settle them nerves down a touch. It inspires hope for Father Johnstone. He hopes — prays, actually — that maybe these men will gentle down, see the error of their ways. Or maybe they'll all get tanked and forget about him. Moonshine sneaks up on you. Old man Clevenger's moonshine smashes your head in with a hammer, and he'd do anything to have a taste of it right about now. Numb the pain. Numb it so much that he wouldn't feel the next series of boot kicks and pistol whips. He watches the Durphy boy drink. Then Tuck Graybel, who downs three times as much as Travis.

Sheriff Morgan, however, doesn't drink. He takes the bottle and begins pouring the contents on Father Johnstone's torso and neck. Booze immediately begins eating the wounds and straw-berry welts on his body, stinging, making his body coil. He's like a salted slug twisting around on the grass, balling up tight and hoping that bottle goes empty quick. Sheriff Morgan taunts him. He spits on Father Johnstone and says that ain't nothing compared to what's coming up next. To Travis he says, you'll do the honors. Sheriff Morgan hands him a box of wooden matches, the same ones you use to get the coals going on the grill. Travis accepts them in his hand, staring down at the little box. Terrified. Strike and drop, the sheriff says. That's all you need to do…then this all will be over. We walk away and never speak of it again.

I can't, Travis says.

Your father could, the sheriff says. He chucks the moonshine bottle out into the distance. They can hear it bounce off the soft ground about twenty yards out. A little girl got hurt…hurt in a way that can't be mended, Sheriff Morgan says. And Danger knows when someone hurts you or your kin, the fix ain't sticking them in a little cage. You let the hellfire eat 'em. So strike and drop, boy…for your pop. He loved this town and he'd never tolerate a child-fucker living among us.

I'm sorry, Father Johnstone says. I'm so, so sorry. Please. Please, don't burn me. I'm sick. I can't help it, he says, crawling with his hands clamped together, begging. He begs Travis to reconsider, but the boy strikes the match. He's disgusted by him, picturing that pale stick-thin frame touching little Betty Graybel, taking off her tiny daisy-patterned underwear and photographing what's within. He made her spread herself apart, telling her this was a grown-up secret game that no one could know about. He said he would give her presents if she played along and never told anyone. Father Johnstone put his fingers inside her, asking little Betty if it felt good, if she liked being tickled like this. He remembers, and the memory excites him, but not nearly as much as when Travis flicks the match at his body.

The pastor tries to bat it away while it hangs in mid-air, but it's no use. He's soaked in old man Clevenger's moonshine, a human torch rag. As soon as the flame kisses the fumes, he's lit. Burning. Rolling on the grass, screaming, cooking. Fibers of his shirt melt into his skin. The plastic buttons heat, lose form, turning to a syrup that chews his flesh. Father Johnstone burns in front of the three men, but only the sheriff watches. Only he has the stomach to witness pain and take joy in it. He watches until the very last tendril of fire dies out, telling the burned body on the ground, you're dead to this town, Mason. I'm gonna leave you out here for the birds to pick at. Tuck and Travis seem relieved by this, but they still can't look at him directly, the skin so cooked it's black. Muscle sinew in the neck is visible, glistening under the high beams like meat soaked in canola oil.

Sheriff Morgan crouches down, spitting onto heated grass, he tells the still-smoldering body, if you survive…if you manage the strength to drag your ass across these fields…you crawl *that* way, understand? He points west, away from Pratt and everything he's ever known. He points to exile. You let the rest of the world see you for the freak you are, Morgan says. You're their problem now, and don't you ever think about coming back, he displays the pistol. Even though the pastor's blinded by the smoke of his own skin, he knows Shelby's there, caked in sticky blood. You get the bullet, he says. No warning. I'll feed your body to the hogs and your head becomes a trophy for my wall, got it? You either die here or stay gone for good. Those are your choices.

…he fades back in.

Bitterness returns to the air and Father Johnstone regains himself, still bound to the metal folding chair with Madeline five feet to his left. He's panting, the skin of his chest burning as if it's just been grilled. Eyes water. The pastor is back in his own head again, but the body hasn't fully let go of the pain yet. It needs a moment to acclimate to reality.

"There's other things I can do with this," Pollux says, poking Father Johnstone in the forehead, the parietal lobe. "I can make you feel bone cancer, heart failure, a lung collapsing. I can make it feel like you're drowning. Or maybe an orgasm…that swell of bliss flushing through your entire body. I can make you feel that for hours, if you'd like. And you want to know the best part?" Pollux asks. "It doesn't break any of your little rules. It's just…feeling," he shrugs. "Electrical signals. That's all they are." Pollux leans in, cradling the pastor's face in his hand softly, lovingly. "We can rewrite the rules together, lead together. Your flock will consist of thousands."

"And you'll never be alone." Mason buttons up his shirt, curtaining the scars behind black cloth. "You'll have love in your life. Her love, if you want it," he nods to Madeline, shaking, bleeding out all over herself. "She can be whatever you want her to be…daughter, wife, whore," he lists off. "Or all three if that's what you're into." Mason smirks, scratching the side of his neck again.

Meanwhile, Father Johnstone is praying. He prays Madeline regains herself, prays the Lord release them from this unholy binding. With every desperate fiber of his person, he prays for Pratt, prays that little Betty Graybel never has to feel Mason's hands on her again. He even prays that Sheriff Morgan stays gone, stays far away from these men who wish to break him down.

"It's futile, Johnstone," Pollux says. "You can stop."

The pastor stares through the window, out into the pale yellow light that the Lord brings down. He admires the work of His Creator one final time, knowing in his heart that he'll soon be with Him in the Kingdom. Father Johnstone will be able to say that he stayed true, resisted the temptations that were laid out before him. He remained devout, despite the small compromises he made on behalf of Pratt and its people. The pastor asks forgiveness for these minor trespasses and cleanses his soul.

"No help will come," Pollux says.

Father Johnstone stares into the light, noticing the small birds still flopping around on the dead earth. Feathers wilt and fall from their flesh. Their skin yields to the disease as lungs swell with poison. The small ones go first, as Mason Hollis said: the insects and tiny field mice. Then birds. Mary won't be far behind. And Madeline—the pastor can't hold out hope for her. He merely prays that whatever these men do to her, they execute it quick and with as little pain inflicted as possible. It's a naïve sentiment, though. She'll be raped, tortured, and sacrificed for the sake of archaic ritual. Madeline's body won't be the only thing to suffer; her soul will be twisted, torn apart, and no one is in any position to prevent it. In these dire times, everyone is worried about themselves.

"I feel it, Johnstone," Pollux says. "Hope draining…despair."

In the distance, Father Johnstone sees an object that's neither animal nor person. It's large, familiar. He'd recognize the blue body and those chrome fenders anywhere. It's the Challenger, manned by an unknown driver. At roughly 40mph the vehicle speeds at the wall right behind Pollux and Mason, but only the former feels the shift. Only Pollux can sense a sudden spike of hope within the pastor, causing his brow to furrow in confusion. He stares at Father Johnstone a moment, attempting to read him, deciphering this change in mood. Pollux turns around, and the Challenger breaks through the wall just in time to meet his gaze.

Book XIII, Exchange & Ascent Theory

There are two forms of cursed state. The first is concocted by a Primary using earth-based materials in conjunction with the required incantation or recitation of passages (reference: curses). Method, ingredients, and their effectiveness vary depending on region and coven. The second form of curse is delivered directly by a god or goddess, usually as penance for disobeying an established maxim. Some scholars believe it is derivative of the 'Forbidden Fruit Principle' in which each deity maintains one specific rule that cannot be forgiven in the event that it is broken, also known as anti-Divine action. The god or goddess bestows either death or powerful curse, a state of being in which the Primary is restricted in their ability, and mind, body, and spirit become de-unified (or: de-harmonized). Attempts to perform Craft will either backfire or result in failure. All joy is suspended, including the sensation of orgasm. Dream state will be poisoned by the deity, tormenting the offender with visions of their crime from the perspective of their victim. If the Primary is to become sick, they will remain in that state with no method of recovery. In some rare cases, the deity will find it prudent to allow the sickness to spread to the offender's surroundings, turning them into what's known as 'a walking plague.' To counteract these effects, first the Primary must find a Secondary of equal standing. As of this writing, Holy men remain opposed to the beliefs and practices of Craft. However, should Primary and Secondary unite, they must find the individual in which the catalyst action transpired and perform the conversion ritual, a process of the utmost complexity and difficulty. It should be noted that Divine and anti-Divine cannot be within the same proximity without the deity intervening in some way, usually in the form of earthly disruption: quakes, storms, or other extreme shifts. Should the curse be passed on to another vessel, mind, body, and spirit will be destroyed—essentially, resulting in a hollowed existence of 'the sacrificed.' They will be incapable of thought, voluntary movement, or verbal communication. The Primary will absorb their power and knowledge, adding it to their own. It is foretold this process would allow a Primary to ascend to godhood.

The Fray

Father Johnstone doesn't know how it happens, but somehow both he and Madeline survive the breach without incurring any additional injury. The same, however, cannot be said for Pollux and Mason, both of whom are lying buried under a sizeable amount of wall rubble and debris: decaying planks of wood, drywall, fiberglass insulation, and numerous shards of glass and ceramic. Through the dust, the pastor can see one hand blooming from the wreckage, blood seeping down the palm and wrist. His Challenger is parked less than a foot away from his knees, lead-colored smoke billowing from under the hood. The engine makes a worrisome clanking noise to the tune of Madeline coughing up fluid in her own lap, heaving hard. Her tongue curls in a U-shape and juts beyond her cut lower lip. She coughs, gags on wall dust and poisonous air.

"You okay?" Dr. Keller disembarks from the vehicle wearing the same clothes from the night before, still stained with the blood and fluid of Helena Wright. He walks along the uneven surface of the debris, careful to avoid the various nails and shards of glass. "Are you hurt?" he tries again.

"We're okay," the pastor says. It feels like a lie considering he can barely breathe and his chest still aches of fire. Madeline is in even worse shape, swaying sick and hacking up torrents of fluid into her own lap. "Can you cut us loose?"

Dr. Keller pulls out a small blade that's clipped to the back of his pants, unfolding it. He starts with the tape around the pastor's wrists, telling him, "Sorry about your car."

"Where's yours?" The tape snaps off Father Johnstone's wrists. He flexes his hands, feeling the blood flow through his palms and fingers in a cool flush.

Dr. Keller saws the tape that binds the pastor's left leg to the chair. "Pratt has been compromised," he says. "Everyone's panicking. Otis Banford decided my car would be better off with him." He saws the tape holding the other leg, careful not to accidently cut into the pastor's ankle during the process. "Be thankful the old models are easy to hotwire. I'm afraid I had to crack the steering column."

Father Johnstone looks at the front end of the Challenger, assessing the damage: a bent fender, various silver slivers from all the scratches in the paintjob, a busted headlight. God only knows what's wrong underneath the hood that's causing all the smoke, yet, it doesn't seem important right now. Only moments ago, he was prepared to die, and Madeline may still be on her way out.

"How'd you find us?" Father Johnstone asks.

Dr. Keller begins sawing at the tape binding the pastor's torso to the chair's backing. "Mary," he says. Father Johnstone feels his torso expand, relief and breath returning to his body. "She led me here about an hour ago. I peeked in the windows and saw you two taped up with Mason Hollis keeping watch. Decided it'd be best to pull out the stops."

Father Johnstone tears the tape away from his mid-section, surveying the debris for signs of Mary walking around. It's odd that she hasn't hopped out to greet him by now. "Where is she?"

Dr. Keller pauses. He looks at the pastor the same way he always does when he's forced to deliver bad news. "The car," he says. "She's not doing well." He stands up, walking to Madeline with the knife ready to cut her loose. "It's in the air. This plague. Birds are falling from the sky," he says, but Father Johnstone is no longer listening.

He steps over the debris with unsure movements, feet tingling from the lack of bloodflow they've endured over the past many hours. The fear of what he may find in the Challenger allows him to look past it, peeking his head into the interior. Mary is curled up in the backseat on what appears to be a sheet from one of the hospital beds. Tiny stains spot the fabric. Black sticky fluid oozing from her mouth and nose. Father Johnstone gets into the backseat to look at her, touch her fur. As soon as his fingers smooth over her body, he notices the unusually coarse texture that's akin to dry wheat. They break off at his touch, ending up with the rest of the strands collecting in the blanket. Mary's eyes look at the pastor, glazed over in a film like cataracts. Fluid leaks from those as well. He doesn't need Madeline to tell him that Mary's on her way out. Dying. It can be heard in every breath she struggles to take.

"Bring the kit," Dr. Keller shouts. "My black bag in the front seat."

Father Johnstone looks at Mary, sick, falling apart before his eyes. The saving grace is that she's still alive. Still breathing. She can be saved. If he gets her away from Pratt quickly enough, he thinks, her health will return and he won't have to lose her. He prays he can do that. As he retrieves Dr. Keller's black case, he prays to the Lord that the Challenger is able to deliver them from the town.

"The bottle," Dr. Keller says. Currently, he's holding Madeline's head up, mouth pried open. Madeline continues to cough, struggle. "Take the cap off and pour it down her throat," he says. "The symptoms match. It's Kurt and Mrs. Wright all over again. We're going to help her purge."

"What is it?"

"Ipecac," Dr. Keller says.

Madeline lunges forward, breaking free of Dr. Keller's grip and plunges her fingers down her own throat. Shoves them all the way down so that two of her knuckles are past her teeth. She gags, shooting fluid down her arm. Vomit erupts on the wall debris and Father Johnstone's pants. Madeline's panting, gasping for air. She repeats the process again, but only a small amount exits this time.

"My way's...faster." She spits. Breathes deeply. Spits again. Her face is pale, sweating. "Epinephrine shot...in the bag,

Johnstone."

"No. You don't need that," Dr. Keller says. "You'll be fine if you rest. It's just going to take a moment."

She spits again, bracing herself on her knees. Recovering slowly. "Don't have a moment." Her eyes lock onto Father Johnstone's, urging him to do it, and he knows exactly why. It's not over yet. Father Johnstone digs the shot out of the bag, attempting to hand it to her but Madeline shakes him off. "Bless it," she says. "Then inject."

The pastor does as she requests. He prays, bestowing the object with the Lord's Divine sanction before uncapping it and shooting the compound into Madeline's upper arm. She winces slightly as the chemical begins to hit her bloodstream, her muscles. Only a few seconds pass before Madeline feels it: her heart pounding in her ears. She inhales sharply and both Dr. Keller and the pastor witness the house moving, bending. Smaller pieces of the debris hover an inch or so off the ground as Madeline pants, smiling. Pupils wind tight and she's standing under her own accord now, wiping the blood off of her face with her forearm.

Strong. Sharp. Renewed.

"Pull the car out," Madeline tells Dr. Keller. She stomps off to the corner of the room where Mason Hollis previously had his workstation set up for translation. It's since been destroyed by the Challenger.

"What about them?" the pastor asks. His eyes check the hand rising out from under various pieces of wall. It has yet to move as far as he can tell, but the cuts continue to pour blood down the palm and wrist.

"I'll deal with them," she says, and Father Johnstone thinks he has an idea of what she means by that. She's not going to leave any loose ends. If it's one thing Madeline Paige never wants to do again, it's the act of looking over her shoulder in fear that Pollux will be behind her. She's done running.

"What about the cleric?" He looks to the other corner where a body lies, stark white and frail. No breath. No life. "He should be buried," the pastor says, remembering something that Pollux mentioned earlier in regards to the afterlife. Limbo, he said. This man would walk through Pratt for an eternity, an infinite spectator, never ascending to the Kingdom. He can't subject him to that, regardless of his alliances.

"Load him up. Quick." Madeline tosses planks of wood and siding over her shoulder, digging through the debris while Dr. Keller and the pastor excavate the body from rubble.

"Do I dare ask what happened to this man?" Dr. Keller hoists the body up by his armpits while Father Johnstone wraps him at the knees. He's surprisingly light, as if his limbs and torso have been hollowed out, not totally unlike a store window mannequin.

The pastor ignores the question for the time being, careful to keep up his end of the body as the legs pass into the Challenger's backseat. He can hear Madeline tossing pieces of wall and structure as she continues to dig around in the corner of the room. She finally finds the object that she's looking for, inspecting the spell book for any damage it may have taken during the crash. It appears to have incurred nothing more than a few small tears on select pages. Madeline makes her way over to the Challenger, placing Book XVIII in the backseat along with Mary and the dead cleric. "Now pull the car out. Wait for me outside."

Dr. Keller tosses his medical bag onto one of the floorboards, and the two men board the car with Father Johnstone at the wheel. He shifts the ignition into reverse, stomping on the gas. The tires kick up dust and gravel-sized chunks of drywall, spinning hard until they catch traction with the floor. Abruptly, the Challenger peels out of what's left of old man Clevenger's living room and onto a patch of dead earth. Mary lets out a disconcerted grumble from all the commotion while Madeline follows the tire marks, walking out of the house and showing the pastor her singed palm, indicating for him to wait there.

"What is she doing?" Dr. Keller asks.

Father Johnstone can feel it already, the sensation of warmth channeling through his body as Madeline prepares to cast. She walks out a few more strides into the yard before she turns around and faces what's left of the house, extending both hands out and pointing them at the living room. Her palms glow, intensifying until they reach a fever pitch—then flame erupts. Fire coats the floor, walls, and ceiling of the living room, eating, burning. Black smoke begins to churn out of the crater of old man Clevenger's home, and Madeline watches, allowing her arms to come down at her sides. The flames eat, char the wreckage, and Father Johnstone knows that she's saying goodbye. Neither Pollux nor Mason will receive their proper burials, and the pastor prays this is the last of it, that their opposing journeys will end in ashes from whence they came.

Madeline flexes her hands, rolling her fingers as she turns to the Challenger where Dr. Keller and the pastor wait. She rounds to the passenger side, opening the door and squeezing into the front seat. "It's either going to hit the gas line or his moonshine collection, so you better back up a little."

Father Johnstone taps down on the accelerator, backing up the Challenger another ten or so feet away from the house. He's not exactly eager to leave. If Mason Hollis is about to die, he wants to make sure of it this time. Rumors and ghost stories aren't going to muddy up the facts, nor will he build up his own legend the way Sheriff Morgan did by being a braggart. As far as Pratt is concerned, the two men being cremated in Clevenger's living room never existed. They don't need to know that they were responsible for the plague that fell over the town. They don't need to know about Craft or how their Lord and Savior was a little more than what the scriptures made Him out to be. In the midst of all the panic a decaying town has brought, Father Johnstone is of a mind that some things are best kept secret. Perhaps this is why Madeline was never as transparent with him as she could have been. It was his purity of faith that made him an ideal partner, and shaking that might have introduced complications—namely, him deserting Pratt and leaving her to fend for herself.

"And I do have feelings for you, Johnstone," Madeline says, reading those intangibles, the pastor's emotions. "I've had them for a while now, but it's easy to make someone look bad when you don't ask them the right questions."

Father Johnstone watches old man Clevenger's home turn to ash, fire spreading to the stale roof shingles. For reasons he can't exactly discern, he remembers the kiss. Madeline's lips caressed his and the relationship took on a different meaning, something not quite paternal but not purely romantic either. Too complex to summarize in words.

"Don't try to define it," she says. "Just know it's there and that I feel it, too."

The pastor turns over his right shoulder, looking to the backseat where Mary is resting in a pile of blankets and looking miserable. As much as he'd like to reach back and hold her, he's not sure if her body could take it at the present time. Symptoms of the plague remain apparent. Mary continues to wheeze and leak from her eyes, mouth, and ears. The pastor can only assume that the debilitating effects will regress at the same pace they originally came about.

"We'll fix her," Madeline says. "All of this. We'll bring back the crop, the flowers and gardens. Purify the water and earth. Repair the damage."

Father Johnstone nods. For the first time in a while, he allows himself to feel relief. The crackle of the flames and the smoke calm him, ease his nerves.

"I could use your help as well…with the people," Dr. Keller mentions, somewhat tentative. He's unsure if he's out of line with the request, or if Madeline can even do it.

"Of course," she says, eyes never wavering from the house.

The same brown eyes that Father Johnstone has now.

"The town needs to be pacified," Dr. Keller says after a moment. "You haven't seen what it's become, and Mayor Farnsworth refuses to address the issue. He's hiding. A pillar should step up in his absence."

The pastor and Madeline exchange a knowing look. Farnsworth's desperation notwithstanding, Father Johnstone has no forgiveness in his heart after what he witnessed. He was going to hand Pollux the town on a silver platter for the sake of commerce, to keep the cogs turning.

"We'll handle him later," Madeline answers for the both of them.

Father Johnstone looks towards the main part of town from the outskirts where old man Clevenger's reclusive hovel lies. Smoke billows from numerous buildings in the distance. Other structures have already begun to collapse under the duress of weakened foundations.

"Do you sense them?" the pastor asks. He continues to watch the fire, the smoke, looking for unusual movement.

"No," Madeline says. "They're gone. We can go now."

Father Johnstone shifts the Challenger into drive, pressing on the gas, although it's not nearly as responsive as it was before Dr. Keller smashed it through a house. He mentally adds his vehicle to the list of things that need his attention. The Challenger and Mary, and maybe the church, too. The few roof leaks the Pratt bake-off was intended to remedy seem small in comparison to what he might be coming back to. His church was already falling apart; the plague may have finished the job.

"And we'll rebuild that, too," Madeline says.

Dr. Keller releases a frustrated sigh, turning to look at Madeline, then the pastor. "She's reading your mind then, I take it?"

"Something like that," the pastor answers.

Madeline doesn't say anything, cooling off one of her palms

by hanging out the passenger side window. Wind cuts through her fingers, still tinged with rot and not pleasant to breathe. Everything smells of poisoned dirt and engine smoke. Even the air itself has a brownish tinge to it, like a smog cloud you'd see in a major city. As the Challenger drives into the main population, people can be seen moving along sluggishly, almost too sick to stand. Stan Cordish, another one of Pratt's debilitated, is in the midst of having his oxygen tank looted by a couple men. Houses are either on fire or collapsing. Stores are being looted for inedible food and tarnished goods. Not even a few blocks away from Kurt Clevenger's property and already Father Johnstone can see he has his work cut out for him. Yet again, the town has turned—but not on any one person in particular. Pratt devours itself now, growing sicker, fearful, more violent with every moment that passes.

Father Johnstone finds himself distracted by all the bedlam happening that he doesn't see what's obstructing the road until Madeline curses, leaning across Dr. Keller's body to yank the wheel hard-right. The Challenger careens into a crack in the earth, smashing in the front end entirely. A swan song of broken engine can be heard as black smoke rises from underneath the folded hood, obstructing their vision along with a windshield cracked to spider webs. They sit tilted forward at an odd angle, breathing smoke, poison, and dead dirt. Dr. Keller mashes his face into the crook of his arm, releasing large hacks and favoring a knee that hit the steering wheel during the crash. Mary grumbles from the backseat, sneezing granulated muck. Fortunately, the body of the cleric cushioned the impact.

"Fault lines," Madeline says.

Much like the trees and beams of structures lose their integrity and decompose, so too does the earth. It dries out, unable to sustain life of crop or garden, then it begins to crack. Father Johnstone attempts to open his door but it's stuck. The passenger side is wedged against a wall of dirt. Air is running out, becoming thinner by the moment.

The pastor reaches into the backseat, grabbing Mary by the scruff of her neck and holding her close. "Pop it," he says, and Madeline places her palms to the roof, magnetically pushing it until it breaks free. Framing warps, flexing out until it breaks and the windows shatter, spilling down the front end of the Challenger in thick kibble. Madeline climbs out first, claiming Book XVIII and scaling over leather seats and the back end of the vehicle. Dr. Keller grabs his kit and follows with the pastor close behind, holding Mary tight against his ribs like a football.

Father Johnstone coughs a couple times, clearing this throat of smoke and dirt. "You okay?" he asks Madeline, but she's staring off into the distance, back in the direction of Kurt Clevenger's still-burning home. A column of smoke rises from the ground and mixes into the brown atmosphere above.

"We have to fight now."

The pastor looks at her a moment, confused until he follows her sightline down the dead dirt road. Beyond a few random looters, he can see them coming: Pollux and Mason, their faces smudged black from soot and smoke. Shoulders covered in dust and small chunks of drywall from the breach. They approach side-by-side, a few bystanders giving pause when they recognize the face of Pratt's most infamous ghost story back from the dead. Healthy, alive, smiling at the pastor from roughly two blocks away.

"Can you fight?" she asks. "Tell me what you want to do."

Dr. Keller stands idly by, both he and Madeline waiting for an answer. People panic, scream. Dying birds flop around on the ground like fish, collected and stuffed into burlap sacks by those hoping to taste unspoiled meat. Another roof collapses on itself. Another fire breaks out inside a residence from a gas leak. Sam Cutting curls up in front of his own hardware store, vomiting in the streets between gasps for soured oxygen. He's robbed by a couple local kids, unable to scream for help or defend himself.

Limbs fall from large oak trees, breaking cleanly like elongated cigarette ash. The Challenger shifts, falling to its side when the crack lengthens. It gets worse, will continue to get worse until the living choke on dead air and the fault lines eat whatever remains. Everything dies. Ends. Returns to dust.

Father Johnstone gives a minute nod. To Dr. Keller, he hands Mary over and tells him, "Keep her safe for me."

Madeline grabs the black medical bag, turning it upside-down and shaking out its contents onto the street. She rifles through the various items, tossing away rolls of gauze and bandages with shaky hands. Veins are popping in her arms and over metacarpals. "Shot's really kicking in now," she says, handing over an oxygen mask and the black medical bag back to Dr. Keller. Book XVIII now rests inside of it. "Page twenty-one. You should have everything you need."

Dr. Keller stands stunned a moment, eyes darting from Madeline to Father Johnstone. In the distance, Pollux and Mason continue to gain ground at a brisk pace. He looks terrified, wanting to help but unsure of his ability to do so.

"It's fine, David. Go," the pastor says. He reaches out, giving Mary one final scratch on the chin. Despite the fact that she can barely lift her head, she gives his fingers a couple of affectionate licks. Father Johnstone smiles, telling the doctor, "You gotta go now."

Dr. Keller purses his lips, nods. He navigates around the fault line and heads down the dirt road at a light jog.

"He'll be fine." Madeline uncaps a syringe and sticks it through the top of a small glass container no bigger than a golf ball. She says, "He's the only medical resource left. They won't hurt him if they think they might need him. Trust me."

"What's the deal with the book?" the pastor asks.

"Insurance." Madeline pulls the plunger on the syringe, filling the plastic chamber with fluid. She holds it point-up, flicking it with her middle finger to shake loose the bubbles and pushing them out. "When you ordain something, you infuse it with holy properties. It's not limited to communion wine and wafers." Madeline gives the syringe a little squirt, readying it for injection. "Bless this for me," she requests.

Father Johnstone doesn't think about it. He doesn't consider the contents of the syringe or what Madeline plans on doing with it. There's no time. They're getting closer, so he makes short work of it, bestowing the Lord's sanction upon the object. One quick blessing, and then Madeline is injecting it into her own bicep, pushing the plunger down hard with her thumb before tossing the syringe behind her in the fault line.

"You're stronger than me," Madeline says. "Always have been. It's why the paint peels and the walls start to bend sometimes...you're too much." Madeline sweats. Her skin flushes and the pastor notices veins popping in her neck and forehead, almost as if she's been holding her breath for too long. "The reality here is that I've been holding you back."

In laymen's terms: the battery is too powerful for the device. Unlike the cleric lying in the backseat of the Challenger, Father Johnstone hasn't once felt weak or fatigued. In fact, he feels more vital than his chronological years should allow.

"What was that?" he asks.

"Morphine," she says. "Now I can be on your level."

She turns and begins to walk toward Mason and Pollux, balling her fists tight and releasing, giving her hands a little shake. Father Johnstone notices small bolts of static flashing around her fingers. This is when Pollux extends his hand out to a nearby parked car, a red station wagon about fifty feet away from him. He pulls up, lifting it off the ground with magnetic force and guides it through the air, still on the approach.

"He's a hunter, Johnstone," Madeline says. She sounds calm, controlled. "The hunter always tries to strike from a distance first. Now get behind me."

The station wagon hovers fifteen...twenty feet above street

level, then a bit higher as it rises past the tops of the buildings. Pollux swings his arm slightly back before throwing it forward, aiming at Madeline and grunting slightly from the effort. 3,000 pounds of vehicle launches through the air, and although the pastor is tempted to dive out of the way, he holds firm, hand on Madeline's hip and feeling a flush of warmth course through his system. He prays for her, prays that she can stop it.

"From Book VII, this is a spell developed by a group of witches in ancient Rome," Madeline explains, watching the station wagon sail closer. They can hear it cutting through the wind now. It's only seconds away from smashing into them head-on. "Primarily, it was used to stop the arrows of Roman soldiers attempting to persecute them," Madeline says cooly. "Today, we'll use it to stop a car."

Father Johnstone sees it at the last possible moment, a thin sheen that has developed in front of Madeline's extended hand. It's just barely visible until the station wagon smashes into it, inciting a violent ripple. He flinches as the front end smashes in and the headlights burst against the transparent wall a mere five feet away, but the sound is all that gets through. Not one fragment of glass or steel touches them.

"Particle barrier," Madeline says, flexing her hands again. She briefly peeks over the station wagon to gauge how close Pollux and Mason are before squatting down, motioning for the pastor to do the same. "He'll toss another."

"And will you stop it again?" the pastor asks.

"We won't be here," she says. "We use this as an opportunity to reposition...over there." Madeline points to the right side of the street, near the hardware store.

"So we run?"

Madeline smiles. She takes Father Johnstone by the hand and tells him, "Walk, actually."

Father Johnstone interlocks fingers with Madeline, feeling hot moisture and her pulse pumping so hard it reverberates throughout her entire appendage. Bystanders marvel as Pollux takes control of another vehicle—a gray pickup truck this time—and lifts it into the air nearly twenty feet above his head.

"So we're seriously just going to walk?" the pastor asks, concern slipping into his voice.

"Watch his eyes. Stay close," Madeline says. She stands, pulling the pastor up by the arm—it's flushing with warmth again. They move off to the right of the smashed station wagon and walk parallel to the edge of the fault line, nearing a cracked length of sidewalk which is littered in various pieces of debris. The pastor and Madeline have since moved ten or so feet away, but Pollux hasn't noticed. His eyes remain locked onto the space in front of the station wagon, arm positioned above his head.

"Does he not see us?" the pastor whispers into Madeline's ear.

"Book IX," she says softly. "Sometimes a witch needs to hide when there's no cover. No caves or trees or tall grass. So they devised a method in which to appear invisible." Madeline nods to the sky, tinged in smog. "They figured out how to bend light around them. Now watch."

Pollux swings his arm forward, launching the pickup truck to the space between the front end of the station wagon and the nearest edge of the fault line. It sails, landing with a loud crunch that dislodges a section of the dead earth. Both vehicles fall beneath street level, sinking into the crater. Mason and Pollux continue on, the latter furrowing his brow, suspicious he's missed his target for a second time. Pollux pauses a moment, motioning for his Secondary to stand behind him. Both men survey the area with extreme caution, unaware they're about to pass their targets.

"He's concerned for his Secondary," Madeline whispers into the pastor's ear. "We're going to play off that."

"Can't you just bolt them?" the pastor offers, remembering what happened to Mary out in the fields. It seems like a reasonable plan of attack, but Madeline is already shaking her head.

"Lightning is composed of electrostatic charges, both in the sky and in the earth, and they're walking on dead ground." Madeline pulls the pastor along, stepping quietly until they're standing just outside the hardware store. It appears to have been looted, although not much compared to the grocery stores and small markets that have been stripped bare in desperation for food. The battery rack by the front register has been cleaned out, but other things like paint supplies and small tools unfit for weaponry remain undisturbed. Madeline turns to pastor. "I got something we can try. Grab some nails," she says. "Quietly."

Father Johnstone backs into the store, careful to step over the various trash and tools still in their packages lying on the ground. He grabs a couple small boxes of ten penny nails from a nearby end-cap, sandwiching them between his palms to keep them silent. Upon exiting, the pastor sees Pollux and Mason stopped in the middle of the road. Thirty feet away, the Primary looks right, then left to where Madeline and the pastor are stationed. He still doesn't see them.

"They've moved," Pollux says. He walks a couple paces away from them, scanning his surroundings. He keeps Mason close behind him who currently is favoring his left arm. Fresh burns from the house fire blacken and distort the flesh.

"I'm gonna give them a little distraction." Madeline says this so quietly the pastor almost can't hear it. "When I do that— throw."

He nods, holding both boxes of nails tightly in his right hand and ready to toss. Yet again, warmth flushes through his body, burning at the tips of his fingers. Father Johnstone looks skyward, noticing a small patch of clouds forming over the far end of the fault line. Although Pratt is covered in a shell of dead earth, the cracks have exposed the healthy soil that lies underneath. Madeline appears to be aiming her hand past Mason and Pollux, close to the spot where the Challenger is buried.

"Almost," Madeline whispers, arm tensing as electrostatic charge builds in the sky and earth. Father Johnstone readies himself, waiting. The first flicker of light manifests in the distance and Pollux swiftly puts himself between it and his Secondary, arms extended and ready to defend. The pastor tosses the two boxes of nails at Mason's back, but neither Pollux nor Mason hear them over the thunderclap. They're still distracted by a cast that seemingly missed the mark, vulnerable to the 200 nails nearing their proximity.

They burst from their boxes and Madeline buries every one of them into Mason Hollis's ribcage, spine, and shoulders. He screams, arching his back and falling onto the dead earth, writhing in pain. Pollux whips around and sees it: his Secondary, nails dug deep into his skin, pouring blood into the dirt. Precious blood. Blood he can use. He yanks on Mason's shirt collar and stands him up, magnetically popping out the nails. They hover around the two men, glistening under the sun as Mason continues to bleed from the holes in his back. So much wasted blood. Pollux cups his hand against his Secondary's back and gathers a palm's worth of it, bringing it to his lips and slurping.

"Nails," he says, talking to himself, a grin spreading across his face. "Where can a guy get nails in this town?"

Before Madeline can fully react, Pollux is shooting every piece of steel in the direction of the hardware store they're stationed in front of—not focused on any one point in particular. The nails spray wide, covering the entire face of the store and shooting through windows. Madeline had attempted to shield them again, but the particle barrier couldn't be formed in time to stop the few that make contact. Four or five stick in her torso; another couple have pierced clean through her right hand. She doesn't wince or cry out in pain. With all the chemicals coursing through her system, the wounds are barely felt.

"There you are," Pollux says, now able to see Madeline and the pastor. She pops out the two nails in her hand and attempts to shoot them back, but he's ready this time. The steel abruptly stops mid-air, crackles against his own barrier, and falls to the street. "I read Book VII long before you did, my dear. You're going to have to show me something new."

Madeline smirks. "Very well."

She turns, pushing Father Johnstone back through the entrance of the hardware store while items jump off the shelves and zip past them. Saw blades, shovels, and power tools— anything metal. It's as if the entire contents of the store are being sucked out by a vacuum. Every box of nails, nuts, and bolts zips past them and out the front entrance and windows, heading towards Pollux where they hit the particle barrier. Cans of paint and tins of brass polish flood by the pastor and Madeline, enabling them to put distance between their party and the one being barraged in hardware supplies just outside.

"There's something you should know," Madeline says, pushing Father Johnstone along through the hardware store as a flurry of screwdrivers and wrenches whips past him. She plucks the nails out of her torso by hand, one-by-one; they fly backwards with the rest. Blood drips from her right hand and the puncture wounds in her stomach as they walk through, splattering on the shop linoleum. Madeline says, "Anything the plague kills can't be brought back. Not even by someone like me."

It doesn't take long for Father Johnstone to surmise what she's referring to. She's not talking about the flock or any specific person. If the plague moves up the food chain as Mason said, that means Mary hasn't got much longer. She was already having a rough time in the car. God only knows how long she can hang on.

"I'm sorry," Madeline says, still ushering the pastor through the hardware store, which is very nearly out of metallic objects to propel backwards. Only a few items such as wood and plastic rakes and ceramic tiling remain on their respective shelves.

"What can we do?" He feels slightly guilty because he knows Madeline can tell that's not the real question. In actuality, what he really wants to know is how he can assist her in killing this man in as little time as possible. On the brink of losing Pratt and the only real family he's ever known, what Madeline foretold has finally become true: he has compromised. He is now willing to cross the threshold, and the Lord need only look into his heart to understand why.

Near the back wall of the hardware store, Madeline checks to make sure they haven't been followed in. "We're going to try something," she says vaguely.

"Can I help?" Father Johnstone isn't sure if he's supposed to go out the back door or wait for further instructions.

"You stay on my back. Keep close," she says. "He's already healed his Secondary by now so we'll bend light again and circle around."

Madeline steps in front of the pastor and opens the back door leading outside. It's raining. Over the sound of metal objects whipping by and making contact with mortar and windows, the patter of the downpour on the roof couldn't be heard clearly. Clouds have rolled in as well, all but cutting off natural light as dead earth loses its firmness. Madeline pauses in the doorway as the rain gets heavier.

"You can't do it again?" the pastor asks.

"He's read everything I have. Can't bend light if you don't have any," she says.

Through the roof, another vehicle plummets their way, slamming nose-first into the flooring a few feet behind the pastor and Madeline. They flinch, flooring cracking underneath their feet. The Ford truck crunches a flashlight display and tips over sideways onto some of the empty racks. Heavy rain falls through the hole in the roof, patting on the truck's driver side. Unlike the first two vehicles that Pollux launched at them in the street, this one was tossed while it was still running, and occupied. Mr. Hudson is hanging limp behind the steering wheel, held in place by a seatbelt. The blood curling around his features makes him almost unrecognizable.

"The hunter knows where we are and is now trying to force us out. He's going to start killing people," Madeline says.

"I can't have that," the pastor says. He looks at Mr. Hudson, limp and bleeding in his vehicle. It's one more person he'll have to bury if he ever makes it out of this alive.

"He knows you'd feel that way. He's playing off your sense of obligation to these people," she explains. "These are pawns meant to draw you to him."

Two months ago, Father Johntone would have taken great offense to Madeline's usage of the word 'pawns' in reference to Pratt's innocent bystanders. He would have lectured her on the importance of life and how they're equal in capacity. That's not the case anymore. His days of thinking in absolutes have ended with Mr. Hudson and whomever else Pollux decides to use to bait the pastor out.

"He'll keep showing you bodies until your guilt gets the best of you. Either that, or he'll toss another car and the roof might collapse in on us," she says. "And if we go outside, we'll be out in the open with no cover."

"You're saying he wants us to come at him head on," the pastor says.

"He always did prefer having the target come to him." Madeline looks at the hole in the ceiling, then the truck. Rain continues to pound through the opening, beating on the vehicle and shop flooring. It pours in so thick the column of wet is almost impossible to see through. "We take high ground," she says.

Naturally, Father Johnstone scans the room for a ladder they can prop up against one side of the truck's entry point, allowing them to climb up to the roof. This is when notices Madeline moving the truck, magnetically tilting it until it's sitting on four wheels again. Mr. Hudson's body, of course, is shifting around on the inside as she does this. He deserves better, the pastor thinks. "No time to move him, I'm afraid." Madeline addresses the issue before he can bring it up. "Get in the bed there. He's moving."

"Pollux is?" The pastor checks the front windows. Not much is visible with all the rain, and the few feet of ground he gains by hopping into the truck bed doesn't help.

"Don't worry. He won't come in," Madeline assures him. "He's got the advantage in open space, so he'll try to force us out to him." She hops in the truck bed, which is now aligned underneath the hole in the ceiling. They're drenched. Blood and dirt washes away from their skin. "When we get up there, you let him see you."

"I'm bait?" he asks.

"He still thinks he can use you," she says. "So he won't kill you if he can help it."

"You don't sound sure," the pastor says.

Madeline smiles in the rain, flashing those campfire eyes and the smile just as warm. "Have faith," she says, and the truck elevates, suspension creaking as the tires hang dead weight on their axles. Standing within the bed, he watches the space between Madeline's crown and the ceiling decrease, shrinking until they're able to see the poorly tarred roof of the hardware store. The two of them jump out of the bed, rolling into the inch of rainwater coating the surface. Father Johnstone looks at Madeline, noticing veins popping in her arms and forehead, skin looking flushed despite the coolness of the downpour. Perhaps it's all the chemicals in her system finally having an adverse reaction.

"You okay?" he asks.

"I'm holding a truck." She looks down. The Ford is still hovering in the middle of the hardware store. "Look over the edge." Madeline nods towards the perimeter.

The pastor finds himself cowering as he walks towards the fringe, concerned that by peeking over he's putting himself at risk to have his head blown off or worse: tampered with again. He has no idea what Madeline plans on doing, but he prays it works. He prays whatever idea she's attempting to execute, that it comes to fruition.

Father Johnstone makes his way up to the front of the building, the various tools and metal objects scattered in the street. They slowly drown in rainwater, muck, and the multi-colored innards of busted paint cans and wood varnishes. No sign of Pollux or Mason. Just an unpopulated stretch of dead road and supplies sinking into the earth. He heads over to the west side of the roof, creeping his eyes over the crumbling edge. Father Johnstone sees the two men sidling the building, ready to ambush the back door. Mason turns. He connects eyes with the pastor, grinning. Pollux immediately whips around, running full-sprint down the alley with an arm extended. Rain begins to twist unnaturally in front of his palm like a small cyclone. The pastor knows it's useless to duck for cover. Whatever is about to happen, a few inches of rotting mortar won't be able to stop it, but he prays he survives. Prays the Lord intervenes.

The truck smashes through the wall.

Madeline tosses the Ford through the hardware store's western perimeter. It throws off Pollux's cast just enough so that it doesn't hit the pastor directly, but rather, takes out all the supporting brick and framework of the corner the pastor is on. He falls with the collapsing roof, losing sight of Mason and Pollux. Madeline watches helplessly as her Secondary falls over twenty feet onto rubble and random metal, calling out for him. Father Johnstone feels a hard snap in his lower leg upon impact. The mud helps soften the fall, but he's now looking at bone fragment bursting forth from one of his pant legs.

"Wait there," Madeline shouts from the roof. "I'm coming down."

Pain hasn't hit yet, but it will. It's on its way. He tries not to look at it, tries not to accept that a half a foot of bone is sticking out of his leg. Madeline can fix this, he thinks. If she can cure a cripple, she can take care of this with ease.

He yells for her to hurry, praying. Father Johnstone prays she can mend his wound. He prays to the good Lord almighty that she reaches him before Mason or Pollux does. With every fiber in his being, he pleads that the truck has finished what the fire at old man Clevenger's did not. If not death, then at least an injury worse than his own.

"Hold still. I'm coming." Madeline navigates the collapsed section of roof in which Father Johnstone lies incapacitated at the bottom. He looks at where the truck came through the wall, and although it's obscured by rain, there doesn't appear to be any movement by either man. There's no way that Pollux could have defended himself in time, he thinks. He was too distracted by the pastor on the roof to even realize it was coming.

Father Johnstone forces a smile. "I think your plan worked," he says.

"Not exactly." Madeline kneels down in the mud, examining the piece of bone sticking out of the leg and swiping wet hair back behind an ear. "I can't just wave my hand and make this better. I'd have to set it first," she says, arms shaking—not from the frigid downpour or chemicals allowing her to ignore her own wounds. It's concern, maybe even fear. Madeline looks at the bone, tentative. She's either unsure of how to do it or scared she might make the situation worse.

She looks away from the bone, gasping, and the pastor turns to see what's caught her attention. He's expecting to see Mason and Pollux, the two of them striding confidently toward a disabled Secondary and Madeline. Fortunately, this is not the case.

"I thought we told you to go home, Keller," Madeline says, pushing off the muck and ready to greet him. He's soaked, pacing through the terrain of rubble and mud in a clumsy fashion. "You're going to have to work fast," she says.

Dr. Keller gives a concurrent nod, stepping over a particularly large section of wall and bringing his eyes down to the pastor's leg. He's empty-handed. No medical bag or tools of any kind. Father Johnstone looks at him, searching for the reason why he would return when he was specifically asked to tend to Mary and the book. His guilt of their original capture might be the event that brought him back.

"How is she?" the pastor asks.

"Fine." It comes out raspy, so low over the rain that it can barely be heard. He offers a smile of encouragement, which puts the pastor's mind at ease somewhat.

"It's my fault. I should have been able to stop it." Madeline hunkers down next to Dr. Keller, watching him examine the wound. She looks contrite. Clearly, her assumption that Pollux would never do anything to injure the pastor was in error. He's lucky to be alive right now, and she's well aware of that. "I can help with the pain," she offers, placing her fingers on the leg and manipulating nerve function. Father Johnstone feels everything below the knee go numb, past his ankle all the way down to his toes.

"Do it. Quick." Even though he's lost sensation in that particular appendage, the pastor braces himself anyway. He waits for the distinct sound of bone snapping over the patter of rain, shutting his eyes tight. There's no need to see it.

The following noise is sharp, as is the gasp that follows.

Father Johnstone opens his eyes to Madeline's ribcage housing a screwdriver. Dr. Keller's fist grips the handle, digging into her. Twisting. Her mouth is gaping, not screaming. Not even breathing. "Imitator spell," Pollux's voice emerges from Dr. Keller's mouth. "See, it's all that junk in your system. You can't feel pain, can't feel your lung collapsing on this screwdriver right now," he says, pinning Madeline's body to the ground, locking her arms in so she's unable to cast. "You can't feel me, either. We'll change that." His frown lines and crow's feet fade smooth, features change, hair goes from thin and white to lush and dark. Even his clothes change. "You'll feel me again—don't you worry about that. I got a little something here for you."

He pulls out a small syringe, capped in a plastic sheath on the needle. It's the M99 shot, the one Dr. Keller gave to Madeline. Pollux plans on knocking her out with it. The pastor screams, curses, tries to intervene. He feels one of Mason's arms slip around his neck from behind and lock him in, cutting his air off.

Pollux removes the cap with his teeth and spits it out, telling her, "Next time you wake up, it's not gonna be taped up in a chair. That was me being nice. You're going to fulfill your duty to me and then you're gonna feel me harvest you for everything you've got, you little cunt." He laughs in her ear, giving it a lick and bringing the needle to her neck, pushing his forearm into her throat to keep her still.

Father Johnstone can only watch as Madeline struggles to breathe, let alone move. Pollux is too strong. She can't budge. The metal is inches away from her skin when the pastor notices the end of the syringe bending like string, then snapping. Liquid bursts out of the plastic housing and Madeline navigates the metal through one of Pollux's eyes. He immediately rolls off of her, clutching his face and screaming.

"YOU CUNT! YOU FUCKING CUNT! YOU TOOK MY FUCKING EYE, BITCH!"

Blood and optical jelly seeps through his fingers, washing away in the rain. He screams. Pollux screams, digging shaking fingers into his eye cavity to pull out the needle fragment. Mason releases the pastor, opting to take Madeline out while she's still wounded and relatively helpless on the ground. He runs full speed through the muck and mortar with nothing but his fists drawn. Instinctively, she thrusts out a hand and flash-fries the space in front of Mason's torso and face. It's so hot the rain turns to steam and burns him, loosening the top few layers of skin and scar tissue. Mason Hollis falls sideways onto the ground, wincing in pain. Father Johnstone can see his face is already bubbling and filling with yellow fluid.

Madeline rolls over to her stomach, crawling on hands and knees to Father Johnstone who is reclined in the wreckage. She doesn't even bother to pull the screwdriver out of her side, panting, "I'm sorry...I'm sorry," so quiet that the pastor can't even hear it over Pollux's screams. He has to read her lips to understand it.

Father Johnstone wants to help. He wants to yank the screwdriver out of her lung so she can heal herself and finish this off, but she shakes her head.

"Why not?" he asks.

Madeline coughs up blood. She lies next to the pastor, putting mouth-to-ear, telling him, "Can't heal...myself. Not this." Even under the cold rain, her breath warms the side of the pastor's face. It reverberates into his neck, his spine.

Meanwhile, Pollux is getting his bearings. Roughly ten feet away, he's hunched over and yanking out the metal lodged in his ocular cavity, bleeding, cursing. The metal all around them begins to tremble and slowly rise out of the ground: the saw blades and nails and wrenches. They're coming to life. Hovering.

"Love you," Madeline says. She cradles the pastor's face in her hand, bringing it to her lips, pecking his cheek. She drags the tip of her nose against his face, releasing hot breath and blood spatter against his neck. Father Johnstone doesn't need to be able to read people like she can. He knows a goodbye when he hears one.

"Don't." He clutches her wrists, shakes his head at her, frowning. The air tastes worse than ever now, and the earth beneath them is oil black. "Please," he whispers.

Madeline kisses him, blood glazing the pastor's lips. It almost tastes sweet. "Don't leave." She says, "They'll need you...more than ever. You'll...figure it out."

She smiles, kissing him on the cheek again. Madeline pushes off the ground and begins striding towards Pollux, heavy-footed and wobbly. Her lung is giving out, and the air she can take in is bitter with poison. Bright lights are crackling her vision, almost as if she's about to drown in the rain from lack of oxygen. Madeline runs through the floating metal, past Mason Hollis who misses in his attempt to trip her up. She jumps onto Pollux's back and wraps her arms around his neck, hanging on for dear life. Even with a burst eyeball, he laughs at her pretension.

Through gritted teeth, he says, "Very stupid, cunt."

Father Johnstone can do nothing but watch as Pollux begins pulls the items hovering mid-air towards Madeline. Nails pin into her back and ribs. A muck-covered saw blade slices her leg so deep the blood comes out in sheets. He can't understand why she's not using her ability to push them away, to defend herself. Then he feels it. He feels that warmth in his skin as another flock of sharp objects stick into Madeline's arms and shoulders, Pollux's attempt at getting her to relinquish her grip. She doesn't let go and Father Johnstone feels the heat in his hands shift to a burn, more intense than anything he's ever felt. It's never been painful like this. Not once.

Then he remembers something Madeline said earlier, not long after she injected morphine into her system: *"Now I can be on your level."*

Father Johnstone and Mason Hollis look on as hot light manifests, and boils the mud beneath Pollux's feet. Nails and screwdrivers begin to melt mid-air, prompting the two spectators to put some distance between themselves and their Primaries. Adrenaline allows the men to forget about their wounds as the light begins to eat, destroy, break down anything within a ten-foot radius.

He watches his love, Madeline Paige, dissolving before his very eyes. So powerful. And bright. The ground dries, hardens, and cracks. Rain boils. Even the air around her begins to catch fire. *"The reality here is that I've been holding you back,"* she told him.

"The intent defines the relationship."

Madeline destroying herself for the sake of salvaging Pratt, to save the pastor and Mary—these too would be considered ingredients. She could have run, he thinks. She could have left all this behind, and now she's burning, screaming. Madeline holds on to Pollux until he is little more than dust and char, unable to suffer him to live a second longer.

She too falls. Dies. Ends.

The rain stops. Clouds clear.

Metal objects plummet dead into the mud, some sticking upright as if they've been planted. Mason and the pastor examine the remains from afar: a hard crater dusted in ash. Random bone fragments and pieces of cloth. Pollux's body is charred, organs cooked. Steam rises off what's left of his body, deforming the air just a little bit more. Madeline lies behind him, obscured, but Father Johnstone has no desire to see her, the damage. He doesn't want to tarnish the memory. Not yet. Not until he has to. For one moment, he wants nothing more than pure uninhibited grief. Madeline's funeral and all that comes with it can be dealt with in due course, but the grief, the feeling—this is all that matters on the fringe of nearly losing everything. Regarding Mason Hollis, his alliance with Pollux was everything he had, and now he's alone again. Alone in the place that burned his body and exiled him to a life of lonely roads and secret shame.

"We're not done, Jairy." Mason picks himself up off the ground, stomping through the mud towards the pastor. He picks up a large wrench on his way and draws back to swing it. Father Johnstone instinctively scoots back but it's no use. His leg prohibits him from making sufficient movement, and the wrench-head ends up making contact with the side of the pastor's kneecap. It bursts open, making a wet popping sound like a piece of dropped fruit. Blood trickles into the mud and the pastor screams. Screams, clutching the wound where fresh pain aches wet and warm.

"I'm not crawling outta here this time." Mason draws the

wrench back again, swinging it into the top of the pastor's hand. Bones crack. Snap. Father Johnstone rolls onto his side, curling up into a ball. He screams into the mud. Cowering. Hiding his broken hand in the muck. "You hear me, don't you?" Mason asks. "You hear me, you fuck?" He brings the wrench down again, on the pastor's ribcage this time. Then his hip. He's crying. Not praying. There's too much pain to even collect a coherent thought. A prayer is impossible at this point.

Mason says, "I'll give you a choice. I'll give you the thing they never gave me, Jairy. You can either be beaten to death in the street or die in the earth." He glances to his left, the fault line. Dark and endless and cold. "How much do you want a proper burial? How much is that worth? You don't even know, do you?" he snickers. "Little cunt never told you nothin'. She had a lot of secrets, that one. Too bad you won't live long enough to know 'em."

The hammer pulls back on a gun.

The barrel kisses the back of Mason's skull.

"Shelby was hoping she'd run into you again," Sheriff Morgan says. "Shelby never did get over Mason Hollis. 'The one that got away,' she called him. Never thought he'd be dumb enough to show his face around here again."

Father Johnstone allows his eyes to slowly peel open. He lifts his face out of the mud and chances a look at the men above him. Mason is terrified. The wrench slips from his fingers, smacking against the mud.

"Does Mason remember what the sheriff told him if he ever came back?"

There's a pause. "Kip. Please."

"No warning. You get the bullet. Your body gets fed to the hogs," Sheriff Morgan says. "And what about your head?" he asks. "Does Mason remember where that goes?"

"You don't want to do this, Kip," Mason says.

Sheriff Morgan pulls the trigger. Shelby cracks and Father

Johnstone watches the bullet exit Mason's forehead, bursting blood and little pieces of skull. He drops dead-weight to the mud with a hard slap, death rattling bubbles in a rain puddle. Executed. The sheriff stands over the body, shifting his eyes to Father Johnstone and looking him over: the busted knee and the protruding bone. Morgan looks not much better. Second-degree sunburn mars his face and arms. His feet are blistered from the hours of walking on hot asphalt and pavement, boots soaked to the sole in blood and pus. Elbows and knees are crusted in weeping scabs and dirt. He's standing over the pastor, Shelby gripped firmly in his hand, fuming at the barrel. No spectators. No one to watch him finish the job. His eyes drift over the wounded leg, assessing the damage. Sheriff Morgan eases Shelby back into his leather holster and adjusts his belt.

"We're even," he says.

His hand grips Mason Hollis at the collar, squeezing so tight the bottom hem of his shirt hikes up. Sheriff Morgan nods at the pastor—not quite like a friend, but close—and he begins walking away. He drags Mason Hollis through the mud, ready to show Pratt a new kind of ghost story. One they'll talk about for years to come.

On the Road with Billy Burke, Secondary

"I believe what I say, Mr. Pollux. I truly do. The Lord has a vengeful side. He's got anger in His heart just like you and I, but He also believes in what's fair. That's why he let me crawl outta Pratt that night...burned up to within an inch of my life. Bleedin'...hurting like hell. He wanted me to use that pain to become Billy Burke...spread His Word in a way it had never been done. He wanted me to find my true calling. My own Divine path. It's like you said, Mr. Pollux: the Man works in mysterious ways. Ways that seems too coincidental even. But you know what? I'm not gonna question it no more. I feel Him...feel His mighty hand guiding us back there...back to Pratt. The Lord wills us to return stronger in our pairing than we could ever be on our own. He wants us to administer our own brand of faith...bring harmony back to the town. You give me purpose, Mr. Pollux. Haven't had a nightmare since we met. That alone I'll be eternally grateful for. You can rest assured I'll be returning the favor ten-fold...help you bring what's coming to Madeline Paige and whoever else needs dealin' with—oh, yes I will. I stake my life on it. Ain't gonna be no runnin' off or crawlin' through the dirt for me this time. We'll be patient...let the winter pass while ol' Mason here keeps an eye on things for you. The Lord wants you strong for this and we've got plenty to learn from each other, you and I. Plenty to learn. When we go back to Pratt, they're gonna see real quick that times are changin'. I'm prepared to die showing them that."

The Relief Effort

Pratt slowly recovers.

After those few initial days of starvation and immense panic, word finally got out about the town experiencing what's now being categorized as an 'ecological disaster.' This is how the local residents and various news outlets are able to explain away the fault lines in the earth, the dead plant and animal life. Even though Father Johnstone knows the true reasoning behind why the water soured and air become poisoned, words like 'plague' and 'curse' would be needlessly alarming now that stability is finally being rediscovered. Far be it from him to destroy what little peace of mind they have with the truth. Some things are best left unsaid, and he has a feeling Madeline would have whole-heartedly agreed with that sentiment.

"Quite the turnout, preacher," Miles Conley mentions. He and his wife are currently toting a couple carts of supplies, either canned goods or fresh sets of hammers and nails for the volunteer workers. People have been arriving in droves for the past three weeks: rebuilding homes and fixing telephone lines. Mr. Conley himself has led more than a few excursions to hunt wild game beyond the county lines, loaning out dozens of rifles that he'd typically sell as merchandise. His only stipulation is that they're returned at the end of the hunt and a share of the spoils.

"Leg's healed up real nice, I see," he mentions. "Let me know if you wanna join in on the next hunt." The Conleys move on, smiling, optimistic. It seems like everyone is breathing a sigh of relief now that the worst is over.

Pratt has changed.

What was once a small town of people 'stuck in their ways' and resistant to outsiders has shifted to something else. In the face of abrupt transition, that old adage of 'love thy neighbor' has spread far and wide. Father Johnstone watches them—both flock and non-flock alike—undoing the damage that nearly ended them. People from neighboring towns arrive with more bottled water and medical supplies. More rations. Pick-up trucks filled with virgin planks of cedar make their deliveries, helping the locals unload before shipping back out to fetch another round of provisions. This process typically goes on until well after dark, at which point families will fire up the grills and share a meal with the people of Aames, Barton City, and the other out-of-town guests lending a hand. They'll swap stories and drink domestic brew out of dirty plastic coolers, chewing the fat until the midnight hours. At dawn the town wakes to do it all over again: rebuilding, repairing, kindling relationships new and old.

His prayers were answered.

He asked the Lord to send aid, to deliver Pratt from its crippled state. Father Johnstone prayed to the good Lord, and with great haste, the Lord responded. He sent them food, laborers, and medical personal to supplement Dr. Keller's sudden increase in demand. The Lord cleansed the bitter air and bestowed regular downpours of cleansing rain. Although to the casual observer these would appear to be nothing more than the tide of misfortune turning, the pastor knows better. The Lord is in every helpful soul that turns up in Pratt; most of them don't even know how they got there in the first place.

"I just thought I should be here," a young man from Junction City told him the other week. "Got in my truck and the next thing I knew I was pulling into town. Kinda odd, now that I'm thinking about it. I've never even heard of Pratt."

It's just like all of those times when he too would randomly appear in certain parts of town. Spells of forgetfulness and long blank periods daunted him to a point of madness—that is, until Madeline stepped in. The pastor can't help but wonder if he's part of the reason these wayward travelers keep turning up, confused and a bit disoriented, but intent on helping in any way that they can. In the end, it's the intent that matters. Father

Johnstone tries to remember that every time he goes over Pratt's recent trials and the death of Madeline Paige.

Her words continue to perplex him: *'The Divine path is full of many detours, but should you stay the course, you'll always find me at the end.'*

Madeline Paige had a Will. Within it she left the pastor her home, all her possessions, and a personal letter sealed in a wax stamp. It was filed with the local records office on the Monday after the Pratt bake-off, within hours of the bleeding episode; Father Johnstone was in a coma at the time. It was way before he knew anything of Craft or just how close old enemies had drawn in. He was at his lowest point, and Madeline brought him back from the edge. Of course, knowing her, she would say that they saved each other. Like a marriage or any other non-standard courtship, this was always a two-person operation. Even so, certain portions of her letter don't add up in his mind.

'Death is the darkest interval, but like love, can be a very powerful ingredient,' she wrote. *'Sometimes death is necessary.'*

It is the puzzle that he's not yet ready to take on—not after all that's happened and the fallout that will haunt Pratt for years to come. Another campfire tale looms, far more grandiose than that of Mason Hollis and his past misdeeds. 'Ecological disaster' is but a soft label for the event that local residents don't understand, and in all honestly, probably wouldn't even if Father Johnstone took them through the paces himself. It's been weeks and he's no closer to understanding the particulars of Pratt's curse, not to mention the correspondence Madeline left behind—specifically, in regards to her burial. It was the first time in three decades the pastor had performed a non-Christian service. No psalms were said. Not one passage of the Good Book was recited as he stood over her body.

'This may be the final time I ask you to do something for me you might not agree with,' Madeline wrote to him. *'But I wouldn't do it unless it was important.'*

Yet again, Father Johnstone found himself in a position of compromising his faith. Yet again, he let Madeline lead him down the path with his eyes shut tight, walking blind behind her and hoping she wouldn't steer him wrong. He prayed for both their sakes that this too was part of their Divine path. Her burial was performed just as she instructed: according to the traditions of the Feri, right down to the smallest detail. Dr. Keller hand-delivered those directions the morning after she died. Madeline's 'insurance policy' as she put it, was a page torn out of one of the many volumes of books that populated her home.

"Maybe not tomorrow, maybe not even this year," Dr. Keller said, "but one day after all this calms down and we've had some time to think on it…maybe then you and I can sit down and talk this out. Until then, I'll keep my questions to myself."

Dr. Keller had witnessed just enough to make him doubt everything he thought he knew about logic and scientific law: a sickness he couldn't diagnose and blood that did the impossible. His rules were broken. Even after Madeline's passing, his beliefs lie in shards like the splinters of dead wood that garnish Pratt's injured streets. Father Johnstone has yet to regress to his former self; the same can't be said for the rumor mill. It continues to churn.

"Ol' preacher is a damn quick healer," people are saying. "Tough nut, that Johnstone."

Not tough. Not exactly. 'Blessed' would be the more appropriate term.

The pastor's hand contained five breaks: three metacarpals and two proximal phalanges. This was in addition to the shattered kneecap and broken tibia that pierced the skin. It was conveyed to the pastor in no uncertain terms that he'd be off his feet for a while. Wheelchair-bound, for starters, then weeks— possibly months—of hobbling around on crutches.

"And you may need physical therapy, too. Men our age don't recover as quick as we once did," Dr. Keller said. "I'm afraid your heroics are going to set you back for a bit."

He was fully recovered the very next day.

The death of friends and enemies alike needed to be handled. In the wake of such destruction, Pratt needed its shepherd more than ever. Lying around a hospital room waiting for his bones to heal wasn't an option, so Father Johnstone prayed. He prayed the Lord restore his health and mend his wounds. He prayed for strength, and the following morning, he found that the Lord had granted it.

'You're capable of more than you realize,' Madeline wrote. *'To walk the Divine path is to be given Divine power.'*

Although a bit sore in the palm, his once-broken hand was fully functional. Cartilage of the knee reassembled, allowing fluid, painless motion. The tibia that Dr. Keller set the previous night had fully mended, leaving nothing more than a faint scar where the bone had punctured the skin. This wasn't another miracle. Father Johnstone was in the gray area, the fringe, that place where almost anything is possible.

"I guess I shouldn't be surprised you're up walking around already," Dr. Keller said upon seeing the pastor sneaking about the halls of Pratt Medical. Father Johnstone was still wearing his hospital gown, ready to make a break for it just like Mrs. Deebs did all those years ago: naked ass hanging out the back and barefoot. He didn't care by that point. He wanted to get out, wanted to see how Mary was doing. He said many prayers in her name, but the effects needed to be seen with his own eyes.

The pastor was given back his civilian attire, his dress shirt, black slacks, and cowboy boots. Although everything had been run through the hospital wash, faint blood stains and light brown discoloration from dead mud remained. A large rip blemished the pant leg from where the bone poked through.

"Are they here?" the pastor asked.

"The morgue," Dr. Keller said. "All three."

"And the book?"

"In my safe," he said. "At home." Dr. Keller watched as the pastor shrugged on the crumpled white shirt, buttoning and tucking it into his pants. "Do you want to see her?"

Midway through pulling on a boot, the pastor paused to think about it. He had grown accustomed to death over the years by vocation, but this was the first time the loss directly impacted him. Hurt him in a way that made his heart bruise. Madeline's last moments were fuzzy. Hair wet, bloody, screwdriver punched in her side and lung collapsing, but brave. Then the fire, he remembers. White fire, so bright it made the pastor's eyes tinge in pain, burning, boiling the mud beneath her feet. She held onto Pollux until they were both charred to death.

"No," the pastor answered, pulling on his boot the rest of the way. He didn't want to see the damage, the life drained from her face. Madeline Paige will always be best preserved in his memory: the campfire smile, and the eyes just as warm. He preferred that memory compared to what lay in wait inside those cold steel basement containers.

"Understandable," Dr. Keller said.

She's dead, and the pastor is still coming to terms with that.

Pratt, on the other hand, is lively in its optimism. Pillars aside, the rest of the town has no idea of Mason Hollis's return and the hell he brought with him. Eye-witnesses were scarce. It's this blissful ignorance that allows residents to focus on the rebuilding effort and the promise of happier times now that the worst has passed. Speculation runs rampant, of course. The pastor will often hear bits and pieces pertaining to levitating vehicles and lightning storms. People are still scratching their heads over how the hardware store was completely emptied into the street and why Mr. Hudson's truck was found parked underneath all the rubble. His wife and two children are especially distraught over this.

"I just don't understand it," Mrs. Hudson said through sniffles. "All he was doing was trying to fetch us some food and supplies. How the hell does he wind up buried under a building? I don't get it."

She's not alone in her bewilderment. Some are simply hiding it better than others.

Father Johnstone strolls through the central portion of Pratt where the market is usually selling honeydew melon and half-gallon jugs of spring cider. Gone are the carts containing produce, floral arrangements, and herbs picked from gardens. Reflecting back on it, Madeline more than likely procured her fair share of ingredients from this very place. It's now spotted in multicolored balloons and booths decorated in streamers and loud patterns. Pies and cobblers everywhere. Piles of oatmeal and peanut butter cookies. Their aromas take over the air, a welcome replacement to the bitter fumes that made breathing a gag-inducing chore.

"You make sure you come by our table at some point, Pastor," Mrs. Whitley says from her station. "I got some rum cake with your name on it."

It's not like the typical bake-off that Pratt's known for. Not once has the pastor overheard any trash talk or ladies conspiring to steal a recipe. The women and wives of the town have grown, evolved, soliciting funnel cakes and sampler bowls of turkey chili for the sake of something bigger than their own *pride*. Now that the air of competition and threat of judgment have been removed, they've rediscovered the joy of cooking. Locally famous dishes and desserts are served to the out-of-town workers: blueberry cheesecake and Mrs. Fran's buffalo hot wings. Between projects, the volunteers will take in a glass of sweet tea with BBQ ham on white or hot dogs off the grill. Already, they're attempting to pretend nothing ever happened.

'Your town may slip back into its old ways,' Madeline wrote. *'You, however, will be forever changed. You'll be capable of more than they realize, so you'll need to act accordingly.'*

Hiding in plain sight.

During the day, Father Johnstone acts as he normally would: he consoles residents of the town and offers reassurance that they are on the Lord's path, he prays with them, guides the flock. He buries their dead, watches over the living. In the absence of prying eyes, he tests the extent of the capabilities Madeline referred to in her letter. The pastor wasn't aware of it until the morning he left the hospital, a distinct change in which he perceived his surroundings. Air and earth had a personality, a varying compendium of moods and gestures that he could read, interpret. He could feel this in the trees that had grown decrepit with rot, the water that had soured at Larpe's Pond. They spoke their own language, and Father Johnstone could finally understand it.

'You will see the world as I saw it,' Madeline wrote. 'You'll feel it in a way that few have.'

The intangibles: a sort of hyper-awareness to one's surroundings, an ability to feel that which normally cannot be felt. Within twenty-four hours of Pollux dying, Father Johnstone could sense the contaminants leaving the air, the sickness passing from all the squirrels and birds on their final breaths. Although the curse had been broken, recovery was going to be markedly slow.

As Madeline once said, "It always takes longer to create something than to destroy it."

So Father Johnstone has been experimenting with these gifts, usually at night once the town has succumbed to the exhaustion of a hard day's work paired with a long night of drinking and socializing. He walks those once-golden fields of wheat, now relegated to acre upon acre of brittle strands and petrified soil. Miles of granulated death. Father Johnstone consults with the Lord, speaks to the earth, and conjures new life in the form of lush stalks of crop. Seeds sink into the womb of the soil, gestate, and sprout from the ground.

The morning after as the pastor takes his morning constitutional, he'll hear all sorts of commotion about how a new crop of corn just spouted in the eastern fields. "Looks like our prayers are being answered," they'll say.

Father Johnstone nurtures the trees and heals the waters of Larpe's Pond. He creates trout and rainbow fish from eggs, then proceeds to multiply them, not unlike Christ and 'The Feeding of 5,000' reading. While the rest of Pratt sleeps, the pastor walks about restoring plant and animal life, bringing the sick and wounded back to a full state of vitality. It's the least he can do for all of Dr. Keller's assistance during his time of need. He's the reason that Mary was returned safely to his arms, and he'll be forever grateful for that.

'You've always watched over the flock,' Madeline wrote. *'Now you'll have the ability to protect them, influence them in ways you never could before. All the materials are there; the decision to use them is up to you.'*

Unbeknownst to the good doctor, Father Johnstone has been providing medical aid to those too frail or elderly to recover on their own. Over the past many weeks, he's been making private visits to those still hacking up blood or struggling to breathe in their sleep. He asks the Lord to guide him to those that require him most, to help him find those in need of his Divine blessing, whether that be in mind, body, or spirit.

"I've had eleven patients with stage IV lung cancer, another fourteen with blood parasites, countless others with walking pneumonia and typhoid," Dr. Keller said to the pastor the other day. "They came in practically on their deathbeds. Then, before I could even fully administer treatment—got better."

"The Lord works in mysterious ways, David," Father Johnstone said, deflecting the credit that was so obviously being given to him.

"Well, if you see the Lord, tell Him Mrs. Leininger has a nasty kidney infection that could use some fighting off," Dr. Keller said. "She's in room 108, at the moment...y'know...just in case

He'd like to stop by."

Father Johnstone cured her that very evening.

At some point, he'll take Dr. Keller up on his offer and have 'the talk,' as he put it. Intangibly-speaking, the man is in a constant state of disquiet. Mason Hollis was the last person he ever expected to wind up on his table, and the strange circumstances of Madeline's demise along with her ex-lover only added to the turmoil. These events piled to all those questions that never got answered while new ones steadily generated. On a daily basis, cancer dissolves and disease disappears. Life-threatening illnesses regress to common colds or minor headaches. He's starting to be regarded less a medical authority and more of an unreliable weatherman of science.

"Heart failure or something like that. Ol' Doc Keller said I had less than a week to live," Mr. Lucas was overhead saying recently. "Was fit as a fiddle the next day. Haven't felt this good in twenty years."

The effects of the plague disrupted by the Divine.

When it comes right down to it though, the pastor knows that Dr. Keller is willing to have his reputation slightly tarnished if it means he doesn't have to see another body buried. So many have already perished, either from illness that had pushed them past the threshold or random accident involving collapsing buildings or unexpected fault lines in the earth. It was fortunate that Father Johnstone had recovered as quickly as he did, if only so he could oversee the process of conducting the funerals and counseling the bereaved.

Including Mr. Hudson, over twenty bodies had to be excavated from some kind of wreckage—usually a house that couldn't hold the roof anymore. It's why Pratt has such a high demand for quality lumber and the hardware to piece it together. Most of the homes were rotted out, and not one time has the word 'termite' been mentioned. Any man in this town can tell the difference between standard wood rot, a bug infestation, and something else.

"You can ask questions until you're blue in the face," Mr. Conley said. "*Or you can get off your keester and hammer a nail or two.*"

Rumors and speculation can wait. There's been too much to do, too many homes to build and roads to bridge. Too many bodies to bury and mourn. That's been the attitude for the past few weeks, and it's this hectic nature that's allowed Father Johnstone to operate in relative secrecy while he works. Today's function is the first time in a while that Pratt has begun to slip back into its normal tone and temperament. Like Madeline said, they'll eventually regress to their former selves, and a bake-off is a conducive environment for that. Twice the pastor has overheard musings of the late Kurt Clevenger.

"Bless the man who buries and prays for the one who attempted to take his life," Mrs. Pitt said. "I daresay we just leave that sorry excuse for a house in ashes. Let the town take back the lot."

"I agree," Mrs. Wyatt responded with a sneer. "And speaking of properties, what's going on with ol' Maddy Paige's place by the daisy hill? Is that going back on the market?"

Madeline's Will and the transfer of the deed haven't been made public knowledge yet. Occasionally, the pastor hears murmurs showing interest in acquiring it, but it's mostly just talk. Economically-speaking, the town has bottomed out. No one is in any position to make any major purchases or take out a mortgage since the grain plant has suspended work and the town is in recovery mode. Even if that wasn't the case, Father Johnstone wouldn't sell.

'Hold on to that house for me, if you would,' Madeline wrote. 'It's not just people that hide in plain sight.'

The many volumes of books have since been stored safely in the basement, hidden behind the old television sets and fans that have long since spun their final revolution. Most of the downstairs content is old bits of junk along with a few normal things like photograph albums and holiday decorations. Josephine Paige, as it turns out, was a bit of a hoarder. She never got rid of anything. Stacks of *The Pratt Tribune* are piled in the corner, warped from age and the recent water damage. At some point, Father Johnstone will have to sort through it all, but a part of him is afraid of what he'll find. Secrets lurk within the home, and he's just not sure he's ready to discover them.

His fingerprints remain abnormally wavy.

His eyes haven't returned to their normal blue.

He can only assume this is part of what Madeline referred to when she said he'd be forever changed, that he'd be permanently locked in the fringe, the gray area where simple prayer becomes reality. It resonates every time he grows a field of wheat or cures a cancer patient. He can communicate with the environment— with Mary, even. Like Madeline explained, the exchange isn't verbal, but a heightened ability to interpret gestures and signals. Whereas before when Mary would whine for something, that could have meant any number of things, ranging from hunger to the need to relieve herself to mild terror due to an ongoing thunderstorm. Understanding the intangibles takes the guess-work out of it. The day of Madeline's funeral was especially hard for her. Mary spent hours slumped on the dirt of Madeline's plot, crying softly. One of the few people that understood her was gone now, and it tore the pastor apart knowing just how much that loss affected her. More so than the countless friends and family members of the pastor has counseled through the grieving process. Not only did he share Mary's pain, but he could feel it transpiring inside her, an ache that would linger. Remorse for not having done more to prevent it.

'Take care of Mary,' Madeline wrote. 'Like you, she's seen things that can't be unseen. She's been pushed past the threshold and felt what's on the other side. Other animals will find her too complex and no human will ever understand her like you can.'

Mary experienced death, disease, and the loss of a friend. Naturally, there have been many periods in which the two of them openly commiserate their recent trials, usually balled up on the couch with the television displaying glimpses of sports highlights between periods of snow. To convey strength and a steady hand, the pastor has not publicly mourned, reserving those moments of vulnerability for the confines of his own household. Mary will crawl into the crook of the pastor's arm, sigh, and attempt to drift off into dreamless sleep. Father Johnstone, unfortunately, can feel it every time she has a nightmare. She feels fear, guilt. In her dreams she's never running as fast as she needs to, never barking loud enough for her master and Madeline to hear.

For Mary, he prays the Lord reward her bravery and let her be at peace. He prays she be allowed happiness and joy again. Unlike the various illnesses the pastor has remedied, Mary's wounds are largely emotional, and therefore, slow to heal. She shows progress, an occasional interaction with a dog her size or a small child, but every other resident of Pratt is regarded with caution, especially men. Her loyalty is to that of Father Johnstone and him alone; everyone else is a potential liability. That goes double for Sheriff Morgan.

"I ain't gonna fuck with you no more...not unless you give me cause to," he said. It was the first interaction Father Johnstone had had with him since he witnessed a bullet rip through Mason Hollis's forehead. The sheriff showed up on civilian clothing: cowboy boots, jeans, and a white T-shirt. Shelby, of course, was strapped tight against his hip, as per usual.

"I left a mess. I'm man enough to admit that," Sheriff Morgan said, nervously fondling the handle of his pistol, avoiding eye-contact. He's never been one to accept responsibility and it made him uncomfortable. Mary, meanwhile, snarled low from behind one of the pastor's legs in the doorframe. "I guess I never thought he'd be dumb enough to come back," he said. "Fuck me for trying to be a nice guy, right?"

"Kip, I don't believe for a second you letting him go was an act of kindness...and I know you don't believe it either," the pastor said, more candid than usual. "You beat this man, you broke him, convinced Travis Durphy to burn him, and then you let him crawl away—not out of mercy—but because you wanted his torment to continue beyond Pratt lines. You liked the idea that he'd be out there suffering. Let's not pretend you did the man any favors."

"So you know about the Durphy boy, then?" the sheriff said, intrigued that Father Johnstone had somehow discovered this information.

"And Tuck Graybel, too," the pastor said. He felt inquiry building up in the sheriff and decided to cut him off, just like Madeline would. "Doesn't matter how I know that."

"But you do—"

"Yes, I realize he deserved to be punished," the pastor cut him off again. "But you let the villain go...let him crawl away angry and full of hate. You let him regain his strength and formulate a plan. Only a matter of time, right?" he recites the sheriff's words.

"Fair enough." Sheriff Morgan fondled the gun at his hip, attempting to find comfort in his old friend. Instead, it brought back a lot of bad memories: Shelby whipping Mason across the face, Shelby leveling to his body, threatening to emit a bullet. Kip regrets not pulling the trigger, and to a degree, so does the pastor. Without a Secondary, Pollux may have refrained from his attack, there never would have been a plague. No death, no burials. Life would have gone on just like normal.

Sheriff Morgan cleared his throat, saying, "It would be best if—"

"I'll never say a word about him, Kip," Father Johnstone told him. Yet again, he was able to determine what the sheriff was about to say before he said it. "I don't need this town getting riled up over ghosts they thought to be dead long ago. You can keep your legend."

Sheriff Morgan paused, looking at the pastor in a way he never had before: with caution. The guise of the schoolyard bully had been beaten out of him on the road, all those hours under the boiling sun, walking on wet blisters. It was out there that he finally felt weakness, an urge to accept death. Sometimes he'd spend miles trying to pull Shelby from his holster and eat a bullet, but couldn't will his arm to execute. His body was no longer his own anymore. He never did figure out how it all happened, only that he couldn't control it. Couldn't stop it, and the pastor had a hand in it. He's a changed man.

"You're not you anymore," Kip said, but not in a disparaging way. An observation. "You're like her now. People been talking about why you haven't preached since old man Clevenger took a shot at you. Maybe she's the reason."

Asking when Father Johnstone plans on taking the helm again has become something of an icebreaker to engage in conversation, he's noticed. Even now, walking amongst the festivities, he's already had eight or nine non-members of the flock ask if next Sunday will be day.

"Sure would be nice to hear what the Lord has to say about all this mess," they'll hint. "Seems like the church was about the only building in town that wasn't affected."

Indeed, not one plank of wood rotted. Not one pillar cracked. Leaky roof aside, the church Father Johnstone has known for over three decades remained immaculate, untouched by the plague. Of course, this led to various theories as well, the main one being that the particular type of wood and varnish combination somehow shielded the building. Others theorized it was another miracle, that Father Johnstone's Divine sanction extended to the structure itself.

'Your power will magnify along with your flock,' Madeline wrote. 'You were always the keystone, but now everyone will know it. They'll feel it intrinsically, all the way to their bones.'

Dr. Keller has been called out for his inconsistent work as of late. People are accusing Sheriff Morgan of being a deserter who left an incompetent fool in his stead. As for the mayor, there's a lot of talk surrounding him. None of it good.

"Andy Farnsworth has barely poked his head out of his house since things went south," Mrs. Colston mentions from behind her pie stand, caring very little for who overhears her discussion. "Word's been going around that he was making some shady dealings with some out-of-towners. Might be time for a change in office."

It's not the first time Father Johnstone has heard this idea being openly discussed in mixed company. Indeed, the mayor has gone into hiding, mostly out of paranoia of what awaits him out in the streets. He knows as well as anyone that Pratt isn't without a sense of *wrath*, no matter how high its spirits are. The town would tear him apart if they knew the details of his arrangement with Mr. Pollux and his associate, Mason Hollis. It would be regarded as high treason, and the backlash would be far worse than anything Father Johnstone saw when his church was flooded with a makeshift mob bearing bats and pistols. Mayor Farnsworth wouldn't even get a chance to speak; they'd drag him from that beautiful home on Waterstone's end and lynch him up on the nearest elm tree. No trial or quarter. Just revenge. 'Settling the score,' as they say.

Father Johnstone often muses whether he'd come to the mayor's aid should violent reprisals come to pass; he hasn't decided. As a pastor, he's obligated to uphold life. As a man living in the fringe, he can't ignore the fact that the mayor's death would be anything if not harmonious.

'Sometimes death is necessary.'

Burying the mayor wouldn't bother him none; he was never part of the flock. Full of hubris, that man. Worshipped himself more than the Lord and wasn't quiet about it. For that, Father Johnstone can spare no concern.

'You'll never be the same,' Madeline wrote. *'Once you stop playing by the rules it's hard to go back.'*

Father Johnstone has been compromised. Permanently so.

After everything that's happened, he doesn't have it in him to assume the helm and recite the Lord's word. He's felt real power surge through his person, witnessed it bring back Mary and save the town. Never again could he utter the line,'Thou shalt not suffer a witch to live' without feeling like a complete hypocrite. He did much more than suffer Madeline's existence. He gave her everything he wasn't supposed to: his support, his love, and a non-traditional burial.

Dr. Keller gave him the directions and the pastor followed them to the letter, saying every word and combining all the listed ingredients: animal organs, select herbs, three drops of blood from the Secondary. Father Johnstone's blood. Dr. Keller wrapped her in a shroud and delivered her to the daisy hill three hours before sunrise. While the town slept, Madeline Paige was lowered into the earth, deep into a pit that the pastor had spent the last many hours digging.

"You sure you don't want to see her?" Dr. Keller said.

He waved him off again. So much had changed in Father Johnstone without his say-so, but the memory, the campfire smile and the eyes—he could keep that. Madeline Paige could be preserved exactly how he wanted to remember her, and no amount of trips through the rumor mill could change that. His faith and relationships would change, pillars would come and go, but Madeline could be absolute. Forever beautiful, buried in the womb of the daisy hill her aunt Josie loved so much. Deep down where the soil was still rich and alive.

In the here and now, Father Johnstone strolls through the commotion that is Pratt, noticing all the colors of the balloons, the streamers, the aromas of pies and cobblers. He can feel the tide turning, the morale of the people rising with every home they rebuild and ill friend that recovers. Pratt is well on its way to finding its feet again, and Father Johnstone—he no longer feels so alone. He has Mary and a dear friend in Dr. Keller. He has the love of the flock and non-flock alike. Even Sheriff Morgan, despite everything, has finally relinquished the grudge. Although the Challenger he poured his soul into is all but totaled, the pastor is fine with that. Father Johnstone has a new project: the Paige household. Pollux left behind a bag of luggage containing the following items: two changes of clothes, two editions of The Good Book, one partially-drank bottle of wine, a sharpened crucifix, some old jerky, and close to $2,000,000 in bundled cash. Father Johnstone figures that should be more than enough to fix the house up, better than new.

The idea appeals to him: working outdoors, hammering lumber with the ballgame playing on the radio. A cooler full of ice-cold bottled beer. He'll pay local kids looking for extra money to help him out while deliveries from the hardware store ship in. The view would be perfect: spring blue skies hanging over a pile of popcorn. Kids chasing each other through the daisies while bumblebees dance from bud to bud, running and laughing, creating their fondest memories over the place where Madeline Paige sleeps past the threshold.

She's in that other place beyond the fringe.

The Visitor

It's worse today.

"You've got to take your medicine now, Mr. Johnstone," Annie says, grabbing a bottle of pills from a nearby desk, which must mean it's around noon. In the mornings, she gives me the eye drops and a pile of supplements. Evenings are for sleeping aids and joint pain. Noon means the heart meds, and with that I either get a bowl of stew or some weak chili. No peppers and barely any spices. Can't have real chili anymore, Annie says. Stuff will burn my mouth right out. Not good for the heart, either. Fat from the hamburger meat clogs up the ol' ticker so much I can feel it wanting to pop. It's worse today, though. The damn thing keeps fluttering every ten minutes or so, but I don't want to worry Annie so I keep my trap shut. She'll make a big deal out of it and I don't want that. I'd rather listen to the ball game and eat in peace.

"I know, I know...I'm gonna turn on the TV in just a minute. Give me a second to make you something to wash those meds down," Annie says, anticipating this part of the routine.

"No lemonade," I tell her. "Too tart."

"No lemonade," she says, pouring out some sweet tea into glass tumbler.

Annie brings over the tea and pills, setting them down on my little plastic bed platter and watches me to make sure I take them. It's not that she doesn't trust me. She does. I just forget sometimes. Little things like what day it is or if I've already opened the mail or not. Ol' doc what's-his-name said it'd get worse before it gets better a few years ago. Young guy named Brian or Brad or something like that. He's the one that took over for Dr. Keller when he finally passed on.

"The machine breaks down at your age," he said. "All we can do is hope the meds take and try to keep an eye on things."

Then he mentioned something about inaccuracies with my medical records and inconsistent blood work. Stuff from way back, right around the time everything went haywire and Pratt had to be rebuilt. I told him

426

it was probably a clerical error, that things must've gotten mixed up during all the commotion.

"Well, that would make sense," he said. "Blood types don't change as you probably know. Odd though."

"Those were odd times," I said.

Back then I could heal a broken bone and cure lung cancer like it was nothing. No one ever got sick, not even during the flu season. There was even a stretch of about nine years when no one in the town died—not even family pets. Nearly a decade without death, mourning, or illness. 'Pratt's golden era,' people were calling it. After Mayor Farnsworth got ran out of town, the crop came back lush and full. Grain-plant workers went back to the factories while the women and wives did their duties on the home front. They were always planning some kind of BBQ or get-together at the newly rebuilt Danger Ranch. Travis finally found the gumption to ride the bull. Never tried to go pro like his pop, but most folks agreed that he could have.

"With the baby on the way, I reckon it's best to keep the ridin' a casual affair," he said with a big wad of jerky in his mouth. After my Madeline took the fear out of him, ol' Travis never touched another tin of chewing tobacco for the rest of his days. "Nasty little habit I never should have started," he told people. "Getting a lot more lovin' from the wife now that my mouth doesn't taste like wet cigarettes."

Heather and Travis conceived during that initial consummation, the same one that left craters in the drywall and broke their furniture. Drake Durphy was born in the dead of winter, hollering and deep purple, but healthy as can be. I remember seeing flashes of Danger in his face, the eyes mostly. He does this squinting thing that the ladies love, but only when he's on the bull ready to be cut loose into the ring. The Durphy stare-down, people call it.

"Not a drop of fear in him," Travis always tells me. "Almost as if someone took my pop's spirit and handed it on down."

Travis normally visits on Sundays. The morning mass will let out and Travis will stop by for a quick visit while his two little girls play on the daisy hill. Over a beer or some hard cider, we'll talk about how things are going on the ranch or Drake's bull riding. Memory is going to hell so Travis knows a story might need to be told more than once, God bless him. Sometimes he'll talk about that day's sermon.

"Feeding of 5,000 reading," Travis will say. "It's about the fifth or sixth time he's done it since you bowed out and I still haven't gotten used to it."

There's always a period of adjustment when a new guy takes the helm, but everyone seems to like the new pastor well enough. He's a good man, conducts his sermons nice and traditional the way folks like, but that's never the reason Travis brings it up. My time as pastor is a bridge back to the past, and the past is still unclear for a lot of folks. When everything got repaired and Pratt was whole again, that was the point when people finally felt like it was okay to speculate. If it's one thing I know—one thing I still remember, anyway—it's that when things get too boring, that's when the rumor mill gets to churning again. Everyone loves a ghost story.

"Such a strange girl, that Madeline Paige," people said. "Strange how her and Father Johnstone were so close. Wonder where she took off to."

She wasn't in Pratt for more than a few months. Madeline made her impression on the town, that's for sure. Folks still talk about where she gone and why she left me the daisy-hill house. It's still the finest property in all of Pratt, so of course people are going to ask their questions. Even Travis and Helena McManus (formerly the widow Wright) bring it up from time to time. I've gotten quite good at keeping secrets though, and losing my memory has made it all the easier.

"Make sure to take your pills, Mr. Johnstone," Annie reminds me, setting down a bowl of reheated beef stew and a couple slices of lightly buttered bread. I pop my meds before I forget again, washing them down with a couple swallows of sweat tea while Annie turns on the tube. Game's already started from the sound of it. I can hear the commentary, the crowd.

"What inning?" I ask, squinting at the screen.

"Second," Annie says. "Bottom of the second. Two out. You want

some more drops, Mr. Johnstone?"

I wave her off. The drops don't do squat. It's like having cold cat piss swimming in your eyes. Surgeries didn't take either. When Dr. young-and-handsome said the machine breaks down, he wasn't kidding. First thing to start going were my joints, especially that knee ol' Mason Hollis took a wrench to. Got to the point where I couldn't get around without a walking cane. Then it went downhill from there: eczema breakouts, hair loss, gum disease, eyes and ears got dimmer as the years passed. Dr. Keller couldn't help nor his replacement. Lord couldn't do anything, either. My gift had run out, and along with it, a few other functions I used to take for granted. That's right around when Mary passed.

"Do you have everything you need, Mr. Johnstone?" Annie asks.

I give her a curt nod, an attempt at a smile to show I appreciate her. My eyes stare at the TV even though it mostly looks like watercolors. Humongous splashes of electric green with white blurs running through them. Can't make out the names of the players or the score, and if I try for too long, I'll just give myself a headache. I concentrate on the stew, let what's left of my ears do the work for me, listening for crowd reaction or the crack of the bat. Mary used to curl up next to me during the games. I miss that. I miss the company. Can't really be mad at the Lord for taking her though. She lived for twice the amount of time most dogs her breed do. After Mrs. Adams lost Missy and Chips to the plague, it was especially hard for her to see Mary trotting around town well beyond her years. Jealousy. She never said anything directly, but intangibly, I could feel her bewilderment as to how a standard terrier lived all the way to twenty-six.

"So I'm going to head out now," Annie tells me, giving me a touch on the shoulder to get my attention. She's been doing this more and more as my condition gets worse, verifying that I'm actually listening. Making sure that I haven't drifted off in my own head. "My replacement will be along any minute, okay?"

"Did you bring the mail in?" I ask.

"It's Sunday, Mr. Johnstone," Annie says.

It gets worse. Every day the machine breaks down a little more, nuts and bolts coming loose in my brain. Sometimes I wake up in the middle of the night from the pain in my knee and feel around for Mary, that warm ball of fur that should be curled up against my gut. My hands will smooth over the cold sheets searching, and it'll take me a minute or so to realize she ain't around anymore. I'm alone and Mary is asleep in the earth where I buried her.

"Hey, cheer up," Annie says. "It's just for the afternoon, okay? And you didn't hear it from me, but word is that my replacement knows her way around the kitchen," she says enticingly. "Maybe she'll fix you up some dessert."

I sigh, giving Annie a little nod. She hasn't said anything to me about it (or maybe she has and I forgot), but I figure she's taking off early to see the doctor. Annie's with child; I can tell. My gift and abilities may have gone out the window, but that knack for reading the intangibles stuck. While I'm struggling to handle a spoon or zoning out in front of the tube, Annie usually daydreams about the baby. She's hoping for a little girl, but whatever the kid ends up being, once it arrives Annie will be out of the picture. Only a matter of time before she formally breaks the news that she won't be my caretaker much longer.

"Just watch the game. She'll be along in a bit," Annie says. "I'm gonna leave the door open for her."

Annie grabs her bag and heads out. It gets worse.

My heart flutters again, giving the inside of my chest a couple jabs. White lights start to prickle in my vision, mixing in with the view of the daisy hill just outside my window. Can't remember the last time I walked through that pile of popcorn, but the breeze always brings the scent of the flowers in. I try to focus in on that, the smell of the daisies flowing into old lungs. Try to settle. Try to find the Lord to hold me together. Just one last little miracle for old time's sake. It's like that for a stretch — five, maybe fifteen minutes of me struggling to sit in my own skin while the game drones on. I can't even remember what teams are playing let alone the inning or the score.

"You okay, Father Johnstone?" a voice asks. A woman. She's

wearing the same basic get-up that Annie does, a pair of scrub pants with a patterned cotton top.

I collect myself, not wanting to look weak, giving her a little nod to let her know I'm fine. Everything's okay. The flutter is already dying off, so I pretend that it's just a little indigestion from my lunch. Clear my throat—maybe a bit too theatrically, coughing. Then it hits me: the way she addressed me that no one really does anymore.

"You called me Father," I say. "Not many people call me that anymore...not anyone your age." I try to look her over but my vision is muddy. Only the broad strokes come through now: slender and pale, a little over five feet tall with dark hair. Smells nice, like soap and perfume.

"I'm older than I look," she says. A small black bag is set down on the bed, which she starts to dig through. Not a medical bag like Dr. Keller used to tote around. A purse. "But you can't tell how old I am, can you, Pastor? Can't see much of anything nowadays...even after two surgeries."

"You can read a file, then," I say bitterly. "Congrats."

"I can do a little more than that," she says, still digging around in her bag. There's a smell coming from it that I can't exactly pinpoint. Like stale dirt, as if she's got a sleeping bag or an old baseball glove in there. "The doctors can't help you because your problem isn't medical," she says. "That's why your vision hasn't improved and your heart is getting worse. You're taking a bunch of pills for something they can't fix...drying out. Remind you of anybody?"

The priest from Barnes. Skin like paper, hair like old attic cobwebs. It was as if Pollux sucked the life right out of him. There was a lot of explaining to do when some folks came to claim his body. Apparently, this man was only supposed to be thirty-nine years old. They had to get his dental records just to make sure they had the right guy, but I remember thinking at the time how he looked aged to death. Put the fear of God in my heart that something like that would ever happen to me.

"It *is* happening to you," she says. "You've been playing two roles in one body for so long that it's finally caught up with you."

She knows me. She knows me well. Intangibly, I can feel it. Then the heart punches against my chest again, harder this time. Less of a flutter and more of a sharp pain. I wince, clutch my chest and try not to scream. Try to look strong.

"You're supposed to pass on today," she says, placing a thumb and a finger on an eye. She spreads them apart, bringing a dropper close to the cornea. "Hold still," she tells me.

My heart prickles, cramps up like old muscle. Hurts so bad my back is arching, having spasms. "Who are you?" I whisper, feeling drops hit my eyes. First, the left, then right. Liquid sizzles, but not in a burning way. It's eating, dissolving the cataracts, chewing up the abnormal cells, and then I begin to see her.

"I couldn't stay away any longer," she tells me, the girl with fair skin and dark hair. A campfire smile, and eyes just as warm.

"Madeline," I say. She's not supposed to be here. I buried her; I remember putting her in the ground and blanketing her in dirt. "How?"

"I told you, Johnstone, there's no afterlife for people like me. We're in a loop, a circle," she says. "Sometimes you come back as a tree or a sparrow or a stone sitting at the bottom of a river. You play your cards right though, you can come back how you want. I thought you would have figured that out by now."

Because when you boil it down to the basic elements, this is all ingredients. Some of them you can see, some not. I remember what she wrote in her letter, that death is a very important ingredient. Been asking myself for years why that was important. I should've been asking myself 'how,' the method in which she passed. White fire so pure that only God could have forged it.

"Sacrifice," I say.

"And you," she says, smoothing her hand over my chest, stopping on the heart. It punches. Punches hard. "You followed the instructions, made it so I could come back," she explains. "You, on the other hand…you won't come back. You'll go on. The end of the Divine path is the beginning of something else for a man of the cloth."

The afterlife. The Kingdom.

"Maybe," Madeline says. She can read me, read what I'm feeling and thinking. She can feel my heart threatening to burst inside me. "Maybe heaven, maybe nothing. You're about to find out in a few minutes."

The punching relents, reverting back to a light flutter. I can breathe again. For now. "Come to say goodbye, then?" I ask.

"If I have to," she says. "I'd rather not. I'd rather you come with me."

I start to laugh but it comes out so dry and wheezy it deforms to coughing. Throat's dry, lungs are dry. "Too old," I say. "Lost the gift some time ago."

"You never read any of those books, did you, Johnstone?" Madeline asks, but she already knows. The answer is written all over my face: I compromised, sat in the fringe for a while, but I couldn't bring myself to go all the way with it. My faith had been rattled enough for one lifetime.

"Put those in the basement," I say. "Never touched them again after that."

"Then you still have a lot to learn," Madeline says, smoothing a thumb over my forehead, the hairline. "It's your choice, though. You don't have to come with me. You can stay here...see what's on the other side. I'd like you to come with me, though."

"How could...?" I trail off, looking at myself, my frail little legs and weak body. My chest hurts and every joint feels like it has broken glass in it. I can barely walk, barely think straight. Even little things like going to the bathroom and showering require two people now. I could never subject her to that.

"You won't hold me back. Not after you're all fixed up," Madeline says. "I can do that, y'know...make you healthy again, young again. You can be even younger than you were when we first met. It's just like the car, Johnstone...you can be restored with the right materials...the right ingredients." Madeline digs around in her bag, pulling out a small glass bottle with a cork stopper. The liquid inside is light green, glowing like a firefly. "This one stops you from going into cardiac *arrest," she says, leveling another in my sightline. "I've prepared others...one to repair your joints and bones, another that will fix your short-term memory. You're in bad shape but you're not past the threshold, Johnstone. Not yet."*

"And what would we be doing once I'm all fixed up?" I ask.

"We see where the path takes us," she says. "See the world."

The world beyond Pratt: mountains, oceans, deserts. The Grand Canyon, Yellowstone, Niagara Falls. Other countries and continents. It hits me that I've been praising the Lord's name and his creations for some decades, but I've seen so very little of them with my own eyes, restricting myself to the small joys of the daisy hill and Pratt's numerous golden fields. I've served long and well, but as many men of the cloth will attest to, it is a lonely servitude. Often loveless, bound to the church and the flock until He takes you. I could let Him take me right now, take me past the threshold and see what exactly is on the other side. Mary's already waiting there for me; I can feel it. She bounds through endless pastures. Then I look to Madeline holding that bottle that could save my life, the black bag of numerous other miracles made especially for me. She'll never enter the Kingdom. She can't. Madeline Paige walks the loop, destined to recycle on earth until the Lord decides there will be no earth left. Maybe a bomb will drop or the surface will freeze over. As it is written, one day all this will end, but right now the world is a beautiful place ripe for exploration. Right now Madeline is here and young and offering something that few people ever get: another chance.

"So what'll it be, Johnstone?" she asks, still holding those bottles. Ready to restore, to revitalize that which has become senile and weak. Madeline smiles, leaning in close. "What path will you choose?"

Acknowledgements

It's only when you get to the end that you realize how many people were involved.

First and foremost, I'd like to thank my publisher Phil Jourdan of Perfect Edge Books. Your belief, support, and patience with this project has been nothing short of stellar and I'll be forever grateful for that.

To my Wendy, thank you for being wonderful, keeping me sane, and allowing me to bounce every crazy idea I've ever had off of you. This job is so much easier when you have love in your life.

A huge thank you to my friend and graphic designer, Jamie Turpin, who took a simple sketch and turned it into a beautiful work of art.

Thanks to Derek Beals and Renee Pickup who served as my beta readers for this book. Your feedback was invaluable.

Thank you to my femme fatale editor, Pela Via. You kicked my ass, ripped my guts out, and I'm better off for it.

To Dennis Widmyer and the good people at LitReactor, thank you for the support and for giving me a literary soapbox to stand on.

A very special thanks to Clint Mansell, Hans Zimmer, and M83 who serve as the soundtrack to which I create.

And lastly, I want to thank my friends. I won't list you off by name for fear that I'll miss someone, but all the dinners, drinks, and conversations we've shared have meant the world to me.

PERFECT
EDGE
BOOKS

"There are many who dare not kill themselves for fear of what
the neighbours will say," Cyril Connolly wrote, and we believe
he was right.
Perfect Edge seeks books that take on the crippling fear of other
people, the question of what's correct and normal, of how life
works, of what art is.
Our authors disagree with each other; their styles vary as widely as
their concerns. What matters is the will to create books that won't be
easy to assimilate. We take risks, not for the sake of risk-taking, but for
the things that might come out of it.